Georgia Hill writes rom-coms and historical fiction and is published by Harper*Impulse*.

She divides her time between the beautiful counties of Herefordshire and Devon and lives with her two beloved spaniels, a husband (also beloved) and a ghost called Zoe. She loves Jane Austen, eats far too much Belgian chocolate and has a passion for Strictly Come Dancing.

@georgiawrites
www.facebook.com/georgiahillauthor
www.georgiahill.co.uk

Also by Georgia Hill

Say It With Sequins: The Rumba
Say It With Sequins: The Waltz
Say It With Sequins: The Charleston
While I Was Waiting

Millie Vanilla's Cupcake Cafe

GEORGIA HILL

A division of HarperCollins*Publishers*
www.harpercollins.co.uk

Harper*Impulse* an imprint of
HarperCollins*Publishers*
The News Building
1 London Bridge Street
London SE1 9GF

www.harpercollins.co.uk

This paperback edition 2018

First published in Great Britain in ebook format by
HarperCollins*Publishers* 2018

A catalogue record for this book
is available from the British Library

ISBN: 9780008212162

This novel is entirely a work of fiction.
The names, characters and incidents portrayed in it are
the work of the author's imagination. Any resemblance to
actual persons, living or dead, events or localities is
entirely coincidental.

Set in Birka by Palimpsest Book Production Limited,
Falkirk, Stirlingshire

Printed and bound by CPI Group (UK) Ltd, Croydon, CR0 4YY

To the people and town of Lyme Regis, Dorset. Thank you for the fabulous holidays.

Spring Beginnings

Chapter 1

Millie wiped the table and then straightened to enjoy the view. Millie Vanilla's Cupcake Café must have one of the best in Berecombe. Situated halfway along the flat promenade leading to the harbour, its wide windows looked straight out onto the seas of Lyme Bay. And what a view! Now, in early January, a chill bit into the wind and the light was crystal clear, making the azure blue of sea and sky deeper and rain-washed. One or two gulls wheeled about in the light breeze, chattering to the skies. Even though she'd lived in the little flat above the café all her life, Millie would never tire of how beautiful her home town was.

She carried the tray, full of empty plates and mugs, back to the kitchen and began washing up. Some people might say she was mad to stay open in the winter. All the other cafés and restaurants in this part of town were firmly shut up until March. Even the chip shop only opened on weekend nights.

But Millie loved this time of year. Yes, it was dark in the mornings, but the winter winds whipped up the sea into towering waves and she fed off the energy from a good storm. There was nothing more exhilarating than a walk along the promenade watching the waves tear into the beach and being deafened by the roar. She frothed the washing-up water in the sink with enthusiasm. Yes, there were only a few people about but she'd pick up a bit of trade from the literary festival later in the month. Besides, there were always one or two week-enders wanting a good foamy latte. There were all her regulars too. Biddy, with Elvis the poodle, would be along in an hour and Zoe and her friends would pop in for hot chocolate; fresh off the school bus and wanting a place to gossip in until it was time to go home. During the low season, Millie relished the luxury of having lots of time to talk to her customers.

'And besides, Trevor,' Millie called through the kitchen door to the cockapoo snoring in his basket by the radiator, 'What else would we be doing? I can't knit and daytime telly bores me rigid.' The dog, worn out from his run on the beach, didn't grace her with an answer.

The familiar jingle-jangle of the bell on the door alerted her to a customer. Wiping her hands on her apron – hand sewn by Biddy and turquoise-blue and pink to match the decor – Millie grabbed her pen and order pad.

There was a stranger sitting at the best table, next to the middle window. A man and alone. It was unusual. Not many men came into the café in the afternoons. She had a few who popped in for breakfast, but men weren't usually, in her experience, afternoon-tea-and-cake type of people.

'Hello there,' she said, pinning on a welcoming smile, 'What can I get you?'

The man lifted his face from the menu and gazed at her. He had dark eyes and blond hair. A striking combination. He was about her own age and very, very attractive.

'Good afternoon.'

Cultivated voice. Expensive-sounding, to match his heavy overcoat. Millie glimpsed a snowy white shirt underneath, with a red tie and charcoal-grey striped suit. Definitely not her usual sort of customer. Perhaps he'd got lost on his way to the Lord of the Manor Hotel? It was far more exclusive and upmarket than Millie Vanilla's.

'What cake do you have?'

Millie relaxed a little. This was much safer ground than dwelling on how hot he was. 'I've some Victoria sponge and a coffee and walnut cake. I also have a light fruitcake, which is iced, and freshly baked scones with jam and cream. Clotted, of course.'

'Of course.' He smiled back.

Millie's heart did a flippoty-flop and her knees weakened. The smile transformed his features. He was gorgeous! Trevor, as if aware of his mistress's agitation, stirred in his basket and gave a little snuffling snore.

The stranger looked at the dog's wicker basket. 'You allow dogs in the café?'

Millie stiffened. No one criticised her café and certainly not her dog. 'He's allowed in the seating area, but nowhere near any food preparation.' She jerked her head towards the kitchen. 'And, as you can see, there's a door separating the two parts of the café. We're very dog-friendly in Berecombe. Always have been. Lots of visitors bring their pets with them on holiday and want to eat out with them. In the better weather we have tables outside on the sun terrace and, of course, there are no restrictions on dogs out there.'

'Ouch.'

'Excuse me?'

'I've obviously touched a nerve. I apologise.' That devastatingly charming smile again.

Millie felt the tension leave her shoulders. He hadn't meant to criticise after all. 'No, it should be me apologising. It's a defence I have to produce every now and again.'

'And you find it's better for trade to have dogs in?'

Who was he to be asking all these questions? Suspicion prickled. 'I do. There's always the occasional customer who prefers to eat without having a dog around, but most people, even if they don't have one of their own, actually like it.'

'Good. Interesting.'

This was getting weird. 'Now, what can I get you?' Millie asked bracingly, to avoid further interrogation.

'I suppose I'm too late for lunch?'

'Not at all. I've some curried butternut squash soup and homemade bread. Or a sandwich on granary?'

'The soup sounds wonderful. I'll have that. And a piece of the Victoria sponge for pudding. Oh – and tea.'

'I have Earl Grey or English Breakfast. The Breakfast tea is from a local Devon supplier and is particularly good. Or I have a variety of fruit and herbal teas.'

'English Breakfast it is, then. Thank you.'

'Thank *you*. Won't be a minute.'

As Millie prepared his meal, she couldn't resist sneaking peeks through the porthole window in the kitchen door. Who was he? Health and Safety? One of those secret review customers? Someone from the tourist board? He'd slipped off his overcoat and she'd been right about the suit. Very well cut and fitted to his long legs. No, he couldn't be any of those. No tourist-board official had ever looked that beautiful. Did people really have cheekbones like that? Trevor, she saw, to her intense annoyance, was now nosing around and making friends. She'd expected the stranger to bat him off but he was tickling Trevor's golden ears, to the dog's great delight. And dogs were supposed to be loyal! Looked like Trevor couldn't resist a handsome man either.

Feeling more than a little flustered, Millie put the soup on to heat and took over a tray with teapot, milk jug, cup and saucer.

'What pretty china,' the stranger exclaimed. 'I like the way it's all mismatched but goes together so well.'

Millie's suspicions grew.

He looked around him with open admiration. 'And I love the turquoise starfish and pink shell mural. You've obviously thought a great deal about the image for this place.'

Millie hadn't. She'd got her best friend's husband to paint it colours she liked and the china choice was forced on her by economy. She'd picked up a load at a car-boot sale. Was he being sarcastic? 'Thank you.' She forced a smile through gritted teeth. 'I'll just go and get your soup.'

Again, Millie watched avidly as the stranger examined his cup, turned the handles of the teapot and hot-water jug this way and that and lifted the saucer to examine the maker's mark. The delicate flowery pattern should have looked ridiculous in his long-fingered grip, but it didn't. Who *was* he?

There was one way to find out. She carried his soup and bread over, determined to ask questions, only to be thwarted as Biddy came in with Elvis. Shaking sea spray off her woollen beret, the elderly woman said, 'Afternoon,' in her over-loud voice. Millie served the stranger his meal and noticed with amusement that Biddy was glaring at him. He was in her favourite seat.

Biddy settled noisily at a table nearer the kitchen and made a great fuss over taking off her coat and settling her poodle.

Realising the interrogation would have to wait, Millie went over to her. 'Your usual, Biddy?' Millie didn't need an order pad for this customer. Biddy always had the same thing.

'My usual,' the woman barked. 'What else? A coffee and scone. And a shortbread for Elvis.'

'Coming right up.' Millie made sure she was facing her as she spoke. Biddy was really quite deaf but could lip-read. When she chose. Millie tried to be charitable and sympathise with how frustrating it must be but suspected Biddy's permanently bad mood was nothing to do with her hearing loss. 'How's Elvis today?' Normally Millie would fuss over Biddy's hearing-assistance dog but she was too aware of the stranger. He seemed to be watching everything that was going on.

'Upset, that's what he is. That bitch has been after him again.'

Millie sensed rather than saw the stranger's shoulders tense. 'What, Arthur Roulestone's retriever? She's as quiet as a mouse.'

'Not when she catches sight of Elvis, she isn't. I swear he makes her randy.'

'Oh dear,' Millie murmured. 'Just as well he doesn't have the same effect on Trevor.' They looked to where the dogs, having had a sniff to say hello, were now studiously ignoring one another.

'Yes well,' Biddy sniffed. 'Folks ought to control their dogs, especially when they're around others that work.'

Out of the corner of her eye, Millie saw the stranger's shoulders quiver. Was he laughing – or about to complain? He'd been friendly towards Trevor, but maybe two dogs in a café was too much?

As far as she knew, Arthur's Daisy never had the energy to raise her head, let alone pester a poodle a quarter of her size, but she supposed Biddy knew what she was talking about. 'I'll just get your coffee.'

Unfair though it seemed, maybe today wasn't the day to let Biddy sit in a corner with Elvis nursing a solitary cup for an hour or two. The sooner she served her, the sooner she might leave. Taking Elvis with her. Millie immediately felt guilty. Why shouldn't Biddy take as long as she wanted? The café was hardly busy. It was just this stranger. He made Millie uneasy. In lots of ways.

She busied herself in the kitchen, served Biddy, gave Elvis a homemade dog biscuit and took away the stranger's empty soup bowl.

'That was absolutely delicious.' He gave her the megawatt smile again. 'Is it really homemade?'

'It is.'

'By you?'

'By me. As is the sponge cake.'

'Then I can't wait!'

He was being friendly. Saying the right things. Even Trevor, tart that he was, liked him – and she trusted Trevor's opinion implicitly. But still, there was something not right about this whole encounter. She couldn't quite place what it was. Maybe she was just unused to dealing with men who made her hormones fizz?

'I'll go and get it.' The sooner he ate and left the better. Then things might get back to normal. *She* might get back to normal.

'Could I trouble you for some more boiling water?'

'Of course,' she breathed. Bugger. He was going to linger.

As she served him, Zoe and her collection of friends clattered in, bringing the fresh January cold with them. They deposited their school bags and coats in a pile and slumped onto their usual corner table, phones in hand.

'Hiya, Mil,' Zoe called.

'Hi, girls. Hot chocolate?'

'Hot chocolate,' they chorused back.

'We've had PE,' Zoe explained further. 'Had to run around the field for hours. Supposed to be cross-country training,' she added gloomily.

'You poor things. I remember it well. Extra marshmallows, then.'

'Thanks, Millie,' came another chorus and they disappeared into scrolling down the screens of their phones.

After distributing mugs of hot chocolate, liberally laced with marshmallows and cream, Millie glanced around. Against the silvered light of the winter afternoon Biddy sipped her coffee, one hand protectively on Elvis' black woolly head and Zoe and the gang were giggling over something on their phones. There was a comfortingly warm fug in the place. She sighed with pleasure; she loved this little café and cherished its place at the heart of her community.

Then she noticed the stranger pushing away his empty cake plate.

'May I have my bill, please?'

'Right away.' Millie had already prepared it. She couldn't wait to get rid of him.

He glanced at the amount and paid cash. 'So, you're Millie?' he asked, putting a note on the saucer.

Blimey. More questions. She forced a friendly smile. 'I am.'

'And you own Millie Vanilla's?'

'I do.'

'Great name, by the way.'

'Thank you.'

In a bid to encourage him to leave, Millie picked up his payment, her eyes widening at what he'd tipped. As he stood up and put his coat back on, she noticed he towered above her. Another point scored. She liked tall men.

'That was really delicious food. And you've got a marvellous place here.'

'Thank you,' Millie repeated. Why didn't he just *go?*

'I hope I can find the time to come back.'

As he went out, Clare, Zoe's best friend, wolf-whistled. The dogs' noses shot up at the sound. 'Who was that?' she asked, her eyes like saucers. 'He's gorg!'

'And totally too old for you,' Zoe replied.

9

Clare rolled her eyes. 'I so totally don't care.'

Zoe craned her neck to view him as he sauntered along the prom. 'Nice bum.'

Millie giggled. 'That'll do, Zoe. I've told you before to stop ogling the customers.'

'Hope he comes in when I do a shift on Saturday, then. He can have my extra-extra-special service.' She waggled her eyebrows comically.

'Oh, Zoe,' Millie put her head on one side with pretend concern. 'Whatever has he done to deserve that?'

Clare poked her friend in the ribs and cackled. 'Yay, Millie's got you there, Zo.'

Something drew Millie to the door. She watched as the man strode towards the harbour, the low sunshine lightening his blond hair. He had a loose-limbed style that was very sexy. Confident, assured of his place in the world. Arrogant almost. As if sensing he was being watched, he turned back to the café and raised a hand.

Millie ducked out of view, blushing furiously. She still hadn't a clue who he was.

Chapter 2

Millie didn't have long to wait until the gorgeous stranger returned. He came in a few days later on a bright, cold morning when the wind whipped up white horses.

'Good morning again,' he greeted her cheerfully.

'Morning.'

He extended a hand. 'As I know your name, I think I'd better introduce myself. Jed Henville.'

'Nice to meet you.' Millie wiped her hand unnecessarily on her apron (bright pink with turquoise stars today). 'Emilia Fudge. But everyone calls me Millie.'

She waited for the laugh. For a quirk of amused eyebrows. For the jokes over her name being as sweet as her cakes. None came and she blushed with gratitude. This guy had class. 'What can I get you today?'

Jed grimaced. 'I shouldn't have anything, really, as I've just had a rather mediocre English cooked breakfast. But when I was in the other day, I couldn't help but notice you do raisin toast. It's my all-time weakness. Is that homemade too?'

'Alas, I can't lay claim to being a bread-maker. My pal Tessa makes all the bread I serve in here. But it's very much made in her home. She's a fantastic artisan baker. I'll get you some of her fabulous raisin toast, then, shall I? Would you like some coffee with that?' Millie smiled and wondered where he'd eaten his very ordinary breakfast and if he'd shared it with anyone. Who was he and why was he in Berecombe? It was a sleepy place and not considered as trendy as Lyme Regis, further along the coast. At this time of year any stranger stood out a mile, especially one as good-looking as him.

'Thank you. I'd love a large latte. It's cold today; I need warming up!' Taking off his stripey scarf, he settled at the same table he'd sat at the other day and spread out a broadsheet newspaper.

He was less formally dressed today, in dark moleskin jeans and a buttery suede jacket. With his out of season suntan, he looked just as buttery and edible himself. So he was in need of being warmed up? Millie could think of one or two things that might do it. She gave herself a shake. Honestly. Grow up, woman! She was as bad as Zoe and her gang going weak at the knees at the sight of a hot man. She ran into the kitchen and put herself to work as a distraction.

The morning passed peacefully enough. Jed had eaten his toast and drunk his latte with enthusiasm, declaring both delicious and had thrown on his scarf and jacket and departed. As she cleared his table, Millie was prevented from watching where he was headed by the arrival of Arthur Roulestone, breakfast regular and owner of Daisy, Elvis's arch enemy.

'Morning, my dear,' he called, as he came in with the puffing retriever in tow. He followed her look. 'Stranger in town, then?'

'Morning, Arthur.' Millie picked up the tray and paused,

with her bottom pushed against the kitchen door. 'You don't happen to know who he is, do you?'

'No idea.' He tapped his nose cheerfully. 'I can keep my ear to the ground for you, though.'

'Thanks.' Arthur was a member of Berecombe's town council. What he didn't know wasn't worth knowing. 'Your usual?'

'Bless you. A trifle chilly out there today.'

'Isn't it just? But I love these crisp days,' Millie shouted from the kitchen.

'I've heard we might have snow later.'

'Snow?' Millie put the tray down on the draining board and poked her head out of the door. 'It never snows here. We don't even get so much as a frost.'

'Not strictly true. I can remember it snowing one winter when I was a boy. Covered the beach. Magical. Funnily enough, I always find it's the coldest just before we get the first of the spring days.'

'Some warmer weather would be welcome and good for business too. But snow, eh? How exciting! Must have been years ago. Before my time.'

'Thank you for reminding me what an old codger I am.'

'Sorry, Arthur. Extra sausage? And one for Daisy as an apology?'

'Accepted with pleasure. Organic sausages from Small's farm, I assume?'

Millie nodded and disappeared into the kitchen.

Arthur went over to the table Jed had just vacated. 'Ah,' he called through to her. 'I see your mysterious customer has left his newspaper. I might just have a quick look.' He bent and picked it up. 'Oh, how disappointing. The *Financial Times*. Not quite my choice of reading matter on a Friday morning.' His brows rose over his steel-rimmed specs. 'Might be a clue to his identity, however! A businessman, perhaps?'

'Perhaps.' Millie stepped around Daisy as she brought over Arthur's mug of tea. 'Strong builder's as usual.'

'Bless you, my dear.'

'And how's the old girl?' She bent to tickle Daisy's ears. 'I hear she's been annoying Elvis again.'

'Well, at least it shows there's some life left in her. She's getting on a bit now. Like me.'

Millie saw emotion contort Arthur's face. She straightened. 'Oh Arthur, you've both got years ahead of you yet.' Goodness knows what the old man would do when Daisy went. They were devoted to each other. 'And if she can still chase after a poodle, there must be hope.'

'Indeed. However, I fear Biddy does not quite see it that way. And Elvis is an assistance dog. Daisy shouldn't interfere when he's working.'

'I think they're secretly very fond of one another,' Millie said, reflecting that the same could be said of their bickering owners. 'And don't worry, Biddy's fine. Never happy unless she's got something to moan about.'

'As my granddaughter Zoe would say, ain't that the truth?'

Laughing, Millie went to get his breakfast ready, confident *her* cooked English could never be described as mediocre.

Chapter 3

Early on Saturday morning, when the sun was just rising over the bay, Zoe crashed in to begin her shift.

'Like your hair, Zo. What colour is it this time?'

Zoe pulled a lock of her purple fringe and went cross-eyed looking at it. 'Plummy Aubergine.'

'Nice. Although I quite liked the shocking pink.'

'Mum didn't,' Zoe said gloomily as she tied on her apron. 'And school hated it. Threatened to suspend me if I didn't tone it down.'

'And Plummy Aubergine counts as toning it down?'

Zoe scuffed her platform trainers. 'Mmm.'

'Well, this is an important year for you. Getting your grades for university and everything.'

Zoe pulled out a chair and collapsed onto it, looking morose. 'Yeah, well, don't know if I actually want to go.'

Millie paused while refilling the cupcake-shaped sugar bowls. Taking the seat opposite Zoe, she sat down and took the girl's hand. 'What's all this about, then, my lovely?'

Zoe gave an enormous sigh. 'Oh, I don't know. Just think there's more to life than batting off horny undergrads and

15

saddling yourself with a humungous debt.'

Millie tried to keep a straight face. 'Well, there's certainly more to university than that.'

'You know what I mean.'

'But it's what you've always wanted.'

'Is it?' Zoe looked up and Millie was shocked to see tears in her heavily kohled eyes. Usually the girl was breezily happy and uncomplicated. Her choice of alternative image being the notable exception.

'Isn't it?' Millie hid her shock. Zoe was an extremely bright girl. University had always been the goal.

'It's what Mum and Dad want me to do. Have always wanted me to do. And Granddad.'

Arthur would be devastated. Zoe was his only grandchild and he doted on her. 'You need to do what's right for you, my lovely.'

Zoe pouted and moodily traced the flowery pattern on the oilcloth. 'You didn't go, did you?'

Millie resumed filling the sugar bowl. 'No,' she said carefully. 'But that was different. I had the café.'

'That your parents ran?'

Millie nodded. 'Until they died.' She bit her lip.

'Aw, I'm sorry, Mil. For making you remember.'

Millie nodded. 'Well, some things are difficult to talk about still.'

'Even after all these years?'

'Even after all these years.'

'That A35. It's a death-trap,' Zoe said viciously.

Millie rose. 'It is.'

'There was another accident on it last week. Friend of Clare's mother. But no one was seriously hurt.'

'Well, road accidents happen all the time, don't they?' Millie clasped the bag of sugar to her as a shield. 'Now,' she said, with a forced brightness. 'We'd better get ourselves ready; we'll have a few frozen weekenders in, no doubt.'

'Yeah, okay.' Zoe got up and followed Millie to the kitchen. 'Sorry.'

Millie turned to her in surprise. 'Whatever for?'

'For doing a downer on you.'

'Oh, Zoe!' Millie put the sugar down and gave her a hug. 'You know you can talk to me. Any time. About anything.'

'I know.'

'Just think carefully about your future, won't you? You're such a clever girl. You could do anything and everything you want.'

'Meaning university?'

'Maybe university, if that's what you really want, but so much more too.' Millie released Zoe and gave her a grin. 'Come on, let's grab a coffee before the Saturday rush starts. I've made some millionaire's shortbread. Fancy some?'

Zoe rolled her eyes and giggled. 'Is the Pope Catholic?'

'Is he? I've no idea. Pretty sure he wouldn't approve of Plummy Aubergine, though.' Millie tweaked Zoe's fringe.

'Showing your age, Mil.'

'Cheek. I'll have you know I still have a two in it. Just about.'

Zoe grinned. 'Yeah, that's what I mean. Pos-it-ive-ly ancient. Totally past it, girlfriend.'

Millie grabbed a tea towel and snapped it at Zoe's rear. 'You, young lady, may not live long enough to get as far as my shortbread. Into that kitchen and begin work this minute.'

'Gawd. Thought the days of child slave labour died out with Dickens,' Zoe said good-naturedly and skipped ahead of Millie and into the welcoming scents of a kitchen, which produced heavenly little squares of chocolate and caramel on shortbread.

Chapter 4

It was cold and still dark as Millie walked briskly up Berecombe's steep main street to the post office. Millie was used to early starts. She'd been getting up at five all her working life. True, getting up at the crack of dawn was far more pleasant in the summer months. But even at this time of year she delighted in the muffled, secretive quality the town had when few others were around. She kissed each letter as she posted it, wishing it a safe and speedy journey to its destination, then turned and walked back down the hill. As she did, she passed the old bank building. The closing of Berecombe's only bank had caused huge distress, especially among her older customers. Not used to online banking and unwilling to trust it, they were now having to go into Honiton or Axminster to do any banking business. More alarming for Millie, a lot of them, having made the journey, were staying on there for coffee and lunch. She'd lost quite a lot of trade that way. She bit her lip; she might have to rethink one or two things to keep her going through to the busy summer season. She just wished she knew what.

She paused to study the elegant Georgian facade. The

building work had been going on for some time now and no one seemed certain about what was going to open. All sorts of rumours abounded. At the moment, its windows were resolutely boarded up and hostile-looking, giving away no secrets. She shivered in the sea fog that was yet to go out with the tide. It really had been a long, dismal winter. The promised snow hadn't appeared but she hoped Arthur was right when he'd said spring was on its way. Walking fast, she clicked her tongue at Trevor to follow and made her way home.

As she unlocked the café, her best friend Tessa arrived, carrying a tray of freshly made breads.

'Alright then, our Mil?' she called out in her broad Brummy tones. 'Got you a load of granary, a couple of white bloomers and fruit bread. That should see you through.'

Millie eyed it thoughtfully. She would have to freeze a lot of it. 'Should see me through a few days the way business has been lately.' She held open the café door and Tessa followed, putting the heavy tray down with a sigh of relief.

'That bad, eh? Time of the year, though.'

'Hopefully. Got time for a coffee?'

'Always got time for one of your coffees, bab.' Tessa plonked herself on the chair nearest the kitchen door and shouted through. 'Looks crackin' in here.' Then she fell silent as her phone pinged and she scrolled through a message.

Millie came through with a cafetière and plate of biscuits and joined her. 'Zoe touched up some of the paintwork on Saturday as we went a bit quiet. She's a good girl.'

Tessa put down her phone and looked around. 'Always loved this pink and blue theme Ken did.' She watched as

Millie poured the coffee.

Ken was Tessa's artist husband. She had met him while on holiday, fallen in love and, three children later, was still in Devon.

'How did his show go?' Millie yawned and stretched out her long legs. She slipped off her Uggs and tucked her feet underneath each other. Glancing at Tessa she thought her friend seemed unusually tense.

Tessa pulled a face. 'Okay, but we only sold a few paintings. And that gallery in Exeter charges a fortune to host an exhibition. Don't think we covered our costs, to be honest.'

'That's a real shame. You'd both worked so hard on it. Here, have a gingerbread man. I made them last night.' Millie pushed the plate over. 'I hadn't realised they charged.' Maybe that was the reason for Tessa's mood.

'Oh yes, they charge alright.' Tessa snapped a biscuit in half viciously. 'We'll have to find somewhere else to do it next time. Maybe provide our own fizz. Got to find a way to cut costs,' she waved a gingerbread man leg in the air, scattering crumbs. 'Otherwise it just ain't worth doing.'

'Can you do another in the summer, when there are more people around?'

Tessa shrugged. 'Maybe but holiday-makers don't want to buy Ken's paintings. Too big to get in the back of the hatchback to trek up the M5, like.'

Millie put down her half-eaten gingerbread man; she'd lost her appetite suddenly. It wasn't like Tessa to be so negative. Something else must be worrying her. 'These would be better iced, I think.'

'Why don't you do them to match the caff? Blue and pink buttons!'

'I might just do that.' Millie laughed, relieved her friend sounded momentarily brighter. She reached for her coffee. 'Speaking of colour, Zoe's got purple hair at the moment.'

'Love that girl!' Tessa nodded. 'Yeah, Ken said as much. She's been hanging round the studio a bit lately.'

'She's having a crisis over whether she wants to go to uni to study English.'

Tessa nodded again. 'Ken says she's got real artistic talent. You should see the water-colour sketches she does; they're ace.'

'Maybe that's what she really wants to do? Probably doesn't want to let her parents down, though. Under all that punk make-up and fluorescent hair, she's a softie. Wants to keep them happy.'

Tessa pointed a stern finger. 'Yeah, but what does *she* want? Going off to study books for three years isn't going to make her happy. All she'll end up with is debt.'

'That's exactly what she said to me. It's awful that kids have to think like that.'

'Well, Ken reckons she ought to get herself to art college.' Tessa pulled another face and spread her arms. 'And not going to uni didn't do us any harm, did it?'

Millie raised her eyebrows. 'No. We're just sitting here at six in the morning, wondering how best to make ends meet.'

'Yeah, well,' Tessa got up. 'A poxy English degree ain't necessarily going to fix that. Agreed?'

'Maybe.' Millie grinned. Tessa's antipathy to academia

stemmed from disappointment in her eldest son. Sean had little scholarly ambition. The Tizzards' hopes were now focused on their middle boy.

Just as Tessa got to the door, she turned. She hesitated before speaking. 'Have you heard what's going into the old bank building?'

'No, what? I walked past there earlier but there was no clue.' Millie began clearing their plates and mugs.

Tessa took a breath. 'It's another caff, Mil. I'm sorry, kiddo.'

'A café?' Millie sank back onto her chair on suddenly weakened legs. Another café. Coming to Berecombe. And opening up as a rival.

She looked around at the sunny turquoise walls, the fairy lights, encased in feathers and twinkling, lovingly put up by Zoe. The tray of tempting breads waiting to be eaten. The tables scrubbed and laid ready for her customers to flock in. Except they hadn't exactly been flocking in recently, had they? And with competition opening up, it could just about sound the death knell for Millie Vanilla's.

Oh God.

'Sorry, Millie,' Tessa repeated. 'Look, I've got to go. School run. Laters, bab.'

She disappeared before Millie had the chance to answer.

Chapter 5

Arthur wandered in later than usual and, very unusually, without Daisy. He rejected a cooked breakfast and sat morosely nursing a solitary mug of tea. In sympathy, Trevor whined and squatted at his feet, but was ignored.

When Millie spotted Biddy pushing open the door, with a cheerful Elvis in tow, she feared the worst. She was in no mood for squabbling pensioners this morning.

'You're early, Biddy. What can I get you?'

'It's allowed, isn't it? Being early. Not a crime. And what else do I ever have? The usual, please.'

Muttering to herself as she worked in the kitchen, Millie wondered if Biddy got on with anyone. Maybe it was the low, dull clouds? It seemed to be putting everyone in a bad mood today. As she warmed up Biddy's scone, Millie could already hear her bickering with Arthur. Biddy was moaning that yet another restaurant was opening up in town. Her heart sank.

She brought out Biddy's coffee and scone, served it and retreated behind the counter, pretending to polish some glasses.

'For once I agree with you,' Arthur went on. 'And it does

the town no favours to have these businesses open in good faith, only to have one poor season and close down again.'

'Hmph,' Biddy snorted. 'Don't see it happen in Lyme.'

Arthur sighed. 'Lyme Regis has always been a special case as it's so popular. And Berecombe's not doing too badly, really.'

'But you've still let this new café open.'

Millie stiffened.

'Apart from myself, the town council were in agreement. Blue Elephant is an international chain. The council felt, with the backing of a big company behind them, it might help the café stay open and provide some continuity. And that's quite a large building to pay rates on. Only a big organisation like that could afford it.'

Millie found the leg of the stool behind the till and dragged it over using her foot. Blue Elephant! She collapsed onto it. It couldn't be much worse. They were huge in the States and had just started to open branches over here, rivalling Costa and Starbucks. They were a Fairtrade company and committed to using organic supplies. With their muffins, granary sandwiches and coffees they'd be in direct competition with what she did at Millie Vanilla's. Even worse, the backing of a large corporation meant buying in bulk across their outlets and almost certainly undercutting her prices. She felt sick.

'But the council is still letting this Elephant place go ahead?' Biddy asked through a mouthful of scone, scattering crumbs.

'I'm afraid so, Biddy.'

'What did you say? 'Speak up, man.'

'I said, yes I'm afraid so,' Arthur repeated.

Biddy snorted again.

'I will endeavour to put forward your feelings at the next council meeting.'

In answer, Biddy slurped her coffee. Silence fell, only interrupted by whimpers coming from a now dreaming and kicking Elvis.

Arthur, sensing their conversation was at an end, came to the counter and paid the exact amount in cash as he always did. 'I'm sorry, dear girl,' he whispered, 'that I couldn't tell you sooner. About this Blue Elephant business. It was all a very hush-hush affair.'

Millie nodded mutely and watched him as he left. Trevor followed him to the door and whined. After hearing the dreadful news Millie wanted to join in.

Chapter 6

To her relief, business picked up a little at Millie Vanilla's over the next few days. The literary festival brought a smattering of people into town. Millie stayed open on the nights events were held and did a roaring trade in warming pea and ham soup and her rich apricot and almond tray bake. She liked the lone customers who came in, pored over a book in a corner and demanded constant tea and coffee. The festival was designed to bring some trade into town in the quiet days after the Christmas season and it was working.

Along with the Yummy Mummies Plus One Dad Group and her other regulars, the W.I. Knitting Circle and the Berecombe B.A.P.S (the Berecombe Appreciation of Paperbacks Society), she was kept busy.

Tessa popped by one evening with her two youngest boys. While the children took Trevor for a run on the beach, she tucked into the apricot cake with relish. 'Oh,' she sighed, 'you should definitely make loads more of this. It's bloomin' gorgeous.' She looked up as the door opened. 'Hello, our Sean.'

Her eldest son stood in the doorway looking coy. 'Hi, Mum.'

A possible reason for his embarrassment arrived a second

later. Zoe, this time with bleached-white hair, fell into the café behind him. 'Oh hello, Mrs Tizzard.'

'Zoe, me lover, told you before, call me Tessa. Grab a pew. What are you having?'

'Well, we're not stopping. We're just on our way to the poetry reading in the theatre.'

Tessa's shoulders quivered with barely contained laughter. 'Poetry reading? Not usually our Sean's thing.'

As an answer Sean grunted.

'You forgot your scarf on Saturday, Zoe,' Millie interrupted, to save him further embarrassment. 'And would you like your wages while you're here?'

'Aw thanks, Mil. I can get Mum her birthday pressie later. There's a craft fayre on in the theatre afterwards. She said she'd seen some nice earrings she'd like.'

'That Susie Evans does some nice stuff,' Tessa pointed out through a mouthful of cake. 'Tell her I sent you and she'll give you a bit off.'

'Oh and she can have a free coffee next time she's in,' added Millie.

'Thanks, Mrs Tizzard, I mean Tessa. And thanks, Mil.' Zoe wound the scarf around her neck and stuffed her wages into the battered satchel she used as a handbag. 'You coming then, Sean?'

Sean, who was looking longingly at the half-eaten slice of cake on his mother's plate, snapped into attention and opened the door.

'See you later, kids,' his mother cackled. 'Don't do anything I wouldn't do!'

Millie pressed a couple of slices of cake, wrapped in a serviette, into Sean's hands. She winked at him in sympathy. 'Bye both. Oh and Zoe, think I preferred Plummy Aubergine!'

Sean scowled at his mother, Zoe waved a cheerful goodbye and then they strode off along the promenade, arm in arm, heads close together.

Millie served scones and tea to a group deep in argument over the latest Booker prizewinner and then joined Tessa. 'Is there something going on between those two?'

Tessa exploded into laughter. 'Bloody poetry. Our Sean? I ask you!' She shook her head in answer. 'Who knows? If there is, it's news to me. Thought they were just friends. Wouldn't mind a bit, though. Zoe's a lovely girl. And she's a good influence on Sean, not counting this sudden passion for poetry.'

'But isn't he going to work at that picture-framing company in Honiton?'

'Yes, bab, it's all set up. It'll suit him. Says he's had enough of exams to last a lifetime. He's never been the most academic of my three. Unfortunately. What of it?'

'Just that it might explain Zoe's sudden cold feet about going to Durham.'

Tessa looked to where, illuminated by the white lights strung up all along the promenade, she could see her eldest walking with his arm around Zoe's shoulders. They stopped for a moment to take the inevitable selfie and giggled at the result. 'You mean, young love? Sweet.'

'And intense. You never feel the same as you do when you're in love at seventeen.'

29

Tessa pulled a gloomy face. 'Don't know. It was so long ago I can't remember.'

Millie laughed. 'Don't get me wrong, your Sean is gorgeous. But —'

'If you had the choice between love and a degree from Durham?' Tessa asked.

'I think I'd choose Durham.'

Tessa shoved in the last of her cake. 'That's what's wrong with you, Emilia Fudge,' she said through a full mouth, 'there's no romance in your soul. When was the last time you had a hot lover on your arm?'

'Don't know. It was so long ago I can't remember.' She winked at Tessa.

Tessa sniggered and got up. 'Better go and rescue Trevor from the boys. He'll have had enough by now. I'm amazed they can see anything on the beach at this time of night.'

'Oh, the lights on the prom reach out quite a way.' Millie stretched her back. It had been a long day.

Tessa observed her friend with affection. 'You look knackered. It really is about time you had some fun, my girl.'

Millie gave a wry smile. 'You tell me when and who with and I'm all for it. Not sure how I'll squeeze in a hot man, though. I work all day and bake all night. And I don't know about fun, but it would be lovely to have someone special to share my life with. I get lonely sometimes.'

Tessa nodded. 'I understand, kiddo. You can have all the friends in the world and still feel lonely without a special person to come home to.' She was silent for a moment and then added, 'Come here.'

'What for?'

'Come here,' Tessa repeated and beckoned Millie to where she was standing by the big picture window. When Millie obeyed, she turned her to face it, standing behind their joint reflection and putting her hands on her friend's shoulders. 'Look at you.'

Millie looked. And pouted. 'You're right. I look knackered.'

'Dead right you do. You're tired because you've just done a fourteen-hour day.'

'Your point being?' Millie was embarrassed, aware that the literary festival group were watching with interest.

'Behind the tiredness, I see gorgeous big brown eyes, that lovely dark hair and legs that I'd kill for. Don't let life be all about work, Millie. Go and find yourself that man. You want marriage, babies, the whole enchilada, don't you?'

Millie nodded, her eyes filling with tears that she put down to exhaustion. Tessa had a point. It had been months since she'd taken any time off. She tried to see herself objectively. Yes, her make-up had disappeared hours ago and while her bob had grown out, her hair was still thick and glossy. Her legs, toned by a lifetime of being on her feet waitressing, were encased in matte-black tights, their length revealed by the flippy short skirts she favoured. Not too bad, she ventured. She bit her lip. 'But where am I supposed to find a man, let alone some fun, Tess?'

Tessa made a face. 'God knows. Pick up a tourist? Or what about that bloke who keeps coming in? The one that Zoe keeps going on about. Wears all that designer gear – Hackett, she reckons it is. Another word for expensive, in my book.

31

Oh, I don't know where you'll find him but get out there, kiddo. Take some time out. Forget the ruddy café for five minutes.'

'And there's me wanting to be the next Mary Berry.'

'Wash your mouth out. There's only one Mary Berry!' Tessa put her hands together as if in prayer. 'Saint Mary!'

Millie giggled. She could always rely on her friend to make her laugh. 'Love you, Tess. Now go and find my dog.'

'Will do. Love you too, honeybun. Tarra a bit!'

Chapter 7

Millie bumped into Jed as she was hurrying up Berecombe's steep main street. Literally bumped into him. Tessa would say it was fate. Millie would say it was because she had her head down against the icy wind blowing sleet against her face and didn't see him coming the other way.

Oomph. Her library books slid onto the pavement as they collided. Trevor barked with excitement.

'Here, let me.' Jed bent down and collected them for her. 'Hello, Trevor,' he said, fending him off as the dog tried to lick his ear. '*Middlemarch* and James Joyce,' he read as he handed them back to her one by one. His eyebrows rose. 'Interesting reading.'

Millie blushed. 'I didn't go to college, so I've been trying to catch up on some books everyone tells me I ought to read.' She held up *Moby Dick*. 'This was for Book Club.'

'How did you find it?'

'Excruciatingly boring.'

Jed laughed. 'My thoughts exactly. I always had a bit of a thing for Mrs Gaskell. Maybe you could try her? Look, I think you're out of luck trying to return them tonight, the library's just closed. I passed it on my way down. Lights off and doors definitely locked.'

'Oh.' Millie's face fell. 'I hadn't realised it was so late.'

'I hope you'll avoid a fine? I have to confess it's been a long time since I borrowed a book from a library. Do they still do that?'

Millie nodded. 'I've got until tomorrow.' She sighed. 'I'll have to try to find time to return them then.'

Jed peered closer. 'If you don't mind my saying, you look rather done in.'

'The café's been busy with the literary festival. I've been rushed off my feet.'

'Well, it's good that you've been busy. Have you finished for tonight?'

Millie thought of the batch of Bakewell tarts she should get in the oven and of the apricots she needed to soak before making another four lots of the tray bake.

Jed filled in the gap left by her hesitation. 'If you have, may I suggest getting some supper in the White Bear? I hear their food isn't too bad.'

'The food in there is lovely.' Millie hopped from one foot to the other. She was freezing. Her nose was like ice. The thought of hot food in the company of an even hotter man was tempting beyond belief. Tessa's words from the other night reverberated. Since when did she have gorgeous men asking her out to eat? Since when had she had some fun? Sod it, she decided, the customers would have to make do with scones tomorrow and she had some tea bread she could defrost.

Some nice salty farmhouse butter would make it special. 'I'd love to,' she smiled up at him.

'What about Trevor?'

'Oh, he hasn't eaten either.'

Jed laughed. 'That wasn't quite what I meant. Do they allow dogs in the White Bear?'

Millie nodded, as much to keep warm as to answer. 'Oh yes, in the public bar, anyway. It's cosy in there too; they'll have a roaring fire going.'

'Sounds perfect. Shall we?' He held out an arm and Millie took it. 'Let me,' he added and relieved her of the books. 'Perhaps we can dissect Herman Melville some more?'

'Blimey, could we not?' Millie, very aware of how close he was, giggled. She leaned nearer, thinking that he smelled heavenly. She breathed in spice and lemon. It wasn't dissimilar to the cardamom lemon-drizzle cake she made sometimes.

'Maybe stick with Gaskell, then?'

They retraced her steps back down the hill, the sleet now at their backs, making their passage easier. Unusually cold weather aside, Berecombe looked beautiful. White lights strung across the narrow shopping street blew gently in the salt-laden breeze coming off the sea. Most shops had closed by now but had kept their window displays lit against the deep indigo of the night. It was postcard pretty.

Millie was overcome by a wave of affection for her home town. She'd never lived anywhere else and had never wanted to. Never needed to. She'd had everything she ever wanted here. Until recently. Risking a glance at Jed's profile, she wondered how long he was going to stay around. With his long upper lip and sharp cheekbones, there was definitely something of the Eddie Redmayne about him. He was posh-boy gorgeous. She breathed out a white cloud of hot breath in longing.

He looked down at her. 'Cold?'

Millie nodded. 'Freezing. Spring can't come soon enough. You?'

'God yes.'

He pulled up the collar of his overcoat. The wind had whipped high colour into his smooth, tanned complexion. The line where his skin met the deep black of his coat made Millie's insides melt with tenderness.

'The Bear's just down here, isn't it?'

When she didn't answer immediately, he said, 'Millie?' and looked penetratingly at her. He put an arm around her shoulders and hugged her closer. 'Warmer now?'

Don't gaze into my eyes like that, Millie begged silently, and then forced herself to get a grip. 'Um yes, thanks. And the pub's just along the passageway off the high street.' She clicked her tongue at Trevor and pointed the way.

'I love these small towns. So complete in themselves.' There was yearning in Jed's voice. 'A couple of pubs, some cafés and restaurants. Enough shops to buy what you need but not necessarily what you want. A strong sense of community. Have you always lived here?'

'Always.'

'And you never wanted to leave? To live somewhere else?'

Millie shook her head as best she could against his shoulder. 'No. As you say, everything I need is here. I'm really happy living here. Settled.' Or I was until recently, she added to herself. She stared up at him. How can I long for a man I know nothing of? But I do. I long, long, long for him.

'Where do you live, Jed?'

'Me? Here and there. Hotels mostly. I go where the work is. I move around so much there seems little point in settling anywhere permanent. Occasionally I rent an apartment, but that's rare. I'm in London mostly. New York sometimes.'

'And you go wherever the company you're working for is?'

As an answer, he nodded.

It all seemed impossibly glamorous to Millie. And alien. She couldn't imagine the life he had.

Trevor halted to sniff at something interesting, forcing them to stop.

Jed turned to face her. 'But nowhere I've lived has had quite the same appeal as here.' He came closer, only a breath apart. 'You have a tiny bit of sleet on your eyelashes,' he said and, with the gentlest of touches, he smoothed it off.

He was very close. If Millie reached up an inch, she could kiss that mouth, with its generous upper lip, could caress that square chin, nuzzle against his strong throat.

'I thought it was never supposed to be this cold at the seaside,' he murmured, his eyes locked on hers.

'It isn't usually.' Her eyes dropped to his mouth again. She ached to kiss it. 'It might snow, they say. At the seaside, it's a once in a lifetime experience.' Like this man. She had the strongest instinct she would never meet his like again.

Trevor, oblivious to what was going on above him, tried to trot off and yanked at the lead in Millie's hand.

'It's too cold to stand around, anyway,' she breathed and wondered if she saw regret in Jed's dark eyes.

Chapter 8

The White Bear was packed with early-evening drinkers and with those having come into town for the festival. It exploded around them as a colourful warm fuzz in contrast to the chilly monochrome outside. Dean the landlord spotted Millie and said he could find them a table in a corner, away from the loudest of the revellers. When she thanked him, he simply shrugged and added that it was the least he could do for someone who made the best flapjacks this side of Weymouth.

After letting Trevor drink his fill from the bowl of water at the door, they threaded their way through and settled on an old church pew in front of a tiny table. There was only just enough room if they sat tightly thigh to thigh. Millie found she didn't mind one little bit.

Trevor tucked himself underneath and collapsed with a sigh as Dean brought over their drinks. 'Half a Thatcher's, Mil, and the gent requested a pint of the local beer.' He put the cider and the pint of Black Ven onto the table. Without ceremony he barked out, 'Two steak and ale pies do you?'

Millie hardly had time to reply, 'Yes please,' before he disappeared back behind the bar. 'I hope that's alright for you?' she asked Jed, who was eyeing his glass suspiciously.

'Sounds delightful. Not sure about the beer, though.'

'It's a porter, a dark beer,' Millie explained. 'It's brewed in Lyme Regis, not far away.'

Jed took a cautious sip. 'It's good.' He took another. 'No, really very good.' He leant back against the pew, making it creak. Looking around at the worn slabs on the floor, at the two-foot thick whitewashed walls, at the heavy beams, he sighed with pleasure. 'This place is great, isn't it?'

'It is.'

'So, you know about beer too?'

Millie grinned, thinking that beer probably wasn't his usual tipple. 'Only the local stuff. I make a mean porter and chocolate cake with it.'

Jed groaned. 'Chocolate cake? I think I've found my perfect woman!' When all Millie did in response was blush, he added, 'Is there anything you don't know about around here?'

'Well, I've lived here all my life, so I ought to.' To hide her pleasure at his compliment, she sipped her cider and then said, 'Where did you grow up?'

'Oh, here and there. Family's R.A.F. so we moved around a lot. I got sent to boarding school when I was eight.'

'Eight?' Millie was appalled. It was the same age as Tessa's youngest son. 'That seems very young.'

'It does, I suppose,' Jed said cheerfully. 'But when your family moves so much it gives you some stability. Most vacs I didn't make it home; I even spent some Christmases at school. Don't look so horrified. I had some very jolly times with Matron's family.'

'Matron? *Matron!* Where did you go – Eton?'

Jed gave her a rueful grin. 'Somewhere like that.'

Bloody hell. Bit different to Berecombe Comp. Millie gulped down more cider. 'I can't imagine spending Christmas anywhere else but home.'

'Is that what you do?'

Millie nodded. 'Or I used to. Now I go to my friend's. Only for lunch, though. Trev and me, we have a good, long walk on the beach first and then get over to Tessa's just in time for the present opening. She's got three boys, so it's great fun.'

'You don't have parents?' Jed noticed the change in Millie's expression and added, 'I'm so sorry, that was intrusive.'

'No, it's alright. It used to be me, Mum and Dad, but they died in a car crash eleven years ago. Since then, I've always gone to Tessa's.'

Jed put his hand on Millie's. 'Now I really am sorry. I had no right to butt in on your most personal memories. Your most painful memories.'

His hand was very warm and firm and Millie's senses danced at his touch. It swamped the inevitable stab of grief. 'It's fine,' she said quickly. 'It was a long time ago. As the café was owned by them, it seemed the right thing to take it over and run it myself.'

'And you've done that ever since? You must have been very young at the time.'

'Yes, I suppose I was. Just about to go away to university to read English Lit.'

'Ah. Hence the books.'

Millie nodded again. She was blurrily aware she was getting drunk quite quickly and hoped their food would arrive soon. 'Hence the books. Trying to catch up a bit. Maybe I'll try your suggestion of Mrs Gaskell.'

Jed nodded. 'She's slightly more fun than Melville. So you gave up your place at uni and stayed here instead and worked at the café? That's amazing, Millie.'

'Oh, I don't know about it being amazing. In a strange way it kept me closer to them. It helped me, you know, being busy, doing what they'd always done.'

Jed took another sip of his beer. 'I can quite see that. I think it's one of the bravest things I've ever heard.' There was a beat before he added, 'You must have seen a few changes in the town.'

Perhaps Jed was attuned to her distress or maybe he'd simply wanted to change the subject. Either way, Millie was glad the conversation had taken a more casual tone and agreed. 'Oh yes. We went through a phase of being popular with surfing dudes; there was a time when the pound was weak and the ferries brought the French and Dutch over in droves and the last invasion was a hippy group who camped out on Mill Field for the summer. They've got some sort of commune Honiton way now. As we're the next stop along from Lyme, we get the visitors who can't find anywhere to park there and find us instead.'

'So there's a lot of tourist trade in the town?'

'There can be. If we have a good season. If the weather blesses us. And families seem to be rediscovering the traditional English seaside holiday again.'

'Sandcastles on the beach?'

Millie laughed. 'Don't scoff! That sort of thing, absolutely.'

Jed spread his hands. 'I wouldn't dream of scoffing, as you so delightfully put it. It sounds wonderful. I've never had that kind of holiday.'

Millie gave him another shocked look. Christmas spent with Matron and no beach holidays; what sort of childhood had he had? Her heart exploded with protectiveness for a little boy, no doubt privileged, but who hadn't seemed to have had the most basic of childhood pleasures. 'At the next opportunity we'll make sure we go on the beach and make the biggest, sandiest sandcastle you've ever seen.'

'Even if it snows?'

'Especially if it snows!'

Jed clinked his glass against hers. 'You're on!'

They smiled at one another, aware of the delicious, dizzying fizz of emotions rushing between them. Of the happy sliding into lust. Of maybe edging, blissfully, into something more meaningful.

The moment was only interrupted by Dean slamming their food onto the table in front of them.

Chapter 9

For the first time since taking over the running of her café, Millie resented the early start. When her phone buzzed and Debbie Reynolds trilled, 'Good morning, good morning!' she snapped it off and put her head back under the duvet. Instead of getting up in the dark, walking Trevor and getting the café ready, all she wanted to do was relish the evening she'd spent with Jed. To pick over every moment. Pulling her knees up she hugged them to herself with glee.

It had been the perfect evening. Enclosed in their cosy corner, it was as if they were in a happy little bubble all on their own. Jed had eaten with gusto, declaring his steak pie the best he'd ever had and ordered another pint of beer. They'd talked – about his childhood spent all around the world, but mostly he'd asked about her. Millie hadn't had anyone so interested in her for, well, she couldn't remember. So used to listening to Biddy moan or Arthur give a weather forecast or Zoe bang on about school, it had been exhilarating to talk about herself for a change. Jed had been an amazing listener, hanging on her every word. It had been immensely flattering. Millie hadn't missed the covetous glances from the other women in the pub either. She didn't blame them. Jed had looked positively edible in skinny jeans and a blue-and-white-striped rugby shirt.

He had insisted on walking her the short distance back to the café and to the steps at the side that led to her flat. It was about as romantic a night as could be. The sleet had stopped. All that was left was a crystal-cold night sky over an inky calm sea. No moon but a sprinkling of stars hanging over a just-visible, rolling coastline. In the distance, the Portland lighthouse beam appeared and dipped from view. There were few other people around and no need to hurry. As Jed and Millie walked along, arm in arm, the sea shifted and sighed, as if indulging in the romance of it all.

If Millie had been hoping for – or expecting – a goodnight kiss, she was disappointed. After a sort of mock salute, Jed had walked off along the promenade into the night, his broad shoulders making a triangle of his coat as he tucked his hands inside his pockets, pulling it tight across his hips. Millie had watched his blond head, made paler by the white lights strung from lamp post to lamp post, disappear around the corner to the hill leading to the shops. Her breath puffed out in a frozen cloud as she rested her chin on the handrail to the steps. She clung on to the metal for dear life. It was the only thing that stopped her from running after him.

It had been one of the best nights of her life.

Millie hugged her knees again and giggled to herself. She knew she was acting like a lovelorn teenager but it was such a novel and delicious feeling to like and be liked back that she couldn't help herself. Enjoying the champagne fizz of emotions inside, she rolled over onto her back and listened to the sea crashing outside.

She must have dozed off because she was woken by Trevor's impatient barking, ordering her to let him out. When she clocked the time, she gave a frantic yell at how late she'd slept. There was no more time for dwelling on mysterious handsome men with melting brown eyes.

Arthur was her first customer. He turned up just as Millie was unlocking the front door and flipping the sign to, "Come in for gorgeous cakes." She'd given Trevor the most cursory of runs on the beach and had got most things ready for another day at the café. The breeze coming off the sea was gentler this morning and there was a brighter blue in the sky. Even the aubrieta, cascading down the low wall that separated the café's sun terrace from the beach, had greened up. Was it too much to hope that spring was in the air?

One look at Arthur's distraught face had all thoughts of Jed and the softening season taking flight. He came in, again without Daisy, but followed closely on his heels by Biddy and Elvis.

'I've been calling you all along the prom,' the elderly lady yelled at the unfortunate man. 'Where's Daisy?'

Ignoring Biddy, Millie steered Arthur to his table in the window and sat him down. She feared the worst.

'Cup of tea, Arthur? Or maybe a pot?' At his nod she smiled and wasn't reassured to see tears gleam behind his spectacles. To her surprise Biddy joined him, sitting opposite. Millie's heart sank. Biddy wasn't the easiest company and her tactlessness was legendary.

'I said, how's Daisy? Fern at the vet's said she was in there.'

'Biddy,' warned Millie.

Arthur cleared his throat. 'It's alright, Millie. You may as well both know, the vet found a tumour. Daisy's got to have an operation.'

'A tumour? That doesn't sound good.' Biddy sniffed.

'Biddy!' Millie rolled her eyes.

'What? No point beating about the bush, is there?'

Millie supposed there wasn't. Concerned that Biddy might upset Arthur further, she rushed to the kitchen, made a pot of tea as quickly as she could, threw a few pastries onto a plate and joined the pensioners at their table.

'You know I always drink coffee,' grumbled Biddy.

'Well, just this once you can have tea.' As the woman began to moan, Millie cut her off with, 'Don't worry, it's on the house.'

There was a silence as Millie doled out mugs and plates and offered round the cakes. She sneaked a dog biscuit to Elvis, who had retreated under the table and was sitting on her foot. 'Go on, Arthur,' she encouraged when he at first refused. 'Try a bit of this tray bake. I soak the apricots in brandy to give them extra flavour.'

'Brandy, I ask you!' Biddy spluttered. 'You'll never make a decent profit by doing that sort of malarkey, young lady.'

'Maybe not, but it goes down a storm and I only make it at this time of year.' So put that in your pipe and smoke it, she added silently.

'Not keen on brandy, me,' added Biddy taking a huge mouthful and chewing with enthusiasm.

'So, Arthur,' Millie resumed, 'Tell us all about Daisy. That's if you can, of course.' She put a hand on his and was distressed to feel it tremble.

He took an enormous breath and began to talk. Turned out Daisy had been under the weather for a while and, on a regular visit for her jabs, the vet had felt a lump on the dog's stomach.

'I don't know how I could have missed it!' Arthur cried. Millie pushed a mug of tea towards him.

Biddy pursed her lips. Millie braced herself for some kind of accusation or dire warning from the old woman. Instead she said, 'Easily done. And some of them tumours grow fast. Besides, Daisy's got such a thick coat, would've been easy to miss.'

Millie looked at Biddy in gratitude. She was being quite nice!

'I had a goldie years ago,' Biddy went on. 'Just like your Daisy. Had her when I was doing my last job. Too busy rushing round the place. Missed a lump just under her ear.'

'But she was okay, wasn't she?' asked Millie, praying Biddy had some consolation for Arthur.

'Oh no. Turned out to be malignant. Had to have her put down. Upset all the girls, it did. Mind you, she was knocking on for twelve.'

Millie winced. Biddy's rare tactfulness had been short-lived.

Arthur drank some tea. 'Good age for a goldie,' was all he said.

Biddy nodded. 'You do what you can, don't you?' she boomed. 'But there's only so much you *can* do.'

'What's going to happen?' Millie pushed the plate of cakes

Biddy's way in the hope of shutting her up.

'They'll have to conduct some tests, I expect, see what it is and we'll take it from there.'

'You got insurance?' Biddy asked.

Arthur nodded. 'But only up to a certain amount. If Daisy needs a very expensive operation ...' his voice trailed off.

'Was going to say, I can always cough up a bit if you haven't. What you looking at me like that for, Millie? We dog-owners got to stick together in times of crisis.'

Arthur dislodged Millie's hand and reached over to Biddy. 'Dear lady, that is a very kind thought.'

Millie looked from one to the other in amazement. Their usual enmity had been completely forgotten. Sliding off her seat she left them to it, praying Daisy would be in the clear – and that Biddy wouldn't say anything more to upset Arthur.

Chapter 10

It was the middle Saturday in January and Millie was going stir-crazy. She needed fresh air. She closed the café early and sent Zoe home. It had been quiet anyway since the literary festival had finished. She decided to drive into Lyme Regis. She had Tessa's birthday present to buy and a sudden need to do some pottering around the town's quirky shops.

It was one of those wonderful gifts of a day at which her part of the coast excelled. Spring really did seem just a few days around the corner. The sky was an optimistic shade of clear blue and you could smell the changing season lilting in on the gentle breeze from the sea. Millie wondered if her thick Guernsey might be a mistake, but it had been her dad's and wearing it filled her with happy memories of him.

She found a parking space and eased her wheezing Fiesta into it, ignoring the sounds it was making. Repairs meant more expense, and money was short. The much-needed refurb of the café might have to wait.

'Can't afford to do both, Trevor my lad,' she said to the dog. 'Maybe we'll start doing the Lottery again?'

She took the dog to Church Beach for a run around and

laughed as he scampered in circles, high on the new smells. Finally, when he'd had enough, he came back to be put on the lead.

'And now for some real exercise, Trevor.' She pulled a face. 'How to spend as little as possible on a pressie without looking mean.'

Trevor's only response was a little whine and a regretful look back at the beach as they made their way to the shops.

Two hours later and an exhausted cockapoo and an over-heated Millie sat on a bench on the Bell Cliff tucking into a pasty. 'Well, I think we've done okay, Trev,' Millie said as she blew on her pasty to cool it down. She pulled off an edge of pastry and gave it to him. 'That "Don't Disturb Me, I'm Baking" mug is perfect for Tessa.' She giggled. 'She'll love how it plays the theme to *The Great British Bake Off*.'

'Talking to yourself, Millie?'

It was Jed.

Millie jumped a foot. Trevor lunged with a bark and her carrier bag slithered to the ground.

'I'm so sorry, I didn't mean to startle you. Here, let me.' Replacing the shopping on the bench, he sat down. 'What are you doing sitting out here? Enjoying the sunshine?'

Millie waved her pasty at the sea. 'I've been shopping and got rather warm. Wrong clothes choice,' she explained further. She squinted at the sun. 'Besides, it's a glorious day and you can't complain about the view from here.'

Jed took off his Ray-Bans and grinned, showing even, white teeth. He pushed his sunglasses onto his head. 'Can't believe you can get days like this in this country – and in January.

It's glorious!'

'I think spring will be early this year. Quite often is around here.'

Jed sat back, taking up most of the room on the bench. 'And I wouldn't dream of complaining about this view. It's fantastic, isn't it?'

Millie nodded and, feeling self-conscious about eating something so messy in front of him, wrapped the remainder of her pasty back into its paper bag. 'You can see Portland today. That's the bump of land far out to the right of the coast. And the sun's just coming onto the red cliffs at West Bay, look. That's where they film *Broadchurch*. And the highest bit of the coast is –'

'Golden Cap. I know.'

'Sorry, was I being boring? Too much of a tour guide?' Millie deflated.

'Millie, you're never boring. It's just that I know Lyme a bit. Ma and Pa had a holiday cottage near Dorchester for a couple of summers.'

'Oh. I thought you said you'd never had a beach holiday.'

'And I never have. Mum didn't like the mess everything got into with sand. So we did days out, the museum here in Lyme, the tank place over at Bovington, that kind of thing. My brother and I liked it best when we had a day by the pool, though.'

'You had a pool? A swimming pool?'

Jed nodded. 'Yes, for a while it was great. Alex and I spent all day splashing about in it. Mum got bored, though, after a few years and bought something in France.'

'Like you do.'

Jed didn't seem to notice her mild sarcasm and answered cheerfully enough, 'As you do. She's sold that now. A restless spirit is my mother. She mentioned she'd quite like a pied-à-terre in Lyme, so I've just been pressing my nose against the estate agents' windows.'

'Along with everyone else, I would imagine.'

Jed laughed again. 'Oh yes. I had quite a crowd to fight my way through.'

'Lyme's very sought-after. It's the thing to do when coming here. Gaze at the houses for sale and gasp at the ridiculously high prices.'

'Actually, I didn't think they were all that bad; certainly not compared to London.' He stretched his legs with evident enjoyment and nodded at the view. 'And you can see why it's so popular. I wouldn't mind living here myself. Have you had much success with your shopping?'

Millie was about to launch into how difficult it was trying to be generous with a limited amount of money, but didn't feel someone who accepted Lyme's property prices so glibly and had a mother who bought and sold holiday cottages on a whim would empathise. 'Oh yes,' she nodded. 'Think I've got what I wanted.'

She looked at his bright-orange puffa jacket and at the collar of his rugby shirt, snowy white against his tanned skin. Who was sun-tanned in January? She spotted the gleam of an expensive-looking wristwatch and the designer logo on his coat. He was a creature from a very different world to hers and her little café in Berecombe. She wondered, fleetingly, whether Cinderella had ever really been happy with her Prince Charming. They hardly had scrubbing floors in common. Millie had to scrub the old lino in the café quite a lot, what with muddy sand being walked in. She couldn't exactly see Jed on his hands and knees, dipping a brush in a bucket.

Millie dismissed the mental image of Jed with soapsuds on his nose with a giggle. 'So is that why you're in the area? To suss out property for your mum?'

'Partly.' Jed replaced his sunglasses. He gave an embarrassed grin. 'You don't say no to my mother and live. She's supposed to be checking up on me at some point.' He paused and then added, 'But I've one or two clients around here too, so I might have a bit of business to deal with. And how did you like the shopping, Trevor?' He bent down and fussed the dog.

The change of subject wasn't subtle and Millie didn't miss it.

'I envy you being able to have a dog. I'm always here, there and everywhere. It wouldn't be fair on it.' He sighed. 'Not enough time, either.'

There was that note of yearning again. The same as when he'd complimented Berecombe. Millie didn't understand it. How could anyone like him be envious of what little she had? 'What do you do, Jed? For a living, I mean.'

He continued to fuss Trevor and didn't answer for a moment. Then seemed to come to a decision. 'I'm a management consultant. Freelance.'

'Sounds high-pressured.'

'It can be.' He straightened and looked out to sea. 'It most certainly can be. I enjoy a challenge, though.'

'And you say you've got clients around here?'

'One or two. Mostly in Exeter. I do some work for the university and for Lodgings.'

'Blimey. They're the biggest chain of solicitors in the south-west.' Millie was impressed.

He named another couple of prominent companies and then returned to tickling under Trevor's chin.

'What does it involve? Your job?'

'Oh, you know, I identify strengths and weaknesses, help to develop strategies, reduce costs. That sort of thing. Help companies do what they do but better, I suppose. And it's always useful to have an outsider look over things.'

'True.'

'I'm the maverick of the family, though. My brother, Alex, is the successful one. Banker in the city,' he added at her blank look.

It really was another existence. For the first time, Millie felt restlessness tug at her, felt the frustration of a life that had been so horribly derailed on that awful day in June. The one when the police had arrived on her doorstep asking if there was anyone who could be with her. The only people she could think of had been the Barts. Owners of The Plaice Place and parents of her best friend at school. Millie had a sudden vision of Dora pushing past them, running into the café and bursting into hysterical tears. Mrs Bart had simply hugged a dry-eyed Millie to her. Millie hadn't cried for a long, long time. Instead, she had given up on school and a university place, to run the café. She'd layered her grief under solid hard work ever since. Had re-named the café and begun to enjoy the life it gave her.

But what if her parents hadn't died? What if she'd gone to university after all, got a job like Jed's or his high-flying brother's? Trevor nudged at her knee and whined a little, bringing her back. It was stupid to think that way. Her life was perfect as it was.

Jed had been talking, explaining more of what his job entailed but she'd missed most of it. She gathered it meant a lot of international travelling. She'd been right. They were from different worlds. Different galaxies, even. She imagined him with a sleek blonde on his arm, at parties, skiing, at one of those resorts where cute little huts were built over a tropical sea. Or did that constitute a beach holiday? She doubted it.

'You're miles away,' Jed said and took her hand in his. 'That's why I don't go on about my job, or one of the reasons, anyway. It bores people rigid. And I'd hate to bore you.'

He was very close. Yes, they were different animals but even Millie, inexperienced as she was, couldn't mistake the warmth in his expression.

'I'm so sorry. You're right, I was miles away.' Fervently hoping her hand wasn't greasy from the pasty and that she didn't have onion breath, she blurted out, 'I'm just a bit worried about how the new café opening up in Berecombe will impact on my place.'

Jed sat back and removed his hand. Perhaps she had bad breath after all?

'I've heard the gossip in town. You're talking about Blue Elephant?' he asked after a long pause. 'I can't see it myself.'

'Can't you?'

'Millie, you've got something very special going on. Millie Vanilla's does exceptional food, great coffee and you've a loyal band of customers on top of seasonal trade. You're at the heart of your community, any fool can see that. I certainly did on my first visit. They all love you, don't they?' He shoved his sunglasses up his nose with one finger and seemed embarrassed at being so serious. 'Plus,' he added, more flippantly, 'you're much nearer to the beach. Practically on it. And that sun terrace you have is a huge bonus.'

Millie wasn't sure she was loved by everyone. It certainly didn't feel that way with Biddy most of the time. 'The terrace is my secret weapon, I agree. It's a fantastic draw in the summer.' She glanced across. 'So you think I'm worrying about nothing?'

'Well, it's wise to be cautious. I wouldn't invest in changing any major stuff for the time being. Sticking with what you know goes down well with your customers and your strong brand.'

Millie laughed. 'My brand? I don't think I have one of those.'

'You may not think it but, yes, Millie Vanilla's is strongly branded. In its own way. And remember your links to your community. Blue Elephant can never hope to emulate that.'

'Thanks, Jed. I appreciate you saying that. Is that some of your management consultancy in action?'

He laughed. 'Sort of. Need a lift back to Berecombe?'

'No thanks. I've got my car.' She rose and he passed her the shopping bags.

'Millie, I know you work all the hours God sends but I'd

like to take you out one evening, if I may?'

Millie looked down at his face, wishing he'd take off his sunglasses so she could see his eyes. Tessa's words rushed back at her. Her friend had been right, she did deserve some fun. When had she last been out with a man before Jed came along? She wracked her brain to no avail. She and Tessa hadn't been out on a girly night in Exeter for weeks either. They'd not even managed a pizza in Lyme.

She smiled at him, making her decision. 'Now the literary festival is over, I'm not staying open late in the evenings, so yes, Jed, you may take me out. In fact, I'd like nothing better.'

Chapter 11

Jed picked her up in a Golf, top of the range, and obviously a hire car.

When he saw her admiring its plush leather interior, he explained. 'I'm never in one place for very long.' There was more regret in his voice. 'So there seems little point in getting a car of my own. I just hire one wherever I am.'

It was one more indication of his peripatetic lifestyle.

'Where are you staying, while you're around here I mean?'

'Oh, haven't I said? The Lord of the Manor.' He steered the car out of its tight spot with ease. 'Do you know it?'

Millie suppressed a laugh. 'Yes, I know it. We're not going there for dinner, are we?'

'No fear,' Jed said stoutly. 'The food's dire. I can't believe the place gets any business.'

'Neither can I. The Simpson family, who run it, have had it for donkey's years but don't like spending money on it. I haven't been in for ages.' She glanced at his profile while he drove. He had a very lovely high-bridged nose and enviably clear skin. 'What's it like?'

'The public rooms are okay, if you like shabby-chic that's

original Jacobean and not designer. But my room is a nightmare. Hot water at random times, the windows have gaps around them bigger than the frames and non-existent heating. I only had enough hot water for the quickest of showers tonight. I hope I don't smell.'

Using it as an excuse, Millie leaned over and sniffed. He smelled heavenly, as usual. 'No, you don't smell of anything you shouldn't,' she said, taking in a lungful of something woody. It made a change to be with a man who smelled of something other than Old Spice, as Arthur invariably did. Along with wet dog on occasion.

Jed concentrated as he turned right onto the A35 before adding, 'But it's the lack of Wi-Fi that really irritates me. The place claims to have superfast broadband but I haven't seen any evidence of it so far.'

'To be fair, the internet is notoriously slow around here. I've never been sure why. Too many hills, maybe? In some places it's hard to get a signal on your mobile, let alone anything else.'

'I've noticed.' He flashed a swift grin. 'How on earth do you manage? To run a business, I mean.'

'Oh, we do okay. Sometimes it's even quite nice to do things the old-fashioned way. You know, on the landline.' She pulled a face. 'Or by post.'

'Do you know, I think I've had better reception in the middle of the desert than Dorset or Devon?' Then he heard, properly, what she'd said. 'Are you poking fun at me?'

'Not at all, but don't you think it's good to occasionally be away from all that social media and stuff? I can't see the point of posting pictures of what you've had for lunch. Fries my brain sometimes.' Millie felt herself tense. They were approaching the spot where her parents had died. Even after all these years, she still couldn't pass it without grief stealing in.

'I think you're delightfully and gorgeously old-fashioned, Millie. And I know what you mean, but customers nowadays expect to be connected to a fast service all the time. And moan like hell if they can't.' He gunned the Golf's engine and overtook expertly. He must have noticed her clenched fists. 'Are you alright? Not a nervous passenger?'

They were past. It was okay. 'I'm fine.' She forced herself to relax and to focus on more pleasant things. On the here and now. On the fact that Jed had called her gorgeous. Well, sort of. 'So, if you're not treating me to an evening of dubious gastronomic delight at the Lord, where *are* we going tonight?'

'You'll see.' With a smile, Jed flicked on some music and they didn't speak again.

It turned out to be a country-house hotel on the edge of Dorchester. As Jed swung the car into the car park, he asked, 'French. Is that alright with you? It's one of my favourite countries and I love the food. This place was recommended to me, so I hope it lives up to its reputation.'

They parked between a Bentley and a Porsche. Millie looked around in dismay. She should have guessed it would be an expensive sort of place. She was going to be completely underdressed in leggings and flowery mini-dress.

Jed read her panic. 'You look beautiful. You always do. Don't worry and try to relax. I want this to be a real treat for you.

Thought it might make a change for you not to cook. I only hope the food comes up to your standards.'

Millie felt his appreciative gaze on her and blushed. She added 'beautiful' to his list of compliments and the glow inside her spread.

The passenger door was opened by a liveried car-park attendant who murmured a reverent, 'Good evening, madam.' Millie tried not to giggle and looked up at the hotel's subtly lit Georgian facade. She wondered just what she'd got herself into.

Her recollection of the evening was of soft music, good wine, fantastically complicated food and impeccable service. From the moment she stepped from the car she wasn't aware of having to lift a finger or even open a door. All evening her needs were not only met but anticipated. Once in the lounge, a soft-footed waiter presented her with a glass of champagne and another brought a tiny canapé of salmon gravlax. Seated at a table, covered in a snowy white cloth, an amuse bouche of different-coloured beetroots and creamy goat's cheese arrived, followed by brill with citrus couscous. The service was attentive and discreet. She didn't have to wait a second for her water or wine glass to be topped up. It was divine and a world away from her little café in Berecombe. Jed, she noticed, had a glass of champagne and then drank sparkling water all night. He seemed not only to be at home in his surroundings but was almost casually contemptuous of it.

Sighing over delicious chocolatey petits fours she said, 'I'd love to travel as you obviously have.'

Jed shrugged. 'If I'm honest, it can get pretty boring. And

mostly all I see is the inside of airports and hotels. I've done some cool stuff, dining with a Bedouin tribe under the desert stars is a stand-out, but it's not much fun without someone to share it with.' He flicked a glance at Millie. 'Just lately I've developed a real hunger to settle down somewhere. Put some roots down. With that special person.'

'Ha!' Millie blurted, aware she'd had quite a bit to drink. 'Gotta find her first.'

Jed gave her a slow smile. 'That's very true.'

Millie licked melted chocolate off her finger and frowned. 'So you mean you'd like marriage, a family, the whole commitment?'

'Yeah. I think it's the right time for me. I've rattled around the world on my own for too long. It would be nice to be in one place, be part of a community, like you are.'

Millie's face burned. It could be the alcohol or it could be the picture that was forming of Jed rocking a baby in his arms. A baby that had his dark eyes and a mop of her unruly hair. Whoa, Millie, she admonished herself. Too much too soon. She gazed at Jed. There was no mistaking the heat in his expression. She finished her coffee in one gulp. 'Still, as I've said, you've got to find that special someone first.'

He smiled enigmatically and then called a waiter over. 'More coffee, please. And Millie, would you like a brandy with yours?'

She nodded. She was bursting with questions to ask him but was too self-conscious – and quite possibly too tipsy. Instead, she tried for nonchalance when spotting a well-known actor and two presenters from the local news. And then, as the alcohol really kicked in, she surrendered herself to the happy feeling of being completely and utterly cosseted.

'Don't know about you,' Jed said, in the car on the way home. 'But I didn't think that wild garlic consommé was a patch on your butternut squash soup.'

Millie giggled sleepily, replete with good food and luxury. She could get used to this. 'It was a lovely evening,' she said, snuggling down into her coat. 'Thank you. You were right, it *has* been a real treat.' She rested her head back and enjoyed the scent of the leather upholstery.

'Good. I get the feeling you haven't had many treats. I was delighted to indulge you.' As he manoeuvred the car out of the car park, he began to explain that the hotel was trying to emulate Le Manoir aux Quat' Saisons, but he still preferred the original. Millie didn't reply; she was fast asleep.

Jed woke her by tweaking her nose gently.

Millie came to, flustered and embarrassed. 'We're back in Berecombe? I'm so sorry, I can't believe I slept all the way!' She looked around. They were parked up on the promenade outside her café.

He rested an arm along her headrest. 'You know, I think you work too hard.'

Millie gazed into his dark eyes, their expression impenetrable, even in the glow from the lights strung up along the prom. He was very close and nerves made her breathy. 'Do I? I've normally got bags of energy. It's just that –'

She was silenced by his kiss. His hand cupped her cheekbone and she found the touch of his long fingers immeasurably exciting. His lips were cool and expert and Millie gave in. Time for a bit of fun, she decided. I don't really know who you are or how long you'll be around, but at this precise moment I don't care. Then his kiss deepened and she stopped thinking altogether.

It seemed only seconds later that he was pulling back.

'Don't stop.'

'Millie, my love, it's late. I'm assuming you have to get up at some unearthly hour in the morning and I have to fly to Paris tomorrow.'

'Oh.'

'I'll be back. It's just for a meeting.'

Millie took a deep breath. 'You could come in, you know.'

He dropped his hand from its hold on her face. 'God, I'd love to Millie, you don't know how much. But it's just not the right time.' He looked down, a frown knitting his brows. 'There are some things I have to sort out first.'

'Oh, I see.'

'No, you don't.' He raked a hand through his hair, making it stand up on end. 'You don't see at all.' He gathered her hands in his. Kissing her fingers, he added, 'And why should you?'

The script wasn't going according to plan. Yes, okay, when she should have been indulging in light banter and pre-coital flirting, she'd fallen asleep in the car and may well have snored. It wouldn't have been pretty. But weren't men supposed to be permanently gagging for sex? And here was the man of her dreams turning down her offer. Maybe she'd had too much garlic soup at dinner? Or she wasn't his usual brand of sleek blonde? Lust shrivelled in her loins. Bugger.

Jed's hand returned to her cheek. He trailed a finger down

her face. 'Do you – can you trust me, Millie? Before this goes any further, there's something I have to do.'

Millie found herself nodding. 'I trust you.' She did. She didn't have a clue why, but she did.

Jed exhaled, as if her answer had mattered a great deal to him. 'Good.'

He reached over and unclicked her seatbelt. He was very near. Tantalisingly so. She could smell his hair and feel the heat coming off his skin. She wanted him so badly it hurt. It actually hurt. She gave a little gasp of need.

He gave her a rueful look. 'Let's get you inside before I change my mind.'

Chapter 12

Millie was in such a state the following morning that she hardly noticed who came in to the café, what they ordered and, more worryingly, what she served them.

What had Jed got to sort?

Why did he have to go to Paris? When would he back?

Why hadn't she thought to ask for his mobile number? Why hadn't he given it to her?

Why did his upper lip jut out slightly more than the lower and made her want to take it between her teeth?

'What is the matter with you, girl? Since when do I eat chocolate cake?' Biddy's sharp voice made Millie jump.

'So sorry, Biddy. It's my special today, but I'll get you your usual scone.'

'And a biscuit for Elvis.'

'Of course.' Millie caught a sympathetic look from Arthur as she glided back into the kitchen. She was walking on air. Who would have thought one kiss could make her feel like this? And if his kiss was that powerful, what would...

'Millie!' roared Biddy. 'Arthur's not got his tea yet.'

Millie forced herself to concentrate. At this rate there would be no Millie Vanilla's for Jed to come back to. Banishing a vision of his long tanned body rumpling her nautically striped sheets, Millie slapped herself on the cheek and went to work.

As she came out, bearing a tray of tea for Arthur and scones for Biddy, Zoe and Sean came in. According to Tessa, Zoe was making the most of any free time by spending it with Sean, working with Ken in his studio.

'Hi, Millie,' Zoe said and blushed. 'We'll sit over in the corner, if you don't mind. Thank you. Oh, hi Granddad,' she called to Arthur. 'Mum said she'd be over later. Got a couple of frozen casseroles for you.'

This was deeply worrying. Zoe never blushed. And she was never that polite.

Millie served Biddy and Arthur and watched, from the corner of her eye, as Zoe and Sean pressed themselves into the corner table and gazed adoringly into each other's eyes. The intensity!

'There's no sugar in this bowl,' Biddy yelled.

Buttoning down the urge to tell Biddy where to go, Millie forced a smile and murmured she'd go and get some.

'What did she say?' Biddy said irritably to Arthur. 'What's going on in here today? I've a good mind to take my custom elsewhere.'

Millie served Zoe and Sean their hot chocolate and was beckoned over by Arthur. 'Come and sit yourself down for a minute, my dear,' he said. He looked comically over his shoulder, as if spies might hear. 'I've got some information about that new place opening on the high street.'

Millie poured herself a coffee and, having glanced around

to check if anyone needed anything, perched on a chair next to Arthur. 'Do I have to give you a password before you tell me anything?' she hissed, wide-eyed.

Arthur looked blank.

'You know, "The moon is full and the sea is calm," sort of thing.'

Arthur raised his eyebrows in a way that made Millie feel about five. 'You might not be laughing when you hear this, my dear. This new café, Blue Elephant, is opening next weekend.'

Millie sat back in dismay, all flippancy gone. 'So soon?'

Arthur nodded.

'I'd been hoping it wouldn't be ready for ages.'

'Apparently they've been beavering away behind those boarded-up windows. Want to catch a bit of the trade as soon as possible. Establish themselves before the new tourist season starts.'

Millie bit her lip. 'I suppose that makes sense.' She could kick herself. There had been no time to think through the refurbishment of the café and she hadn't even tried out any new menus. She looked around. Who was she kidding? Biddy always had her coffee and scone, the kids drank hot chocolate and Arthur was loyal to his pot of tea. They weren't exactly the customers to go for the sort of exciting flavour combinations she'd eaten last night. She couldn't see Biddy enjoying brill and citrus couscous. With a heavy heart, she tuned back in to what Arthur was saying.

'They're opening a Blue Elephant in Berecombe,' he was saying, 'and Taunton and Honiton is next on the list and then

Exeter. That's if all goes well here.'

Millie snorted. 'And why shouldn't it? With so many branches close together they'll be able to buy in bulk cheaply. And completely undercut my prices.' She put her head in her hands and groaned.

'I'm so sorry, my dear, but I thought you'd like to know.' Arthur's voice was full of concern.

She forced herself to look him in the eye. 'Thank you, Arthur. I appreciate it.' Then a thought struck. 'How do you know all this?'

'Dennis, the chairman of the trading committee, told me.'

'Fuck.' Millie caught herself. 'Sorry, Arthur.'

He gave a small smile. 'A certain level of profanity is acceptable in the circumstances, my dear.' He patted her hand. 'But you have no need for concern. This café and the Blue Elephant place are two very different animals, as Zoe would say.'

'Maybe.'

'Now, don't look so gloomy. Think about it. You've lived alongside Kosy Korner and The Plaice Place all these years.'

'I have. But you've got to admit they both offer different things. People go to a chip shop for, well, chips and the KK does its roast dinner carveries. The Blue Elephant will sell the same things as me – coffee, cake, sandwiches, that type of thing. They'll be in direct competition with me.'

Arthur straightened. 'I'm positive it will all be fine. When the tourist season begins there's trade enough for everybody.'

'That's the problem, Arthur. I've got to *get* to the next season.'

'Things that tight, eh?' He looked shocked.

Millie didn't trust herself to speak. She nodded.

'Oh, my dear, I'm so sorry.'

'Arthur, I don't know what I'll do if I don't have this place. I can't do anything else.'

He patted her hand again. 'I'm sure it won't come to that. Look, I'll get my thinking cap on, shall I? See what I can come up with.'

'Oh, Arthur, would you? Thank you.'

'Best be off. Don't want to leave Daisy too long.' He stood up.

Now it was Millie's turn to look shocked. 'Oh, Arthur, I feel awful, I haven't even asked after her!'

Arthur's face clouded. He tucked his scarf around his neck. 'I'm still waiting for test results. Never an easy time, is it?'

Millie rose and gave him a hug.

He shook her off. 'Now, dear girl, don't be too nice to me. That's when the waterworks start. I'll be off.' And, with a quick wave to Zoe, he'd gone.

'What were you two whispering about so secretly?' Biddy asked, obviously miffed at being left out of the conversation.

Millie said the first thing that came into her head. It wasn't a complete lie. 'Oh nothing much. Think Arthur's worried about vet's bills and poor Daisy being so ill.'

'Hmph, he needs to man up,' Biddy said, sourly. 'Eyes too near his bladder. Always said so.'

Millie ignored her, collected Arthur's plate and mug and went into the kitchen. All romantic thoughts of Jed had fled.

Chapter 13

If Millie needed a diversion from worrying over the café, she got it on her early-morning dog walk across the beach two days later.

Trevor saw him first. With a delighted bark, the dog belted across the flat wet expanse of sand.

The sun was shining in Millie's eyes, so she could only see his silhouette but she'd know his walk anywhere. Confident, covering a lot of ground in a short space of time. Summed the man up, really.

Jed. He was back!

She ran up to him, but wasn't in time to stop Trevor from jumping up and covering his jeans in wet sand.

'Hi, Millie. Thought I'd join you,' he yelled over a volley of barks.

'I'm sorry,' she gasped, horrified. 'He really shouldn't jump up at people like that.' She bent to grab the dog's collar and missed. She straightened. 'Oh, Trev, get down!'

'It doesn't matter. These are old.'

Millie, eyeing the cut and the material, quietly disagreed. They looked thoroughly designer to her. Not that she had much experience to go on. 'He really shouldn't get into the habit of jumping up at people.'

Jed fussed the dog, who danced around and barked some more. 'It's my fault. I called him over. I really don't mind, you know. It makes a nice change to get out of a suit sometimes and be scruffy.'

'Is that your idea of scruffy?' Millie looked down at her own cropped jeans and knee-length baggy grey sweater. It was another of her dad's. She pushed her hair, made curly by sea spray, off her face and laughed.

Jed looked abashed. 'Well, it's all relative.'

With Trevor finally calm, Millie put her arm through Jed's and turned westwards, in the direction of the café. 'What brings you out this early?'

'Thought I'd see what the attraction of a dawn start was and join you on your early- morning dog walk. Oh, and you know, it's too nice a morning to waste.'

'Isn't it just? Glorious. And it's a spring tide today. The sea has gone out a long way. Loads of space for Trev to run.'

They wandered nearer the edge of the waves, where the dog was trying to tug a deeply buried bit of wood out of the sand.

'And he never gives up hope with that. Stubborn and persistent, that's my Trevor.'

'Wonder who he gets that from?' Jed said, on a smile.

'Hey!' Millie jabbed in the side with her elbow.

'I believe you promised me a sandcastle building lesson.'

'What? Now?'

'Well, the thing is, I have to do this thing called work and

73

you seem to spend all your waking hours running the café. I find I have to make the most of any time I have with you. So, yes. Now.'

Millie stopped and smiled up at him. The chilly air had freshened his complexion and brought an impish gleam to his dark eyes. 'You're on.'

He clasped a hand, cold from the wind, around the back of her neck. His thumb hooked around her earlobe and he brought her face closer. 'You could teach me so many things, Millie,' he murmured against her lips. He began to kiss her and then yelled.

Millie felt icy sea water hit her wellies and shrieked with laughter as Jed danced around trying to avoid the incoming tide, which had soaked his expensive-looking boat shoes.

She grabbed his hand. 'Come on then, Scruff Boy. Let's go and find ourselves a bucket and spade.'

They ran over to a shack on the very end of the promenade, where it met the lane that led to the harbour. The dilapidated sign over the shop read: Barney's Beach Supplies.

'Looks in need of a bit of TLC,' Jed observed.

'It's the rough winter weather. Always plays havoc with any paintwork on the front. Barney will repaint before the season gets going proper and it'll look beautiful.' Millie looked up at the front of the boarded-up wooden shed with fondness. 'He does candy floss and yummy toffee apples in October before he closes up.' She disappeared around the back and yelled out, 'Barney always keeps a few buckets and spades back here. He does an unofficial lost-and-found service in the summer.' She reappeared, brandishing a couple of spades and three faded plastic buckets. 'Come on, let's find us the right sort of sand.'

'There are different sorts of sand?' Jed queried.

'Oh, you have so much to learn, my lovely,' Millie responded, looking pityingly at him.

Jed grinned. 'Apparently so.'

'Bet mine will be bigger than yours.'

'Are you challenging me?' Echoing her tone, he added, 'Oh, Millie, you have so much to learn!'

Millie gave him a quick peck on the lips and then bobbed out her tongue. She ran out to sea, to the flat sand, a euphoric Trevor at her heels and screamed as Jed began to chase her.

Squabbling like children, they worked furiously to build the biggest castles possible, in a race against the tide.

Watching all their hard work crumble into the sea, Jed put his arm around Millie's shoulders. 'I can't believe I've got to the age of thirty-three and not done this before.' He kissed the side of her head. 'And you know what?'

'You're starving?'

'How did you know?'

Millie giggled. 'Lucky guess.' She put her arms around his waist and hugged him to her. Standing on the beach of her home town and feeling his warm, solid body next to hers, she wondered if she could be any happier. Lifting her face to the sun and to the salty spray, she said, 'I love it here so much.'

Jed tightened his arm around her. 'You know what, Millie? So do I.'

Back at the café, they toed off their wet shoes.

'These are never going to be the same again,' Jed mourned

as he examined his ruined loafers.

'Oh dear,' Millie said, without sympathy. 'Totally unsuitable for sandcastle making.' She adopted a lofty expression. 'What you need is a pair of wellies like these.' Taking her foot out of the left one, she held it up and dripped water from a sodden pink sock. Her face fell. 'Ah. Think I've sprung a leak.'

'Yeah, that's exactly what I need, Millie!' Jed caught her as she giggled and unbalanced. He kissed her soundly. 'You make me laugh. You make everything so joyous. How do you do that?' He kissed her again.

'I don't know,' she replied, emerging blinking from the kiss. Wrinkling her nose, she said, 'Maybe it's something I put in my famous bacon sarnies?'

Jed groaned. 'Speaking of which ...'

Chapter 14

The following Saturday Millie locked up the café for the afternoon and went along to the grand opening of Blue Elephant. As she flipped the sign to, 'I'm so sorry, you've missed our lovely cakes!' and turned the key, her heart sank into her Doc Martens. The café had been as silent as a tomb and just as gloomy all morning. She was in no danger of losing trade by closing early. Even the weather refused to sympathise. It was a gloriously fresh and blue day and the sun beat down hard on the concrete of the promenade. Millie shoved on her heart-shaped sunglasses and hid behind her hair. This wasn't going to be easy.

As she neared the steepest part of the high street there was an air of palpable excitement. Approaching Blue Elephant itself she was accosted by someone in, of course, a blue elephant costume. He gave some passing children a bunch of blue balloons and thrust a glossy leaflet into her hands. It was, inevitably, elephant-shaped and exclaimed she could get a free muffin with her coffee today. Passing the acoustic trio cheerfully playing 'Nellie the Elephant', she went in. No expense had been spared for the launch, it seemed.

She paused for a moment to get her bearings. No trace of the old bank remained. Instead, the entrance hall rose uninterrupted to the ceiling, with a mezzanine level running around half. A spiral staircase led up to the second floor and it had been discovered by the town's teenagers, who were running up and down, shrieking and giggling. The walls of the café were painted a chalky blue and there was a stunning abstract ammonite-themed mural on one. It had streaks of denim blue and sandy yellow, which was echoed in the striped material covering the banquettes and chairs. Millie took a breath. She'd half-hoped for more naff blue elephants or a cartoon theme. She was disappointed. Even she had to admit the decor was supremely tasteful. And the place was packed. Of course it was. It was the reason why Millie Vanilla's had been empty all day.

Zoe appeared at her elbow. She tugged her arm. 'Hi, Mil. Come to vet the competition?'

Millie gave her a weak grin and nodded.

'Hand over your voucher and I'll grab us some coffee. Quick, there's a free table over there.' Zoe pointed in the direction of a table where two customers were just leaving.

Millie made her way over to it, saying hello and goodbye to the people she knew as she went. Lots of them were her regulars. Perching on the very edge of a bench, she waited for Zoe and looked around. Mr and Mrs Levi, who ran the bed and breakfast on the front waved, as did Percy the butcher, who was sitting with Dean from the White Bear. Millie murmured a greeting to Dave Curzon from the newsagent and to Lola, his girlfriend, who ran a veggie restaurant in nearby Colyton. Even the Simpsons from the Lord of the Manor were here.

Zoe returned, with Sean in tow. They were carrying polystyrene cups of coffee and a paper plate of muffins.

No pretty mismatched pink flowery crockery here, Millie thought bitterly. And no washing up either. But, then again, it was not very eco-friendly. A little glimmer of hope dawned. Maybe that was something she could emphasise at Millie Vanilla's? She was careful to use eco-friendly and reusable products.

Sean found Zoe a chair and toed it over for her to sit down. The girl looked around, a half-impressed, half-horrified expression on her face. 'Awesome, isn't it?'

Sean agreed with a muttered, 'Well sick.'

Zoe sniggered at him. She turned to Millie. 'Do you want the bad news or the really bad news?' She pushed a coffee over.

Millie couldn't trust herself to answer. She took a sip of her latte instead. It was delicious. Pinching off some muffin she found that was good too.

Zoe, watching her with concern, said, 'That's the one bit of bad news. The coffee and cake is good. The other bad news is they've got a barista from Rome.' Her eyes widened. 'A real-life Italian barista here in Berecombe. And to top all that, he's bloody gorg!'

Millie pushed her food away. How could she hope to compete with all this? She felt like crying.

Zoe put her hand on hers. 'Don't worry, Mil,' she said stoutly. 'It's busy today 'cos people are getting freebies. And there's the novelty value, of course. But it won't last. Things will settle down.'

'Will they?'

''Course they will. Can't see old Biddy or Granddad in here, can you? Or the knitting circle.' She leaned closer. 'And here's the killer, they don't let dogs in. That'll reduce their trade by at least half come the tourist season. Chillax, Mil.'

Millie looked around. At the happy faces, at the buzzy atmosphere, at the children running about trailing blue balloons. Looking at the glossy dark-wood tables, the chandelier tinkling from the ceiling, the state of the art coffee-making machines, she despaired. In comparison, Millie Vanilla's seemed all at once dated, shabby and insufferably twee.

Her misery was interrupted by Sean exclaiming he'd just seen his mum go through a door marked 'Private', accompanied by a bloke in a suit. Millie's mood worsened. What the hell was Tessa doing here? And, more importantly, what was she doing having talks with the enemy?

Chapter 15

'Right,' she said, a week later, to her audience of Arthur, Zoe, Sean and Biddy, plus a snoozing Trevor and Elvis, 'I need an action plan!'

She'd spent all week poring over the net and making muddled notes, but wasn't much closer to coming up with a cohesive plan. All she'd succeeded in doing was having long, restless nights tossing and turning. Usually her white and gull-grey decorated bedroom was her sanctuary. She'd deliberately painted it soothing, calming colours so it would be a quieter comparison to the café's more frantic decoration downstairs. But since going to Blue Elephant's launch, sleep had evaded her. She'd lain awake until the first heavy steps and squawks of the herring gulls sounded on the roof. Then she'd fallen into an uncomfortably heavy slumber punctured by weird dreams of Jed running up and down Blue Elephant's spiral staircase.

This morning, she'd woken, unrefreshed, to a turquoise sea and a sun so bright it hurt her eyes. It seemed Arthur was right, spring was determinedly on its way. And, with the better weather, came tourists. It was time to do something positive.

'*We* need an action plan,' declared Arthur, his eyes gleaming. 'We'll show the buggers.'

'Way to go, Granddad!' giggled Zoe.

He harrumphed and pushed his specs back up his face. 'Yes well, you know what I mean.'

Despite the sunny weather, her little gang of faithfuls had congregated in the café to discuss what could be done.

There had been a noticeable dent in Millie's trade already. The café had been deserted for much of the week. Once the season proper began, she anticipated she'd still be popular with tourists using the beach, but those window-shopping in town would favour Blue Elephant. She just hoped her dog-friendly policy would bring in a few customers turned away from the new boy on the block. The real crowning glory was Millie Vanilla's sun terrace and its uninterrupted views across the bay. Once the weather really warmed up, it would be a huge asset – and one that a converted bank building most definitely lacked.

To Millie's disappointment, most of her regulars had jumped ship already. The Yummy Mummies hadn't been seen all week and the knitting circle had been lured away by the promise of cheap pensioners' specials. Even Zoe's gang of girls seemed to prefer Blue Elephant. Zoe, however, was confident they'd return. Clare had reported back that staff actively pushed additional orders, asking if a giant cookie or slice of cheesecake was needed to go with their hot chocolate – and getting stroppy when their suggestions were refused. To make matters worse, in Clare's opinion, the staff had made it clear that once everything had been eaten and drunk, customers should make themselves scarce. It turned out Blue Elephant wasn't tolerant of a group of schoolgirls loitering over one drink all afternoon.

Stick all that in your trendy pipe and smoke it, Millie had thought. Even with your hot Italian barista, the fight is on!

Buoyed by the realisation that not all was perfect in the rival camp, Millie distributed coffee, tea, hot chocolate, a specially made upside-down pineapple cake and dog biscuits and called the meeting to order. She outlined a few thoughts but explained she was open to anything they could suggest.

'So, anyone got any ideas? Anything to say?'

'Cake's brilliant,' Sean said, through a mouthful.

'Not quite what I had in mind, Sean, but thank you for the compliment.'

'Cheaper prices,' Biddy yelled out, making Trevor jump. 'Or free things?'

'Good point, giveaways always go down well,' Zoe agreed.

'I can't do that indefinitely,' Millie pointed out. 'I haven't got the luxury of the profit margins Blue Elephant will have.'

'Could you buy any supplies in more cheaply, my dear?'

'No, Arthur. That's one thing I'm not compromising on. Organic produce and homemade food. That's what people know me for.'

'And quite rightly so.' Arthur put his hand on Millie's. 'But I'm happy to have a look at your accounts. See where economies can be made.'

'Thanks, Arthur. I'd appreciate that. I'm pretty good at them, but a fresh pair of eyes might help.'

'Ice-cream in the summer?' Sean put in.

Millie pulled a gloomy face. 'I don't want to encroach on the Icicle Works,' she said, referring to the ice-cream parlour. 'And besides, I don't want to wait until the summer before getting anything new going.' She paused, thinking. 'I could add in an ice-cream option with my apple pie or fresh strawberry tart, though, couldn't I? Good idea, Sean!'

Sean blushed rosily and concentrated on eating his cake.

'What about themed weeks?' Zoe added. 'You know, something to go with Valentine's Day.' At this she and Sean glanced at each other and giggled.

'That's an interesting idea,' Millie said, slowly. 'What sort of thing did you have in mind?'

Zoe shrugged. 'I dunno. Heart-shaped biscuits?'

'Pink iced cupcakes?' Sean said. As his reward Zoe hugged his arm to her and kissed him soundly on the cheek.

'Love Heart sweeties on the tables,' Biddy added, somewhat unexpectedly.

'And heart patterns in the froth on the coffee!' Zoe said, bouncing on her seat with excitement. 'It could so work! Clare and the gang would love it.'

'And it wouldn't cost too much extra on top of your usual outgoings,' Arthur added, ever practical.

'Sean and me could do up some flyers,' Zoe said. 'Could easily do some A5 ads on the Mac.'

Millie looked at her loyal group of friends with gratitude. Tears welling, she reached out and grasped the hands of Arthur and Zoe, those nearest to her. 'Oh, you guys. You're amazing.'

'There's Chinese New Year and Pancake Day, Easter and –'

Millie cut Zoe off. 'Oh, my lovely, that's great but,' at this she paused, 'I really don't want to seem ungrateful, I really don't, but as fantastic an idea as themed weeks are, I don't think they'd be enough. I need a really big event to re-launch Millie Vanilla's.'

'A party,' Sean said. 'That's what you need. A party.' His eyes became enormous. 'A huge party!'

Everyone stared at him. Sean's usual utterings were infrequent and monosyllabic but he'd been inspired during this meeting.

'What sort of thing did you have in mind?' Millie asked. 'I can't really see myself hosting a rave or anything like that.'

'Mil,' Zoe said scornfully, 'that's so over.'

'Yes, well, you know what I mean.'

'We don't want any of that kind of trouble,' Biddy sniffed.

Sean shifted in his seat and pushed his plate away. 'Nah, we could have a beach party, here like.'

'Ooh, ooh, ooh, a *Valentine's* Beach Party,' Zoe squeaked. 'It would be cooler than a very cool thing!'

Millie looked from one young eager face to another. 'Now that might be an idea.'

'Or a tea dance?' Biddy's voice boomed into her thoughts.

'What an excellent idea,' Arthur said, in rare agreement.

'Oh, Granddad, a party would be better than some naff dance! Can we have fireworks at the end?' Zoe sneaked a glance at Sean. 'It would be sooooo romantic.'

Biddy began to protest that young people wanted it all their own way and had they any idea how many older folk would appreciate a good old-fashioned afternoon of dancing? Zoe began to argue back and then Arthur tried to mediate.

Millie heard it all as if muffled, through water. Ideas were tumbling into her head so fast and furiously she could barely make sense of them all. 'Let's do both!' she announced. At their stunned silence, she explained. 'We'll start with a tea dance in the afternoon, lovely Valentine's-themed cupcakes –'

'What did you say? Cupcakes?' Biddy bellowed. 'They were called fairy cakes in my day.'

'Alright Biddy, fairy cakes. Lots of lovely good-quality tea, scones and clotted cream –'

'And jam,' Arthur put in.

'And jam, of course. From Small's. Strawberry. My Victoria sponge –'

'Oh, your sponge is lush,' Zoe added.

'Thank you, Zoe. Dress code pretty dresses and smart casual for the men.'

'With ties.'

'With ties, of course, Arthur. And then we roll into a beach party for later. Let's hope the good weather keeps up.' Millie stopped. 'Oh,' she said. 'I don't have an alcohol licence.'

'Alcohol's so over, Mil,' Zoe said. 'Isn't it, Sean?'

Sean didn't look as certain. 'I can get hay bales to sit on,' he offered. 'I know George Small.'

Millie nodded. 'Thank you, Sean, that's a fab idea. I've got a really good recipe for pink-coloured fruit punch. We could serve that instead.'

'The tea-dancers would like that too, I reckon,' Biddy suggested. 'I've got a recipe for a slut-red raspberry and chardonnay jelly you could use. One of Nigella's that is. Ooh, I'm looking forward to this. Reminds me of the good old days with the girls. We used to have some rare old parties.'

Millie looked askance at Biddy. She often mentioned 'her girls'. Fellow office workers, she assumed. She knew Arthur had been an accountant, but wasn't sure what Biddy had done as a career. The slut-red jelly had come as a surprise. She put her hand on the older woman's. 'I'm glad you're looking forward to it.'

'And we can have heart-shaped ice cubes!'

'Yes, Zoe, we might be able to manage those too.' Millie grinned at the teenager. 'What about those fireworks?'

'I can sort all the paperwork for that, my dear,' Arthur offered. 'Consider it done. Dennis at the council owes me a few favours.'

Millie looked at her band of friends with affection. A motley bunch they might be, but none were more loyal. 'I can't tell you how much your support means to me.' Her voice quavered. 'It'll be a new beginning for Millie Vanilla's.'

'Well, spring's the right season for new beginnings, isn't it?'

Millie replaced her hand over the older woman's. 'It is, Biddy. It is.'

'Millie,' Arthur began and then cleared his throat before continuing. 'Millie, I don't think you realise how much affection the town has for you. And for the memory of your dear parents too. I think you'll find once folk realise what they might be about to lose you'll have people flocking to the parties. Both of them.'

'Thank you, Arthur,' Millie said through her tears. 'Thank you everybody.' There was a pause before she pulled herself together. Finding an unused serviette she blew her nose. 'To a new Millie Vanilla's!' she announced, with a raised pink, flowery teacup. 'To spring beginnings!'

'To spring beginnings!' Sean and Zoe chorused.

'To a new Millie Vanilla's,' added Arthur and Biddy in perfect unison. They caught one another's eyes and there was much blushing and coughing and chinking of pink china.

Millie watched them out of the corner of her eye. Was it possible? Was it just possible there was a romance going on between the bickering pair? How intriguing – and delightful! Then something hammered all matchmaking – and enthusiasm for a re-launch – out of her. She looked around at the café. At the shabby chairs and chipped tables. At the sea-shell mural, which she had once loved and which now looked so tired. At the scuffed lino on the floor.

'What am I going to do about how this place looks, though?' she sighed, putting her head in her hands. 'How on earth am I going to get it looking as good as Blue Elephant?'

Chapter 16

The weather continued to improve. Despite it being only February, an early spring had definitely sprung. In celebration and relief, people shed their heavy coats and emerged in butterfly-bright t-shirts. The sunshine and warmth brought out happy smiles and relaxed the hunched shoulders of winter.

In anticipation of the good weather bringing in tourists, the town opened up, like a flower to the sun, for the new season. Nico scrubbed down his ice-cream kiosk and furiously polished the windows. The Plaice Place extended its opening hours, sending waves of hot chips-and-vinegar scent enticingly across the harbour end of town. Those lucky enough to own a beach hut began the annual clean and paint routine and hung bunting across the doors before settling down for a rest with a book and a flask of tea.

Early one morning, before the town had properly woken up, Millie stood on the café's sun terrace breathing in the mild salty air and raising her head to the sky. She closed her eyes to better enjoy the lull and swell of the sea as its rhythm beat through her. The sun warmed her face and there was a cackle of a gull swooping overhead. Even the bird sounded relieved that the long winter was over. Spring was here. She could smell it. Trevor barked in excitement and she heard his claws scrabbling on the sandy concrete, scampering to greet someone. Opening her eyes, her heart leaped into her throat as she saw Jed watching her.

'I'm sorry, I disturbed you. I caught you day-dreaming.' He grinned and pushed his sunglasses onto the top of his head.

He wore skinny chinos and a pink polo shirt, a sweater rolled loosely around his shoulders. He looked just like what he was – privileged and wealthy. He could have stepped straight out of a Boden catalogue. His effect on her was so acute, she said the first thing she could think of, 'I was wondering if it was time to put some chairs and tables out here.' She cursed herself. As if he'd be interested.

In this, it seemed, she was wrong. Replacing his glasses, he came forward, nodding. 'Absolutely, it's definitely warm enough, or it will be later in the day. You're always up so early. It's barely gone eight.' He bent to fuss Trevor, who was going into ecstasies at seeing him.

Millie laughed. 'The alarm goes off at five. I've already walked Trevor and baked today's specials.'

'Oh, how I hate the smug early-riser! More importantly, what are your specials? I'm starving.'

'As ever! I've a red-velvet chocolate and beetroot cake, some coffee and walnut and a batch of savoury scones.'

Pushing Trevor off gently, Jed came even closer. He stared intently at her lips and ran a finger lightly over them. 'I don't know how you do it, Millie. They sound so good. Have I ever told you how much I love your cooking? A real taste of home.'

He bent and kissed her, his lips warm from the sun. 'You taste of home.'

This time Millie lifted her head and surrendered to Jed rather than the early-morning sunshine. And he was far more exhilarating. She let herself open and he deepened the kiss. Holding her around the waist, he pulled her in against his hardness. She thrust her fingers through his silken hair. She wanted to drown in him, in the sensations that were overwhelming her senses.

Jed rested his forehead against hers for a moment. 'Millie, Millie, Millie, you don't know what you're doing to me. I want to eat you up. I want to smother you in some of your famous clotted cream and lick it off.'

Millie stood back, swaying slightly. She felt unhinged by longing. She knew she must look it. 'Sounds messy,' she whispered, in an attempt for control.

Jed caught her to him again. 'Oh, it would be delightfully, sinfully messy.' He kissed her again. 'And so much fun.'

It was all threatening to get out of hand. Millie didn't know whether to be furious when Tessa's cheery voice interrupted them – or relieved.

'Morning, kiddo. I'll just go and put the bread inside then, shall I?' She went past with a giggle.

Peeling herself off Jed and giving him a regretful glance, Millie followed Tessa into the café.

'I see you're finally getting your fun, then, our Mil.' Tessa slammed the basket of bread onto the nearest table.

'Well I was.' Millie pulled a face. 'Before you so rudely interrupted.'

'Soz.' Tessa giggled and peered out to where Jed was playing with Trevor. He was leaning against the low wall that divided the sun terrace from the steps down to the beach and was trying to teach the dog to shake paws. 'Heard he took you to some swanky-wanky place the other night. Zoe's right, though, he's a treat for the eyes. Get a load of those thighs. You could crack walnuts with them. Blimey.'

Millie decided she'd better bring Tessa to order. 'Invoice?'

'On top of the bloomers,' she replied, still staring blatantly at Jed. 'Gotta love a blond man, haven't you?' She screwed her eyes up to see better. 'Come to think about it, he looks familiar. Where have I seen him before?'

Millie, shoving the invoice into a folder behind the counter, didn't reply immediately. 'You've probably seen him about town.' She looked up, amused to see Tessa still staring. 'He's not easy to forget, is he?'

'You're right there, bab. Bugger, hope it's just the weather making me hot and not an early menopause. He's got hormones I'd forgotten I ever had going bananas.'

Millie giggled. She couldn't disagree. 'You got time for a coffee?'

Tessa finally focused. 'No kiddo, I'm running late this morning. Gotta go.' She gave an earthy cackle. 'I'll leave you to the tender mercies of your hot friend out there.' Fanning her face comically, she swept out.

Millie heard her trill goodbye, waited until the coast was clear and then dragged a couple of chairs into the sun. 'Can I get you a coffee, Jed?'

He slid off the wall in such a sinuous way, Millie had a

sudden and very intense longing to forget all about the café and drag him up to bed.

'I'd rather get you.'

He pulled her to him for another kiss. Millie's insides went to liquid and her legs threatened to give way. She pushed him off. 'Coffee? Toast?' she asked on a breathless giggle.

'Well, I am hungry,' he replied dangerously, gazing at her lower lip with intent. 'I have a deep, deep hunger for you.'

'You'll have to make do with raisin toast, I'm afraid.'

'Can't I have you on toast?'

'No!' Millie pushed him away and enjoyed his pout. 'God, you're so gorgeous when you sulk.' She let him kiss her one more time and then escaped to the safety of her kitchen.

Thirty minutes later, Jed sat on the sun terrace on one of her rickety chairs, his feet up on the wall, staring out to sea. He drank the last of his coffee. 'It's so bloody gorgeous here. Devon heaven.'

'There talks a man full of food.'

Jed gave her a wicked look. 'You've satisfied one kind of hunger, certainly.'

'Wish you'd stop flirting. I've got a day of work in front of me.'

'Do you really wish that?'

'No. But it's true that I've got to work. There's loads to do.' Millie went on to explain the plans for the café's re-launch. 'That's why I'm trying out the beetroot and chocolate cake, to make the right colour for a Valentine's party.' She glanced back at the café. The bright sunshine made it appear all the more scruffy this morning. She frowned.

'Something wrong?'

He was always so quick at picking up on her mood. She wished she could do the same with him. Sometimes to her Jed was a riddle wrapped up in an enigma. 'I'm confident I can put on a good party, but the café itself just looks so tired.'

Jed batted a hand at an overly persistent gull that was after toast crumbs and paused before he answered. 'Your windows are an asset; the way they look out onto the sea. Have you ever thought about putting in the kind that open like doors? Then you could bring the outside in and those customers who couldn't find a table out here wouldn't mind eating inside so much. They're not patio doors exactly, but a bit classier. Really popular in bars and restaurants in Scandinavia, Stockholm especially. You could also install heaters out here to take away the sting of the cold. Then you could use this space for more of the year.'

As Millie had never been further north than Birmingham, she hadn't a clue what a Stockholm bar might look like, let alone their fancy windows. Patio heaters were something she'd long wanted to buy but had never been able to afford; she'd need at least eight. And that was the crux of the matter. His ideas, although appealing, sounded way too expensive. 'Sounds great,' she answered, eventually. 'But I can't afford to splash out on a big revamp. That's going to have to wait until next year. That's if I still have a business.'

Jed gave her a keen look. 'That bad, eh?'

Millie nodded, miserably.

Jed shifted uncomfortably. There was a beat. 'Well, we'll simply have to do a paint job, then.'

Millie sat up. This sounded more like what she had in mind. 'I could sand the tables down, paint them something pretty. I love ice-cream colours, you know, cream and baby pink and pistachio green.'

'They would be gorgeous, but do you still want to keep the mural?'

'Yes, I love it, although it needs touching up.'

'I suppose we haven't much time, have we, before the party, I mean?'

Millie shook her head.

'Then can I suggest sticking to the colours in the mural – turquoise and pink – for the moment and we'll add in some hot pink and lime green into the scheme to freshen it up. You can always change the colours next year, when you do your complete overhaul. Do you know what's under the lino?'

'No, but it's horrible, isn't it? Went down in my parents' day.'

Jed grinned. 'And it's seen better days. If there are floor-boards underneath we can paint them white. How are you fixed this weekend?'

'But I have to open the café!'

'Are you expecting much trade?'

Millie shrugged. These days she never expected much trade, but she wasn't going to admit as much to Jed. 'Rain's forecast, but you never know.'

'Then you'll just have to take a chance. Far better to close down completely and then open with a dramatic flourish. How long have you got until the party?'

'Just over a week,' Millie answered, a little dazed by his

enthusiasm. For someone who had told her he was a management consultant, he seemed to know an awful lot about interior design.

Jed jumped up and stretched. 'Better go and buy some paint, then.' When Millie rose to join him, he shook his head. 'You stay here. Plan the menu with lots of old-fashioned sticky stuff and carbs. All my favourites. See you later.'

He'd kissed her and was gone before Millie had time to react. She heard him gun the engine of the Golf along the promenade road. 'Better rally the troops,' she said to the gull that was attacking the leftover toast on her plate. 'I think we'll need some help.' She giggled. 'Do you think two loved-up pensioners and a couple of teenagers are up for a bit of D.I.Y. this weekend? Come on, Trev,' she said to the dog. 'At this rate we'll have to tie a paintbrush to your tail as well. It's about time you earned your keep.' She gathered the plates and mugs and went into the café, humming. With Jed's enthusiasm filling her with a warm glow, she felt more positive than she had for a long time.

Chapter 17

The promised rain blew itself out in the night, leaving a warm, breezily-perfect seaside Saturday. The troops had answered the call to arms. Zoe dragged a sleepy Sean along, Arthur and Biddy came in bickering as usual and Sean had even persuaded an embarrassed Ken to come. He explained that Tessa couldn't make it as she had a lot on.

'Don't worry, Ken,' Millie laughed. 'I'll make sure I have something really evil for her to do as penance.'

'She's made a whole load of sandwiches for us for later. On her best granary and seeded. Shall I stick them in the fridge?' Ken gave a shuttered glance at Sean and disappeared into the kitchen.

Millie's heart sang. Tessa was such a good friend. 'That's nice. I'll get some bacon and eggs on for everyone and, as soon as Jed turns up with the paint, we can get started.'

On cue, Jed appeared, laden down with the first of the cans of paint. As Sean helped him carry in the rest, Biddy came over and began unravelling lengths of material from a plastic bag.

'Thought you'd like these,' she boomed. 'Seem to be back

in fashion for some reason I can't fathom.' She held up a length of bunting, beautifully crafted into exquisite little triangles.

'Oh, Biddy,' Millie gasped. 'They're perfect.' She turned one or two over, examining the perfect stitching. 'The colours are just right. Pinks and greens and I love this sea-blue pattern.'

'Well, I knew the right colours from the aprons I make for you.'

'And they're even slightly padded.'

'Won't look as flimsy as some you can buy,' Biddy said gruffly.

Millie flung her arms around the older woman. 'Thank you so much. I love them!'

'Oh, enough with your fuss. Where's this breakfast you promised us? Army can't march on an empty stomach, can it?'

By lunchtime, the café was already looking transformed. Millie had squashed down her panic at missing out on any customers and had instead made the most of the sunshine by getting everyone to pile up the chairs and tables outside. Ken had brightened up his mural, repainting the turquoise to make it even more vivid. He'd also begun to add snatches of gold paint as highlights. Jed had peeled back a corner of the lino and declared there were floorboards underneath. He and Sean stripped it out and had sanded half the floor in readiness for painting. Meanwhile, Arthur took charge on the terrace. He divided the chairs and tables into three groups and had Millie painting some white. Zoe was in charge of the hot pink (which today matched her hair) while he applied the lime green. Biddy, having peered at the colours in the paint pots, had disappeared for a while. When she returned she set herself up in some shade outside and began furiously sewing cushion covers in similar fabrics to the ones she had used for the bunting, but in bright pink and green.

Millie balanced her paintbrush on top of the tin. 'Break for lunch in a minute, guys?' To the groans of relief, she went over to have a look at what Biddy had been doing. 'They're going to look fabulous.' She perched on the wall and picked up one cover which Biddy had already finished.

'Don't you get paint all over them?'

'I won't.' Millie turned it over, peering closer. 'It's so beautifully stitched.'

'We can get some cheap foam from Dorchester market and cut it into the right shapes for cushions.'

'That's a great idea, Biddy.'

Sean, Jed and Ken joined them on the terrace. They brought out the enormous trays of Tessa's sandwiches and put them on one of the unpainted tables. Zoe cheered and began to distribute food. Everyone looked a little paint-stained and weary but wore huge smiles.

Millie watched for a moment as her team ate as if starving. She felt truly blessed to have such good friends. She turned her attention back to the cushion covers Biddy was sewing. One had an appliqué pattern. The patterns clashed and yet worked together perfectly. 'You're so clever. I couldn't do anything like that in a million years.'

'What did you say?' Biddy looked up.

Millie repeated, making sure she enunciated her words.

'Yes well,' Biddy sniffed. 'It don't do if folk are all good at the same thing. And cooking's what you do.'

It was the closest to a compliment Millie had ever heard Biddy utter. To anyone. 'Thank you, Biddy. That means a lot. Is that what you did as a career; sewing?'

Biddy glared at her over her glasses. 'Seamstress? Oh no, I only sew for a hobby. For a job, I was a madam.'

Chapter 18

Maybe it was the enclosed space that made Biddy's words louder. Or maybe she had her hearing aid adjusted incorrectly and felt she had to yell. Whatever the reason, the statement bounced off the wall behind her and out into the small group. All eating ceased as they, as one, turned to her.

Silence.

'Sorry Biddy, you were a *what?*'

Biddy starred at Millie, owlishly. 'Thought you knew. Don't make no secret of it. I was in charge of a house in south London.'

'A house of –'

'Ill repute they likes to call it.' Biddy shrugged and the gesture made her seem much younger and altogether far more mischievous.

The penny dropped. 'Your girls! The ones you talk about –'

'Ah! My girls. Had twelve of them working for me. Some for nearly twenty years. Good times.' Biddy suddenly became loquacious. 'Had some very eminent clients, we did. Although we had a real problem when the gardener decided to chop the nettles down.' She leaned nearer but didn't bother to lower her voice. 'Some of the clients liked a good thrashing with them. Never saw the attraction of it myself, but each to his own.'

For once Millie had absolutely nothing to say.

'Way to go, Biddy!' Zoe cackled.

'Don't you "way to go" me, young lady.'

'No indeed.' Millie rose, stunned. 'I'll make some tea, shall I? And find some lemonade. I made some earlier.' She rushed for the sanctuary of her kitchen. Splashing cold water onto her burning face, she giggled. Who would have thought it? She was beginning to see Biddy in a whole new light.

Unfortunately, it seemed, so was Arthur. When she returned to the little group outside, bearing a tray of drinks, it was to uproar.

Zoe took a glass of lemonade from her and muttered, 'Biddy and Granddad are having a mega row. Turns out Biddy loaned Granddad some money for Daisy's op and he's got some beef about it coming from her,' at this Zoe made speech marks with her fingers, 'ill-gotten gains.' She rolled her eyes. 'As if!'

'My good man,' Biddy was roaring, 'that money came from an ISA!'

'I want no part of it. You can have it back.'

'Come on, Granddad, if it means Daisy can have the operation,' Zoe coaxed.

'No, Zoe, I'll return it.' Arthur pulled himself up to his full five-feet five. 'I'd rather take out a loan on the house than take dirty money.'

Biddy stood up, sewing materials dropping unheeded.

Millie was relieved to see Jed grab Trevor's collar and try to soothe him. The dog was dancing around, over-excited at the raised voices and she didn't want a needle embedded in his paw.

'Dirty money, you say,' Biddy screeched, to the alarm of a family strolling on the prom. 'Dirty money! Ah, yes, there's always those who take that attitude. The ones who walk past you in the street, hanging on the arms of their wives and sneering at you. And you can be sure they're the same men who come knocking at your door, wanting to be dressed in a nappy and bottle-fed!' She gathered her stuff and shoved it into a plastic bag. 'Millie, I will continue my sewing at home, if I may. I know where I'm not wanted!'

Whistling for Elvis to follow, she swept off, her nose in the air and scraps of material dangling out of the bag and sweeping a trail on the sandy pavement.

'Granddad!' Zoe cried. 'Honestly, how could you?'

Arthur turned on her. 'I do not want to take anything from a woman like that.'

'What do you mean? She's your friend. What she did in the past doesn't change that.'

Not for the first time Millie admired Zoe's wise, old head. Feeling the need to calm everything down, she said, 'Come on, let's sit down and have a cup of tea. Jed, can you take this tray, it's making my arms ache.' She nodded to the only other table they hadn't got around to painting yet. 'Put it on there, would you?'

He came to her and, relieving her of it, whispered in her ear, 'What a shame Biddy's gone. I'd rather hoped to hear more about what she did with the nettles.'

Millie gave him a withering look. 'Sit down, Arthur, and have some tea. There you go,' she passed him a mug. 'It's just how you like it. Strong and sugary.'

'It all goes on in these seaside towns, doesn't it? Who would have thought it of Biddy, of all people?' Jed sat on the wall, looking highly amused.

'I would for one,' Zoe put in. 'Have you seen the size of her house?'

Jed shook his head.

'It's the big one on the hill, just past the newsagents. You need to have done something interesting to bring in the filthy lucre to pay for that.' She gave a knowing wink. 'Hey, I guess we really are talking filthy lucre.'

'Zoe, my girl, I would prefer you to stop talking like that,' Arthur said, sharply.

'Sorry, Granddad.'

The group sat in silence once more, reviewing their opinion of Biddy.

'Wonder if she used dogs? In the business, I mean,' Zoe piped up. 'She said she's always owned one.'

'Zoe!' Arthur roared.

'Not helpful, Zoe,' Millie admonished. She motioned for the girl to have another sandwich in the hope of shutting her up.

'Is Daisy's operation very expensive?' Jed asked unexpectedly. He helped himself to a glass of lemonade and emptied it in two swallows.

Millie thanked him silently for changing the subject and

then cursed as the question appeared to upset Arthur even more.

'Yes,' was the only answer Arthur could manage.

Millie saw his hands shake as they gripped his mug of tea. Some of it slopped out onto the white concrete. Sean and Ken, having grabbed a drink, edged away and went to sit on the wall at the far end of the terrace, ostensibly watching an impromptu cricket match taking place on the beach.

'It's likely to be about five thousand quid,' Zoe said, when it became obvious Arthur couldn't trust himself to explain further.

'Jeez.' Jed's eyebrows rose. 'I had no idea it would cost so much.'

Arthur remained silent for a long time, drank his tea and visibly pulled himself together. Then he began to speak. It was as if he was relieved to talk about something else, no matter how equally distressing. 'The X-Rays show that the old girl's lump is in an awkward spot.' He chewed his lip. 'It's one reason I missed it. It's growing quickly now, for some reason. They don't know why. And the tests have come back, but they're inconclusive. No one knows if it's malignant.' He shuddered. 'We won't know until she's had the operation and they examine the tumour.'

Millie sat next to him and put an arm around his thin shoulders. 'That's awful. Poor, poor Daisy.' She went on, as gently as she could, 'But why did you need to borrow from Biddy? Are you sure your pet insurance couldn't cover the cost?'

Arthur sniffed, removed his glasses and polished them

busily. His face looked strangely naked without them. And vulnerable. 'Daisy's only chance of survival is to go to a specialist surgery unit in Bristol. It's beyond my policy.'

'They have such places? For dogs?' Jed asked. 'I never knew.'

Trevor put his front paws on Millie's lap and, for once, she didn't tell him to get down. She reached for his curly head and tickled under his chin for comfort. She was pretty sure Trevor understood every word of what was being said. His excitement at the shouting had dissipated and he was as dejected as the rest of them. She gazed into his brown-button eyes. He was so dear to her. She could only too easily imagine the pain of being in Arthur's position. Maybe she could forgive the man's harsh words to Biddy. He must be worried out of his mind. The trouble was, he'd now lost his only chance to pay for the operation. She wished she were in a position to help.

'Let's just hope the tumour is benign,' she said, going for briskly optimistic, the words sounding hollow, even to her.

The group sank into yet another silence. An even gloomier one this time.

'Which vet do you use, Arthur?' Jed asked.

Arthur began to explain. Millie only half-listened. Jed had been wonderful today. Refusing to take money for the paint, labouring until he was hot and grubby-looking and now he was taking a real interest in Arthur and poor Daisy. He seemed really concerned about them. Love for him blossomed. As Arthur talked, she drank in Jed's beautiful face and the warmth in his dark eyes. She couldn't take her eyes off him. If she'd thought she'd been in love before, with other boyfriends, the feelings she'd felt for other men paled into insignificance to how she felt about Jed. This was on a whole other level. Despite all her worries, a joyful love for Jed filled her. It was both scary and exhilarating. And yet, a little wormy voice of caution inside her warned, *you've only known him for a few weeks!* She silenced it. 'I don't care,' she muttered. 'I love this man. I could love him with my whole being. Spend my life with him. Have his children.' Realising her mouth was dry she reached for a glass of lemonade and drank it down in one. She was suddenly very, very hot.

'You okay, Mil?' Zoe asked. 'You're a bit flushed.'

She gave the girl a tight grin. 'I'm fine. I hate to say this and I hate to be unsympathetic about Daisy, but I suppose, if everyone has eaten, do you think we ought to go back to work?'

And, to good-natured groans and mutterings of what a slave driver she was, they did.

Once everyone had said weary goodbyes, with the promise to return the following day, Millie turned to Jed and offered to cook him supper. To her disappointment, he refused, saying his parents were staying in Lyme and they expected him for dinner.

She went up to the flat, her entire being on fire from Jed's goodbye kisses. Trevor, worn out from all the excitement, trailed up the steps behind her, his tail drooping. It had been an exhausting day, even without the emotional fallout from Arthur and Biddy's argument. Millie prayed they'd make up. Zoe had promised to pop over to Biddy's in an attempt to build bridges.

Too preoccupied to eat, Millie opened a bottle of wine and drew her favourite chair to the picture window, which was the best feature of the flat. It mirrored the ones in the café below and looked straight out, across the beach, to open sea.

The days were lengthening. No matter how wild and wet a winter they'd had, spring was usually quick in coming to this part of the coast. Millie opened a window. Along with the chatter of people wandering past below, the breeze brought in warm salty air from the sea and the distant cackles of gulls before they settled for the night. Trevor came to her and rested his head on her knee, giving a heartfelt sigh.

'Know what you mean, Trev. It's been quite a day.' She tugged gently on his woolly ears and enjoyed the warmth of his little body against her leg. Maybe it was just tiredness but she'd never felt more content. However, any relaxation was short-lived. Stretching out muscles stiff from painting, Millie got up, ignored Trevor's grumbles and took her wine to the kitchen. She had work to do.

Chapter 19

Millie forced herself up and out of bed early the following morning. She needed to walk Trevor before another day working on the café. On her return from a blissfully solitary walk on the beach, one of the perks of rising at daybreak, she unlocked the café and stood for a minute, appraising the work done so far.

She'd been worried the bright colours they were adding might be too much – too busy in such a small space. Jed and Sean had given the floor its first coat of white paint before finishing yesterday and she could already see how it would calm everything down. Once the re-painted furniture was back in, it would be perfect. Or as perfect as her present budget allowed.

'Hi, Millie.'

Millie turned to see Tessa standing in the doorway. She began to tease her friend about bailing on her yesterday, but then saw her pinched and tense face.

'Can I have a word?'

'Of course you can. Let's sit outside, though. I can't guarantee the paint's dry in here.'

They perched on the low wall next to the aubrieta, which had suddenly blossomed into a vivid purple cascade.

'Is everything alright, Tess? The boys are okay, aren't they? Sean looked hale and hearty yesterday. It's not Ken? He did look a bit preoccupied, come to think of it, but he's done a fantastic job on retouching the mural. It's as good as new.'

Tessa looked out to sea and blinked in the bright sunshine. She shook her head. 'No, everyone's fine. I've got something to say to you. Something that won't be very good to hear, kiddo.'

Millie's stomach did that peculiar flipping-over thing that happens when you fear you're about to receive bad news. She'd rarely seen her best friend so serious. She reached out a hand. 'God, Tessa, what's wrong?'

'Don't be nice, Millie, alright? I've got this new job, see.'

'Well, that's a good thing.'

'Making bread.'

'Even better.' Millie forced a jolly note into her voice, but she knew what was coming. Just knew it.

'Blue Elephant have taken me on to do their range of artisan breads.'

Millie nodded. Part of her noticed how far out the tide had gone this morning. A man was throwing a tennis ball to his Labrador. The dog was barking excitedly. A family were heading out to the rocks at the edge of the harbour wall. Making the most of the low tide to do some rock-pooling. The sun hit hard off the wet sand and made her eyes water. It made it difficult to see. Part of her was aware Tessa was still talking. Giving reasons. Making excuses.

'And it means I won't have time to do both. I just won't be able to supply you with bread as well as them and they –'

'Pay more,' Millie finished. She added in a monotone, 'Of course they would.'

'Aw, Millie, I'm so sorry, it's just with Ken not bringing much in and that exhibition of his making a loss, I didn't have a choice. The kids aren't getting any cheaper and Louis looks like he'll get to university and –'

Millie put up her hand to stop the flow of hopes for Tessa and Ken's middle son. 'Was that why you were at Blue Elephant on the afternoon of their launch?'

'Me? Oh, you saw me, did you? Yes, the manager asked me to go in for a meeting. To discuss the range he wants me to develop. They want me to start immediately, but didn't give me much choice in the matter, to be honest.' Tessa added lamely. 'Where will you get your bread from now?'

'Bread?' Millie tried to focus. 'I don't know. I can make some, but I'm not a bread- baker in your league. Haven't got the time.'

'Maybe Berringtons will let you have some?' Tessa named the town baker. She was obviously trying to be helpful.

'Yes, that's possible.' Millie stood up. She couldn't face talking to Tessa any more. Was afraid of saying too much, of ruining their friendship beyond repair. 'And now, if you don't mind, I've a busy day in front of me.'

Tessa stood too. 'Yeah, okay.' She turned to go and then stopped. She turned back to Millie, who was staring unseeing out to sea. 'Mil, I'm really sorry. I hope – well, I hope you'll be able to see why I had to do it. I hope –'

'Yes, Tessa?' Millie's voice was steely.

Tessa flinched. 'We can still be friends, right?'

Millie stared at her. The rational part of her understood Tessa's decision. But this was her friend. Her best friend. It felt like the worst kind of betrayal. 'Time will tell, Tessa,' she said quietly, desperate not to let the hurt show. 'I think we just need some time apart right now, don't we?' And, with that, she turned on her heel and went into the café.

Chapter 20

It was a slightly depleted work party that trailed in an hour later. Not surprisingly, Ken didn't show up, although Sean did. When Arthur arrived, with Zoe in tow, they made a huge fuss over a wriggling Trevor.

'No, Biddy,' Zoe whispered, when Arthur was busy checking whether the paintbrushes had been properly cleaned the night before. 'She's still dead cross over what Granddad said, but she promised to do some sewing at home.'

Poor Biddy. With all the fuss over Daisy's operation, her hurt had been overlooked yesterday. 'Is she okay?' Millie asked.

Zoe pulled a face. 'Seemed like it. Guess she's used to it, what with once being a sex worker. Must make you hard as nails. I'll try to work on Granddad. Got a feeling if he does some major-league grovelling, she'll come round.'

'I hope so. Friendship's important.'

'Yeah and those two are besties, even though they argue like mad.'

Millie wondered if her own friendship with Tessa would ever recover. Pledging to keep herself busy, she hoped it would stop her dwelling on what Tessa had done. Hard work had eased the grief once before in her life and it might be the salve again.

It was a repeat of the day before, in many ways. After Millie had cooked a huge breakfast, they got to work. Jed and Sean worked on the floor once more. They sanded down the white paint from yesterday, giving it a distressed feel and then concentrated on the walls not covered by Ken's mural, painting them white too. Arthur and Zoe gave the furniture they'd painted yesterday a quick second coat and put it in the sun. Once dry, Millie had a go at sanding edges and corners, to make it look shabby chic.

Once they got the okay from Jed, they carried it all back inside. It had been the quickest of make-overs and not the most thorough but it was a definite improvement. As Millie had hoped, once the brightly painted tables and chairs were in place, the whole look came together. The shabby-chic effect even disguised some of the more hurried paintwork.

They stood on the sun terrace, gazing in at their hard work.

'It's absolutely gorgeous,' Millie breathed, hardly able to believe they had achieved so much in just two days.

'It's mint,' Zoe put in. 'Biddy's getting the cushion covers over tomorrow,' she added in a whisper, as Arthur came to stand with them to admire their handiwork.

'My dear girl, what an alteration!' he said.

'It certainly is and I couldn't have done it without you guys.' Millie put her arms around Zoe and Arthur. 'You've been brilliant,' she managed, before her voice broke with emotion.

Jed slung an arm around Sean and added, 'Can't beat team-work.' He grinned over at her making her feel happy and a bit dizzy all at the same time.

The café did, indeed, look transformed. The white floor and walls gleamed against the pink-and-green furniture and the touches of gold that Ken had applied to his pink-and-turquoise mural added glamour.

'It just looks all pulled together,' Millie began, 'without seeming too –'

'Contrived,' Jed finished for her.

'Exactly!'

They gazed happily at one another.

Arthur, as if sensing the intimacy between them, coughed and disentangled himself. 'Well, I'd best be off. Don't like to leave Daisy on her own, even if all she does is sleep at the moment.'

'Oh Arthur – and everyone else, before you go,' Millie said, 'I've got a present for you all. It's only a gesture, I'm afraid, but I thought, no I *needed* to do something to thank you for all your hard work. Just hang on for a minute, will you?' She disappeared into the café, carefully avoiding some of the still-wet paint and went through to the kitchen.

She returned a minute later, carrying a tower of cake boxes and with an excited Trevor dancing around her ankles. 'Like I said, it's only a gesture and doesn't in any way ...' her voice trailed off. She'd been up half the night baking the cakes. It was the only way she could think of, or afford, to thank them, but it seemed too little a reward.

Putting the boxes carefully on one of the tables they'd left outside, she handed Jed the first one. 'Victoria sponge for you. I know how much you like it. Fresh cream, of course.'

Beaming, Jed opened up the box. 'Millie,' he exclaimed, 'you've iced the top in Millie Vanilla's colours!'

He folded back the card lid for the others to see. Iced in pink and turquoise were the words, "Jed, I can't thank you enough, but hope this sugary sweetness will."

'I love it,' he said, his dark eyes warm.

'A special apricot, brandy and almond tray bake for you, Arthur, and I've done some doggie biscuits for Daisy too.' She handed him his boxes.

'Oh, my dear girl, you shouldn't have! My favourite! And Daisy will love hers too.'

'Chocolate and marshmallow for you, Zoe. Natch!'

'Natch!' Zoe answered and took her cake. 'Thanks, Mil, that's ace. Think Mum might nick a bit of this.'

'She's more than welcome.'

'And Sean, I hope you don't mind sharing but I've made you all some cupcakes. I know Tessa and the boys like them too.'

Sean took his box, then put it back down on the table and enveloped Millie in a bear hug. 'Thanks so much, Millie,' he whispered in a voice gruff with emotion. 'What Mum did to you was wrong. I told her, you know. I'm dead against this new job.'

For the first time Millie could see what Zoe saw in him. Letting him hug her in his scrawny grip for a second, she fought against tears. 'Thank you, Sean. I appreciate that.'

Millie picked up the last boxes and handed them to Zoe. 'Scones with cream and jam for Biddy and shortbread for Elvis. Could you get them to her?'

'No prob. Sean and I will drop them off on the way home.'

'Thanks, Zoe, and thank you all so much.'

'Yeah yeah, we get the picture,' Zoe said, stopping the mood getting maudlin. 'What does Biddy always say about people who cry too much?'

'Eyes too near the bladder,' Arthur supplied.

'That's it. She wants to see you, Granddad, by the way. I think flowers are the order of the day, don't you? Come on,' she slipped an arm through his. 'We can order them online. Next-day delivery and she'll be made up. After you've said sorry, of course.'

'Zoe, my girl,' Arthur laughed. 'How did you get so wise so young?'

'Dunno,' she replied wide-eyed. 'It's just a genius talent I have.' She kissed his cheek. 'Or good genes.' With Sean trailing in their wake, carrying the mountain of cake boxes, they wandered off in the direction of the promenade. As they went, Millie could hear Zoe instructing Arthur on just how best to win Biddy round.

'Well, Emilia Fudge,' said Jed coming to her and slipping his arms around her. 'I think this weekend has been a success.'

Glancing into the café and then refocusing on him, she agreed, 'Well, Jed Henville, I think you might just be right.'

The kiss that followed was as sweet and satisfying as any of the cakes she baked.

Sweeter.

Chapter 21

'Can you stay for supper tonight?' Millie tried to keep it light, not wanting to seem desperate. She'd kept the hurt that Tessa had inflicted to herself all day. Had been too busy to dwell on it, but now all the work was finished, she felt the tension in her shoulders soften and, with it, a need for human comfort. The tears threatened a return.

'I think that's an offer I can't resist.' Jed grinned boyishly. 'And of course I'm –'

'Starving. Of course you are!' She laughed. 'Taken as a given. Reaching up, she tweaked a long lock of hair that flopped over his tanned face. 'You have the most fetching streak of white paint.'

Jed pulled a face. 'Do I?'

'And another smudge of it on your nose.' Millie reached up to kiss it.

'I might need to borrow your shower.'

'I think that can be arranged.'

He followed her up to the flat, with Trevor weaving between their legs and getting in the way.

Millie unlocked the door and, feeling self-conscious, led

him into the sitting room. It must be very different to the places he was used to. She needn't have worried. Jed went straight to the window and stood, hands on hips, drinking in the view.

'What a fantastic place to live!' He turned to her, eyes alight. 'You look right out over the sea. You must never tire of it.'

Millie joined him. It was true. She nodded. 'The view's never the same two days running. But I love it best in the winter when it's stormy.'

Jed put his arm loosely around her shoulders. 'I can imagine. Do the storms ever reach you up here?'

'They can do. I've had one or two windows smashed by pebbles thrown up by the sea. It's not much of a sacrifice to live here, though.'

'I can see why you love it so.' Jed turned her to him and pulled her closer. His mouth found hers and his hand cupped her breast.

She pushed him away. Reluctantly. Much as she wanted this man, she needed a shower first. 'I'll sort you out some towels.'

Jed nodded but the desire in his eyes was unmistakable. 'And then food. I've an idea I'll need all my stamina for later.'

Millie went first, leaving Jed engrossed in the news on TV. While he showered, she frowned over the meagre contents of her kitchen cupboards and wondered what to cook.

When Jed emerged, with wet hair and smelling of her almond-blossom shower gel, she nearly jumped on him there and then. Practicalities won by a nose.

'Just salad and some new potatoes, I'm afraid,' she explained, as they sat at her tiny table in the kitchen. 'But I've made some mango chicken to go with it.' She tried to concentrate on the food and failed. Jed looked gorgeous with his hair damp and curling around his collar. The thought of all that clean, tanned skin under his shirt and chinos was making her weak with desire.

'Sounds great. And we've cake for pudding!' Jed was obviously only thinking of one type of hunger.

'Oh yes, your sponge cake. Hope it's okay. I rather threw them together late last night.'

'It'll be perfect,' Jed declared confidently. 'Everything you touch is perfect.'

Millie laughed, embarrassed. 'Not sure about that.'

He reached over and took her hand. 'It's true,' he said, simply, gazing into her eyes.

They knew what was coming. The promise of it vibrated in the air. Thrummed between them. And they both knew that the longer they deferred it, the sweeter it would taste.

'I'll open some wine, shall I?' he added.

Millie couldn't speak. Could barely breathe. Was hollowed out with desire for the man. She managed a nod.

He rooted around in the fridge and found the half-full bottle of white she'd begun last night. He filled their glasses. 'You know, I really admire how you're right in the middle of your community.'

'Am I?'

He sat down and picked up his fork. 'Yes, of course you are. Look at this weekend. None of it would have been possible without your friends rallying around.' He began to eat. 'It's something I really envy. I've never had that. Experienced that. I've been thinking, by the way,' he leaned forward, enthusiasm warming his dark eyes. 'What you need is a marketing strategy.'

'Do I?' Whatever she'd expected, it wasn't this. She sipped some wine.

'You don't actually need to change much. Actually nothing. Just emphasise what you already do, what you're known for. Have you got a mission statement?'

Millie nearly choked on her wine. 'A what?'

'Something that sums up what you're all about.'

She shook her head.

'Can you tell me what you're all about? In as brief a sentence as possible?'

Millie shrugged. She wanted to concentrate on another kind of strategy, the one to get Jed into her bed as quickly as possible. But he was waiting for an answer. Taking this seriously. He seemed as involved in this as he had been with Arthur and Daisy. She thought for a moment. 'Well, I'm committed to organic, locally sourced supplies and all my food is home-cooked.'

'Yeah, that's a start. It's definitely what you're all about, isn't it?' Jed speared a piece of chicken. 'Maybe we need to work on the wording a little. God, this is gorgeous, Millie.'

'Thank you. So, what do I need one of these mission statements for?'

'Well, you don't really,' Jed admitted. 'It's a bit of a gimmick, but it helps to shove what you're all about under people's noses. The tourists down from the city will really go for it. You could get Ken to paint it on the wall. And you need a slogan. To go on your advertising.' He ate silently for a minute. 'What about, "Come to Millie's and meet your next best friend!"'

Millie began to see what he was getting at. She nodded enthusiastically. 'I love that! And I was thinking of expanding the menu –'

'No,' Jed's voice was firm. 'Stick to what you're good at, what you're known for. Have a limited menu chalked up on a blackboard and when it's gone, it's gone. Gives the impression that everything is freshly cooked.'

'Everything is!'

Jed raised his glass to her. 'Exactly! Promotes the idea that you have to get it while it's hot and fresh – that sort of thing. Maybe add a fish special?'

Millie pushed a cherry tomato around her plate. 'I've thought about that. I don't want to set myself up in competition with the Sea Food Shack and The Plaice Place. It's how Berecombe works,' she explained. 'We all stick to what we're good at – and known for – and don't step on anyone else's toes.'

Jed nodded. 'Okay. Fair point. What about this utterly delicious mango chicken? Has this ever made it onto the menu?'

Millie shook her head and said with a rueful grin, 'Never thought the likes of Biddy and Arthur would go for it.'

'You might be right there.' Jed laughed. 'One alarmingly exotic special a day won't give folk a cardiac, though. They'll still have their scones and tea. Where do you get your recipes from, anyway?'

'Mum's notebook. She collected recipes as well. I've still got them in a big folder. Some go back years.'

He sat back. 'And there's your first *Millie Vanilla's Cook Book*. It'll be a best-seller,' he added triumphantly.

'Do you ever stop?' Millie laughed.

'Nope.' He gave her a flirty look from underneath dark lashes. 'Aw, Millie, it's just that I think the café is a really special place, you know I do. I just want it to be the success it deserves.'

Trevor nosed at his knee in the hope of a tid-bit. 'Of course, the main advantage you have is that you're completely dog-friendly. You make your own dog treats as well, don't you? We'll have to add that to the menu.'

'Or have a separate special dog's menu!' Millie cried. 'That would be amazing.'

'Brilliant! And have you thought about doing any merchandise? Get your slogan on aprons, oven gloves, those hessian bags for life you can get. I've seen people giving the aprons you wear admiring looks. Bet they'd sell all day long. Where do you source them?'

Millie was loving his enthusiasm. 'Biddy makes them for me. I get the material from Dorchester market.'

'Well, tell her they're great. So retro. Do you think she'd like to go into production?'

Millie gave him a big-eyed look. 'After what she revealed yesterday, I think she's probably capable of anything.'

Jed laughed. He stretched his arms over his head and yawned, making the chair tilt back on two legs. 'I've really enjoyed this weekend.' He rolled his neck to ease out the kinks.

'What, painting out a crappy old café?'

'Millie, really, don't you mean, Millie Vanilla's, where the food is home-cooked and you can meet your next best friend?' He grinned widely. 'Yes! I've loved it. I enjoy doing things with you. You must have realised that by now. Working alongside you.' His chair thumped back onto the floor as he leaned forward. He reached for her hand again. 'And now, drink your wine, Emilia,' Jed said, with an unmistakable glint in his eye. 'I really think it's time I took you to bed. I intend on doing a whole load of far more enjoyable things with you. And I think it's going to take quite some time.'

Flustered, Millie replied, 'We haven't had the cake yet.'

'You know what? I think I'd rather have you for pudding.'

Chapter 22

Millie woke to the sound of a herring gull stomping about on the flat roof above her. Rolling over and pulling the duvet up she thought, not for the first time, that they must wear hobnail boots to make that amount of racket. Coming up against the solid warmth of a long male body in her bed jolted her awake properly.

Jed!

He was fast asleep with his back to her. She could hear his quiet, regular breathing. She let him sleep, enjoying the view far too much to want to wake him. Stifling a giggle, she took time exploring him with her eyes. She liked how his hair was slightly too long at the back and trailed into a little point at the nape of his strong neck. She liked, even better, the memory of thrusting her hands into the blond strands, pulling to bring him further into her, wrapping herself around him, desperate to have all of him. His shoulders were wide, his arms satisfyingly well-muscled. The memory of him balanced above her, his face alive with the pleasure she'd given him, sent quivers of desire through her.

She'd been insatiable last night. Need for his body had

blanked everything else out. Worry over the café, her sadness about Tessa both forgotten. She let a sigh escape. He was a beautiful man. And the perfect lover.

Trailing a finger lightly over the smooth skin of Jed's back had ripples of remembered pleasure shuddering through her. She trickled a touch along his side and over his perfect behind. Who would have thought she could get so turned on by a man's bum? Jed's was firm and just so squeezable. She gave in to temptation and found her wrist gripped.

'Beats an alarm call any day,' Jed growled.

Giggling, Millie slid over him, getting impossibly turned on by the feel of his taut, hard body beneath hers.

'Morning, lover,' she said and nipped gently at his lower lip.

'Morning, my love.' He ran a hand up her thigh and then to her breast, a thumb finding the nipple and making her shiver. 'Somehow I don't seem to be able to get enough of you.'

Millie shot him a wicked look. Raising herself up, she concentrated on following the trail of fair hair from his chest, fascinated by how it darkened to a tawny brown at his groin. Cupping him, she breathed, 'I know exactly what you mean,' and kissed his startled mouth.

Afterwards they lay wrapped around one another, watching a slab of dawn light slide across the ceiling and listening to the boom and hiss of the sea.

'I don't think I've ever been happier, Millie. I love you. I love you so very much.' Jed kissed the top of her head softly. 'You know, you mean home to me.'

Millie didn't want to move, didn't even want to breathe, she was afraid of breaking the spell. It was the most perfect thing anyone had ever said to her. Here was a man who loved her and who she knew, without any doubt, she loved back.

'And I love you,' she whispered back. 'I love you right back.'

Chapter 23

The following days were a whirl. Millie had never been busier – or happier. She managed a deal with the bakers that guaranteed a supply of bread for the short term. Not as exciting a range as Tessa's, but it would do for a while until she found an alternative. She baked and froze as much food as she could, in preparation for the parties and even had to borrow space in one of the Barts' freezers. Zoe and Sean were doing a wonderful job at making flyers and getting them put around town and there was a palpable buzz about the parties. It seemed Arthur had been right; she was valued and loved by her community.

It would have been easier – and more effective – to close down and open with a flourish on the day of the parties, but Millie couldn't afford to. Instead, she opened for just a few hours each day, allowing her time to cook but also the opportunity to trial the new menu. She lost count of the positive comments about the café's new look and customers were equally enthusiastic about the specials. Millie even persuaded Arthur to try her mango chicken, which he declared delicious.

What's more, the weather stayed warm and sunny. Perfect

for an evening beach party.

Jed stayed most nights, helped Zoe and Sean distribute publicity and took Trevor out for marathon walks when Millie was panicking about getting everything done. She hardly slept; the nights were too full with exploring Jed's body and the days were a blur of work. She was running on adrenalin and white-hot love.

In an unusual lull, she and Zoe sat on the sun terrace. It was late afternoon and the café was empty. It felt most definitely like the calm before the storm. Millie pushed her sunglasses onto the top of her head, closed her eyes and turned her face greedily to the sun. It was reflecting off the white-painted walls and she could feel her bones drink in the heat. She was exhausted but the happiest she'd ever been.

The café was beginning to attract its old customers back. The W.I. knitters were back, as were the B.A.P.S. Even Clare and her friends had returned, saying they didn't feel welcome at Blue Elephant and already the novelty had worn off. Besides, Clare had pointed out logically, Blue Elephant had no outside space and it was a waste of the spring sunshine to mooch indoors. 'Gotta get some rays,' she'd said.

For the first time in a long while, Millie was daring to feel confident in Millie Vanilla's future.

'These cupcakes are so lush,' Zoe said as she helped herself to another.

'Mary Berry recipe,' Millie murmured, without opening her eyes. 'The woman's a genius. Lots of vanilla.'

'Love the pink icing. So pretty.'

Millie smiled. Since meeting Sean, Zoe had softened. 'How's

school going?'

'Okay.'

Millie swung her feet off the wall and gave Zoe a keen look. 'Have you decided anything? About uni, I mean.'

Zoe sighed. 'Everyone thinks it would be a mistake not to go. Waste of my talent, they keep saying.'

'Your considerable talents,' Millie added, with a grin.

'Sean thinks I should. Go, I mean.'

'He's a bit of a star, that boy.'

'Aw, Mil, that's the problem. I don't want to leave him.' Zoe's voice quavered.

Millie reached over a hand. 'He'll still be here. You'll be back for Christmas, summer. And there are trains to Durham. He could visit. Might even be possible to get a flight from Exeter.'

'Suppose.' Zoe looked unconvinced. 'Ever get the feeling you've met the right man at the wrong time?'

Millie suppressed the unkind thought that Sean could hardly be described as a man – yet. Her thoughts strayed to Jed and how he'd been last night. He'd held her tightly and whispered he loved her again and again. He'd found home, he'd repeated in amazement. To him she was his home.

'Millie?'

Millie brought herself back. 'Sorry, Zoe, I'm a bit tired.'

'I bet,' Zoe said mischievously. 'What with a hot lover and all.'

'Yes, well, I believe we were talking about *your* love life, young lady.'

'Gawd, she's "young ladying" me now,' Zoe said to Trevor,

who ignored her as he was too busy snoring in the sun. 'Now I know I'm in for a lecture.'

'Are you worried Sean might not be faithful?'

Zoe squirmed uncomfortably. 'I think Sean will be more loyal than a very loyal thing. I'm more worried about me.'

'Ah.'

'Oh, Millie, why can't everything stay the same? Why can't I stay in Berecombe with Sean?' Zoe reverted to a young child, bottom lip jutting out while she scuffed her trainer against a pebble.

'I don't know the answer to that, Zo. Think it's called Life.'

'Well, I wish Life would get on its horse, ride off into the sunset and leave me alone.'

Millie frowned. 'A very strange image. Do you think Life looks a bit like Death? Can't imagine either riding a horse, though. Especially one of those dozy ponies George Small has on his farm.'

It wasn't much of a joke, but it raised a smile from Zoe, even if it was a very tiny one.

She sighed. 'Trouble is, Mil, I want both, if I'm honest. I want to go to Durham. I loved it there when I went on the open day. And the course is ace.' She stared out to sea and watched a family with several children paddling in the shallows and shrieking at the cold water. 'But I really love Sean. I really, really love him.'

'Enough to sacrifice getting a degree?'

Zoe stuck a finger into her cupcake and sucked icing off it. 'What good will an English lit degree do me?'

'I don't know, my lovely, but I suppose it's a sign to the

world of your intelligence and commitment. Depends what you want to do, I suppose.'

'That's just it. I don't know what I want to do!' Zoe turned on Millie, all passion and flying dyed hair. 'I don't know if I want to do art. Ken says I've got the talent if I want to go for a fine arts course. But that would mean changing options, going somewhere else. Ken had to do a foundation course on top, so that would mean four years away.' She flung herself back in the chair, which creaked ominously. 'Before Sean, before meeting his dad, I was so certain what I wanted to do and now it's all such a mess. It's doing my head in with all the thinking about it.' She screwed up her face, trying not to cry.

Millie pulled herself higher on her chair. It was hard seeing the usually carefree Zoe so upset. She took off her sunglasses and thought rapidly. 'It's not a mess at all,' she said, with a calmness she certainly didn't feel. Goodness only knew, she wasn't the person to counsel a seventeen-year-old. She thought back to how everything had seemed so black and white when she was in sixth form. A place at university to study, like Zoe, English literature. Weekend clubbing with best friend Dora, going out with Rick. The future rolling out in front of her. A golden time, glistening with promise and uncomplicated freedom. And then the car accident. And everything had burnt to ashes. Rick off to Manchester, Dora to drama school in London. And she'd stayed in Berecombe to pick up the shattered fragments of her parents' lives. She shook her head. No good thinking like that. She glanced at Zoe waiting desperately for advice. Was she projecting her own lost ambitions onto her? Possibly. But it would be a crime for Zoe not to go to university. She was far cleverer than Millie had been at the same age. And had far fewer responsibilities. She should go!

'Zoe – you could have it all.'

'How?' Zoe blew her nose hard into a tissue, making Trevor start.

'Go to Durham, if you get the grades, that is.'

'Millie!' Zoe was scornful. ''Course I'll get the grades.'

'Okay, then. Do your degree. The terms aren't all that long. You can see Sean when you're able and in the breaks you can work with Ken in his studio developing your art.'

Zoe subsided. 'A compromise, then?'

'Ah. I think that's our friend Life's speciality. That and horse-riding,' Millie added.

'Sounds like hard work.'

'That's Life's other surprise. Most of it is bloody hard work.'

'Thanks, Mil. You really know how to cheer a girl up.' Zoe was gloomy.

'Anytime.' Millie made to get up – there was a cider and sultana cake waiting to come out of the oven – but stopped and took Zoe's hand in hers. 'Talk to your parents, though, won't you? Talk it through with them.'

'And Sean.'

'Of course. Sean too. Good girl.'

'Millie,' Zoe protested. 'I'm nearly eighteen. All growed up.'

'So you are, Zoe,' Millie said softly. 'So you are.'

Chapter 24

It was inevitable, in such a small town, that Millie bumped into Tessa.

Millie had popped in to see Biddy and was hurrying down the high street, a scampering Trevor at her heels. It was two days before the parties and she still had loads to do. She was desperate to get back to the café. She saw Tessa coming out of the chemist's on the opposite side of the street. Millie walked on, hoping she hadn't been spotted but Tessa waved and nipped across the road in front of the bus, which was groaning its way up the hill to Axminster.

'Hi, Millie,' she said cheerfully enough. 'How are you doing?'

Millie let Tessa fuss Trevor before trusting herself to answer. 'I'm okay.' She tried for a civilised tone but was aware it sounded forced.

'I loved my birthday present. Thank you so much. Gave me a right giggle when I opened it.'

Millie had given the mug to Sean to pass on to his mum. It had been the first time in many years she hadn't celebrated a birthday with Tessa.

'Heard the café's being re-launched.' Tessa nodded, her expression eager. 'Sound! Hope it's going well?'

'Yes thank you.'

'So, I'll see you around, kiddo?'

'Probably. Got to go. Lots to do.'

'Aw, Mil, please don't be like that.' Tessa caught her arm.

Millie turned back, startled to see tears in her friend's eyes.

'I'm sorry, Millie. I'm really, really sorry. I thought you'd see why I had to do it.'

There was a pause. Tessa had been her best friend and she missed her so much. 'I do, sort of,' Millie admitted and looked down, scuffling her feet. 'I just feel a bit –'

'Shafted. Yeah, I get that. If it's any consolation, the new job's crap.'

'Is it?' Millie looked properly at Tessa for the first time. She was grey with fatigue.

'They keep on at me to reduce costs, cut corners with cheaper ingredients. Non-organic stuff, like. Keep upping the targets too. I just can't bake what they want, the way they want it. My bread's too expensive.' She gave a little hiccough. 'And I've missed you so much, kiddo.'

Millie wasn't quite ready to forgive. 'You've caused me a lot of hassle.' She jerked her head towards Berringtons. 'I had to do a deal with the bakers.' One look at Tessa, who was now distraught and had tears streaming down her face, had her opening her arms. 'Oh I've missed you too, Tess. So much.'

They hugged, ignoring a startled tourist passing by and an overexcited Trevor, who was jumping up and trying to get in on the action.

'Oh, babe, can I come back? Can I do some stuff for you again? I've got some great ideas. Only I can't get out of my contract for a bit. It's a bloody pain. Oh, I'm so sorry!' Tessa's words jumped over themselves and were soaked through with tears.

Eventually everything calmed down. Millie passed Tessa some tissues and they mopped each other up.

'You've got mascara all down your cheek, I always told you to wear waterproof,' Tessa sniffed. 'Here, let me get it off.'

'You don't look too hot yourself,' Millie countered. 'Get down, Trevor,' she added to the dog, who was beside himself, sensing the drama.

'Never was a pretty crier, me.' Tessa scrubbed her eyes. 'Should have seen me after each of the kids were born. Total mess.'

'Your Sean's a bit of a superstar.' Millie blew her nose and pocketed the tissues.

'He is an' all. Can't be too awful a person if I produced him, can I?' Tessa glanced at Millie, checking they were alright.

'No. Although I think he's got most of Ken's genes.'

Tessa grinned. 'If you're back to insults we must be okay now.'

'Of course we're okay.' Millie hugged her again then wagged a finger. 'Don't start crying again! I'm on my way back to the café. Fancy a coffee?'

Tessa put her arm through Millie's. 'You bet! Think we've got some catching up to do, haven't we?' She gave Millie a keen look. 'For a start, I want all the goss on this hot man you've got in tow.'

Millie grinned at her friend. 'I think we have. Not that we'll have much time to chat. Got far too much to do and I've got just the job for you.'

Tessa groaned. 'Well, I suppose I deserve that. Come on then, kiddo. We'd better get a move on.'

Chapter 25

It was two in the morning and Millie couldn't sleep. As she sat in front of the computer, waiting for it to start up, she rubbed a weary hand over her face. Maybe it was the thought of the day ahead that was keeping her awake – or maybe it was what Tessa had told her.

They'd chatted while cleaning the big picture windows, making them sparkle in the last rays of the sun, which was glowing pink and orange as it sank into the sea. After telling Millie what an awful company Blue Elephant was to work for, Tessa had dropped her bombshell.

Millie jumped as the computer sprang into life. She put in her password. With her finger poised over Google, she hesitated. She was about to find out the truth.

Taking a deep breath, found the right key and pressed before she had time to think any more. To back out. She entered the name Tessa had told her to look for.

The room went very still. Millie's existence shrank to the rectangle of light in front of her and the information displayed. A short paragraph written in stark black and white. But they were words that turned everything on its head.

The roar of the surf outside faded and was replaced by a louder one in her head. Her throat hurt with unshed tears. She blinked them back, rubbed her eyes and repeated the search. It brought up the same result.

An incandescent fury consumed her. If she thought Tessa's betrayal had been bad, it was nothing to this. She slammed the laptop lid down and stalked up and down the sitting room, with a fierce energy fuelled by rage. And then, just as suddenly, the anger left her. She fell, boneless and trembling onto the sofa. Trevor crept next to her, pressing his little body against hers, sensing her distress.

Millie put her head in her hands, finally letting the tears fall. Trevor whined and licked the salt from her cheeks. She gathered him up and wept into his fur.

Chapter 26

There was no denying it, the afternoon tea party was a raging success. The sun shone, the guests flocked to the café dressed in their best, the food was appreciated and tea was dispensed in gallons from brown-Betty teapots borrowed from the W.I. Arthur put himself in charge of the music and a series of big-band favourites echoed around the walls of the sun terrace. The newly painted chairs and tables were put at the edge, leaving a space for dancing in the middle. Even the most elderly and frail joined in, not quite ready to let go of the dance steps of their youth. Biddy's bunting fluttered in a warm spring breeze and the movement was echoed by the women's pretty dresses as they danced.

The local newspaper sent along a journalist who interviewed Millie and a photographer who ate his own weight in cupcakes. Then they stayed to dance, promising to come along to the evening do as well. The party even gathered an audience of tourists and dog-walkers, who cheered and clapped at the end of each dance and took endless shots on their phones.

One part of Millie, the non broken-hearted part, enjoyed

it all immensely. Over the years she had learned to be good at hiding her feelings and, today, she had never been more grateful for it. If she appeared blank-faced and exhausted she let people put it down to hard work.

Zoe came over after executing a nifty jitterbug with Beryl, aged seventy-eight. 'Oh this is so much fun!' she panted, out of breath. 'It's completely awesome. Everyone's said how much they've enjoyed the Valentine's-themed week too. Well done, Mil.'

'Well done yourself,' Millie managed. 'You and Sean, and Arthur too, have worked on this just as hard.'

'Has Granddad told you about Daisy?' Zoe flung herself down on a lime-green chair.

'No. I haven't had a chance to talk to him yet.'

'Come on,' Zoe slapped the wall next to her. 'Sit down for five minutes. You haven't stopped all afternoon. You look knackered.'

'Well, thank you.' Millie perched on the wall.

'Sorry, Millie. You know what I mean, though. Burning the candle at both ends. Isn't that what Biddy would say?'

'Something like that.'

'In the Mood' rang out, silencing them for a moment.

'Oh, get a load of this! Clare dancing with Granddad! Hang on, I've got to get a pic.' Zoe raced off, took the picture on her phone and returned, laughing. She showed Millie. 'Never thought I'd see that, although she's the biggest *Strictly* fan going. She's going to get so much grief over this!'

Millie looked at the photograph, shielding the screen from the bright sun. Arthur and Clare had huge grins plastered across their faces as they attempted a sedate jive. She smiled. She was very fond of Arthur and it was good to see him having so much fun. She handed the phone back to Zoe. 'At least she persuaded Arthur to give up being DJ for five minutes. What's this about Daisy?'

'Oh, yes,' Zoe said, her attention on the phone as she scrolled down. 'Apparently, and this is weirdness beyond a very weird thing, a mystery benefactor has paid for the operation. Daisy was taken in yesterday, had the op, all went well and the best thing of all, the tumour's benign.' Zoe grinned. 'Isn't that the greatest news ever? She got driven to Bristol in a special doggie ambulance. Must've cost a packet.' She looked up. 'You don't look very relieved.'

'I am.' Millie forced a happy face. 'Of course I am. I'm delighted for Arthur and Daisy.' She knew exactly who had been behind it all. Who else would have the money for such a grand gesture? It would make what she had to do later all the more difficult. The music seemed too loud suddenly, the sun blinding her as it bounced off the terrace's white walls. She had to get away. She watched as Arthur chivalrously led a beaming Clare back to her chair, where she sat with her great aunt. 'Look, Zoe, I think I'm getting a headache,' she began, 'and I need to check on Trevor, he's been cooped up in the flat –'

Zoe, however, had other ideas. 'Hang on a mo', Millie. You might be about to witness a first in Berecombe's long and illustrious history.'

'What?' Millie couldn't help but be irritable. She was genuinely developing a headache and needed to take something before it took hold. She still had a long day ahead of her before she could crawl into bed and cry.

'Look,' said Zoe wonderingly. 'Granddad is about to ask Biddy for a dance. I think The Big Berecombe Reconciliation might be about to unfold!'

They watched as Arthur approached Biddy, who was sitting in the shade with some friends, Elvis on her knee. The music prevented them from hearing what he was saying but the meaning of his gestures was clear.

Arthur placed his hand on his heart and put his head on one side. Conciliatory. Then he bowed down low, holding out one hand. Biddy gave him an old-fashioned look, raised her brows and appeared to consider the matter. Millie and Zoe held their breath, then watched as Biddy handed Elvis to her neighbour and took Arthur's hand in hers.

Arthur led her into a space that had magically appeared in the middle of the group of dancers. He bowed again before straightening and placing a reverent hand on Biddy's waist. Biddy rested her hand carefully on his shoulder and they began a stately dance to a slow version of 'Begin the Beguine'.

Millie and Zoe sighed in unison.

'I think that was the most romantic thing I've ever seen,' Millie said, through tears.

'Way to go, Granddad.' Zoe turned to Millie, her eyes shining. 'Told him the flowers and grovelling apology would work.'

Millie watched as Arthur and Biddy danced. They were gazing into one another's eyes with rapt attention. It looked as if their friendship, or romance, or whatever they had, was back on track. She was deeply glad for them. If only it could always be as easy as that. For what had been done to her, flowers and an apology, however grovelling, just wouldn't be enough.

Chapter 27

The day, one that should have been filled with pleasure, ground on relentlessly. Millie thought it would never end.

The afternoon tea party segued into the evening celebrations. Biddy and Arthur and their friends said their farewells, saying how much everyone had enjoyed themselves and wasn't it good to have some old-fashioned dancing for a change.

Arthur's parting shot was a suggestion that it should become a regular event, one for which maybe she should think about charging. 'It's been wonderful, my dear. What a new start for Millie Vanilla's! Enjoy your fireworks,' he added, as he kissed her goodbye. 'Dennis knows what he's doing; he'll put on a rare old show.'

Millie watched him as he led off an excited Trevor. Arthur was looking after him for the night as the dog hated fireworks. She felt oddly forlorn and vulnerable without Trevor at her side.

Zoe and Clare stayed on to help and were joined by Tessa, who brought Sean and Ken. They rearranged the chairs and tables on the terrace, this time in romantic twosomes. They added candles, Love Heart sweets and roses in bud vases and tied-on heart-shaped pink balloons. It made the café look very different. Sean changed the music to something more contemporary and the transformation from tea dance to Valentine's party was complete. As dusk fell and the sea became an indigo backdrop, the candle-lit tables looked impossibly romantic.

The headache that had been niggling at the edge of her brain all day, intensified. As the thump of Rihanna started up, Millie wasn't sure she didn't prefer the dance tunes of earlier. Gritting her teeth, she forced herself to enjoy what was turning out to be a hugely successful day for Millie Vanilla's.

Gradually couples arrived. They began dancing, sat entwined over glasses of fruit punch or lolled on the hay bales in the secretive darkness of the beach.

Millie, having served the food and drink and reassured herself everyone was having a good time, found a quiet spot on the wall and sat down. Her exhaustion made everything seem as if it was happening a long, long way away.

'This is a bit of alright.' It was Tessa. She sat down beside Millie and put an arm around her. 'Lucky the weather held. Could almost pretend it's May. Well done, kiddo.' She peered closer. 'You okay?'

'I'm fine,' Millie lied. 'And thanks, it's going well, isn't it? I was a bit worried we'd get gate-crashers, but George Small is doing a great job as a bouncer.' They looked to where the burly farmer's son was standing guard.

'Take a tank to get past him,' Tessa giggled.

Then Millie spotted Jed. Striding along under the white

lights of the promenade. That easy, confident gait. As if he owned the world.

He came up to them. Tessa took one look at Millie's face and said, 'I'll be over there if you need me, kiddo.' Then, with rare tact, she melted away.

'Millie, my darling!'

She let him pick her up, twirl her around. She even let him kiss her.

'The place is looking marvellous. *You've* made it look marvellous. And I hear the tea dance went well. I'm so sorry I couldn't make it. Ma wanted to discuss the house she's thinking of buying. It's pretty cool, actually. In Lyme, just up the hill, fantastic sea views, swimming pool. She's quite keen on it. I can't wait to show it off and introduce you to her. She's going to love you. I love you, my Millie Fudge. My darling girl.'

His eyes were sparkling, his face aglow with excitement. When she didn't respond he quietened.

'Is everything okay? Is there a problem with the party?'

He caught her hands to his chest; she could feel his heart beating. Regularly. Not the jumping-about, dancing-all-over-the-place rhythm that hers was doing.

Loosening his grip, she took a deep, shuddering breath. Everything over the last few hours had been building up to this moment. To this confrontation. Looking into his concerned eyes she thought she'd never been more angry with anyone. Not even with her parents for dying so needlessly and leaving her all alone. She wasn't going to blurt it out, but couldn't help herself. She'd been bottling it all up for too long. Before she knew it the words came tumbling out. 'When were you going to tell me, Jed?'

'Tell you what, my love?'

'That your real name is Jeremy Fitzroy-Henville and that you've been working as a management consultant for the Blue Elephant chain of cafés. The company which opened a branch in my home town and threatened to put me out of business. Might still close me down.'

Jed's face tightened. A beat pulsed in his throat. He pulled his thumb into his temple, massaging it. 'Who told you?' he whispered, barely audible over the thump of the bass. He didn't look at her.

Millie laughed, but there was no humour or warmth there. 'Tessa told me she saw you go into a meeting at Blue Elephant. So I looked you up. Good old internet, eh? It comes in handy when your lover has lied to you.'

She turned away and looked out to the black sea, screwing her nails into her palms to stop herself crying. She was so damn furious with him.

'Millie?' Jed caught her by the arm.

'Get your hands off me!' she spat.

He dropped his hand and it hung limply against his side. 'Millie, whatever I've done, I've never lied to you.'

'How can you say that!' She turned on him, eyes ablaze.

'Because it's true. I never lied. I told you I worked as a management consultant.'

'Oh yes, you told me that.' Millie's voice was bitter. 'You just happened to forget to mention one of your biggest clients! And,' she added, 'Jed Henville isn't your name!'

'It's the one I go by. Jed's been a nickname since I was at school. I drop the double-barrelled surname as it's such a mouthful. I haven't lied to you about that,' he insisted, 'Jed Henville is my name.'

Millie stamped her foot, forcing the zillion things that were rushing crazily around her head to steady. She needed to think rationally. 'Why didn't you tell me you work for Blue Elephant?'

'Because I don't, Millie.' Jed's voice was rich with frustration. 'I was asked in as a consultant. I don't work directly for the café chain.'

'It's the same thing, Jed,' Millie shouted. She jabbed a hand into her chest. 'To me it's the same thing. You're in the enemy camp. Why didn't you *tell* me?' Then her eyes went big with horror. 'Was it part of some plan? Pick the brains of the competitor, distract them with flowery words and big gestures? That night in the pub. All those questions you asked! Has this all been a big joke to you? Have I meant so little to you? Oh, my God, do you actually even love me?'

'Millie,' Jed paled under his tan. 'You mean the world to me!' He thrust a hand through his hair. 'I know,' he whispered, 'it's all such a mess.' His face crumpled as if in realisation of what he might lose. 'But you must understand I love you. More than I can say. More than you'll ever know.' He shrugged helplessly. 'That day we met in Lyme. I'd just got the call. They knew I was in the area – I really have been house-hunting for my mother, I promise. I tried to get out of it, but I'd done some work for one of their American cafés and I still had to fulfil my contract.' He gazed at her. 'They insisted I do the work, Millie, otherwise they threatened to withhold my fee.'

'I might have known it would come down to money with you!' Millie interrupted.

'Let me finish. That's not what I meant.'

'I don't want to hear it.' Millie put her hands on her ears.

He gave a gutsy sigh. 'Then hear this. You don't know how much I've hated myself, not being able to tell you.'

'Then why didn't you tell me, Jed?' she snarled. She directed him to a quieter corner of the terrace, away from Tessa's watchful gaze. Most of the couples were dancing on the beach by now. A stiffer sea breeze had got up. It made the Valentine's balloons jerk on their ribbons and the candles flicker wildly. The cheap romance of it all seemed, to Millie, to mock their argument.

'I don't know!' Jed was shouting with frustration now. 'I was clutching at straws, at anything to keep us together.' He took a deep breath, got himself under control and went on more calmly. He took her hands and drew her closer and, despite herself, Millie craved his touch. 'God, I tried to tell you. I wanted to. I so nearly did. But then I had to sit in on a few meetings in the Berecombe branch and I was put in a really awkward position. I *wanted* to tell you, Millie,' he repeated, 'but by then it was too late because I'd fallen in love with you. I love you so much, Millie. And I knew the moment I told you the truth, I'd lose you.'

'And you have, Jed.' Tears streamed down Millie's face. The anger had gone, she was too hollowed out by the emotion to sustain it. It was replaced by a deep, weary sadness. She gulped, unable to go on for a moment. 'Because I'm not sure I can ever trust you again.'

Jed nodded. He brushed a hand over his eyes. 'Jeez, Millie,' he said on a breath. 'I've fucked this up, haven't I? I've fucked it up good and proper. But you know I love you. Whatever else you think of me, believe that. And I'll never ever stop loving you.'

He opened his arms and, after the briefest of hesitations, she flew into them. Desperate for his touch one more time.

'Can't we work this through?' he said against her hair. 'Can't we talk about it?'

'I love you, Jed. I don't think I'll ever not love you.'

They stood wrapped tight into one another, feeling the agony of what must happen next spike to and fro between them.

At last Millie tore herself away. Wiping her face, she said through thinned lips, 'You'd better go.'

'I can't go. I can't leave you.' His shock was palpable.

'You'll have to, because even though I love you more than life itself, I can't –' tears bubbled up again and Millie fought for composure. 'I can't trust you and I can't love you completely, not as I'd want to love a man, without trusting you. You're not who I thought you were. And ... and I just don't know what else you've lied to me about.'

Even as she was saying it, Millie wondered what she was doing.

'I'm not going to go. I'm not leaving you.' He took her in his arms again. 'I promise the only thing I didn't tell you was that I was doing work for Blue Elephant.'

The name of the hated café on his lips made her shudder. And hardened her resolve. 'Oh, Jed, don't make this any more difficult than it already is.' She forced the words out. 'Whatever we've had, no matter how wonderful it was, was based on lies.'

'I didn't lie to you!'

'No, perhaps you think you haven't, Jed. Perhaps you haven't lied explicitly, but you've lied by omission and that's the same to me. It's what I can't live with.'

'This is madness. Why can't we start again?' Jed broke away from her, his body rigid with anger.

Millie's anger rose to meet his. 'Based on what, Jed? Sex? Even you have to admit we're two different people.' She gestured to the party raging around them. 'This is what I am. The café, Berecombe, my friends. You spend so much time travelling for work, you don't even have a house to live in. However was that going to work? I'll never be what you are. I'll never fit in with your lifestyle.'

Jed stared at her in shock. 'I've never wanted that from you. I've never even thought that way.'

'Where do you spend Christmas, Jed?'

'What? What the fuck has that got to do with anything?'

'Where do you usually spend Christmas?' Millie repeated.

Jed thrust a shaking hand through his hair. 'It depends.'

'Tell me.'

'Dubai once. Cancun. Diving in Sharm before the troubles. St Lucia in Aunt Marina's villa.' He looked bewildered. 'Tell me why this should matter.'

'Not Devon, then?'

'No, of course not. It's nice to get some sun in December.' He stopped at her look. Realising what he'd said. 'Are you really throwing away what we have on the basis of where we spend *Christmas?*'

Millie stamped her foot again. He just wasn't getting it. Hell, she wasn't sure she was. Adele began singing in the background. The slow dances had started. The mournful notes smothered her. Millie felt she was drowning. She mustn't weaken. Screwing up her eyes in an attempt to get her thoughts straight, she replied, 'No, of course not. But it's an example of how different we are, maybe of what we want. Look at your clothes. How much did that jacket cost?'

Jed looked down at his orange puffa coat. 'I don't know. Four, five hundred?'

'The fact you don't even know is enough. I buy my clothes in Hospice Care. It's a charity shop,' she went on when he looked blank. 'We don't fit, Jed,' she said sadly. 'We don't fit together.'

His lips compressed into a hard white line. 'That's it, then. You're throwing away what we have on the basis of clothes and holidays.'

Millie saw his colour rise.

'That's snobbishness, Millie.' He spat the words out. 'Inverted snobbishness.'

'No, it's just being realistic. How long do you think you'd be happy with what I can offer you?'

'I'd hoped forever. I'd hoped I'd found home with you, Millie, but obviously that's not good enough for you. *I'm* not enough for you.'

'That's not what I meant, Jed!'

'No? That's what it sounds like. You know, perhaps you're

right?' He shook his head, suddenly defeated. 'I don't think you know me at all. You certainly don't understand how much I love you. Well, perhaps you need to know this. I was prepared to give it all up for you. That meeting I went to in Paris? I told Blue Elephant I would no longer work with them. That they could sue me for breach of contract if they wanted. They were welcome to keep their fee. Happy now?' He glared. 'But maybe you're right, maybe it's time I went. I'd give up the world for you, Millie, but it still wouldn't be enough. There might be a time we can discuss this rationally but now isn't the moment.'

'Jed?' There was a beat before Millie realised no sound had actually come out of her mouth.

He came to her again and wrapped her in his arms. 'We're both too mixed up at the moment. Too much has been said.' He tightened his hold. 'Just remember this. I love you, Millie.' Releasing her, he took her face in his hands and gave her one last hard kiss. His lips burned into hers. Tracing a shaking finger down her face, he added, 'you'll always mean home to me. Maybe, one day we might even begin to think about making a home together.' He shook his head, sadly. 'But not now.'

He turned on his heel before she could respond. As she watched him walk away, a part of her heart tore away and followed. Every particle of her being wanted to run to him. To hold him in her arms. To start again. His words were slowly sinking in. Was it possible, was it just possible that he was as kind, generous and honourable as he'd always seemed? And she'd thrown it all away. Thrown what they'd had away.

What they might have had.

What had she done?

Jed paused at the end of the promenade and turned to face her. He stood, a tall shadow, silhouetted against the white lights and then walked around the corner and disappeared from view.

Tessa found her, minutes, or hours later – Millie couldn't tell – and forced a small glass into her hand. 'Illicit booze. Don't tell the kids we've got alcohol. Thought you might need a drink, kiddo.'

Millie downed it in one. The whisky traced a fiery trail down her throat and made her choke. She realised she was shaking.

'Better?' Tessa slipped an arm through hers. 'It's been a fantastic night.' She kept the tone conversational, as if knowing any hint of sympathy would worsen Millie's distress. 'And interesting news, Zoe's just told me who paid for Daisy's op. Lover boy Mr Hunk himself. Your Jed. Wasn't that amazing of him? Maybe he's not as bad as we thought?' When Millie remained silent, she went on gently, 'And spring is definitely in the air. Time for a new start, eh? Think the caff's going to be a real winner. We'll show that lot up at Blue Elephant!'

Millie couldn't answer but put her head on Tessa's shoulder. 'Yes,' she whispered, eventually. 'A new start. Spring beginnings.'

She watched where Zoe and Sean were dancing close together, their feet hardly moving, their bodies as close as possible. She remembered Biddy and Arthur's happy faces at the tea dance. Thought about how beautiful the refurbished café looked. How much they'd all achieved. But for her every-thing felt at an end. Spring beginnings? For the café, maybe. For her friends, undoubtedly. As far as she was concerned, she was certain she'd just said good-bye to the best thing she'd ever known.

'You're all in,' Tessa said softly. 'Come on. Let's find you another drink and something to eat to soak it up. And then you can tell Auntie Tess all about it.'

As they began to move, the crowd whooped and sighed as the first of the fireworks erupted. It soared high above them, blasting the night sky into a vivid red and orange.

Millie watched it sear a dazzling trail over the sea. She imagined the hiss as it hit the inky water. She and Jed had been as spectacular, but they had turned to ashes just as fast.

She allowed herself to be led back into the café. Back to her home. She wasn't sure she'd ever feel happy again.

Summer Loves

Chapter 1

April was a beautiful month in Berecombe. As Millie walked an excited cockapoo across the deserted beach she could feel the early morning sun on her face and a sea breeze lifting her hair, lilting and gentle. It was a most glorious morning and something she used to take great pleasure in. She threw Trevor's tennis ball, shading her eyes to see where it bounced on the hard, flat sand. A movement on the harbour wall caught her attention. A figure stood there. Tall and masculine. Millie's heart faltered. She screwed up her eyes to see better but he was just a silhouette against the morning light. It couldn't be Jed, could it? It had been weeks since he'd left Berecombe. Since she'd angrily sent him away. Trevor skidded to a halt beside her and jumped up, tennis ball in mouth, eager for her to continue the game. Bending down, she took the ball from him and threw it. When she looked towards land again, the figure on the harbour had disappeared.

Of course it hadn't been Jed. Why would he come back to Berecombe? With a heavy heart, Millie turned to return to the café. She had the Yummy Mummies and the W.I. Knitting Circle coming in this morning, so would be busy. Last night she'd slaved over getting a batch of Battenberg cakes ready and still wasn't happy with them. She was finished if her baking was going off-kilter, she mused, as she trudged over the softer sand near the prom. It was almost as if the kitchen sensed her mood. Ever since Jed left, part of her heart had gone too. She couldn't seem to throw herself into things with the same enthusiasm. Even her baking was something to be done more as a chore rather than a pleasure. Jed would have loved the Battenberg. She stamped the sand off her feet, exasperated at how her thoughts kept circling back to him.

She unlocked the café door and inhaled the familiar sweet smells. Forcing herself to think positively, she grinned down at a sand-covered dog. 'At least Dora is back in town, though, eh Trevor?' Going through to the kitchen to switch on the kettle, she called back, feeling a little more cheerful, 'And life's never boring with Dora around!'

Chapter 2

If one more person pulled her duck's tail or made one more lewd remark about 'little duckies' Dora would seriously lose it. She tugged at her escaping tights and waddled through the White Bear's public bar, rattling her money tin. 'Buy a number for the duck race,' she called. 'Raise some money for a good cause.' She'd have serious words with Millie later. How the hell did she get roped into this? It was little more than ritual humiliation.

'Oi oi,' called a man in a lecherous voice. 'What have we got here?'

What got into these men? It was barely nine o'clock. Had she been away from her home town so long she'd forgotten all about these riotous Friday night drinking sessions? No, alcohol alone couldn't excuse their behaviour; it must be the duck outfit that got them going. Male hormones obviously went into overdrive at the sight of a woman dressed in yellow feathers and red tights.

Dora adjusted her duck head to peer down at her latest assailant. He reached out and pulled her tail hard.

'That's enough,' she yelled. 'I've had enough. You can buy

a duck for that.' She held out her money box as a demand for payment. And swore. Hard.

'How much?'

'They're a pound a duck.'

'I don't see any ducks,' he sniggered. 'Apart from you.'

'No,' Dora explained, for what seemed the thousandth time that evening. 'You buy a number and then come along to the river tomorrow afternoon. All the ducks will have a number on them. We set them off and if yours wins, you get a prize.'

'What's the prize? You?'

Dora was having difficulty containing her temper. Her feet hurt, her head was sweaty from wearing the ridiculous duck headdress and she wanted to go home. Why was it such hard work separating people from their money? It was only a measly pound.

'You get a fifty-pound voucher to spend at Millie Vanilla's, the café on the front.'

'So tell me again why I've got to buy a duck?'

'I think the idea is it raises money,' another voice interjected. 'For the Arts Workshop. Am I right?'

Dora froze. She knew that voice.

With difficulty, she turned her head to the left. The drunk man had a friend. A man who was sitting next to him and who had been screened out of her sightline by her ridiculous duck head.

Shock reverberated through her. It was him.

It was not the way she wanted to bump into the guy she'd fallen so hopelessly in love with in sixth form. Whose heart she had broken when her parents had insisted that Berecombe's bad boy wasn't good enough for her. The years spent acting in the States vaporised. She was seventeen again.

Mikey Love.

Still with that gypsy-dark hair, although it was now threaded through with silver and not quite so unruly. Still with those wicked blue eyes and the grin that made you go weak at the knees and completely at his mercy. Whatever that involved. Sheer charisma. She'd never met a man with as much, even in the torrid world of American television. She hadn't seen him for years. Since leaving Berecombe. Had never set eyes on him again. Until this moment.

'Someone up there must really have it in for me,' she muttered, the yellow felt headdress muffling her words.

Someone really *had* got it in for her. Millie and Tessa chose that moment to catch up with her. They'd obviously been treated to a drink and had given up all thought of fund-raising. Both held a glass of white in one hand, their duck head in the other. Deeply uncool, seeing as it was Tessa's Arts Workshop they were raising money for.

Her bad temper was affecting her judgement. It seemed she was wrong.

'Ooh, laters, babes,' Tessa cooed. 'Just spotted Dennis. A local councillor should be good to cough up a few bob.' She made her way through the crowded bar, cheerfully batting off the stares and wolf-whistles.

Dora could admire the woman's self-confidence, even if she found her loud voice grating. They must breed them tough in Birmingham.

Millie came up to her with a kind smile. 'Just sold my last

number. What's been holding you up?'

Dora glared at her through the yellow. 'Maybe you weren't being molested all night,' she hissed. 'My legs will be black and blue after this.'

'Oh I know, my lovely,' Millie sympathised. 'Me too. Swiped more than one bloke with a wing and then guilted them into buying a duck. How many tickets have you got left?' she asked. 'I'll take a few and sell them for you. Actually,' she reconsidered. 'You know your trouble? You're getting all hot and bothered. Take your head off.' Without warning, Millie yanked off Dora's headdress, leaving her marooned like a headless chicken, or rather duck. If anything, Dora now felt even more of a fool. At least, with her outfit complete, she made sense. Now, with an enormous yellow body out of all proportion to her head, she knew she must look ludicrous. What was more, with red hair and pale skin, Dora did not do heat in any way that was attractive. She knew perfectly well her face was scarlet and shiny with sweat and her hair flattened and greasy-looking. She scrunched up her eyes, waiting for the inevitable and tried to brave it out. With any luck, in this state she might be unrecognisable.

'Dora!'

'Fuck.'

'Oh my God. It is isn't it? It's Dora Bartlett. Or should I say Theodora Bart?' Mike sounded amused. 'You've learned to swear in a very unladylike way since you left school.'

'Oh my,' said his friend. 'Now we can see what the filly looks like. Or should I say duckling?' He roared at his feeble joke.

'That's enough, Phil.' Mikey stood up. 'Forgive him, he's had a bit too much to drink.'

'Well, I had to try the cider now I'm in the West Country,' Phil protested and turned to someone. Dora heard a very female giggle.

She opened one eye to see Mikey staring at her. Oh, how she remembered those naughty blue eyes. What the hell was he even doing here? The last thing she'd heard, he was working in London.

'Hello Mikey,' she managed eventually. How could he still make her legs go weak, her insides churn around in the most delightfully revolting fashion, just as he had when she'd been seventeen and in his thrall.

He came closer, or as close as the fat feathery costume allowed. 'Hello Dora. It's lovely to see you again,' he said quietly.

'Isn't it,' she mumbled, refusing to meet his eyes.

Millie, her eyes on stalks, interrupted. 'Mikey, wow! Whatever are you doing back in Berecombe?'

'Back working in the Regent,' he said, naming Berecombe's little theatre on the sea front. 'Putting on *Persuasion* as a fund-raiser for it. The old place is looking a bit sad. Needed some cash input, so thought I'd help.'

'Oh yes,' Millie continued. 'You've made quite a name for yourself, haven't you? Directing or something. Up in London.'

'I've had some success.' The modest words belied his tone.

He'd always been so sure of himself, Dora thought. Some said brave, bearing in mind his background. Some said cocky. It depended on your point of view.

'How nice.' She couldn't keep the edge from her voice. She hated being wrong-footed like this. If she'd thought, coming back here, she'd bump into him, she would have gone to her villa in Siena. But something had called her back to Berecombe and, besides, her parents had been due a visit. If fate engineered a meeting with Michael Love, then Dora would infinitely have preferred it to be when she was looking at her best. In control. The very image of the successful actress.

Millie was completely star-struck, however. She'd always had a soft spot for Mikey when they were all at school together. 'Ooh lovely, one of my favourites. I love *Persuasion*. When's it on?'

'Later in the summer. Early days yet, we haven't even cast it.' Mikey directed his words to Millie, but his eyes were fixed on Dora.

'Are you Theodora Bart? It is, isn't it? Oh. My. God.' A Sloaney female voice. Very young. Very gushing.

The evening just got worse. A fan.

The woman Dora had heard giggling with Cider Phil stood up and joined them.

'I absolutely love you in *The English Woman*. I literally can't wait for the next series. When's it due out?'

Dora tried to pin on a gracious smile but was desperate to get away. The duck costume was making her claustrophobic, her red tights were far too big and threatening to fall down and she couldn't bear Mikey's gaze. 'Thank you,' she said in cool tones. 'I'm afraid I'm not sure about the next series.'

'This is Kirstie Fielding, my first assistant director,' Mikey explained. 'And one of your biggest fans.'

'I'll say,' Kirstie went on. 'When I found out you and Mike came from the same town, went to school together, even, I was literally so thrilled. And I can't believe I've met you! And in a duck costume too! I've just got to get a selfie with you.'

'Phil and Kirstie?' Millie laughed, thankfully interrupting. 'Really?' She turned to Mikey. 'And you're no longer Mikey?'

He gave a regretful look. 'Dropped the "y" when I left Berecombe. We all need to reinvent ourselves, occasionally, don't we?'

He left the words hanging but Dora knew his inference. Panicking, she clutched at straws. 'Look, I'm so sorry but we have to go. I've still got a ton of ducks to sell.' As Kirstie got her phone out, she put up her hand. 'No really, no pictures. The fund-raising isn't about me. It's about the Workshop.'

'No doubt we'll bump into each other again, Dora.'

'I'm sure we will Mikey. I mean Mike.' She grabbed Millie's arm in a vice-like grip, but before they could escape Millie rattled Dora's tin at Mike.

'How many have you left?' he asked.

'Twenty-five.' Dora said it as a challenge, sticking her chin out. 'Pound a duck.'

The challenge was accepted. 'I'll take them all,' Mike said, with a defiant gleam in his eyes.

Dora peeled off the last numbers from the sheet, took his money and, with barely a thank you, steered Millie away. She shoved her unceremoniously through the crowd to the door. As they left they heard Kirstie's *Made in Chelsea* tones complaining that you should never meet your heroes as they always disappoint.

Chapter 3

'How could you show me up in front of him, of all people?' Dora fell onto the sofa in Millie's flat.

'Who?' Millie dropped her duck head with a relieved sigh. 'Ooh, it's been a long night. My feet are killing me. No, Trevor,' she warned as the cockapoo nosed it with interest.

'Mikey Love, that's who. Or maybe we ought to call him Mike now.'

'Yeah, he's definitely more a Mike now he's all grown up and gorgeous. Mind you, he was gorgeous at school too.' Millie's voice was dreamy. 'All the girls had a crush on Michael Love, although I seem to remember he only had eyes for one girl.' Getting up, she went into the kitchen and foraged in the fridge. Brandishing a bottle of white and two glasses, she added, 'Think we've earned this. Tessa was really grateful we helped out.'

'So she should be.'

Millie poured the wine. 'Why are you so cross?'

'Those men! They treated us like shit.'

'All in good fun. Millie shrugged. 'They didn't mean any harm. You just need to elbow them where it hurts.'

'Is it always like this on a Friday night now?'

'What do you mean?'

'So much drinking.'

'Think you're a bit out of touch with us commoners,' Millie observed. 'Maybe you've lived in LA for too long? It was just ordinary Friday night banter.' She passed over a glass. 'Here, have some of this.'

Dora sipped her wine and tried not to grimace. It wasn't the smooth white Californian she was used to. Maybe she *had* been in the LA bubble for too long? After all, when was the last time she'd been out without a protective entourage? Granted, it was more necessary in the States as she had a bigger fan base there. Putting her wine down, she slipped out of the duck costume, kicked off the horrible tights and lay spread-eagled on the sofa in only her underwear. 'Oh, that's better,' she sighed, feeling better immediately.

Millie laughed. 'I'll open a window. Cool you down a bit. Going to be a hot summer, I think. It's boiling now and it's only April.' After opening the window and letting the sea breeze float in, she disappeared to her bedroom and changed. Five minutes later she flopped down on the chair near the window and cackled. 'If only your adoring fans could see you now.'

Dora didn't bother opening her eyes. 'They've seen me in less.'

'Wasn't quite what I meant.'

This got through. Dora giggled and sat upright. She took another sip of wine and found it tasted better this time. 'Oh, I'm sorry I'm such a grouch, Mil. Too hot, too tired, too jet-lagged.'

'Too spoiled?'

Dora pursed her lips. 'You might have a point. God, I'd love a smoke.' She gestured to the rejected duck costume, 'But if all this yellow polyester caught light it would start a fire that would wreck half the town.' She poked it with a disdainful toe.

'You've never smoked,' Millie exclaimed in horror.

'Keeps the weight down.'

'Dora, you hardly weigh anything now.'

Dora shrugged. 'A size zero is the norm.'

'Oh my God, that's awful.' Millie drank her wine in one go as a protest.

'That's the reality of acting in the States. If you're under forty, they'll only cast you if you're a lollipop head and, if you're over forty, they don't cast you at all.'

'Just as well you've still got another ten years, then,' Millie observed drily.

'Fifteen. I took five years off and go backwards a year with every birthday.'

'What a way to make a living. Just as well they pay you so many squillions.'

Dora giggled. 'True. And there are other perks. Lovely beach-front house in Malibu, hot chauffeur permanently on call.'

'Well, it's no wonder you found Friday night in the White Bear a little plebeian.'

'You been reading those books again?'

'Have to get my education where I can. Some of us didn't make it out of Berecombe.'

Dora was silent for a moment. For all her problems, she

had at least escaped to go to drama school and, more importantly, still had both parents. No matter how strained her relationship was with them. Poor Millie had had her entire family wiped out in one cruel second when a drugged-up idiot had driven head-on into her parents' car. 'I'm sorry, Millie. I'm turning into a real spoilt LA bitch.'

'Yes you are,' Millie agreed, without rancour.

'Love you.' Dora saluted her oldest friend with her glass before drinking it dry and holding it aloft for a refill. That was the beauty of a proper friendship; you could pick up where you left off.

Millie topped up Dora's glass. 'So, is this just a flying visit again?'

'It will be if you continue to force me to dress up as a duck,' Dora complained. 'I'd hardly got off the plane before you attacked me with a feathered head.'

'Sorry. Zoe was going to do it, but she's knee-deep in A-Level revision. So come on, how long have we the pleasure of Berecombe's most famous export this time?'

Dora paused, took a deep breath, then said, 'Can you keep a secret, Mil?'

'Me? You know I can.'

Dora sighed and stared morosely into her glass. 'Might be back for good, as the sainted Gary Barlow would say. Long story short: ratings plummeted, show pulled. No more made.'

Millie sat up. 'That's awful.' She shook her head. 'But it's the most popular thing on the box over here. Zoe loves it.'

'Well, you're two series behind, so you've still got something to watch.' Dora fiddled with a long strand of hair, trying to

171

control the urge for a cigarette. She was trying to give up. 'It's the way American TV works. As soon as a show gets even a whiff of a ratings drop, it's axed. You have to admire the business ethic, I suppose. It's all about the profit.'

Millie wasn't sure she did. It sounded far too ruthless for her and, besides, she was off anything American at the moment. 'So, what are you going to do?'

'Shack up with Mum and Dad for a bit. I haven't seen much of them over the last few years. Walk on the beach if I can borrow Trevor. Have lazy mornings in bed. Have a holiday, enjoy myself!'

'Get to know Mikey Love again?'

Dora gave her friend a shuttered look. 'No way. Not going near that heap of trouble again. Nope. Me and Michael Love belong firmly in the sixth form. I do not intend to rake up all that shit again. Ever!'

Millie thought her friend protested too much. She'd seen the looks flashing between Mike and Dora. And who could resist a man who looked like he did? She finished her wine in silence. Dora and Mike had been besotted with one another when they'd all been in sixth form. They'd been the hottest couple in school. Surely feelings that intense never really went away? In the pub they looked as if they wanted to jump on one another and rip their clothes off there and then.

With them both in town, it was going to be an interesting summer.

Chapter 4

The afternoon of the duck race was bright and sunny. Dora, used to the endless sunshine of California, rejoiced. Millie had explained she hoped for a good turnout, for Tessa and Ken's sake. This new Arts Workshop was their latest venture and they were trying to raise money to renovate a venue in town. It seemed an excellent idea to Dora too. There had never been very much for kids to do in Berecombe. Boredom was one reason why Mike had got into trouble so much. Hopefully an arts centre would help other young people. She was all for it. And at least she didn't have to dress up as a duck this time.

Checking out her reflection in her old bedroom at her parents' house, she gave herself the once-over. Dora wasn't a vain person, never had been, but years of living and working in the most image-conscious city on the west coast had made her able to view her looks objectively.

Still too thin, as her mother had pointed out this morning. Red hair, one of her distinguishing features as an actress, long and waving now it wasn't being ruthlessly straightened by the studio's hair department. Bluey-green eyes, which changed colour according to the light and pale, almost translucent, skin. The summer dress she'd chosen, patterned in greens and blues, suited her perfectly. It made her look tall and willowy, when in reality she was only average height. An expert at changing her appearance, today she was going for a demure vicar's wife vibe. A wide-brimmed straw hat borrowed from her mother and her favourite sunglasses and she was ready.

She dropped her parents off in town and drove down Berecombe's steep hill, turning off along the lane by the river to find somewhere to park. Concentrating, as she still wasn't used to driving on the left, she squeezed the Mini into the only space available and followed the crowds to the start of the duck race.

There was a carnival atmosphere, families with small children clutching at balloons and ice creams ran along the riverbank, from where the ducks would be launched. It was fun, she decided. And very, very English. She manoeuvred her way through the crowd and found Millie and Tessa on the wide pebble beach on the bend of the river. A long meadow stretched down to the tree line of willows, which were shading the riverbank. It couldn't have been more English.

'Hi Dora, you're just in time,' Millie kissed her on the cheek. 'Tessa's so pleased you've agreed to start the race.'

'All right, campers,' Tessa yelled. 'Last chance to buy a duck and then they're off. Don't forget the top prize is a voucher to spend at Millie Vanilla's: Berecombe's friendliest caff.'

'What's the second prize, Tessa,' some wag called. 'Two vouchers? Only joking!'

Dora looked around to see who the joker was – some

middle-aged man – and caught sight of Mike standing high up on the meadow. He was with Phil and Kirstie and another man, tall and blonde. Before she could control it, her body reacted, as it always had, to Mike and she willed herself to turn back to Millie and Tessa. She could still feel Mike's gaze burning into the back of her neck. 'Insufferable man!'

'Oh don't worry your bones about him,' Tessa said with a grin, misunderstanding her. 'There's always one and it's usually him. I got him to buy thirty tickets, so he's cracking out the jokes in revenge. Very witty, Dennis,' she yelled to the man. 'Now crawl off under your stone.' She turned to Dora. 'You ready?'

'I'm not sure what to say.'

'Just keep an eye on my boys and when they release the ducks, say the race has started. You'll be fine, bab. No takers, then?' Tessa yelled, once more to the crowd. 'Right, I'll hand over to our very own, home-grown Hollywood star, Theodora Bart!'

Dora glanced over to where Tessa's three sons were standing knee deep in the middle of the river. As they held up sacks full of little plastic ducks, she took a deep breath, prepared to project and called out, 'I declare this duck race well and truly started!'

She wasn't sure what she expected. A casual stroll to the bridge, where the River Bere met the sea, maybe. She certainly hadn't anticipated the mad dash of duck racers running along the riverbank, the squealing, the competitiveness.

As the ducks bobbed and meandered their way down the river, the crowd yelled with excitement and ran alongside.

Dora let them go. The kitten heels she thought matched her floaty dress so perfectly proved themselves totally impractical. As she picked her way along the gravel beach, taking care to avoid the cowpats, she was left well behind by the crowd.

'Ouch!' Her heel caught on a piece of flint. She would have stumbled had it not been for a strong arm on her elbow.

'Careful there, can't have you going arse over tit in that rather lovely dress, can we?'

It would be him, wouldn't it?

Mike picked up her sunglasses, which had flown off her face as she tripped. 'Here you go. Undamaged.' He peered at them and whistled. 'Chanel. Nice. Just as well they're in one piece, then.'

He was looking edible. Loose white shirt, scruffy faded denims and a red-and-white spotted scarf at his neck. It didn't quite conceal the rugged chest exposed by the open buttons of his shirt. Dora's mouth watered. He'd never been as well muscled at eighteen. His shoulders had been far narrower and he certainly hadn't the thick covering of dark chest hair. She itched to trail her nails through it.

'Dora? You're staring.'

'Am I?' Snatching the glasses back, she put them on. There was a smear of dust on one lens but she didn't bother cleaning them; she needed the protection – and not from the sunshine.

'Can I walk with you to the finish line?'

She shrugged.

They followed the excited jumble of people, some of whom were paddling in the river, shrieking at the cold, in order to rescue their duck, lodged against a branch or rock.

They walked in silence, but eventually even Dora thought she was being ungracious. 'Thank you,' she said, at length.

'You're welcome.'

'It's been a while.'

'Certainly has.'

Of course, he wouldn't make this any less awkward, would he? She cast about for a subject matter with which to fill the silence. 'Who was the blonde man with you? The one who was so impeccably dressed?'

Mike gave a knowing grin. 'Thought you might notice him. Knows Phil slightly. Jed. Friend of Millie's, apparently.'

'That's strange. She's never mentioned him. Your friend Phil, he looks like a banker.'

'Financier. He invests in pet projects I have going.'

'So you have to keep him sweet, no matter how much a drunken boor he is.'

'What a very Dora word.' Mike laughed. 'Boor! He's actually a nice guy as long as he keeps off the scrumpy.'

'I'll take your word for it,' Dora said sourly, then added, 'Where's the finish line?' as her ridiculous shoes were beginning to pinch her toes. She never had to walk anywhere in LA.

'Ken Tizzard's at Bere Bridge. He and his team are catching the ducks before any get lost at sea.'

'It's mad.' She stumbled and winced as her ankle turned over. Mike took her elbow again and his hand was hot on her bare skin.

'But a great way of raising money for a good cause, don't you think?'

She'd forgotten his ability to make her feel small-minded. 'Of course,' she replied coolly. God he smelled good. Had he always smelled like that? She couldn't remember.

'I've enjoyed *The English Woman*.'

'Thank you.' She was surprised. 'You're obviously a busy man, I'm amazed you have time for television.'

'I don't normally.'

'Of course, you're two seasons behind over here.'

'Of course.' Mike echoed her lofty tone. 'But a friend sends me the streaming links so I'm up to date.'

'Oh.' He'd always had friends who supplied him with anything he wanted. 'What did you think of it?' She hated herself for being desperate enough to ask.

'Yeah. Good. Usual American shouting-and-waving-hands-around style of acting but it's tightly written. You're wasted in it, though.'

She stopped. They'd nearly reached the old mill beyond which there was a proper path. The once-abandoned building had been restored and its grounds tidied up. It looked as if someone lived there now. She banished the image that sprang up of her and Mike kissing passionately in the shelter of the long grass that long, scorching summer so long ago. Before it had all gone sour. She remembered the feel of his generous lips on hers, his eager hands inching under her t-shirt. Their hot panting breath. The fact that they were in the open, barely concealed by the meadow grass, had made it all the more illicit and exciting. Her throat closed with lust. When she and Mike were together nothing else had seemed to exist.

'You're staring again, Dora. And looking flushed.' Mike was

looking at her intently.

Fuck. He remembered too. How could he not?

Dora tugged her brain back into the conversation. Flustered by memories, she went on the defensive. 'It's the network's biggest-grossing show. I hardly think my time is wasted.'

'Oh Dora, Dora. You know that's not what I meant.' Mike chuckled, a throaty sound, which took her straight back to when they'd shared his post-coital cigarette. She'd had to eat an entire packet of extra-strong mints before daring to go home. If Mum and Dad thought she'd been smoking, they'd have killed her. Still would.

'I've got to go. I'm meeting my parents in town.' She knew she was coming across as prissy but it was her only defence against the desire that was curling in her loins. For him. Always for him.

At the mention of her parents, Mike's face closed.

Millie came running up to them. 'Mikey, I mean Mike! You've won! One of your ducks came in first.' She waved a piece of paper at him. 'Here's your voucher. I do a great afternoon tea if you fancy it. Maybe bring Dora?'

He turned to Dora, his blue eyes glittering. 'Maybe I'll just do just that.'

Chapter 5

Millie and Dora were sitting on the terrace of the Old Harbour Inn soaking up the last rays of sun.

'Can't believe we have to drink wine out of plastic cups,' Dora moaned.

'Health and safety,' Millie murmured and topped up their glasses. 'Still, the view alone makes up for it.'

She was right. the Old Harbour Inn was a little further west than the café and had views over to the beach on the other side of the harbour. It had the best view of the setting sun.

Dora sat back and inhaled the salty, vinegary, seaweedy smell of her youth. It was good to be home. 'Do you remember when we thought an alco-pop was the height of sophistication?'

Millie giggled. 'I think it was, back then.' She swirled her wine around her glass before taking an appreciative sip. 'Thank God things have changed a bit. Tessa's really grateful for all your help, Dor.'

'Not sure I did much but, bruises on my ducky bottom aside, I was glad to help out. Things all right between you two?'

'What do you mean?'

'I don't know, you just don't seem as close as you used to be.' Dora tapped her nose. 'Call it actor's intuition.'

'Well, we had a bit of a falling-out a few months ago.'

'I knew there was something. What happened?'

Millie explained how Tessa had agreed to supply bread to the Blue Elephant café, Millie Vanilla's biggest rival. 'She's back baking for me now, when she can. Blue Elephant are making it hard for her to get out of her contract,' Millie sighed. 'It's a real pain. I'm still having to get some bread from Berringtons.'

'Ooh Berringtons,' Dora said. 'Remember their lardy cake? And their ham rolls were good too. Standard lunch at sixth form, I seem to recall. Don't tell me Berringtons have gone downhill.'

'I never understood how you ate lardy cake every day for two years without putting on an ounce.' Millie shook her head. 'Their bread is fine for sandwiches but, with the new menu I've got, I need something a little more unusual. Tessa's been developing some rosemary bread, which is wonderful, and her walnut bread is gorgeous. It's just that she hardly has time to breathe, let alone make bread.'

Dora, starved of carbs for eight years, salivated. 'But you two are okay now? You know she's never been my bag, but I know she's a good friend to you.'

Millie nodded. 'The whole family has. They're my sort of adopted family, I suppose.' She stroked a sleeping Trevor's silken tummy with a bare toe.

'He's gorgeous, Mil. I'd love a dog but –' Dora was interrupted by a couple asking for an autograph.

'I told my Lee it was you. It is Theodora Bart, isn't it?' the woman trilled. 'We saw you at the duck race this afternoon.' They insisted on a selfie and a chat and by the time they'd gone, most of the pub's other drinkers were staring.

'Do you mind if we go, Millie. It'll only encourage others if we stay.'

'Of course,' Millie murmured, casting a regretful glance at the half-full bottle.

Dora followed her look. 'We'll take this with us, shall we? Find somewhere secluded on the beach and hide. Grab the glasses.'

Giggling they tripped across the cooling sand and sat where the wooden groyne met the path which ran in front of the beach huts. Sheltered under the lip of the concrete path, which ran parallel to the promenade, they were more or less hidden.

'I feel about fifteen again,' Millie giggled as she flopped down. 'We always used to come here to gossip.'

'Best thing is you can still see all of the beach. Perfect for spying. Refill please.' Dora held out her glass.

'Does that happen often?'

'What?'

'People asking you for autographs.'

'Not so much over here, although it depends. Not often when I'm going incognito like tonight.' Dora gestured to her enormous sunglasses and straw hat. 'It's just if one person recognises me it seems to spark others off. Half of them don't even know who I am. They just assume I'm famous enough to warrant a signature and a selfie. Once a guy got me to sign his arm and then had a go at me as he was disappointed I wasn't Bonnie Wright. You know, out of the *Harry Potter* films?'

Millie screwed up her eyes. 'I suppose you do look a bit like her. Not really thought about that before. Cor, my bestie the celeb! Not really thought about *that* before either!'

'Yes well,' said Dora, evenly. 'Just remember, I'm really only Dora Bartlett, who held your hair off your face when you were sick the first time you got bladdered. And listened to you wax lyrical about, oh, who was it?'

'Rick.'

'Oh yes, he of the floppy fringe, soulful brown eyes and poetic tendencies. Whatever happened to him?'

'He went to Manchester to do electrical engineering. Living in Watford now. Everyone seems to leave here.'

Dora ignored her friend's mournful tone. 'Okaay. Living the dream, then.'

Millie snorted. She leaned against Dora. 'I've missed you. I can never get hold of you when you're in the States, you know.'

'Yeah well, the schedule gets pretty crazy.'

'It's so good to have you back, Dor.'

'Get off, you soppy mare. Never took much to get you drunk, did it?' They watched as Trevor rolled on his back, wriggling into the sand, getting his golden-brown coat covered. Millie went suddenly rigid against her. 'What is it, honeybun?'

'Oh God. It's him. He's back. Jed's back.'

Chapter 6

Millie pointed a wavering finger at a tall blonde man walking along the promenade. He vanished behind the beach huts only to reappear towards the harbour end of the prom.

Dora lowered her sunglasses to see better in the gathering dusk. 'Oh, I saw him earlier at the duck race. He's friends with one of Mike's cronies. Some city type, I guess.' She squinted at Jed's disappearing form. 'Mike said you knew him.' She peered at Millie, who had gone white beneath her tan. 'Come on, then, spill the goss.'

She filled Millie's glass with the last of the wine and settled back against the groyne, a now snoring Trevor lying on her feet.

'He's a man I know. Knew. He came into the café in January and I fell for him.'

'Don't blame you, he's gorgeous.'

Millie nodded. 'Kind too. He paid for Daisy's operation when Arthur couldn't afford it.'

'Daisy?'

'Arthur Roulestone's golden retriever.'

'Ah. So why does the reappearance in Berecombe of this totally gorgeous, beautifully dressed, and apparently kind, man give you a nervous breakdown?'

'Oh Dor. He's the man I love. Will always love. But –'

'But?'

'He just happens to work for Blue Elephant.'

'No shit!'

Millie nodded. 'Or rather, as he was at pains to point out, he's their management consultant or something. Or was. He's stopped doing work for them now.'

Dora relaxed. 'Not so bad, then.'

'Not if you don't count him overseeing the opening of the branch here and not telling me. The café which may yet put me well and truly out of business.'

'Ouch.' Dora finished her wine and crushed the plastic glass. 'And it's the not-telling you that really hurts?'

'Yup.' Millie stared gloomily into her wine. 'That and the fact that he and I come from different worlds.'

'What do you mean?'

'Oh, he travels the world, is never in one place longer than five minutes, skis, dives, has holidays in St Lucia. That sort of thing.'

'Oh, that sort of thing.' Dora sounded amused.

'Don't laugh!'

'I wasn't laughing, honey. It's the sort of life I had until recently. It doesn't stop us getting on, does it?'

'Of course it doesn't. But you're not my lover, are you? And you'll go away too at some point, won't you? And I'll still be here.'

'It wasn't like Millie to be self-pitying.' Dora put an arm around her. 'If he loved you, he'd give it all up, wouldn't he? To be with you?'

'What and live in Berecombe and run the café with me?' Millie gave a hard laugh.

'Maybe that's what he's looking for?'

'He said once I was home to him,' Millie said wistfully.

'Well, there you go, honeybun.'

'But I'd never be enough for him. I know I wouldn't.'

Dora stared at her friend. It wasn't like her to be defeatist either. 'Millie, you're one of the kindest, most generous people I know. And you're beautiful.' When Millie snorted derisively she added, 'Yes, you are. You look just like Keira Knightley with added curves. And you're brave. Far braver than me. I couldn't have taken on what you did when your parents died. You know me, I'd collapse in a fit of the vapours.'

'You did an awful lot of crying. I think you did my share too.'

'Well, I loved them too, don't forget.'

Millie let her head sink onto her friend's shoulder. 'Oh Dor, you're such a good pal.'

'Even though I have the temerity to go skiing and have been known to holiday in St Barts?'

'Even that.' Millie's voice was slurred.

'Good, there's hope for me yet, then. I think, my lovely, we'd better get you home and to your bed.' She picked up their discarded bags, the crumpled wine glasses and the bottle and put the loop of Trevor's lead around her wrist. 'Come on, my sandy boy. You need to go home too.'

As they meandered along the promenade, towards Millie's flat, Dora's mind was busy plotting how to get her best friend well and truly hooked up and back with the delectable Jed.

Chapter 7

'It's just one big social whirl in Berecombe nowadays, isn't it?' Dora slugged back her wine and surveyed the crowd milling about at the launch of the Arts Workshop.

'Hello Dora. Standing on the edge of the party and looking superior as usual? Bit Mr Darcy, isn't it?'

'I really don't have to make any effort at that, Mike.' It came out more diva-ish than she meant. Whenever he came near she felt herself reduced to a stereotype. The truth was she was lonely and a bit self-conscious. Tessa and her husband Ken were the focus of everyone's attention, something she was more used to being, and Millie was busy overseeing the catering. The venue they'd decided upon for the Workshop was an old youth club tucked away in a grimy part of town next to the tennis court and children's playground. The interior was rundown and filthy. She felt distinctly uncomfortable and out of place and Mike's presence wasn't helping.

'It's hardly the sort of thing I'm used to.' Whoa! Where had *that* come from? Was she channelling Scarlett O'Hara now?

'No, I don't suppose it is.' Mike's voice was dry. 'I suppose it hasn't occurred to you that you could use your celebrity status, however limited, to help them fundraise?'

She turned on her heel. 'Putting aside the fact I already have, I don't suppose you have either? Or is your celebrity status even more limited?' She smiled archly and was pleased to see the barb hit home. There was a fascinating pulse beating at the base of his throat. Dora stared at him, a desire to either hit or kiss him warring. Her gaze dropped to his mouth. Oh, she definitely wanted to kiss him. Maybe to find out if it was as good as the memory. Mainly, to kiss him until she left him gasping for mercy. Deliberately and very slowly, she licked her lips and then looked him straight in the eye. He gave a sort of strangled gasp and she knew she'd won this round.

He blew out a breath, looking as if he longed to get away. From nowhere Kirstie appeared and claimed his arm. She gawped up at him, adoringly. 'Darling, there are literally millions of people you need to meet.' As if only just realising Dora's presence, she added, 'Oh hello again, Theodora.' She gave a cat's smile.

'Kirstie.' Dora looked from Mike to the girl. So this was how it was? She might have known. The disappointment felled her like a physical blow. How had she been so stupid?

Mike cleared his throat. 'Dora, I'll introduce you to Jed, shall I? Only be nice to him, he's had his heart broken.'

'Oh Mike, you silly boy. I'm sure Theodora will be lovely to Jed.' Kirstie batted a hand at Mike's arm. She turned a baleful gaze upon Dora. 'Won't you?'

'I'll try my best.' Dora gave them her best celebrity mile-wide smile and was gratified to see both blink. She drank her wine down in one and gave the empty glass to Kirstie. 'Put that somewhere, *won't you?'*

'Who is going to be nice to me?' A deep, cultured voice sounded behind them.

'Ah, Jed,' said Mike. 'Dora here is panting to meet you.' Mike gave Dora an evil look and allowed himself to be led away by a sullen Kirstie.

In her head Dora stuck out a tongue at them. Then she pulled on a professional veneer and put out her hand. Jed. 'How nice to meet you.'

'Jeez, you're Theodora Bart!'

'This is very true.'

'Sorry, did I just go all fan-girly?'

Dora laughed. 'You did, rather.'

'It's just that I love *The English Woman*. I travel a lot so have to download it. Saved many a lonely night in a hotel room.'

'I'm very gratified you like it. And it's plain Dora when I'm here in Berecombe.'

Jed lifted a couple of fresh glasses from a tray being circulated by the Tizzards' eldest son and passed one to her. 'Then Dora it is.' He clinked glasses with her. 'It's a complete pleasure to meet you.'

Dora drank the wine and observed him over her glass. A smooth operator, confident and assured; she'd met many like him. Expensive clothes and a permanent suntan, he was good-looking in a glossy blonde way. Not remotely her type, but she could see how he had dazzled poor Millie. For a second she very much hoped his heart had been thoroughly broken. Then remembered her pledge was to get these two together.

Well, there was no time like the present.

'So, I understand you know Millie?'

'Yes. We went out a while back.' He wrinkled his high-bridged nose attractively. 'Well, I suppose we never really went out much. She was always working too hard.'

'That sounds like my friend Millie.'

'How do you know her?' His almost pathetic gratitude at being able to talk about her made Dora warm to him a little.

'We went to school together. Berecombe Comp.'

'Along with Mike?'

'Yes, we were all there together, although Mike was known for his absences rather more than his attendance.'

They looked to the middle of the crowd, where Mike was deep in conversation with the town councillor who had made the feeble joke at the duck race. He must have heard his name being mentioned, or the old sixth sense was working, as he raised his head and looked straight at them.

Dora, to her horror, felt herself blush. She took Jed's arm and steered him away. 'You know Millie's here tonight, don't you?'

Jed's face went through a tumult of emotion. Joy, fear, apprehension, need. Dora watched him, fascinated. He'd make a marvellous actor, with such mobile and transparent features. She melted further. If Millie had fallen for him, then he couldn't be all bad.

'She's in charge of the catering for this.'

'Do you think she'd want to speak to me?'

He seemed to assume Dora knew all about his and Millie's relationship.

'I'm not sure.' At the corner of her eye, Dora caught sight of Millie perfecting the buffet. Watching her friend disappear into the kitchen, she turned her laser gaze on Jed. 'How did you two leave it?'

Jed looked down, scuffed his expensive-looking brogues and sighed. 'I was a twat. She told me to disappear out of her life.' He glanced up. 'Which was completely justified, I have to say.'

'So I understand.' Dora smiled, she was beginning to like Millie's Jed a great deal. 'Well, if you know you're in the wrong and Millie feels she has had the last word, all, in my opinion, is not yet lost.'

Jed looked at Dora, starstruck but also with total and abandoned admiration.

She turned him towards the kitchen door. 'She's in there. Whenever in doubt, seek Millie in the kitchen.'

Jed gave her a grateful look and went. Dora returned to the margins of the party, sipped her wine and hoped she'd done the right thing.

Chapter 8

'Hello Millie.'

She started. She'd know that voice anywhere. It was inevitable, she supposed, if he was in town, that they'd bump into one another. 'Hello Jed.' Passing the tray of smoked salmon canapés to Clare, who was waitressing for her, she forced herself to meet his eyes. She drank him in. Thinner than she remembered, but browner. The suntan emphasised his fine cheekbones and there were new highlights in his blonde hair. He looked like a well-bred racehorse, nervy and on his toes before an important race. She gulped. He could still make her heart race and her knees buckle. But part of her, the ever-cautious part, remembered her fears over the long-term compatibility of Cinderella and Prince Charming.

'How have you been?'

She nodded. 'Okay thanks.'

'And the café?'

'Doing quite well.' She added in a rush, 'Thank you for helping Arthur out. With Daisy, I mean. He couldn't afford the operation.'

Jed shrugged. 'He's a nice man. Daisy, I'm sure, is a nice

dog.' His brown eyes burned into hers. 'But I really did it for you, Millie. Arthur is a friend of yours and I could see his being unhappy made you unhappy too.'

'Oh.' Millie swallowed. Every fibre of her being yearned to gather Jed in her arms and tell him she loved him, had always loved him, would never stop. 'I said some things back in February.'

For the first time, Jed smiled. 'You did and I deserved everything you threw at me.' He spread his hands. 'How could you not be angry?'

Clare yelled from the kitchen and Millie gave Jed an apologetic look.

'I know, work calls.' As she turned to go, he added, 'Millie, do you think we could get together sometime? To talk things over? I'd like that.'

Millie was about to nod but the little voice of caution that always wreaked havoc between her and Jed piped up. 'I don't know, Jed. I'm not sure that's a good idea.'

His face tightened. 'I don't understand you, Millie,' he said through clenched teeth.

'Did you think we could just start up again? Just like that?'

'Yes. No. Yes. Maybe?' He shrugged helplessly.

Millie looked at him. She doubted if anyone had ever said no to Jed. All his life everything had fallen into place for him. A golden boy with effortless charm. Well, she wasn't going to be the latest in a line of easy conquests. He'd lied to her! 'It's just not that simple, Jed. And maybe, if you don't like that,' she added, as his angry expression deepened, 'You'd better keep away from me altogether!'

Chapter 9

'So, how did it go?' Dora took a slug of wine, thinking she could get used to the stuff Millie had stashed away.

They were holed up in Millie's flat, sharing a bottle of wine and a bowl of Kettle crisps. It was Sunday night and it seemed the thing to do.

'What do you mean?' Millie's voice was guarded.

'Last night between you and Jed?'

Millie concentrated on stroking Trevor. She hesitated before answering and then blurted out, 'Oh Dor, it was such a shock seeing him like that!' She hugged the dog to her and buried her face in his fur. 'I told him ... I told him to go away.'

Dora spilled wine on her white skinny jeans. 'You did what?'

'I just couldn't face him,' Millie continued miserably. 'I mean, I knew he was in town, but I didn't think he'd turn up at the launch party. I had no idea he even knew Mike!'

'He doesn't, not really. He's a friend of that idiot Phil.'

'Oh.' There was a pause. 'How do you know?'

'Mike told me. I had a little conversation myself with your Jed. I rather fell for him actually. And he's –'

'Not your type!'

'No need to shout, Mil.'

'Sorry,' Millie mumbled. 'Hands off, though.'

'Wouldn't dream of it, honeybun.' At Millie's glare, Dora put up her hands. 'Honestly, I really wouldn't go there if you paid me. But others might if you don't sort this out. A man like that won't stay around here for long.' As soon as she said it, Dora knew it was the wrong thing to say. 'I don't mean –'

'But that's just it, Dor. Why would a man like that want to stay in Berecombe?'

'Then maybe you need to give him a reason?'

'Perhaps.'

Dora, annoyed at Millie's mulish tone said, 'On the other hand, he could be your ticket out of here, you know.'

'And what about the café, Millie? Who's going to run that? And who says I want to get out of Berecombe anyway?'

Dora sighed. Time to tread very, very carefully. 'Millie, I know that the café was your parents' dream but that's just it, it was your *parents*' dream. Is it yours? Haven't you longed for something else?'

'Yes!' Millie yelled, making Trevor yelp. 'Of course I have, but how can I? I have to carry on with the café, make a living.'

'If you got together with Jed you could probably afford to put in a management team.'

'And become what? One of those women who have nothing to do but have lunch and gossip? You know that's not me, Dora. And besides, I've always earned my own money.'

'But it's kept you trapped here.'

'It's where I want to be, or it was until Jed Henville came

along and ruined everything.'

'Or rather, made you question everything.'

Millie blew out an enormous breath. 'I'm not sure what I want any more. I don't know how I can even begin again with Jed.'

'Do you want to?'

'I'm not sure of that either.'

This was going to be a harder task than Dora thought. 'Look Mil, when I had my little chat with Jed last night I thought he was rather desperate to get back with you.'

'Did you?'

The look on Millie's face so echoed that of Jed's it made Dora even more determined. 'What about a challenge?'

Millie threw herself back on the sofa. 'God Dor, we're not kids any more.'

'You always enjoyed my challenges.'

'Like the one where I had to nick the flag out of the town hall? And then there was the knitted graffiti.'

'One of my more imaginative ones, I agree. Okay, so I challenge you, Emilia Susanna Fudge to –'

'Please don't say I've got to go out with him!'

'One step at a time and stop interrupting. I challenge you to talk to Jed and explain your feelings. That you and he are from different worlds, that you feel inadequate and chained to your parents' café by some misguided grief and sense of loyalty to them.'

'Bit harsh, Dor,' Millie huffed.

'Okay, the last bits were, but you have to agree that you tie yourself to that café because you want to keep your parents' memory alive.' Dora took a breath, wondering if she'd gone too far.

'Wouldn't you feel the same?'

'Quite possibly, honeybun, quite possibly, but I don't have anything like the relationship with my parents that you had. I hope it wouldn't stop me from being with the man I love and who obviously adores me.' Dora watched Millie flush and waited.

'All right then.'

'So my challenge is accepted?'

'Suppose.'

Dora drank her wine in triumph. Piece of piss, this matchmaking malarkey. Her feelings of accomplishment lasted two seconds.

Millie raised her head, a mischievous look on her face. 'But I have to give you a return challenge.'

'Oh. Okay. Yeah.' Dora shrugged.

'Then I challenge you to take on the role of Anne Elliot in Mike's production of *Persuasion*.'

'That's not fair!'

'Why?'

The image of Mike, with Kirstie's hand on his arm, flashed into Dora's vision. Of his blue-eyed, penetrating gaze across the shabby space of the Workshop last night. To work with him, be close to him on a day-to-day basis would be torture. Exquisite but mostly torture.

'I couldn't –'

'Why not? Do you think my challenge is going to be easy?'

Dora slid herself up Millie's sofa and glared at her best

friend. Of all the things she could have asked. As ever, when feeling threatened, she channelled her inner diva. 'I have starred in one of American TV's biggest-grossing shows. I trained at Central. I am nationally and internationally known. I can't act in a cheap, tin-pot production of *Persuasion* in a shabby little theatre in a not very well-known seaside town in Devon!'

'Why?' Millie's tone was unforgiving.

She couldn't tell her the real reason. That she was still in love with Mike. Always had been. And, even worse, that he had a perky little blonde called Kirstie attending to his every need.

'Why, Dora?' Millie repeated. 'Why can't you do Mike's play? If you don't there's no deal. I won't talk to Jed.'

'Oh alright, I'll do it!' Dora yelled. Then threw a cushion at her friend to shut her up.

Chapter 10

Dora was confused. She'd contacted Mike (through gritted teeth) and he'd asked her to meet him here, in the Regent Theatre on the far end of Berecombe's sea front. She'd assumed the meeting would be a private affair. The theatre, however, was buzzing with people. She spotted Kirstie briefly, who waved hello and promptly disappeared. A group in the unofficial theatre uniform of ripped jeans and black t-shirts were earnestly discussing a large piece of paper – stage designs maybe and another group of youths were sweeping and collecting litter in black bin bags. They were chatting loudly about the latest Bond film.

The place felt very different. It had been a second home to her for the two years she did A levels. She'd spent more time in here, with Mr Latham and the drama group, than she had revising. Until her parents had tried to put their foot down.

An assistant, who looked about twelve but who was gratifyingly star-struck, led her to the front of the theatre. There was nothing to sit on and no one had offered her as much as a coffee. It wasn't how she was usually treated when negotiating a role. It couldn't have been further from how things were organised in LA. She suppressed a frustrated giggle.

The theatre was tinier than she remembered. There was a small stalls area and a narrow balcony running in a horseshoe around the walls. It would barely seat a hundred people when the seating was replaced. She understood it had been taken out for a craft fayre, which was held once a month. That was new since she was last in Berecombe. The walls and floor-boards were painted a matte and rather sinister dark blue, making it seem even more compact. At the opposite end to the stage she recognised the kitchen and bar, currently hidden behind scruffy steel shutters that didn't quite fit. The stage itself looked to be in fairly good repair but there was a motley collection of buckets and containers where the house seats, if the Regent went in for that sort of thing, would be. Water dripped mournfully through the roof. Dora wondered where it was coming from; it hadn't rained since she'd been back. She was peering up, trying to work out the cause of the leak when Mike's voice startled her.

'There you are.' He was accompanied by a large dark-haired man, who looked vaguely familiar. 'This is Greg Symon. I'm sure you know him from *The Gates of Almonhandez*.'

'Of course.' Dora extended a hand. 'How nice.' She'd caught some of the series, a *Game of Thrones* rip-off in which Greg had been out-acted by the rest of the cast, including the horses. She hoped he had nothing to do with Mike's production.

'Greg's our Captain Wentworth.'

Shit. Dora composed her face. 'Wonderful!' How the hell was she supposed to act besotted with this plank? And what was he doing back in the UK? She could only assume he had lots of time on his hands. *The Gates of Almonhandez* had been pulled after the first season.

'It's an honour to meet you, Theodora. I've always admired your work.'

I bet you have, Dora said silently. It's probably given you an acting lesson or two. 'Thank you so much, Greg. And may I say how much I enjoyed *The Gates*. So innovative.' She was alarmed to see the tops of his large ears turn pink.

'Thank you. Coming from you, Theodora, that means a huge amount.'

'It's Dora,' Mike put in, curtly. 'Now we're back in Berecombe.' He gave her a hard look. He knew she'd been lying. 'Did you know Dora grew up here, Greg? Her parents ran the fishan-dchip shop.'

Dora swept him with a beatific smile. He wouldn't belittle her that way. 'They did indeed. And still do, as a matter of fact. They also now have three fish restaurants, including Samphyre. It's tipped for a Michelin star.' She raised her brows at Mike in challenge.

'Really?' Greg said, impressed. 'In Exeter? I ate there last month. It was magnificent.'

'Thank you, Greg. I'll make sure to let my parents know. They're so proud of their achievements.'

'Could we get down to the matter in hand, do you think?' Mike's voice was brittle. 'I want you to read the scene where Anne meets Wentworth, Dora. Where he re-enters her life as a successful sea captain. They meet each other seven years after he was jilted by her. Do you think you're up for that?'

'I think I can just about manage. Of course, as you haven't sent me a script, I haven't had a chance to look at it. It'll be a sight-reading, but I think I'll cope.' Dora gave Mike a thin smile.

'I'll get Lily and Josh to read in for Mary and Charles and we'll get going, then.' Ignoring her sarcasm, he yelled for Kirstie, who went to find them. 'If we could get a move on I'd be grateful. I've got quite a few to audition today.'

Dora stopped dead. 'Auditions?'

'Yes.' Mike became very busy studying his script. 'I've got at least another three Annes to see today.'

'I'm auditioning?' Dora exploded.

'Of course.' Mike met her fury. 'You didn't think you'd get this by not auditioning? That's how it might work in American television, but I audition every actor in one of my productions.'

For a moment Dora was too incensed to speak. Then she caught the slightest of quirks at the corner of Mike's mouth. He was bloody well testing her. 'You ba '

'Come on, Dora. Not too big for your boots to audition, surely?'

'Oh Mike,' Greg began, 'Surely someone of the calibre of Theodora shouldn't be asked to –'

'Where do you want me?' Dora cut Greg off. She glared at Mike, knowing full well he needed her far more than she needed him. Her celebrity status alone would send the publicity for this production stratospheric.

'If you could stand stage left, please, Dora,' Mike said serenely. 'And Greg, could you enter from the other side?'

As she began to stalk off, he stopped her.

'You'll need a script, Dora.'

Ripping it off him, she concentrated on finding her spot.

On the phone to Millie later, she explained what had happened. Expecting sympathy, Millie couldn't stop laughing.

'Oh poor Dora! But you'll make a fantastic Anne. You know you will. And so does Mike.'

Dora made an unintelligible sound. 'And precisely what have you done to keep up your end of the bargain?'

'Ah. Well. Been too busy today. Rushed off my feet in the café.'

'Likely story. I need to scrap the idea of Anne Elliot. Think my talents would be better served as an Emma instead. She had far superior match-making skills.'

As an answer, Millie just laughed some more.

Chapter 11

Dora was used to read-throughs. Every project she'd ever been involved in had begun with one. It didn't stop her hating them with a passion. A read-through always seemed so pressurised. It was usually the first time the entire cast gathered together. There was always a certain amount of sizing up the others, wanting to prove why they had been granted the part over everyone else. And then there was the dilemma; should you simply read your lines and be accused of not trying, or actually invest in the role and look as if you were showing off? You couldn't win either way. No, read-throughs were never easy. Dora felt she had added pressure heaped upon her. She was the big name in the cast and had to judge it pitch-perfect. The fact that Mike would be directing added a whole other dimension to her discomfort.

After the nervous greetings over coffee, 'the who should sit where' farce and a particularly shaky start from the girl playing Mary Musgrove, everyone forgot their self-consciousness and settled to the task, letting the words work their magic. It was a fairly faithful version of the book and began with Anne arriving at Uppercross having closed up the family home.

Dora had felt sorry for Greg, as Wentworth only came in once everyone else had hit their stride. Any sympathy fled when she realised how awful he was. They'd all had full scripts for over a week now. Many had begun to learn their lines, or at least become familiar with them, so that today wasn't as much of an ordeal. It looked as though Greg had never opened his. He fluffed lines, stuttered over them, frequently lost his place and, at one point, dropped the whole script on the floor. Mike announced a break while Greg scrambled to put his pages in order. It had completely interrupted the flow that had begun to develop.

Dora cornered Mike during the tea break. She came straight to the point. 'Just whose bright idea was it to cast him as Wentworth?' she hissed.

'What's the matter, Dora, not a big enough star for you?'

Dora bit off an expletive and just about prevented herself from stamping her foot. 'You know that's not it! I'm not like that.'

Mike raised one dark brow. 'I don't know anything about you, Dora. Until your momentous duck impersonation, we hadn't set eyes on each other since your father decided I wasn't good enough for you over ten years ago. Since then our lives have taken very different paths.'

It was all said in an undertone and without malice, but Dora could sense the bitterness behind the words. She couldn't argue with him. It was all true. She too remembered that awful night when her father came home from the restaurant early and found them in her bed. She screwed up her eyes against the memory. Of Mike scrabbling for his clothes, of her father's hand gripped around his arm, leaving great red marks. She'd never seen him again, although she'd hunted all over town. Her parents told her Mike had left Berecombe. Most assumed he'd ended up in prison. It was only when his name re-surfaced in the theatre world that she found out he'd been at the Old Vic theatre school.

She took a deep breath. 'I don't give a shit whether Greg has won an Oscar or has just come out of drama school. I just want him to be a damn professional. Which, even with your lofty attitude, can see that that isn't happening. He's bringing the whole thing down, Mike. Even Lily and Josh, the kids from the youth group, are doing better.'

Mike seemed to consider his words before replying. 'You're right,' he admitted eventually. 'He's –' He began to say something and changed his mind. 'I'll have a quick word.'

'Thank you.' She turned to go and then said, 'Oh and is it really necessary for Kirstie to take photos every second?'

Mike smiled. 'Ah, that I can do nothing about. It's for publicity.'

'It's very distracting,' Dora grumbled. 'For the less experienced, I mean.' She caught his look and gave in. 'I'll just make sure I give her my best side, then, shall I?'

'You don't have a bad side, Dora. Never did.'

There was a beat of longing in the air and then he disappeared to find Greg.

Whatever Mike had said to Greg during the break had an effect. Greg was slightly improved and the rest of the run-through went more smoothly.

It was still exhausting though.

'I'm glad that's all over. These things always wreck me,' Dora said to Ellie, who was playing her sister Mary. She shoved her water bottle into her bag. 'It's been a very long day.'

Ellie gave her a gratified smile. 'I'm so glad you said that. I haven't done many. I can't work out why I'm so knackered.'

'Nervous tension, I suppose.'

Ellie nodded. 'Must be. I've got to admit, I was so in awe of you when we started that I completely mucked up the beginning. Couldn't believe I was sitting next to Lorna Peters from *The English Woman!*'

Dora smiled. She could remember being in the same position when meeting more- established actors. 'You did fantastically. Everyone, including me, is petrified at the first read-through and Mary's not an easy character to get a handle on, is she? Hardly sympathetic.'

'Tell me about it.'

Dora put a hand on Ellie's arm. 'Relax, honey. You'll get there. Take your time to get to know the character.' Ellie was gorgeous. Blonde, smiley, curvaceous. If anything, she was far too attractive to play Mary Musgrove. Dora thought she might like her.

'Look, a few of us are going up to the White Bear. I don't suppose you'd like to join us?' This was added shyly, as if Ellie imagined Dora would have her chauffeur on hold to whisk her off to a private jet.

'Oh, that would have been lovely but I promised a friend I'd meet her.' As Mike walked past, Dora added, 'I can't come, I'm afraid.'

Mike obviously had only heard the last part. 'Got something

better to do, Dora?'

Dora gave him her most diva-ish look. 'Something better than drinking warm beer while having to look at your ugly mug?' she said, her nose in the air. 'Hard to believe, but yes.'

She refused to explain she was only meeting Millie for supper. Let him stew, she decided, as she swung her bag onto her shoulder. Let him stew.

Chapter 12

Millie took a deep breath, eased the kink out of her shoulders and pushed open the door to the coffee shop. Lyme was heaving with visitors and she'd driven around for twenty minutes trying to find a parking space, ending up at the park-and-ride. She was late. Hot, flustered and late.

Over dinner last night, Dora had heckled her remorselessly over failing to keep her part of the bargain. She refused to accept Millie's plea of embarrassment and confusion as excuses.

'The man wants to talk to you,' she'd said, giving her a very steely Dora look. 'He still loves you. Any fool can see that.'

'But nothing's changed,' Millie had protested.

'So change it.' Dora leaned forward and waved an asparagus spear, dripping butter everywhere. 'Come on, Mil, you're lots of things and courageous is one of them. Grab life by the balls, baby.'

'God you're so American sometimes,' Millie had responded, to which Dora had simply sniggered.

So, leaving Millie Vanilla's in the hands of Clare who, having decided A levels weren't for her, was filling in time by working in the café. She was proving herself more than capable, so Millie was confident she could give herself the morning off.

This coffee shop was a deliberate choice. She wanted somewhere which was completely disassociated with her and Jed. And besides, she could do a quick bit of research while she was here.

Even though she was late, Jed was nowhere to be seen. Collecting a large latte she spotted some girls leaving a table near the window and sat down. Sneaking a quick look in her mirror, she checked her appearance. Apart from looking slightly flushed, she was amazed at how calm she appeared. No one looking at her would detect the racing pulse, the flipperty beat of her heart. 'Well, Dora, I've met your challenge,' she murmured to herself. She wondered if ringing Jed and arranging to meet but him not showing up would be enough for Dora. She doubted it. Getting out her phone, she was about to ring her and then remembered she'd be deep in rehearsals.

'Hello, Millie.'

There was that voice again. Expensive, smooth. Seductive.

'I'm so sorry I'm late. I couldn't find anywhere to park.'

Millie looked up at him. Again, she couldn't help herself from gazing, feeding greedily on every detail. He wore a pink linen shirt and white skinny jeans and should have looked effeminate but didn't. There had never been anything effeminate about Jed. Ever. She swallowed. He looked like a raspberry ripple ice cream and she wanted to lick him. All over.

When she didn't speak, Jed ran a hand through his hair. He was tense, she realised.

'I'll get a coffee,' he muttered and disappeared.

Millie sipped her coffee. It was good. Not as good as hers but better than that in Blue Elephant and, for some ridiculous reason, it gave her courage.

Jed sat down. They swapped nervous banalities about how busy Lyme was, that maybe it was because of the lovely weather. How nice it was in here. Then a heavy silence fell.

'I've missed you, Millie.'

'I've missed you too.'

'Then why can't we be together?' Jed dashed a hand over his eyes. 'I don't understand.'

Millie sighed heavily. 'I'm not sure I do, not really. Well, there was the matter of you not telling me who you really were, I suppose. That you'd done work for Blue Elephant.'

Jed blew out a breath and stayed silent for a minute. 'I know. I was an idiot.' He took her hand. 'But there's also the matter of me being truly who I want to become when I'm with you, Millie.'

Millie felt his touch burning on hers. She gulped. 'I don't know what you mean.'

'Then let me explain. Please. In lots of ways I've had a charmed life. Money, a good school, one of the best universities, a string of jobs. And, believe it or not, I've never taken any of it for granted, although I'm sure from the outside it looks that way. But it's always felt hollow, Millie. There has never been a centre to my life. No permanent home, no ties, lots of travel but never anyone to come home to.'

Millie held her breath.

'I found that in you. Or thought I had. I found the still centre of my chaotic life. I found home. I found love. With you.'

'We're so different, Jed,' she whispered.

'Are we?' Jed frowned. 'Because that's just it, I don't think we are. In essentials I think we're very alike. Hard-working, loving, looking for something lacking in our lives. Something I thought we'd found in each other.'

'But what future do you see for us?' Millie willed herself not to cry.

'I don't know, Millie. We never had a chance to talk about that, did we?'

'No.'

'Would you like there to be a future for us, Millie? Because I'd like that. I'd like that very much.' He blew out a long breath. 'Look, I know I let you down. I just hope, no I'm begging, that you can learn to trust me again. Do you think you can?'

'I don't know, Jed.' Millie raised her tear-filled eyes to his. 'I don't know. Maybe. I want to, Jed. There's just something stopping me.'

He lifted her hand to his mouth and burned a kiss onto her palm. 'It's a start, Millie my darling. It's a start.'

Chapter 13

Each day, Dora drove into town, squeezed the Mini in next to Millie's ancient Fiesta behind the café and strode along the promenade to the theatre, swinging her arms and lifting her head to the salty breeze. The fifteen-minute walk was energising. She dressed down in scruffy sweats, hid her hair under a cap and went make-up free. The few dog walkers who were around took no notice of her. It was a simple but exquisite pleasure having Berecombe sea front to herself.

To her surprise, she was enjoying being part of the production. The eagerness from the locals in the cast was contagious and she liked the other professional actors, especially Ellie, who was funny on and off stage. It had been too long since she'd done any stage work and she hadn't realised how much she'd missed the theatre. It was only Greg who was pulling everything down.

This morning they were, once again, rehearsing the moment Anne saw Wentworth after refusing him seven years previously. To focus on the crucial scene, Mike had only called in Ellie, Greg and Dora. Kirstie flitted in and out, but now she'd got over the fan-girly nonsense, she was professional and

214

efficient. Dora could see why Mike had employed her. She tried not to think of Kirstie's other talents and how those were deployed. It did no good to dwell on Mike and Kirstie. No good at all.

She greeted the others and then went to stand in front of the stage, breathing the dusty, slightly sweaty, smell of the theatre. Mike emerged from the gloom at the back. Dora blinked. He had a way of moving like a cat. You were only aware of his presence if he chose. Maybe that was why he made a good director? No bullying, no bombast, surprisingly little ego, he simply watched, then made a quiet suggestion that was somehow perfect. Another revelation; she was loving working for him.

'Morning guys. Are we ready to do this, this morning?' He slapped Greg on the back.

'Um yes, Mike. Hi. Morning.'

As the two men exchanged greetings Dora watched, puzzled. Mike was the consummate pro, he put in more hours and pushed himself harder than anyone. She could see his heart and soul was in this but she wasn't sure why. Rumour had it he'd been offered an important Shakespeare but had taken this on instead. It must mean a great deal to him – to give something back to the town. It made it all the stranger why he should cast Greg in such a key role.

Pinning on a smile as Greg, whatever he lacked in acting skills, was a nice man, she got herself into position, closed her eyes and focussed on getting into Anne Elliot's head.

An hour later and it was clear Greg still wasn't getting it. Or, if he was getting it, he was unable to convey any of it.

For the first time Mike was becoming impatient. 'Break,' he called. 'Take twenty, everyone.'

The relief was palpable. It was exhausting going over the same few lines time and time again and never feeling they'd nailed it.

Dora refused a coffee, she found the cravings for a cigarette were inevitably linked with caffeine and rummaged in her bag for her water bottle instead. When she looked up, Mike was leaning against the edge of the stage looking pensive.

'Where's everyone gone?'

'Out for some fresh air and a smoke, if those two things aren't mutually incompatible.'

Dora thought longingly of the space outside the theatre. It was a large cobbled courtyard, bounded by seawalls and looked directly onto Lyme bay. She smelled the ghost of nicotine in her nostrils and nearly caved in. The expression on Mike's face stopped her. He sat on the edge of the stage and looked utterly miserable.

'Why *did* you cast him?'

Mike gave her a rueful grin. 'He's Phil's brother.'

'Ah. And without him in the cast —'

'There's no financial backing.'

'Figures.'

'He's not working out very well, is he?'

Dora pursed her lips but stayed silent.

'He had real promise early on. I remember seeing him as Ariel and he was great.'

For the life of her Dora couldn't imagine the lumbering, wooden Greg as *The Tempest's* fantastical sprite. 'There's no drink or drugs problem?' she asked. In her experience it was the most common reason for a fall off of early talent.

Mike winced and shook his head before taking a while to answer. 'None that I know of, barring the odd cigarette.'

'Woman trouble?'

'We've all had our fair share of that, Dora.'

'Ha ha.' Dora levered herself up onto the stage to sit beside him.

'He's happily married,' Mike added.

'Not like us, then.' Dora tried to keep her tone light.

'Not like us. You never married either, then?'

'Always too busy. You?'

'The same. Right pair, aren't we?'

'We haven't done the town too bad for a couple of Berecombe Comp sixth form no-hopers.'

'You were never a no-hoper, Dora.'

There was a silence as their thoughts escaped back to a simpler time.

'Why does this mean so much to you, Mike?'

'This production?' He pursed his lips. 'Well, I don't like to see the old place so run down. If something isn't done about the roof soon, it'll be too late to save it.'

'This town doesn't owe you anything. What's the real reason?'

Mike gave her a quick and very charming smile. It lit his blue eyes with humour. 'Could never pull the wool over your eyes, could I?' He sighed gustily. 'Wasn't easy coming back here.' He pushed a hand through his hair, making it even more dishevelled and making him look years younger. 'I wasn't happy living here.' He glanced at her. 'Well, there were moments. Snatched moments of sheer bliss, but mostly it was hell.'

'Your dad?'

'Yeah, him and other stuff. You try growing up with a petty criminal for a father. It's not much fun. He died in prison, did you know?'

'I didn't.' Dora put her hand on his and left it there. 'I'm so sorry, Mike.'

'Yeah well, by that time I was away in Bristol and things had been bad between us for a long time.'

'But he was still your father.'

'Yup. Mr Latham took me in. When we split up, old Joe tried to sort me out.'

'Our drama teacher?' Joe Latham had spent his retirement running the youth drama club. 'He was a lovely man.'

'You're not wrong there. Saw the potential in people. Certainly saw it in you and tried really hard to steer me in a more positive direction than the one I'd been heading for.'

'So you went to live with him?' Dora was intrigued.

'He took me in that night when ... the last night we were together. Dad didn't want to know and got sent down soon after anyway, so old Joe Latham let me kip in his spare room.'

'I let you down,' Dora said suddenly. 'I should have fought for you. I'm sorry.'

Mike turned his hand over and threaded his fingers through hers. 'You were seventeen, Dora.'

'Old enough.'

'An over-protected, spoiled, innocent seventeen.'

'Not all that innocent.' Dora's mouth twisted at the memory.

Mike's fingers tightened. He laughed. 'Maybe not that innocent. God, the sex was good, wasn't it? So intense. Was it because we both knew it was wrong?'

Dora laughed to cover the excitement of touching Mike once more. The feel of his warm, firm hand in hers was shredding her nerves. 'It wasn't wrong, I suppose, more forbidden. But you're right, it was amazingly exciting.'

'Never been like that with anyone else, Dora.'

He felt very close. She could feel the warmth from his body, smell his clean, soapy skin, feel the rough wool of his sweater through the sleeve of her thin t-shirt. Dora couldn't bear the idea of Mike sleeping with anyone else. She shook his hand off. 'Yes, well, we were very young,' she said, in a tight voice. 'A lot's happened since then.' She jumped off the stage and concentrated on screwing the cap back on her water bottle.

'I'm partly doing this for him,' Mike burst out suddenly. 'For Mr Latham. I think it would be a fitting memorial for him.'

Finally meeting his gaze, she said, 'I agree, Mike. I think it would be too.' She knew, no matter how much she longed to, that she couldn't back out now. She couldn't let Mike down again. And she, too, owed Joe Latham.

Their intimacy was broken by the sounds of the others returning. She pulled a face. 'But what are you going to do about Greg?'

Chapter 14

Mike had an idea about how to improve Greg's performance. He was going to model the role of Wentworth himself.

Dora knew he had acting talent; it wasn't that which was a worry. It was the parallels of the story that were disturbing her.

There was a sharp tension in the air when she and Mike took to the stage. Greg looked uncomfortable, but then he always did. Maybe he resented being shown up? Ellie looked scared, even though she was excellent in the tricky part of Anne's hypochondriac of a sister. Even Kirstie, who normally wore an air of forced jollity, had a nervous twitch. Dora wondered why and then realised. If they upset Greg and he backed out, there would go the funding – and Mike's dream.

She got herself into position, surprised to find herself shaking, and decided to channel her nerves to use as Anne's. Closing her eyes, she felt the hair on her arms rise as she heard Mike, as Captain Wentworth, say to Mary:

'Morning ma'am. I've come to ask about the boy.'

Wentworth and Mary greeted one another, with Mary chattering on that her son was recovering from his fall.

Dora steeled herself to open her eyes and greet the captain herself. She had one line in this scene. One short line. All the emotion had to come from her body language. The poignancy must be unspoken but clear, even to those sitting right at the top of the theatre, in the gods. Gripping the chair behind her, she said, 'Good day, Captain Wentworth.' Forcing herself to leave the security of the chair, she took one tiny step forward and reverenced. When she straightened any nerves fled in appreciation of Mike's acting. But maybe there was no need of stage skill. The parallels of the story of *Persuasion* were only too obvious to them both.

Wentworth's body froze. He appeared to want, simultaneously, to rush forward and gather her in his arms but also to retreat as fast as possible. He stared at her, his eyes burning with a passionate resentment at the woman who had been persuaded to reject him as an unworthy suitor. The moment hung in the air. Even the dust motes stilled. It seemed to Dora to go on for seconds. Hours. Years.

Then Wentworth recollected his manners and breeding, gave a curt nod, said goodbye to Mary and turned on his heel.

Dora turned to face the auditorium and grasped the chair again. She was trembling violently. She half bent, one arm clasped across her middle to quiet the tumult of emotions.

'Shit. That was so awesome,' said Ellie, completely out of character – and historical period.

Dora sank onto the chair. Uttering four words had exhausted her. She vaguely heard Mike giving notes to Greg – on much the same lines as the ones she'd given herself.

'So you can see there are very few words spoken between Wentworth and Anne but this is a crucial scene,' he said. 'The first key scene in the play between them. It's vital that you get the subtext over. Of course they still love one another. Have never stopped. She's certainly always loved him but assumes he hates her. And Anne never thought she'd have to face him again. They're covering the cracks with social niceties but they're being torn apart in the worst possible way inside. Somehow, you've got to convey all that. Ready to have a go?'

Mike leapt off the stage and resumed his position as director. 'Places, everyone. Let's go again from Wentworth's entrance.'

And Dora, the consummate professional, got ready to do it all over again.

Chapter 15

After another three days of rehearsals just as intense, Dora gladly accepted Ellie's invitation to go to the pub. The force field of her love for Mike was becoming downright irritating. The craving she had for cigarettes was nothing in comparison. She needed a drink and she needed to unwind.

She and Ellie linked arms on the steep walk up Berecombe's main street to the White Bear. It was Thursday night and Dora hoped the pub wouldn't be crowded. Mike had announced he had to return to London tomorrow, so there was an end of the week vibe among the merry band of players. As they walked, head down to concentrate on the incline, Dora half-listened to Ellie's enthusiastic chatter but had her mind on what called Mike back to the capital so urgently. She couldn't imagine what his life was like in the city. He never mentioned where he lived or in what, who he mixed with or what he did in his spare time. Glancing over at a giggling Kirstie, who was fawning over him, she could have a good guess.

To her dismay, the Bear was as packed as before.

'Still, at least you're not dressed as a duck this time,' Mike said cheerfully. 'Drinks orders please,' he called. 'First round is on me.'

Dora was tempted to order a bottle of champagne just to spite him but refused to be so childish and meekly put in for a vodka tonic instead.

As there was quite a crowd of them and they were a noisy bunch, Dean, the landlord, opened up his small function room at the back. It doubled as the skittles alley and smelled damp.

'Oh, the glamour of the acting life,' said Dora as she collapsed on a red-velvet chair, which had definitely seen better days.

Ellie giggled and joined her. 'For some of us, being bought a drink by your director is as good as it gets.'

'Point taken.' Dora clinked their glasses together.

'I've never asked, not really. What brought you back to the UK? Looks to me as if you've made it in the States.'

Dora gave Ellie a fleeting look. She didn't know her well enough to trust her completely. Not yet. 'Oh, you know,' she said, affecting an airy tone. 'Only so much sunshine and perfectly teethed muscle men you can take. It's good to have a fresh challenge.'

'Speaking of muscle men, do you think Mike will ever get Greg into shape? I hate to say it of a fellow actor but he's crap, isn't he?'

Dora pulled a face and nodded. They looked over to where Mike and Greg were deep in discussion.

'And I hate to say this too, but it would be so much better a production if Mike was Wentworth,' Ellie went on. 'When he did that scene with you it was electric. I thought the scenery would combust. It was hot, hot, hot.'

'Talented man, is our Mr Love,' was Dora's only answer. As ever, Mike sensed he was being talked about. He looked over and saluted them with his glass.

'God, he's gorgeous,' Ellie sighed. 'I'd heard he had killer looks, but the reality is so much better than the rumour. I'm curious Dora,' Ellie went on. 'I've seen the way Mike looks at you. Did you ever, I mean have you ever ...?'

Dora forced a laugh. 'He's probably looking at me and wondering why he cast me. No, we're just old school friends, Ellie. I try to never mix work with pleasure. I think it's unprofessional.' Aware she was in danger of sounding pompous, Dora stood up. 'Now, come on, it's the end of the working week. What'll you have next?'

As she passed Mike, he stretched out a hand and stopped her. 'What were you and Ellie talking about?' He glared at her. The heatwave was official now. It had been in the seventies for the whole of May and a scorching summer was promised. The temperature in the Bear's scruffy function room, however, instantly dropped to arctic.

Dora smiled up at him, ignoring how sexy he looked in his threadbare jeans and white-linen shirt. 'Oh, you know, how it's never wise to have a relationship with one's work colleagues.' The contrary devil in her nodded over in Ellie's direction. 'Think you've got a fan there. And you've got to admit, she's gorgeous. And talented.'

Mike gave Dora a cool look. 'Which is precisely why she got the part. But I happen to agree with you. Never a good idea to play too close to your own doorstep.' He arched a brow. 'So maybe I should follow your advice?'

She went to leave but he put his empty glass into her hand. She looked down at it in surprise. Mike used to be a beer drinker, but this glass held the remains of orange squash.

'You'll probably remember what I drink, Dora, but this time make it a pint of squash. I'm driving later.'

Dora met his look with a challenging one of her own. 'Oh, you'd be surprised what I remember about you, Mikey,' and fled before she gave in to temptation and kissed his face off.

When she returned, perilously carrying three drinks on a battered tin tray, Mike was nowhere to be seen. 'Typical,' she said to Ellie as she balanced it on the edge of a table. 'I buy him a drink and he's not here to take it. Where's he gone?'

'Not sure, maybe he's gone back to London already. He announced he expects us to be scripts down next week, that we'd had long enough to learn our lines, and disappeared.' Ellie sounded gloomy as she took her wine off the tray. 'Cheers, Dora.'

'Cheers,' replied Dora absently. She drank her vodka. 'Scripts down already? Seems a bit soon to me. Won't be popular.'

'It wasn't.'

Going without the comfort blanket of a script in your hand was a hurdle to get over during the rehearsal process. Even if the actor knew his lines, to have them to refer to made everything else fall into place. Having no script to clutch onto often put rehearsals back a stage or two before everyone regained confidence. Timing was crucial. Too soon and you risked nerves failing just as the actor was getting to know his character. Too late and the rhythms and patterns of gestures were in danger of being stifled by the encumbrance of a script. Dora thought Mike had called it too soon and wondered why.

'That's my long weekend gone, then. Better get learning those lines,' she said to Ellie.

'I know,' she answered, nodding vigorously. 'Bummer, isn't it?'

Looking over to where Greg was at the centre of a particularly loud group, Dora wondered how he had reacted to the news. His eyes had been glued to his script all week. 'Well, Mike's an experienced director,' she added, still staring at Greg. 'He knows what he's doing.'

Chapter 16

The evening turned raucous. Some locals spilled into the back room, one or tourists strayed in and some not so friendly banter started up between them over an impromptu game of skittles. Dora thought it was time to leave. It was exactly the small town mentality she'd tried to put behind her. 'Why can't people just get on?' she murmured, as she pushed through the crowd.

'Hey,' slurred a northern voice. 'You're that bird off the telly!' The man in question thrust his red face into Dora's. She flinched. He stank of beer and sweat. Smiling politely, she tried to shrug off his grip.

'You are, aren't you? You're that bird from that Yank show. What is it, Gary? That American thing your Stacey's glued to?' He turned to ask his friend and Dora took the opportunity to escape. Hearing the words, 'It's that Theodora summat or other,' behind her, she fled. Taking the wrong door, she ended up in the pub's tiny car park rather than the alley that led to the main street.

'You seem to make a habit of running out of that place.' It was Mike locking the door of an expensive-looking silver car.

'Don't I just?' said Dora a little bitterly. 'Thought you'd gone home.'

'No. Went to collect the car. Thought I'd drive up to London tonight. Less traffic.'

Dora cast an anxious glance behind her. She could hear the northern guy's voice getting nearer and had no desire for an awkward conversation with him. If she was friendly, he'd misunderstand. If she was standoffish, he'd claim she had no time for her fans. Experience with drunk male fans had taught her you just couldn't win.

Mike saw her expression. 'Problem?'

Dora nodded.

'Get in, then. I'll give you a lift home.' When he saw her hesitate, he added, 'Don't worry, my drink-driving days are over.'

'You never drove when drunk,' she said, as she slid into the car. It was a Mercedes she noted. 'Nice car.'

'Thanks.' Mike was silent as he concentrated on easing it out of its tight spot. 'And you're right. I never drove when I was drunk. That was my dad's speciality.' He turned right up the high street and overtook the last bus to Axminster. 'Where are you staying?'

'At my parents',' Dora answered, embarrassed to have to admit it.

Mike said nothing, but his silence was deafening.

'Thought I'd see a bit of them while I'm here,' she added, defensively. 'Haven't seen much of them in recent years.'

'How have they taken the news that you're working with me?'

'It hasn't really arisen in conversation. Besides, if you hadn't noticed, I'm all grown up now. Who I work with is up to me.' She shrugged. 'And if they have a problem with it, I'll go and stay at the Lord of the Manor.'

Mike winced. 'You don't want to go to that extreme. I hear it hasn't improved.'

They travelled the rest of the journey to Dora's house in a charged silence.

Mike pulled up in the only gap on the street available, a short distance away. 'I won't park in the drive. Don't want them to think I have designs on their daughter again,' he said as he killed the engine.

The light was only just going, but Mike had parked under some conifers, which darkened the car interior. The only sound was the engine ticking and a distant gull calling mournfully.

'What was the problem in the pub?'

'Oh, just a drunk and over-attentive fan.'

'You okay?' Mike's voice was sharp with concern.

'Fine. It's just I've managed to go about fairly incognito recently, it caught me by surprise.' She felt Mike nod.

'Would you be willing to do some publicity when the time comes? I don't want it to cause you any problems, though.'

She turned to him. 'Of course I will. I'd be happy to.'

'Would you?' He rested an arm along the back of her seat. 'Even though your period of anonymity would end.'

'Yes. I know how much this means to you, Mike. And I know I can bring some attention to the production.' When he didn't answer, she added, 'I'm really not the walking-ego diva you think I am, you know.'

Mike traced a finger over the nape of her neck. He appeared to be concentrating very hard on doing so, his eyes narrowed and dangerous. His touch made her shiver with excitement. 'I've never thought that about you, Dora.' He shifted nearer.

'No?'

He shook his head and kissed her.

It was like coming home. Every muscle relaxed into the familiarity of him. And at the same time every nerve flared into life at the excitement of touching him once again. It was a releasing of a long, pent-up breath. One that she'd been holding for years. The missing years. She remembered the shape of his jaw as she held it, the feel of his stubble raking her skin, his warm breath, his skilled lips.

His hand reached under her t-shirt for her breast and caressed it, finding the nipple with an expert thumb. They knew so much about how to please each other. Had never forgotten how their bodies melded into each other as if the fit was meant. Had always been meant.

She thrust a hand through his curls, bringing him closer and the press of his muscled chest made her moan with need. She found a gap between the buttons on his shirt and heard desire catch his breath as she raked her nails over his skin.

His mouth found where he knew she was most sensitive; where her neck met her shoulder. She arched up violently, craving to feel as much of him against her as she could.

He was first to break away. 'Christ, Dora,' he said, on a ragged breath. 'I'd forgotten how good snogging in a car could be.' He rested his forehead against hers.

She giggled a little. Need for him was making her ache.

'Remember those afternoons on Woodbury Common?'

He shuddered. 'Don't I just.' He kissed her again. 'We spent hours necking. The frustration nearly killed me.'

She grabbed his collar and pulled him to her. 'I know exactly how you felt,' she murmured against his lips. Her hand reached down and found his hardness. She got as far as unbuckling his belt when his hand stopped her.

'Dora,' he said on a strained laugh. 'What are you doing? We're in a car in the suburbs of Berecombe.'

It was a bucket of ice to her senses.

She reared back, appalled at herself, at what she had been about to do. There was a horrified pause. 'No,' she snapped, shame at her behaviour making her frosty. 'We're not teenagers any more, are we?' She fumbled for the door handle, desire for Mike replaced by an urgent need to get away from him. As far away from him as possible. 'I'll see you next week.'

She got out and stood on the pavement for a second, trying to pull herself together. There was no way she could greet her parents in this state. She shook her hair into place and wiped off what was left of her lipstick.

Mike leaned over the passenger seat and called out, 'You bet you will. You owe me a pint.' He sounded uncomplicatedly cheerful.

Dora slammed the car door shut and it was only as the red tail lights disappeared around the corner that she remembered Kirstie.

What the hell were she and Mike playing at?

Chapter 17

Millie glanced at her watch for the umpteenth time. Dora was very late and it wasn't like her. Glancing up at the sound of the restaurant door opening, she saw Jed framed in the doorway. Her heart simultaneously leaped and sank – if that were possible.

He looked just as shocked to see her. 'Millie! How great to see you. I was expecting Mike and Phil. Are you joining us for dinner?'

It had to be a set-up. It was so typical of Dora. When they'd caught up with how the challenges were going, Dora hadn't bothered to hide her disappointment that her match-making wasn't going to plan. Dora was never happy when things didn't go her way.

'Sit down, Jed,' Millie said as he hovered by her table. 'I can explain.'

After she'd told him what she guessed had happened, they'd laughed a little and decided they might as well stay.

Once their first course was eaten, Jed sat back and grinned. 'Well, I've got to say, I'd much rather spend the evening with you than Mike and Phil. Don't get me wrong, Mike is great, but a little of Phil goes a long way.'

'Not sure he's Dora's favourite person, either.' Millie reached for her water glass. 'Thank you,' she added to the waitress, who removed her plate. 'That was delicious. It makes a change not to have to cook myself.'

'Do you come here a lot? Sorry. That sounded corny, didn't it? I'm nervous.'

'Oh, Jed,' Millie sighed. 'However did it get to this? We were always so relaxed with one another. It was so easy between us.'

He reached for her hand. 'And it can be again. If I can only get you to trust me.'

'The mad thing is, I can see exactly why you didn't tell me. I can see what a difficult position you were in.' Millie bit her lip. 'Dora says I'm too attached to the café, that it's all to do with my parents' death. Maybe I overreacted?'

Jed caressed a thumb over Millie's knuckles. He shook his head. 'I don't think you did. The café is your livelihood, as well as being your parents' legacy. And you were bound to be concerned when Blue Elephant opened in direct competition. Of course I don't think you overreacted. I was a complete idiot not to be honest with you. And, if you can understand my position, I can certainly sympathise with yours. I just knew, as soon as I told you who my client was, that I'd lose you. And I did.' He hesitated. 'Actually, I have something to tell you.'

Millie tensed.

'I've given up the management consultancy work. As of March I became officially unemployed.'

'Jed!' Millie gasped. 'Why ever did you do that? I thought you loved your job?'

'I do. Well, I did.' He looked down and kneaded a piece of bread into a ball. 'I used to love it. Working with different companies, seeing the world. I met some great people. But the job changed.' He looked up. 'Instead of companies wanting help to be the best, it became more about cutbacks, saving money, raising profits for shareholders.' He paused and drank some wine. 'And how best to shaft their competitors. It lost its appeal for me when it became purely about the money.' He looked at her from under dark lashes. 'And it really lost its appeal when I discovered I wanted to be in one place. With one person.'

They smiled at one another. Tentatively. As if they knew there was the tiniest of chances they could start again. It was humming in the air. Millie felt the knots of worry, of uncertainty, starting to unravel. But only a little.

'Oh.' To stop herself blushing, she busied herself with her wineglass. 'So, what have you been doing with yourself ?'

'Stayed with Alex in London for a while. You remember I have an older brother?'

Millie nodded.

'Couldn't get a grip on his lifestyle, though. It's manic. He never takes any time off. The hours he works are crazy.'

'I know how that is.'

Jed laughed. 'Too right.' There was a pause while their main courses were served and then he went on. 'I'm worried about him, to be honest. He always took life way too seriously and now he's in danger of burnout. It's quite common in the city, I'm told.' Jed forked up some of his chickpea kofta and added, 'This is so good.' He raised his wine glass, 'Thank you, Dora!'

Millie giggled. His attitude to food was joyful. 'Supposedly the best vegetarian food in town. This place is always booked up. Maybe Dora pulled her celebrity card to get us a table?' They concentrated on eating for a few minutes, then Millie asked, 'Are you staying at the Lord of the Manor again?'

Jed pulled a face. 'God, no. Wanted something a little more homely. I'm in a very nice B&B in Axminster. Mrs Silver is looking after me. Fresh towels and bedding every day, a cooked breakfast and unlimited wi-fi and all for a fraction of the price of the Lord.'

'Sounds perfect.'

Jed gave her a meaningful look. 'Almost.'

'I hope her cooking isn't as good as mine.' Millie stifled a quick pang of jealousy and wondered how old Jed's Mrs Silver was.

He took her hand again. 'No chance of that.' He paused and then teased, 'Although she does a mean bacon sarnie.'

Millie laughed. 'Can you be bought for so little?'

'Only by one woman.' The expression in his dark eyes was eloquent.

'I'll remember that.' She raised her glass and chinked it against his. 'Can I be honest and admit how lovely it is to see you again, Jed? I was a bit worried, after we'd met in Lyme, that you wouldn't ring.'

Jed clinked his glass in return. 'I wasn't sure how to play it, to be honest,' he admitted.

'And you can be certain I'd take offence whatever you did.'

Jed's brows rose. 'Well, there was that.' He grinned. 'It was more that I had a proposition to put to you and I wasn't sure how to ask.'

Millie drank some wine and held her glass for a refill. 'Sounds ominous,' she said. 'I may need some more of this excellent white.' When he'd refilled their glasses, she added, 'Fire away, then.'

Chapter 18

'You want to what?' Millie exploded.

'I'd like you to consider me investing in the café.'

Aware her jaw was slack, Millie forced her mouth to close.

'It would be a completely legit arrangement,' Jed went on. 'I wouldn't dream of doing it any other way. We could get someone to look over any contract.' He slid forward and took her hand. 'Oh, but Millie, think about it, we could go ahead with all those refurbishments you've got planned. We could make Millie Vanilla's somewhere even more special.'

'I don't know what to say.' It came out on a gasp.

Jed released her hand. He screwed up his face. Here I go again. Jumping the gun. You don't have to say anything yet. Think about it.' He smiled. 'The last thing I want to do is rush you into something you're not totally happy with.'

'And you'd come on board as an equal partner?'

'As I said, think about it. It would be what you want.' He shrugged. 'I'll be happy with whatever you think would be right for the café.' He gazed at her, a little uncertain. 'I just want to help you make the café a raging success.'

'Well, it would solve one problem,' Millie began, slowly. 'As you know, I'm desperate for investment.' She picked up her wine and stared into it, as if the answer lay in her glass.

'And create another?'

'Jed, we started off in a sort of relationship.' She gave him a tight smile. 'Maybe, perhaps, we'll get back together. At some point in the future.' When he beamed, she rushed on, 'I'm not saying it's a definite possibility, but if we do get back together what happens when you invest all this money and it doesn't work out? We could end up being stuck as business partners and hating one another.'

'I'll never hate you, Emilia Fudge. You're the love of my life.' He said it completely matter-of-factly.

'Oh.' Millie wasn't sure, but she thought she was seeing stars, she was so dazzled by his words. And he really seemed to mean them. But it was all happening so fast. Much too fast. She gulped the last of her wine down. Not wanting to acknowledge his declaration, she concentrated on business. 'Well, you've always been great at coming up with ideas for the café and you're always bursting with enthusiasm –'

'So, what's the problem?' Jed said impishly, taking the sting out of the words. 'Maybe you should just grab me by the balls and take me to bed?' At her look of horror, he added, 'Joke. It was a joke, Millie!'

Millie relaxed a little. 'Well, it isn't as if I haven't tried that,' she said, acknowledging the heady passion of when they first met. 'I suppose I wasn't backward when coming forward. Think a sort of red haze of lust took over.'

'I didn't complain.' Jed gave a roguish grin.

'But,' Millie took a deep breath; it had to be said. 'And I

can't believe we're having this conversation, Jed. This might be about building a relationship for life, not just how good we are in bed.'

'Always helps if it works out in the sack, Millie.'

'Helps if your partner doesn't irritate the hell out of you the following morning. Especially if he's going to be your business partner. Not to mention the big trust issue.'

Jed subsided. 'Point taken. So what are you going to do?'

Millie sighed. 'I think we need to take it slowly. I think we need to take *everything* slowly, Jed.' She shook her head to clear it. 'I can't rush into this. There's too much at stake.' She met his gaze at last. 'And I've got to know if I can really, really trust you this time before I decide anything.'

'Fair enough.' Jed's lips twisted. 'To be honest, just the fact that you're considering anything to do with me is more than I hoped.'

'Oh Jed.' Aching to touch him, Millie reached over and took his hand. 'Just give me some time, eh?'

'Sounds like a plan. Take it slow. Then grab me by the balls.'

Millie giggled.

'Tell you what, what about dating? You know, nice meals out, moonlit walks on the beach. Getting to know each other.'

'And no sex?' Millie was mournful.

Jed's eyes gleamed. 'Not until you're ready. As you say, take it slow. Learn you can trust me and then everything else might, just might, fall into place.'

'I think that's what we'll have to do.'

'Could be romantic, Millie.'

'It could be very romantic, Jed,' and she smiled at him.

Chapter 19

It had been yet another disastrous rehearsal. Having his script taken away from him had made Greg even more nervous. It was clear he was still in the very early stages of learning his lines.

'Always takes me an age to get them bedded in,' he apologised.

If he wasn't such a nice man, Dora would have strangled him.

Everyone was far more on edge and nervy than they should be at this stage of the rehearsal schedule. Mike wanted to do the first complete run-through the following week and, in all honesty, Dora couldn't see Greg surviving. Her mood wasn't helped by the fact that, since she'd arrived in Berecombe two months ago, there had been an ominous silence from both her US and UK agents. Originally her desire to succeed in this production had been for Mike and Joe Latham's sakes. Now it looked as if a success in this was the only thing that might reinvigorate her career.

And it all depended on Greg Symon.

Dora lingered until the others had gone. She needed to talk

it through with Mike.

They hadn't mentioned what had happened in the car. Mike had been distant. Professional and incredibly busy, but definitely distant. So Dora had picked up on his vibe and returned it.

Her parents had been furious that night. Not because she'd stumbled in with a face red with stubble rash but that she'd completely forgotten she'd left the Mini parked at Millie's. Her father had had to drive her mother into town to rescue it. Dora had escaped to bed, to lie unsleeping, her body twitching for Mike. It had been an uncanny throwback to when she was seventeen.

'I owe you that pint,' she said to him now, as he gathered his things and began to switch off the lights. 'And I really need to talk to you about Greg.'

His blue-eyed gaze flickered over her and he'd simply nodded. 'Let's go back to my digs, then.'

Dora, envisaging a bed and breakfast along the lines of the one Millie had told her Jed was staying in, was surprised when Mike's Mercedes purred up a long drive to a house on the outskirts of Berecombe.

He drew up next to a double garage attached to a chalet bungalow. It was so completely not what she expected that she burst out laughing.

'What?' Mike asked, only slightly put out.

'You're living here?'

'Yup. Belongs to a friend. It's his holiday home, but he's not using it this summer. I quite like it in a retro-seventies way.'

Dora peered up at the big picture windows and white weatherboarding and said, 'Retro is right.'

'Don't be such a snob. It's great inside. Come on in and see for yourself.'

Mike was right. The house did improve once you were inside. He led her to the sitting room and pressed a button on the wall. It opened the bi-fold doors, which ran the length of the southern wall.

'I think this is what sells it.'

The doors opened onto a vast patio with superb views over Berecombe town and towards the sea. The sun was setting on yet another gloriously hot day and the sky was filled with scarlet and tangerine as it dipped its toe into the sea over to the west.

'Oh my God,' said Dora, going onto the patio. 'This is gorgeous.'

'Worth putting up with the naff outside?'

Dora couldn't take her eyes off the view. 'More than.'

'Find yourself a chair and I'll get us a drink. I've only got soft stuff in. Elderflower cordial. Is that okay?'

'Lovely.' Dora settled into a recliner and watched the changing colours drift down from the sky into the sea. 'This is heaven,' she said as she took the tall glass Mike offered. 'A little bit of paradise.'

He sat next to her. 'Cheers,' he said as they clinked glasses. 'The owner doesn't get to use the place very much.'

'He must be mad. I'd be here all the time.'

'Wouldn't argue with you there.'

'And who knew it was here? Tucked away up that driveway.'

'Hasn't been built all that long. Despite the seventies look, it's a new-build. All mod-cons. Fantastic kitchen and bath-rooms.'

They sat in silence until the light went and indigo washed the sky. Dora watched in fascination as the lights came on in town. Pinpricks of diamond in navy velvet. She could see the string of lights along the promenade, the neon glow from Berecombe's only supermarket, the white lights along the main shopping street. It felt very removed being up here. A little like being a Greek god and watching the mortals at play.

'You wanted to discuss Greg?'

Dora sighed. It seemed a shame to spoil the mood with discussing work, so she said so.

She felt Mike shrug in the dark. 'You were desperate to talk about him.'

'I was, you're right.' She went on to explain how she felt Greg was bringing the production down, how nervy everyone was.

Mike's only response was, 'Yes, I can see that.'

'I mean, I know you've been working extra hard with Greg, and everything, but whatever you do, whatever any of us do, doesn't seem to make any difference.'

There was a silence, then Mike began speaking. 'You know I said Greg is Phil's brother and that funding is tied up with him being Wentworth?'

Dora nodded.

'Well, it's true, but there's a bit more to it than that. When I first started working in the theatre in London, I was still carrying the baggage of Mikey Love, the Bad Boy of Berecombe.

244

I had a chip on my shoulder the size of a King Edward. The size of a whole sack of them. The problem was, for the first time I had no Joe Latham around to help. Yes, he could be on the end of the telephone, but it wasn't the same. By this point he'd got ill anyway. He died just before I got the job at the National.' Mike paused and when he went on, there was raw emotion threaded through his voice. 'I'll never stop regretting that he didn't know I'd made it.'

'I'm so sorry, Mike.'

A plane cruised past high overhead, on its way to Exeter airport, its lights flickering against the dark sky. The dull rumble was the only sound for a while.

'Yeah well.' Mike cleared his throat and continued. 'I went through a bad time. Drinking too much. Sleeping around. Got a reputation for being difficult to work with. My career was nearly over before it had a chance to begin.'

Dora thought of the type of people common in the theatre world; public school, well- heeled. None would make life easy for a scarily talented but working-class bad boy from a little seaside town. An outsider. She could well imagine how hard Mike had had to work to prove himself. 'I guess I know what you mean.'

She felt him glance at her in the dark and then he carried on speaking. 'None of that is a big secret, but this is. Greg met me when we were both starting out. He's RADA, did you know?'

Dora found it hard to believe, but just murmured, 'No, I had no idea.'

Mike went on as if she hadn't spoken. It was as if he was

telling himself the story. 'I'd just got the National job, he was spear-carrying in *Troilus and Cressida* and we hit it off. Greg had struggled in school like me, but for different reasons. He's dyslexic. Said it made school hell and he got out as fast as he could. Joined a drama group, found he could act a bit. We got on like a house on fire, shared a flat in the West End for a bit. Drank a lot. Womanised. Fancied ourselves as the new Terence Stamp and Michael Caine.'

The reference was lost on Dora but she stayed silent, not wanting to interrupt Mike's flow.

'Only the thing is, Greg can drink and then stop. I was developing a problem. The more I drank, the more I needed to. Greg found me one night passed out in the alley next to the flat. I was out cold, lying on the bin bags. Turned out his uncle liked a drink and he recognised the signs. He got me to AA, supported me through the shitty times when I needed a drink and the times I gave in and had one. So I owe Greg big time. When he went to the States to do *Almonhandez*, I couldn't be there for him. He had a crappy time. His dyslexia means he can't learn his lines very quickly, can't remember any moves until he's blocked them over and over again. The way they make American TV was too fast-paced for him. You must know all about that. It annihilated his confidence. He came back a broken man. Trust me, I wouldn't have cast him in anything this important if I didn't think he'd be up to it. But I know he can act, I've seen him in enough things to know he's got real talent. I thought something small like this would help him get back into it.'

Dora was silent for a moment. It made Greg's difficulties

make sense; she'd worked with a few dyslexic actors and should have recognised the signs. 'So you called for scripts down early to level the playing field?'

She felt the warmth of Mike's look even in the dark. 'Always said you were bright, Dora.'

'It's a wonderful gesture, Mike, but it's risky, isn't it? If he doesn't raise his game, Greg could ruin the whole production.'

'He could. I'm betting that he won't.'

'I hope you're right.'

'Dora, I'd appreciate it if you could keep all this to yourself. I don't mean about me being an alcoholic – there have been enough rumours about that for people to guess the truth – but Greg doesn't want the cast treating him any differently or giving him the sympathy vote.'

'I won't say a thing.'

'Thank you.'

Dora finished her drink, the ice having long since melted. Mike using the word 'alcoholic' had brought her up short. He didn't have a slight drink problem, like a lot of people she knew. He didn't go on the occasional bender. He'd called himself an alcoholic. It sounded so much more serious. 'How do you cope?' she asked suddenly.

'What do you mean?' There was humour in his voice.

'Oh I don't know, going to pubs, being offered a glass of wine at the Arts Workshop do. Being around people who drink.'

'It depends how I'm feeling. Who I'm with. Whether I can be bothered to go into the whole boring thing. Sometimes I just say I'm driving – people don't challenge that. Or I say

I'm on a health kick, doing a month off the booze. It's got a lot easier recently. Lots of people have a dry month, or give up alcohol for charity. And if people are really persistent I just tell them the truth; that if I have one I'll have to have another and then another.'

'It sounds so hard,' Dora said, in a small voice.

'It is hard. It won't ever stop being hard. Once an alcoholic, always an alcoholic. I'm going to have to work at it for the rest of my life. But you know what they say, it's one day at a time. And there's one huge advantage.'

'What's that?'

'Sober sex is truly mind-blowing.'

Dora gulped.

Mike stood up. He reached down a hand. 'Come on, I'll show you around the house. The bedrooms are worth the entry fee alone.' His hand was very hot and firm on hers.

Chapter 20

Mike was right. The house was something else. A simple layout but with large, square rooms, which would be filled with light during the day. It reminded Dora of her Malibu house a little – the one she'd had to give back at the termination of her contract.

She sensed Mike was enjoying showing her around. He had always been very aware of their different social status when they'd been teenagers. The chip on his shoulder had a long history.

She dutifully admired the bathroom, with its enormous shower and extremely vulgar Jacuzzi bath and followed him into the master bedroom. In here, Mike didn't switch the lights on. Instead, he pressed a button to let the curtains flow back. The room had the same aspect as the sitting room – and the same view.

Dora was immediately drawn to it. 'Beautiful,' she breathed. She turned to Mike, a potent shadow in the dark. 'We come from a really wonderful place, don't we? I think I'm only just realising that.'

He came to her and slipped a casual arm around her

249

shoulders. 'Agreed.'

'I know you're doing what you're doing for the theatre and old Joe, but I'm amazed you want to have anything to do with Berecombe.' She felt a tremor of humour run through him.

'There were times I never wanted to set foot in the town again. And I suppose I never needed to. Most of my work is London based.' His arm tightened. 'But as I got older, I could see things differently. Not everyone was gunning for me. Remember Mrs Hart at primary school?'

Dora nodded.

'I was always one of the first kids to arrive.' He shrugged. 'Never much to stay at home for. As soon as I got to school, Mrs Hart would bring me in from the playground. Scrub me up, give me breakfast, got me to clean my teeth, sorted some clean uniform.' He laughed. 'She even bought me a new pair of shoes once. And there was old Jerry at the newsagents. He sussed I was stealing from the shop in the summer holidays. Grabbed hold of me, sat me down in the back room and gave me a right talking to. Thought he was going to shop me to the old man, but instead he made me a mug of tea and a bacon sandwich and gave me a job. Dad never really fed me, so out of term time and without a school meal I was starving. Jerry got me working all hours. Kept me out of trouble a bit and I had some cash to buy food. So, it isn't just Joe Latham I owe big time. It's the town too.'

Dora put her arms around Mike's waist and rested her head against his chest. He felt adult and solid. The epitome of the successful man returning to his home town. A world away from the neglected child he'd just described. She'd never known about his childhood – he'd never wanted to discuss it and they were usually too busy kissing to talk.

'I had no idea things were so bad.' She snuggled into his warmth. 'Why weren't social services doing anything?'

She felt him kiss the top of her head. 'That's a nice, middle-class thing to say, Dora.' His laugh took the sting from the words. 'Dad was savvy enough to keep any do-gooders at bay. When he was sober he was charm personified. Could call birds down from the trees. And when things got really heavy, we'd decamp off to Aunty Debs in Truro.'

'So that's why you disappeared so much?'

'Yup. Debs was lovely. Fed me up, sorted me out. She wanted me to live with her permanently but Dad insisted I was the only family he had.'

'I'm sorry you had such a shitty time.' It seemed a completely inadequate thing to say, but she had to say something.

She stepped from Mike's embrace, needing some space. Her perception of him was changing. Yes, he was still deeply desirable; yes, a fragment of the rebellious youth remained. She still loved him as she had when they teenagers. But a new respect for the man he'd become was developing. He had a strength of character she'd never needed. She'd sailed into Central, had got the part in the States almost immediately, had achieved an enviable lifestyle. Until recently. Mike had been the only thing denied to her. Ironic, considering he was the thing she'd most desired.

She looked out to the view again. A fingernail moon had

risen and everything had turned monochrome after the fiery colours of the sunset earlier. A trail of silver shimmered across the shifting waters of the sea. It seemed to lead to them and to the potent atmosphere that had sprung up. She turned to Mike, aware that he was watching her. 'What a wonderful place to live. This house, I mean. Well, Berecombe too, I suppose.' She thought of her privileged upbringing, so different to Mike's. 'You take it all for granted as a kid.'

He came closer. He had a curious expression on his face. 'Do you really think it's so great?'

Dora nodded. Her throat had closed at his nearness and she'd lost the power to speak.

'I'd have thought it wouldn't compare with how you've lived in the States.'

Somehow Dora knew he wasn't just referring to a house. 'No, it's lovely. I would love to live somewhere like this.' She thought she'd said it but it was possible it had come out as a strangled whisper.

Mike traced a thumb down the side of her face. He was so close she could feel his hot breath on her skin. See the glint of vivid blue through the veil of black lashes. 'Dora. It's been so long.'

The kiss, when it came, was measured. Skilled. Grown up. A world away from the one in the car. This was a kiss that meant business.

Dora surrendered to it, pulled him to her to feel his heat. Snaking a hand around him, she hooked her fingers around a belt loop. Hearing him groan as he nipped at her earlobe, she gave in to the deliciousness coursing through her. Again, she felt she was coming home. The only one she'd ever known or ever wanted.

She also felt something vibrate.

Mike sprang away as if scalded.

Dora took his vibrating mobile from his back pocket and stared at the screen. 'Oh look,' she said, one brow arched. 'It's Kirstie.'

'Sorry Dora, I'll have to take it.'

She stared at him for a second in disbelief. 'You do that, Mike.' Then she turned on her heel and was out of the house in seconds.

'Idiot. Idiot. Idiot fucking woman,' she cursed as she stalked down the long drive back to the main road. It was only when she got to it that she realised she had no way of getting home.

With a furious sigh she took out her phone and rang her father. He was going to be so mad.

Again.

Chapter 21

It was Sunday and Jed had been very mysterious on the phone. He'd asked Millie to meet him on the harbour at nine, but she was to leave Trevor behind. The dog had his own little holiday booked – he had a day of being spoiled rotten by the Tizzard boys ahead and would come back sandy and exhausted.

As requested, Millie was wearing a bikini under her dress. She perched on the edge of an ancient iron bollard and inhaled the unique fish and diesel smells. She didn't often have time to walk around the harbour and had forgotten how pretty it was. A seagull glided past with a cackle. It landed not far from her, cocking its eye at a discarded crab claw. Millie watched, amused, as it did a one-step-forward and three-step-back dance before it dived on the claw and flew off. Millie watched it fly low across the water and saw Jed walking towards her with Davy Pascoe. She knew Old Davy, he ran mackerel fishing trips for the tourists in the summer season.

She waved at them. Standing up, she brushed herself down. As they got closer, she asked, laughing, 'We're not going for mackerel, are we?'

'Morning, Millie. May I say how gorgeous you're looking?' Jed gave her a kiss on the cheek.

'Ooh, I think you may. Can I return the compliment?' As ever, Jed looked Boden-perfect in turquoise skinny jeans and a loose white shirt. Today, he'd topped it off with an elegant straw fedora. He tipped the brim and grinned. 'Your words gladden my heart.'

'Don't hear no compliments comin' my way,' grumbled Davey.

Millie took the old man's arm. Hugging it to her, she giggled. 'Now, don't tell Jed but you know you've always been the man for me. Trouble was –'

'Couldn't fight off the other women, I knows. 'Tis always been my problem. All them lemmings coming after me.'

At Jed's puzzled look, Millie explained, 'Lemmings are tourists.'

'Ah. And no, Davey's not taking us mackerel fishing, although I'd love to do that one day. I've chartered his boat for a day out.'

Millie wrinkled her nose. 'Wont it be a bit fishy?'

'Have a care, missy,' Davey complained. 'You got me private boat today. Don't use that for no mackerel. Got a nice little Hardy Commander.'

Millie gazed at Jed, who shrugged. 'No idea either,' he said, 'But I believe it has a motor and a cabin. Speaking of which, hadn't we better get going?'

'Well, I'm rarin' to go,' Davey muttered. Was just waiting for you two to get done with the pretty talk.' He sucked on his teeth.

Jed held out his arm to Millie. 'Shall we follow our captain?'

'Better had. Davey gets a bit cross if you don't do as he says.'

'I 'eard that.'

Once settled at the stern on a bench seat, which smelled, if anything, of new plastic, Millie turned to Jed. 'So what *are* we going to do?'

'Davey's taking us on a cruise. Thought it would be fun to see the coastline from the sea.'

'Oh, that's going to be amazing!' Millie clapped her hands. 'And we couldn't have a more perfect day for it.'

She was right. As they chugged past the Dead Slow sign out of the harbour entrance, the boat picked up speed. Millie shaded her eyes against the bright sun bouncing hard off the sea and gazed entranced at Berecombe's promenade as it came into view from behind the wall.

Jed leaned forward. 'There's Millie Vanilla's,' he shouted, above the noise of the motor.

Millie admired the view of her café. 'So it is. I've never ever seen it from this angle. Those geraniums I potted up look good, even from here. Doesn't it all look pretty?'

Jed grinned. 'It does.'

The boat followed the line of the town until they reached the theatre and then turned and went further out to sea to navigate the rocks at the eastern end of the bay.

Millie shivered in a wind that whipped off the water.

'Come here,' Jed said and she slid over to him. Snuggling against his warmth, with his strong arms around her, Millie was in heaven.

'Relax,' he said, keeping her hands warm with his. 'It's your day off. Relax and enjoy the view.'

So she did.

The route took them past the golden cliffs at West Bay and along the great stretch of Chesil Beach. The boat rounded Portland, past Weymouth, and eventually headed into a tiny bay. Davey tied up alongside a jetty and helped them out.

'See you two later,' he called and waved.

Millie waved until the boat got smaller and smaller and then disappeared out of view.

'What do you think?' Jed asked.

She turned her back on the sea and looked about her. The beach was a perfect fingernail of soft white sand. The only things in sight were three beach huts painted in ice-cream colours and a steep track leading up the cliff behind them. Without the sound of the boat's motor, a hush fell. Even the seabirds, wheeling on a current above, were silent.

'Oh Jed. It's perfect.' Holding his hand, she followed him along the rickety jetty and, taking her flip-flops off, sank her toes into the sand. 'However did you find it?'

'Friend of Alex's owns the hotel it belongs to. He called in a favour. It's completely private and we've got it to ourselves until the tide turns.'

Millie danced around in giddy circles. 'Really? I love it!'

Jed laughed and headed to the central beach hut. 'Should be all we need in here, even a kettle if it gets cold.' He glanced up at the azure sky above them. 'Don't think that's going to be a problem somehow.' He turned and grinned at Millie, who was holding her face up to the sun, greedily drinking it in. 'Swim first and then crab sandwiches?'

'Perfect.' Then she heard what he was saying and checked herself. 'Where can I get changed?'

Jed nodded to a pink-and-pistachio-striped hut. 'Towels and things in there.'

'Give me five minutes.'

Opening the hut door, Millie stared in amazement. It was the most luxurious beach hut she'd ever been in. A full-length mirror reflected light back at her. Two benches padded with striped fabric lined either side and an inviting white robe hung from a bleached-wood hook. Wonder of wonders, there was even a stand with body and face creams and every soothing aftersun and lip gel a woman could want. Millie picked up a bottle and sprayed experimentally. Eau Dynamisante. 'Gorgeous,' she breathed.

Two minutes later she stood ankle deep in the sea, feeling shy and hugging a towel around her. It was ridiculous. Jed had seen her wearing much less. The sound of him opening a door behind jolted her into action. She threw off the towel and did a hasty belly flop into the sea.

'Bugger, it's cold!' she spluttered as she surfaced to find Jed treading water next to her. He was shivering slightly.

He shoved sopping hair off his face, his teeth gleaming very white against his brown face. 'Race you? Not that I particularly want to, but I think it's the only way I'm going to keep warm!'

Chapter 22

While Millie made tea, Jed gathered some driftwood and lit a fire. Wrapped up in the robes, they sat leaning against each other, toasting their frozen toes and eating crab sandwiches.

He gave the fire a poke and new flames curled out, sending smoke into the blue sky. 'Thawing out? Always forget how cold the English sea can be, even in May.'

'Especially in May! I'm just about warming up.' Millie clutched her mug in both hands. 'The tea's helping.' She wedged the mug in the sand and tucked her hands into the sleeves of her robe. 'It's all been lovely, Jed. Such a treat.'

'Good. You on for another date next Sunday?'

'Depends what you've got planned,' Millie giggled.

Jed tapped his nose. 'Secret.'

'Another secret?'

'Another lovely one, I promise.'

Millie pretended to consider. 'I might be free,' she said, airily.

Jed gave her an old-fashioned look.

'Of course I'll be free. Seriously, though, once the season

really gets going I won't be able to take Sundays off. Unless Clare is happy to take over.'

'I understand.' He gave her a look that warmed her far more than any amount of tea could. 'I'll just have to make the most of you while I can, then.'

Millie blushed, turned to pick up her mug and hid her face in it.

Jed shoved another piece of wood into the fire.

'Channelling your inner boy scout, Jed?'

He gave a twisted grin. 'Never became a scout, although I think I would have loved it. We always travelled about too much for me and Alex to join anything long enough to make it worthwhile. I was in the officer-training corps at school. I loved that. Thought about the army for a bit.'

'Did you?' Millie was surprised. 'I can't see you in the army, somehow.'

'Neither could they.' He pulled a face. 'Turns out I'm not very good at taking orders. A bit gung ho, they said.'

'Now that trait I recognise.'

He shrugged and smiled. 'Ma always says I rush into things without thinking them through.'

'She might have a point.'

'Uniform was nice, though.'

Millie toed him gently. 'Now that does sound like you.'

'Suppose I've never really found what I want to do. Or hadn't until recently. Ma's always on at me to get a career sorted. To settle down with one thing, as Alex has.'

Millie frowned. 'She can't be pleased you've given up the consultancy work, then.'

'It hasn't gone down too well.' He gave her a glance from under dark lashes. 'Ma thinks I'm rushing into this.'

'You've talked to her about the café? About us?'

Jed nodded. 'Of course. She's coming down soon. You'll get to meet her. Alex too.'

'What's she like, your mum?'

Jed leaned back on one elbow. His blonde head was very near and Millie longed to reach out to it. He smelled deliciously of the sea.

'Tough,' he admitted. 'She was hard on us as children. Had to be, with Pa away such a lot. She didn't have a lot as a child. Always said her parents were piss-poor. I never met them; they died when I was a baby. As a kid Mum took on anything paid she could find. Newspaper rounds, working in shops, doing another job in the evenings. Got herself to Lucie Clayton. Was quite a successful model for a while, made the cover of *Vogue* and then met Dad.'

'She sounds impressive.'

'She can be.'

'And made all her money herself? I really admire that. I can't stand these trust-fund types. You know the ones, like on *Made in Chelsea*? They always seem to have money handed to them without ever having to work for it.'

Jed gave her a sharp look, then focussed on the horizon for a second. 'Can't say I've ever seen it, but yes, Ma's definitely a self-made woman.' He was reflective for a moment, drawing an intricate pattern in the sand with a twig. 'She had to give it up when she married Pa. It just didn't fit into RAF life and then Alex and I came along. I think she misses it. Wanted girls, apparently.' He gave a short laugh. 'Probably would have started up a modelling dynasty. Apart from my love of clothes, I suspect I'm a sad disappointment to her.'

It showed a rare and surprising insecurity and Millie was touched. 'I'm sure you're not. How could you be?'

'Yeah well. Enough introspection.' He yawned and stretched, the robe gaping open to reveal his muscled chest. 'How about we get into some dry gear and make sandcastles? After my last lesson, I think it's something I'm really rather good at.' He trailed a hand along her naked foot. 'And if you don't put on some clothes soon, I think I'll go mad with frustration. All I can think about is the skin underneath that robe you've got on. It's driving me crazy.'

As Millie got up and glanced back at the length of him stretched out on the sand she knew exactly what he meant.

A few hours later, Davey's boat came cruising into the bay just as the tide was turning. Millie took Jed's strong hand as they clambered aboard. They sat, once again, on the bench in the stern of the boat. They didn't talk, just held each other for warmth and comfort as they headed west into the sun. Millie was thoughtful. It sounded as if Jed had a troubled relationship with his mother. She wasn't entirely sure she was looking forward to meeting her.

Chapter 23

The entire cast had gathered at the theatre for the first run-through. The bucket was still present, with water dripping occasionally through the ceiling from the offices above. Dora placed her chair fastidiously to one side of it and glared up.

'Should really get something done about that.' It was Greg. He flung his chair down next to hers with a clatter. 'Kirstie thinks it's a central heating pipe.'

Dora shivered. 'This place has heating?' She pulled her woollen jacket closer. She'd quickly learned that even when it was seventy outside, the inside of the theatre remained icy. As it was likely there would be a fair bit of sitting around today, she'd come prepared. She wrapped the shawl she'd borrowed from her mother more tightly around her neck and snuggled down.

Greg collapsed onto his chair and laughed. 'Well, *Persuasion* is set during the autumn, isn't it? At least we won't have to act being cold.'

She was about to reply when Mike strode to the front of the theatre, levered himself onto the stage and began to speak.

Dora found she couldn't make eye contact with him. Although she was still furious and eaten alive with jealousy over him and Kirstie, frustratingly she still loved him. And always would. It seemed Michael Love was a habit too hard to kick. She ground her teeth. Giving up nicotine had been easy in comparison. It was all so hopeless. Forcing herself to concentrate, she listened as Mike gave them a pep talk followed by their notes.

During the little time she wasn't on stage, she hung around, refusing to take a break. She watched Mike at work. She couldn't help herself. Somehow, despite the killer phone call, what he'd recently confided made her love him all the more. The hormone-driven rebellious lust for Berecombe's bad boy had been replaced by a deep admiration for the man he had become. He had overcome so much and, despite it all, he'd risen to the top of his profession. Watching how he gave notes to some of the younger, amateur members of the cast – or 'the kids' as they'd been nicknamed – during the lunch break, her heart swelled with pride at what he'd achieved. Had become. And then, seeing Kirstie waiting patiently to one side, her heart shattered at the knowledge he would never be hers.

There was nothing for it. She had to put up the barriers. Her heart was breaking into jagged pieces, but she'd die rather than admit it.

The day dragged on interminably. Some of the kids hadn't grasped that it was a run- through and kept stopping. When they didn't receive the usual prompt or suggestion, their performance dived-bombed.

'First run-through,' muttered Greg as they were waiting in

the wings for their cue. 'Nearly as bad as the read-through.'

Dora smiled at him. His performance hadn't been good, but then no one's had been. It wasn't the point of a run-through.

'I think the kids are rather discouraged,' she whispered.

'Bound to be. Mike will give them a pep talk later. He's excellent at that sort of thing. Force of nature, is Mike.'

Dora peered through a tear in a side curtain. Mike was sitting with his legs astride a backwards-facing chair. His hair was sticking up any old how and he had a coffee stain down one sleeve of his shirt. He was fiercely concentrating on what was happening onstage, his brows knitted, a scowl on his face.

How she loved him. And how he must never know. Her pride would simply not allow it. She'd do the best job she could and then walk away, leaving him to Kirstie's tender mercies.

'Uh-oh, that's me.' Greg shook out his hands and bent his head from side to side to iron out the kinks in his shoulders. Then he strode onto stage. Dora willed herself to forget about Mike and went through her mental preparations to get back into character as Anne. 'Get the job done,' she muttered. 'And get the hell out.'

Chapter 24

'Oh God, where the fucketty-fuck is it?' Dora hunted through her bag for her shawl. It had been a long day. Two run-throughs and brief notes from Mike and the rest of the cast had staggered up the hill to the Bear. Not able to face Mike with the inevitable Kirstie hanging off his arm, she'd refused the invitation, claiming exhaustion. If only she could find her mother's shawl, the sooner she'd be out of here and into a hot bath the better. The exhaustion was real; she was bone-tired and, ridiculously, close to tears.

'Your language really is something.'

It was Mike. Of course it was Mike. He was always first in and the last to go home.

'Looking for this? I found it backstage.'

She wanted to wrap him up in it. To tie him to her. To kiss him until they had no breath spare. Instead, she snatched it off him and stuffed it unceremoniously into her bag.

'You're welcome,' he said, mildly.

'You know, if this place was properly heated or ventilated I wouldn't need to wear three hundred layers. If I lost that shawl my mother would kill me. It's cashmere.' Viciously, she shoved it further down her bag.

'I can see it's very precious.'

Dora ignored his sarcasm and straightened her aching back. 'Oh you can, can you? I'm amazed.' She pointed vaguely in the direction of outside. 'It's eighty degrees out there and you have us working in these inhumane conditions.' One of her favourite parts at drama school had been Martha in *Who's Afraid of Virginia Woolf*. The woman was blasting her way through again. Maybe in rebellion against goody-two-shoes Anne Elliot. Dora squared her shoulders for a fight.

'I'm sorry. I'm sure it's not what you're used to.'

Dora could hear the stifled laughter in his voice. It made her even madder. 'You can bet that's right. For weeks I've put up with it. Crap coffee, amateurs who haven't a clue, ruddy Greg Symon, who is useless and that fucking annoying drip from the ceiling. It's like Chinese water torture.' She moved closer to Mike, so close she could see his eyes glittering. All humour had gone.

'I've starred in one of the highest-ranking network shows in America. I've got a beachside house in Malibu and a villa in Siena. I've been nominated for three Emmys and won a Golden Globe. And you've got me working here.' She gestured wildly to the shabby interior. She edged closer. Annoyingly, Mike still hadn't risen to the bait.

'Go home, Dora. You're tired.'

It was too late. Now she'd begun she couldn't stop. All the frustration poured out of her. One part of her could hear the silly, spoiled notes spike her voice and make it ugly and shrill. 'What sort of director has us do two run-throughs? In one day!' She drew herself up. 'It's clear you have no idea what you're doing.' She jabbed him in the chest. 'It's a tin-pot production in a tin-pot town and the sooner I'm out of it the better.'

Mike grabbed her hand and held it against his chest. She could feel his heart beating wildly, matching her pulse. 'You're welcome to leave at any time, Dora,' he said on a level whisper. He brought his face next to hers. 'In fact, as you've made your feelings abundantly clear, why don't you just do that?'

She met his look. 'And where would that leave you? Your biggest name.' Raising her chin defiantly, she sneered, 'Wouldn't be much of a show without me, would it?'

'Cut the diva crap, Dora.'

'Cut the crap, Mike, and kiss me.'

The kiss slammed her against the side of the stage. He crushed her to him with a savagery she hadn't known him capable. She grabbed onto his shirt and heard the sharp sound of tearing. Holding her by the waist, he lifted her up onto the stage and pressed himself between her legs. Furiously, he unzipped her fleece and tore at her t-shirt. His cold hand meeting her overheated flesh made her boneless and her head lolled onto his shoulder in ecstasy. His other hand flipped her short skirt and his fingers found her. Somehow, Dora found the strength to wrap her legs around his waist and the movement tugged him into her. He moved expertly and, instantly, she felt the spirals of pleasure radiate from her core. She came in seconds and sagged against him exhausted.

He held her until her pulse slowed. Too satiated to move, she nestled against him, needed his solid male warmth.

There was a distant thump. It was the outside door to the

theatre opening, Mike sprang back, his eyes still dark and dangerous with lust.

'Mike? Are you still here?'

It was Kirstie. They could hear her moving about in the foyer, sliding the window to the box office to peer inside.

Kirstie!

This man meant nothing but trouble. When would she ever learn? Dora mustered all her strength and pushed him off. She straightened her skirt and smoothed down her top, giving him a narrow look. Through thinned lips she hissed, 'I despise you! Don't you ever *ever* touch me again.'

Mike came back to her. 'Don't worry, I won't.' He laughed without humour. 'Not until you ask me again, Dora.'

Then he turned on his heel and left her.

Dora let out a long, shuddering breath. She slid from the stage on shaking legs and gathered her things. Shoving her sunglasses onto a sweating nose, she pulled her hat down low and swept past Kirstie and Mike in the foyer. They were bickering about who should lock up.

'And Mike, what have you done to your shirt?' she heard Kirstie squeal. 'It's literally ripped in half.'

Summoning every vestige of acting skill she possessed, Dora swept past them and trilled, 'Night darlings.'

It was only when she was clear of the theatre, and well along the promenade, that she felt tears trickle down from underneath her glasses.

Chapter 25

Again, Millie had instructions, but this time they came on a postcard, which accompanied an extravagant bunch of lilies and roses. She arranged them lovingly in a vintage and slightly chipped vase and put them on the café counter.

'Someone's got it bad,' was Biddy's comment. 'Another date?'

'Yes,' Millie replied, determined not to let Biddy's cynicism spoil her mood.

'What you doing this time?'

'I don't know yet. I'm being collected on Sunday morning.'

'Well, you just be careful. That one's too smooth for his own good.'

As Millie waited for Jed to pick her up, she could see how some might think Jed was a bit too confident, cocky even. Thinking back to the vulnerability he'd revealed when talking about his mother, she was beginning to see chinks in the glossy, well-groomed armour. She thought she rather preferred that Jed.

He drove her eastwards and Millie wondered if they were heading for the beach again. It was yet another warm day, so a few hours there would be welcome. However, Jed's latest instructions hadn't included bringing anything to swim in. She supposed, as it was a private beach, they could go skinny-dipping. Glancing across at Jed's chino-covered thigh muscles as they bunched when he changed gear, she thought she'd be able to cope.

When he pulled into the car park of a steel-and-glass hotel, just outside Poole, Millie didn't know whether to feel disappointed or relieved.

He led her into the foyer. 'Jed Henville and Millie Fudge,' he announced. 'Here for the couples' spa day.'

Millie watched, amused, as the receptionist blushed at his good looks and gave them directions.

'A spa day,' she marvelled, as they made their way towards the hotel's treatment centre.

'Don't tell me, you've never done one.' He picked up their joined hands and kissed her wrist.

Millie's mouth twisted. 'I'll give you three guesses.'

'Thought it might be just the thing to iron out some of the strains of your working week.' He pulled her to him and kissed her and then kneaded her shoulder. 'Too tense, Millie.'

Millie didn't think it appropriate to let him know her tension was coming from the touch of his lips on the sensitive skin of her wrist. 'Lead on, then,' was all she managed.

Two hours later, she lay on a couch in one of the treatment rooms, completely and utterly spent. Her eyelids were so heavy she didn't bother opening them when she sensed Jed lying down on the neighbouring bed.

'Having a good time?'

Millie stretched and yawned. 'Oh my goodness, I feel good.

Exhausted, but good.'

'You look it. What have you had so far?'

Sitting up, she reached for her glass of water and sipped. 'I couldn't decide, so I had the lot. A hot-stone massage and a seaweed body scrub.' Millie lifted a leg experimentally. She was relaxed but strangely weak too. 'Oh and a mandarin skin-brush treatment. Supposed to get rid of the toxins. What about you?'

'Had a really deep shoulder massage. Broke my collarbone a few years ago skiing and the muscles tighten up every now and again.'

'What next? Lunch? Can we go in robes like this? I'm feeling way too chilled to get dressed.'

Jed laughed. 'Yeah. Think that's allowed. But we're booked in for some beauty treatments next.'

'Together?' Millie was faintly shocked. She thought back to the gruesome face packs she and Dora had indulged in as teenagers. She had no desire for Jed to see her with a rock-hard, pea-green face.

'Well, we are on a couples' spa day.'

As it was, she needn't have worried. She was too busy surrendering to bliss to feel embarrassed. One assistant gave her a facial and then a light make-over, while others attended to her feet and hands. She'd never felt so pampered. She was vaguely aware Jed was having something similar, although she hoped it stopped at having his nails painted ruby red.

They decided to dress for lunch after all and took a table near the restaurant doors, which opened onto a terrace and then a magnificent view of Poole Harbour.

'The weather has been astonishing this year,' Jed said as he sat down. 'We could be anywhere on the Med.'

'I've never been,' Millie responded, trying to keep the wistfulness from her voice. For some reason, she was feeling wobbly.

'Well, take it from me, on a day like this Dorset takes some beating.' As the waiter fussed about with napkins and their starters were served, he added, 'Would you like to travel sometime?'

'I'd love to.' Millie drank some water. The treatments had made her thirsty. 'Trouble is, as I've never been anywhere, I wouldn't know where to start. I've always wanted to go to Thailand. Old Davey's granddaughter is there at the moment. She travels all the time. And Dora says Italy is amazing.' She stared out at the view with narrowed eyes. The sun on the terrace dazzled and she blamed that for the sudden tears. The massages and treatments had wrung her out. She felt teary and a little vulnerable. 'Dora's been all over the world with her job, even Tessa's got as far as India. Everyone's done so much more than me and I've hardly been out of Berecombe. Everyone goes away. Leaves me.' There was a heavy pause. She gave herself a little shake. 'I'm so sorry, Jed. It's really not like me to be maudlin. I'm usually too busy to over-think things.'

He gave her a concerned look. 'Sometimes having a massage can get to you like that. You had some pretty intense stuff done. It can get emotional.' He shrugged. 'Or it could just be dehydration.' He topped up her water glass.

'Yeah. Sorry. Food's delicious, by the way. I love scallops.'

'Good. Sea bass to follow and then chocolate pudding.' They ate in silence for a while. 'Is that why you find it hard to trust people, Millie?' he asked suddenly. 'Because you feel they all leave you?'

Millie dropped her fork with a clatter. 'Do I?' She replaced it with a shaking hand. Did she really find it so hard to let people in? To trust them?

Jed reached out a hand and covered hers, quietening it. 'I think you do. Deep down I think you're unwilling to really trust. And let's face it, it is hard. Opening yourself up, letting yourself love. Truly love. Because you run the risk of them hurting you.'

Millie was silent for a long time. 'My parents left me, she whispered eventually. 'I loved them so much. And then one day they weren't there.' She stared out to sea again. 'Mum hadn't even made the bed. I lay in it on the night of the accident, on the night they died and I could still smell them. When I woke up in the morning I thought I was little again. That I'd had a nightmare and snuggled in with them. Only they weren't there. They'd never be there ever again.'

A solitary tear escaped. Jed thumbed it away with a gossamer-light caress. 'Now I'm the one who should be sorry,' he said, his voice hoarse with emotion. 'For asking too many crass questions and spoiling your day.'

She took a deep breath, coming back to herself. 'You haven't, Jed. It has been a lovely day. I feel thoroughly spoiled. I don't know what came over me. The grief for my parents,' she shrugged, 'It's always going to be there. It just breaks through more forcefully sometimes.'

'And it makes me love you all the more.' He took her hand and kissed the inside of her wrist again. Only this time it was a tender gesture, which made Millie's fractured heart tremble. 'Would you like to go? Shall I get the bill?'

'Did you say there was chocolate pudding?' There was a ghost of a smile on her tear-stained face.

'I did.'

'Think that decides it, then.'

Afterwards, she walked back to the car on shaky legs. Jed tucked her in gently, fastening her seatbelt for her. On the journey back she clutched a rug to her like an invalid and watched, unseeing, as the bumpy Dorset countryside sped past her.

He might, just might, have a point about the trust issue. Maybe it was time to move her life on.

Chapter 26

Jed had promised to pick her up at eleven. Millie sat on the low wall that ran along the promenade and peered impatiently at the line of cars cruising for a parking space.

'They'll be lucky,' she muttered to Trevor, who was sitting next to her and panting.

The sun blazed down on another impossibly hot day. The sea front was already rammed with tourists and any spaces had long gone. Crowds bustled past, wafting the scent of factor thirty in their wake.

A toot of a horn from a familiar grey Golf five cars down had her grinning. It was Jed. She ran to where his car was stuck in the queue, bundled Trevor in the back and then got in the passenger seat.

'Morning. Another gorgeous day. And morning to you too, Trevor,' Jed added, as the dog licked his ear. He gave Millie a keen look. 'Feeling better?'

Millie nodded and concentrated on directing him down some back streets away from the chaos of the sea front. Once they were on the open road they both relaxed.

'I'm so sorry I was late. It's taken me the best part of an

hour to get from Axminster and most of that was trying to get along the front at Berecombe.'

'It's the lovely weather. Brings all the visitors to town.'

'You can say that again.'

'It's the lovely weather –' Millie began with a grin.

'Ha ha.' Jed glanced at a signpost and flipped the indicator. Turning right, he said, 'Who have you got running the café today?'

'Clare. She's been wonderful. I probably shouldn't say this with so much glee, but her dropping out of doing A levels has definitely been my gain.' Millie took off her straw hat and fanned her hot face. 'I don't think her parents approve, but she's all set to try for catering college. She's just got to check out what qualifications she needs. I'm hoping she'll work at the café while studying part-time. For the first time ever I've got someone I'm confident about leaving in charge.'

'While you play hookey?'

'While I have a day off!'

'And this the busy season too. Nothing short of scandalous, Emilia.'

'Well, if a good-looking man asks me out I have to accept.' She saw his cocky grin and added, 'But as he was busy I had to go out with you instead. Where are we going this time?'

He grinned. 'You'll see, not far. Somewhere away from the crowds.' He flicked up the air conditioning and the interior of the car filled with blessedly cool air.

'Sounds heaven,' Millie said and leaned back on the head-rest, idly watching as the road narrowed and the Devon hedges closed in on them.

After another twenty minutes of winding lanes, Jed pulled the Golf into a rough clearing, where only one other car was parked.

'Ah, that's a shame,' he remarked. 'I rather hoped we'd have the place to ourselves.'

'Where are we?' Millie looked around with interest. The clearing was overhung with trees that tapped lightly on the car's roof. It was like being in a green cave. Even in the hot weather, it was cool and tranquil. 'It's gorgeous.'

She pressed the window release and it slid down. Her nostrils filled with the aroma of rich damp earth. In the distance she could hear water trickling. 'You know, I don't think I've ever been here before.'

'Well, I'm glad about that. Come on, let's find somewhere to sit and eat our picnic.' An impatient whine came from the back. 'Sounds like Trevor could do with stretching his legs too.'

Millie released Trevor from the back seat and, with a delighted bark, the cockapoo immediately began 'hoovering' a scent trail. Keeping half an eye on the dog, Millie followed Jed to the boot, from where he produced an old-fashioned wicker hamper and a blanket.

'I'll take the picnic hamper if you could carry the blanket,' he said. 'Follow me.'

Whistling for Trevor to follow, Jed led them through an opening in a steep bank and to a huge shady clearing, which was surrounded by a steep circular ridge. Away from the road and the car park, and the heat of the day, it was quiet and soothing.

'What an extraordinary place,' Millie said, looking around in astonishment. Finding a flat spot without tree roots, she spread the blanket on the ground.

'Isn't it? Apparently it's an ancient hill fort or something. Iron age, I think I read somewhere.'

'Well, whatever it was, it's amazingly peaceful today. And so cool under the trees.'

Jed paused from taking food out of the basket. 'There's something magical about it, isn't there? Wouldn't be surprised if Titania and Oberon popped out from behind that beech tree over there.'

Millie giggled. 'Neither would I. Now there's a thought. It would make the most incredible setting for *A Midsummer's Night Dream*. You're right, there's definitely an other-worldly feel to the place.'

'Completely agree. The ramparts make it a natural open-air theatre. Perhaps we should suggest it to Mike? He could put it on next.' Jed opened a bottle of champagne with a satisfying pop. He poured her a foaming glass and handed it over. 'Bit lively due to the journey, but still cold.'

Millie took her flute. She eyed it in wonder. 'Jed this is real crystal.'

'If you're going to do something, you might as well do it properly, I've always said.' He peered into the hamper. 'Lobster or chicken?'

Millie shook her head at him with a fond grin. 'Oh, lobster please, if you insist. Think I could force some down.'

Jed handed her a plate. 'There's lemon mayonnaise to go with it and some great sour dough bread. Salad and – ah –

here we go, napkins.'

Millie batted off an excited Trevor and laughed. She took a mouthful of lobster and closed her eyes in bliss. 'Delicious. I don't eat it very often.' She peered in to see what else was in the basket and was gratified to see some plump strawberries and a pot of clotted cream. 'You've done an amazing job,' she said, suddenly suspicious.

Jed had the grace to look embarrassed. 'Can't claim to have done all of it. I suggested one or two things and Mrs Silver put it together for me. She's an extraordinary woman. Fantastic cook, member of the Axe Valley Runners. Did the Grizzly this year,' he added, referring to the notoriously arduous beach and cliff-top marathon. 'Says it's one way of using all the calories up.'

'Ah.' Millie put down her plate and fed Trevor a tiny nugget of lobster.

Jed must have caught her tone. 'Hope I'm as fit as she is when I'm her age.'

'And what age would that be?' Millie tried for nonchalance.

'Oh, mid-fifties or thereabouts.' Jed gave Millie a grin and saluted her with his chicken drumstick. 'She's got grown-up children, that much I know.'

'Ah,' Millie repeated but this time in a relieved voice. She couldn't believe the jealousy that had shot through her at the mention of Mrs Silver's name. Clinking her glass gently against Jed's she said, 'Thank you for doing this. It's such a treat. And thank Mrs Silver too.'

'I will.'

Millie met Jed's gaze. As ever, he'd picked up on her mood

instantly. The expression in his dark eyes was warm and loving. The sunny weather had deepened his tan and her fingers suddenly itched to run them over his smooth, brown skin. Through his silky, sun-lightened hair. He'd hurt her so badly earlier in the year. About as badly as anyone could. Could she trust him again? Something, somewhere deep inside her began to melt the last vestiges of betrayal he'd inflicted.

Trevor suddenly bounded over to the picnic basket, ruining the mood. He thrust his long nose into it and Jed snapped shut the lid, saying, 'No, boy, you can't have any more of your mistress's lobster. I've got some biscuits for you somewhere.' He reached behind him and produced a bag of expensive dog treats.

'You're spoiling us, Jed. There's a danger we could get used to this sort of treatment.'

Jed didn't meet her eyes. He concentrated on feeding Trevor biscuits, a little at a time. 'I'd be happy to spend a lifetime spoiling you, Millie,' he said quietly.

Chapter 27

Sleepy and replete with good food and, in Millie's case at least, good wine, they lay in the flickering shade of the trees and dozed. Trevor lay at their feet, snuffling and twitching his paws in his sleep. Millie inched her hand over to Jed's and entwined her fingers with his. With a contented sigh, she closed her eyes.

They must have slept for some time as, when Millie awoke, the sun had moved lower in the sky, making the shadows longer and more dense. With the sense that something wasn't right, Millie shivered and sat up. The little patch of grass on which Trevor had stretched out was empty.

'Jed, Jed, wake up. Trevor's gone!'

She scrabbled to her feet, looking around her urgently. 'Trevor!' she yelled. 'Here boy.' Clasping her arms around herself, she shouted again. 'Trevor! Get here now!'

Jed got to his feet and brushed himself down. 'Right. You stay here in case he comes back and I'll go and look for him.' Seeing Millie's stricken expression, he came to her. Taking her by the shoulders, he kissed her gently on the forehead and added, 'He won't have gone far, he's devoted to you, and besides, we've still got food left. He knows there'll be the possibility of treats.'

'It's just so unlike him. He never leaves my side. Oh Jed!' Millie ended on a wail.

'He's probably just followed a rabbit trail or something. Don't worry, I'll find him for you. You stay here and keep calling him and I'll work my way around the ramparts and –' He broke off as Millie gave a relieved grin at something over his shoulder.

'Trevor, you naughty boy. Where have you been?' She bent down to fuss the dog. 'And just what have you got there? Drop. I said drop it, Trevor!'

Trevor was reluctant to give up whatever he had and, instead, scampered around them, shaking it ragged.

Jed held up the packet of dog treats. 'One left,' he said. He passed it to Millie, who bribed Trevor into sitting. The dog eventually got the message and, with an indignant grumble, dropped the bundle of white material on the ground.

While she was clipping on Trevor's lead, Jed picked up the dog's treasure. He dangled the bra from a little finger.

'If I'm not very much mistaken – and I have very little experience in these matters, you understand – I believe this is a lady's undergarment,' he said solemnly, with a wicked twinkle in his eye.

Relief about Trevor's safe return was making Millie giggle. 'Where on earth has he got hold of that from?' She clapped a hand to a horrified mouth. 'When we parked up, there was another car!'

'And this belongs to the owner?' Jed made his eyes go round.

'What *has* she been doing?'

'Or what have *they* been doing?' said Millie. 'If you understand what I'm saying.'

Jed nodded. 'Think I just about get your drift.' He gave Millie a doubtful look. 'We'll leave it at the entrance to the car park, shall we?'

Trevor, however, seemed to have other ideas. He tugged hard on his lead. 'Do you know, I think Trev might know the whereabouts of its owner.' Millie looked up at Jed. She pulled a face. 'I feel ever so guilty about this. After all, Trevor's my dog. Maybe we should try to get it back to her?'

'We could just leave it in the car park, somewhere obvious for her to find.'

'Wimp,' Millie teased.

The matter was decided by Trevor pulling so hard at his lead that Millie found herself being dragged off.

'Looks like we have no option,' Jed said with a grin. 'Silent obs though, *mon capitaine*.'

'Absolutely,' Millie said over her shoulder, Trevor still straining at his lead. 'And you, young man,' she directed at the dog, 'Have caused enough trouble.' She shook a reproving finger. 'Not a sound!'

They let Trevor lead the way. After about ten minutes of stumbling around in a zigzagging way, he eventually led them to a pile of half-rotten logs at the far end of the circular clearing. He nosed at something on the ground, tail wagging furiously.

'Matching panties,' Jed whispered with a grimace and, finding a stick, hooped the underwear onto it along with the

284

bra. 'What else are we going to find?'

'I truly dread to think, but we've got no option,' Millie replied. 'Those look like silk to me. We've got to return them now, they're probably really expensive.'

Again, they let Trevor take the lead and another five minutes later, behind an enormous chestnut tree, they came across a pair of men's trousers.

'You've done a really thorough job, Trevor,' Millie groaned as she collected them and folded them into a neat parcel. 'What else did you find to leave discarded on this trail?'

They followed Trevor to where he found more clothes – a white shirt and a summer dress – until, after a hard climb up the steepest part of the ramparts at the furthest most point of the fort, they stopped to catch their breath. In the next field along, just the other side of a high Devon bank, and only visible from this vantage point, lay two prone figures. Two completely naked prone figures.

Millie ducked down, grabbing Trevor's snout to stop him barking. She caught Jed's eye and stifled a giggle.

He slid down next to her and grinned. 'What do we do?' he mouthed.

Millie shrugged. 'I don't know,' she whispered back. She risked another glance at the sunbathers and then froze. 'Oh. My. God.'

'What is it?'

She turned to Jed, her eyes enormous. 'I think it's Biddy and Arthur!'

'What?' Jed peered over the ridge, became convulsed with silent laughter and then crouched back next to Millie. 'I really need to unsee that.'

'You and me both. Wonder why they haven't got their dogs with them?' She glanced at Trevor. 'Probably wanted some peace and quiet,' she hissed at the dog with a grimace. 'Look at the trouble you've caused.' She sighed. 'I suppose we ought to get their clothes back to them, somehow.' She nodded to the little huddle of garments. 'I think Trevor's managed to snaffle the lot. They can't drive home stark naked.'

Jed nodded in the direction of the field. 'It doesn't seem to be bothering them at the moment.' He grinned.

'No because they don't realise they can be seen.' Millie leaned against a thick tree root and shook her head. 'I know it's funny, but Arthur would be mortified.'

Jed's eyebrows rose. 'From what little I know of Biddy, I think she'd take it in her stride.'

'You're not wrong there.'

'I just hope there were no nettles involved.'

Millie thumped him, laughing. 'Don't! Let's hope they were just sunbathing.' Once again, she risked poking her head over the rampart. 'They haven't moved an inch,' she whispered back. 'I think they're asleep.'

'Or dead.' Jed pulled a face.

Millie thumped him again. 'Don't even think that!'

'I suppose I ought to take their clothes back to them. Can you stay here and keep Trevor quiet?'

Millie did a mock swoon. 'My hero.'

Jed gave a ragged grin. 'Well, it's one way to win your undying love.'

'Maybe.' Millie grinned at him and contemplated telling

him she'd never stopped. She nodded towards the field. 'How are you going to get them back without being seen, though?'

Together they scanned a possible route.

'I suppose if I duck down behind that hedge, I could sneak the clothes to just by the entrance to the gate. They'll find them there. They might think it a bit odd, though.'

'Oh, they'll probably blame kids or something. At least they'll have something to wear.'

Jed looked at the underwear. The last thing they'd found and the item that had got Trevor most excited was Arthur's baggy white y-fronts. 'Have I really got to touch those?' he asked, with a fastidious wrinkle of his nose.

'And there's me thinking they bred them tough at Eton.' Millie bundled up the offending item inside the dress and wrapped the trousers tightly around. 'There, that's the lot, as far as we know.' She thrust them at him. 'Good luck.'

He gave a weak grin. 'We, who are about to die, salute you.'

Millie grinned. 'Get on with it and make sure you don't get caught.'

'If I get caught with Biddy's knickers in my hand, I think it might be the nettles for me.'

'Think it would be a lot worse than that,' Millie said drily. 'Don't forget, I know Biddy very well.'

Jed gave a look of true horror, shoved the bundle of clothes inside his shirt to free his hands and began, cautiously, to navigate the rampart's steep southern face.

Millie clutched a wriggling Trevor to her and watched with baited breath. At this point, Jed was clearly visible. Once at the bottom of the slope, he ran to the hedge and ducked down. Luckily, as it was a Devon bank, it was solid and high and rich with greenery. Millie was certain he couldn't be seen from the field on its other side. He edged along until he came to the open gate, sneaked a glance round, put the clothes on the grass and then sprinted back. Looking up at Millie and realising the bank was going to take ages to climb up, he mimed that he'd go along the bottom of the ramparts and meet her back at the car. She gave him the thumbs-up and, clutching Trevor's lead, retraced her steps.

Millie had made two trips back to the car, carrying their picnic things by the time Jed returned.

He threw himself into the Golf. 'Time to get out of here,' he exclaimed. 'Don't think I'm cut out for a life of espionage. Value my balls too much.'

'Ah,' said Millie. 'Then again, James Bond never had to face an adversary quite like Biddy Treeby. And, if she'd caught you, the safety of your balls would be the least of your worries.'

'Ouch,' Jed winced. 'Just as well we got away with it, then.'

'Indeed.' Millie smiled at him. 'Besides,' she added airily, 'I'm quite fond of your balls too.'

Jed did a double-take. Seeing the look on her face, he gunned the engine. 'Perhaps we'd better get home and try them out.'

Millie pressed the down button on the window and lifted her face to the breeze. 'I think we better had,' was her only reply.

Chapter 28

The blinds made it softly dark in her bedroom. The windows wide to the rhythmic sounds of the sea. It all seemed to happen in slow motion, in silence. Little need for words.

Millie stood in front of Jed, drinking him in. With infinite care, she unbuttoned his shirt and inched it off his shoulders. Concentrating fiercely, she trailed a finger over his smooth, brown chest, over the muscles in his shoulders and onto his biceps. His skin smelled of hot sun. Her finger found his nipple. Bending forward, she licked it, experimenting. She felt him tense.

Her fingers tripped along the ridges of six pack and she unbuckled his belt, unzipped his fly. He stopped her hand. With a look from eyes darkened with love, he whispered, 'My turn, Emilia.' Lifting her, he carried her to the bed. He took off her clothes, kissing each newly exposed expanse of skin with agonising tenderness. Time stilled. The only thing that mattered was Jed and the feel of him on her. Surrounding her.

Later, much later, when he slid into her at long last, it felt completely and utterly right.

Chapter 29

Once Dora had stopped laughing, she managed to splutter out, 'Biddy and Arthur? Of all people! She must be leading him astray.'

'And I think he's probably enjoying every single minute. More wine?'

They were in Millie's sitting room, the windows flung open to the sea air. The June heat had built up to an uncomfortable intensity during the day and thunder was rumbling in the distance.

Dora soothed a trembling Trevor and regarded her friend. 'So what happened, then?'

'I've no idea. I'm assuming they rescued their clothes and put them back on. Haven't seen either of them since. For which I'm very grateful. I don't think I could look either of them in the eye.'

'I didn't mean that, hon. I meant between you and the gorgeous Jed.'

Millie smirked.

Dora sat forward, making Trevor start. 'I knew it,' she exclaimed. 'I *knew* you'd slept together! That smug, satisfied look on your face says it all.' She pointed an accusing finger. 'Tell all, girlfriend!'

'Well,' Millie began. 'I believe the man in question puts a certain part of his anatomy in –'

'I didn't mean that!' Dora roared, making Trevor whine and scrabble to hide behind a cushion. 'What happened to taking it slowly, going on romantic dates. Waiting until you trusted him again?'

'Please don't terrify my dog,' Millie answered mildly.

'Sorry, Trevor. Come here, baby boy.' Mortified that she'd scared him, Dora put down her wine and rescued the quivering cockapoo. Picking him up, she cuddled him close. She nuzzled her face into his soft fur. 'I hate thunderstorms too, little one.'

Satisfied that Trevor was content, Millie considered her answer. She hadn't been sure why her feelings towards Jed had changed so drastically. Or rather, why they had reverted to how she'd felt about him before. Maybe it was because he'd been so thoughtful and careful around her lately. Maybe she was beginning to see just what a difficult position he'd been in – what would she have done in his place? Maybe she was just weary of putting her life on hold and yearned for them to get back together?

'I don't know why I decided to forgive Jed,' she said, at length. 'Maybe I decided life was simply too short to hold a grudge.' She sipped her wine and continued. 'It was the twelfth anniversary of my parents' accident this week. Did you realise?'

Dora shook her head.

'Mum was thirty-eight when she died. Just thirty-eight. So young. Not all that much older than me now, really. She met

Dad when she was sixteen. Said he was the love of her life. Never looked at another man all the time she was married to him.'

'Just think how much more she might have had to enjoy.' Dora sighed. She'd been fond of Millie's mum. She had been a much more motherly figure than her own.

'Exactly!' Millie shrugged. 'You never know what's around the corner in this life.' She refilled her glass. 'Oh, I know how corny I'm sounding, but I just want to enjoy things. I've worked ever since I was seventeen. I want to take my foot off the accelerator for a while. Have some fun.' She waved her glass at Dora, the wine sloshing dangerously. 'In fact, Tessa told me that exact same thing not that long ago.'

'Well, if there's one person who knows about having fun, it's Tessa, Dora said drily.'

Millie laughed. 'I know you're not keen, but she's okay, really.'

'As long as she's a good friend to you, honeybun, that's all that matters.' Dora held out her glass in salute. 'Be happy, my darling. That's something else that matters too.'

Millie smiled. 'I'm aiming to be.'

'What's the plan with the café? You still going to let Jed invest?'

Millie shook her head. 'Still thinking about that. One thing at a time. It was heaven, though, you know, the other day,' she said in dreamy tones. She looked up and gave a gutsy sigh.

Dora regarded her friend fondly. 'Well, I'm glad. For what it's worth, I think Jed is a keeper.'

'Thank you.' Millie brought herself back to earth with an

obvious struggle. 'It's still early days and, despite appearances, we are taking it slow. What's more, Jed's happy to. He's letting me dictate the pace.'

'Emilia Fudge, I do believe you're enjoying the power!'

Millie shrugged and giggled. 'Might be.' She drained her glass and put it on the floor just as the first clap of thunder sounded. 'We need this. Let's hope it clears the air. It's been stifling.' Getting up, she added, 'You need something to soak up the alcohol? I made some bacon and cheese straws earlier. Trying some old recipes of my mum's.'

Dora's mouth watered. 'Might squeeze a few down. Just to take my mind off the storm, you understand.'

'I've made a huge batch. Take some back to your parents, if you like.' Millie disappeared into the kitchen and returned bearing a couple of plates piled high with pastries.

'Ooh Mil, they smell gorgeous. Let me at them. Just realised I'm starving. Today was as bad as ever.'

Dora had popped in to see Millie on return from yet another disastrous rehearsal, craving wine and sympathetic company.

'Still not going well, then?'

Dora helped herself to a cheese straw and spoke through a mouthful. 'Got the techie run-through next week,' she moaned. 'I'm dreading it.'

Millie frowned. 'What's a "techie run-through"?' She leaned forward and fed Trevor a morsel of pastry.

'It's when the lighting and music and all the other technical stuff gets married to the acting. Always takes forever and it's never a true run-through, no matter how hard everyone tries. Greg is still a plank of the finest oak and Mike is stressing everyone out.'

The latter part of the statement was a lie. Mike wasn't stressing anyone out except for her. Since their encounter in the theatre, Dora couldn't relax around Mike, or even look him in the eye. After tossing and turning through sleepless night after night, she found herself falling into a dead sleep in the early hours. She was woken heavy-eyed by the shrill beep of the alarm and threw herself into the coldest shower she could bear in order to wake up.

She bitched at everyone and was being given a wide berth. Dora hated herself, but at least being ignored meant she had to communicate as little as was necessary. The only person who shouldered her moods and happily batted away her spiky comments was Greg. His forbearance and sheer niceness put Dora into an even worse sulk.

She tried hard to snap out of it, but her nerves were shredded and every pore in her skin crawled with irritation, with unresolved lust for Mike. With jealousy.

But she wasn't going to admit it to anyone. Not Greg, certainly not Mike and most definitely not Millie. Dora didn't want to rain on her loved-up parade.

Millie gave her a close look. 'Are you nervous about it? You seem ever so jittery.'

Dora didn't answer.

'Maybe it's the storm,' Millie added kindly, her words almost drowned out by a clap of thunder. 'You were never that keen on them. Look, why don't you stay over tonight and then you can have another drink?' She got up to shut the windows as the rain began to hammer down. 'Save you driving home in this weather.' Without waiting for an answer, she went into the kitchen to find another bottle.

Dora lay back against the sofa, soothing the trembling dog. The scent of wet sand from outside assailed her nostrils and made her throat close. The rain battered the windows as a flash of lightning speared across the room. Another clap of thunder shook them. Trevor whined and stuck his nose into the crook of her arm.

'Ssh, little one. It's okay,' she murmured to comfort him. 'They never last long. It'll be over soon.' She wished, with her whole being, that she could get over Mike as quickly. 'Oh, Trevor,' she said into his fur as she gathered him close. 'I think I'm conquering my fear of storms. If only I could get over Mike so easily.'

Chapter 30

The technical rehearsal was, as predicted, a nerve-shredding affair. It seemed to take ages.

Albie, the lighting director, and usually the most laid-back member of the crew, had a loud and very public row with Kirstie over the non-appearance of a new lighting rig. Dora witnessed the music director and Mike nearly come to blows over the ancient electrical system. The drip from the roof over where the third row stalls seats should go continued and the final straw was news that the promised painters, commissioned to repaint the interior of the theatre, had been delayed on another job.

Dora, unable to stand the atmosphere a minute longer, fled outside for some fresh air and privacy. At the side of the theatre, where a narrow path ran between it and a low sea wall, she came across Mike. He was leaning against the outside of the theatre, one foot on the sea wall and staring out to another uncaringly hot and sunny day.

Dora stopped in her tracks. Mike had just, uncharacteristically, called a long lunch, claiming he had to make some phone calls. He had obviously needed the same privacy she craved herself and she had no wish to disturb him. While every nerve in her body urged her to propel forward, she couldn't face him in a situation like this. During rehearsals it had been bearable – just. Any emotion crackling between them was smoothed over by simply having to get the job done. It was killing her, but she'd managed to be coldly professional. But here, in this intimate space, looking out on another impossibly beautiful day, she wasn't sure she would be able to contain her feelings. She began to retrace her steps and tiptoe away.

A herring gull wheeling past too close and cackling had him look up and in her direction.

'Dora.'

She couldn't see much of his face. He wore sunglasses and a battered straw trilby pulled low. He was shrugged low into the collar of his shirt and looked as if he was desperate to disappear.

Her heart went out to him. She'd never seen anyone radiate so much misery. All her angst, her nerves, melted away. However she felt about him, whatever their crazy, mixed-up relationship, she cared too much about him to ignore his hurt. She approached cautiously.

'It'll be okay, you know.'

'You think so?'

She went nearer. 'I know so. Albie will get over his tantrum and the electricity will work. In the dark, no one will notice that the theatre hasn't been painted and the whole thing will be a triumph.'

Mike gave a short laugh. 'And how do you know all this?'

Dora spread her hands. 'Because there's a moment like this in every production. When all seems lost. When it feels it will never be ready. But it always happens in the end. It's the magic of theatre. And this one will be no different. In fact, I'd go as far to say this particular production will be an absolute triumph.'

'You seem very certain.'

'I am.'

'Why?'

'Because it's being directed by you and I believe in you.'

Mike scrubbed a hand over his face, dislodging the hat to the back of his head. It made him look even more rakish than normal. He gave a tight grin. 'You believe in me? Even after all that's happened. After everything I've done to you?'

'You haven't done anything I didn't want to happen, Mike,' Dora said softly and laid a hand on his arm. The linen of his sleeve smelled hot in the sun.

He turned to her and kissed her. It was infinitely tender, another variation in his array of kisses. This one felt as if it came from the very depth of his soul.

Everything melted away. The sharp saline from the sea crashing onto the shore below was replaced by the fresh, soapy smell of Mike's skin. The feel of the rough stone of the sea wall on her back drowned out by his lips on hers. The sun arrowing down became an urgent heat inside. Everything crystallised into this: his lips on hers, his warm hands as they held her body close. She never wanted it to stop.

He broke away. 'Oh Dora, Dora. I can't seem to stop wanting to kiss you.' In that trademark gesture, he traced a gentle thumb down her cheek and raked her face with his gaze, as if seeing it for the very first time. 'I can't seem to stop wanting you.' He rested his forehead against hers and blew out a breath. 'I know it'll all be okay. I was just having a black moment. A very black moment.' He shuddered.

A breeze drifted in the smell of beer from a nearby pub and Dora understood. She tightened her hold on his sun-warmed back, willing him strength.

'But it feels good to hear you say you believe in me. In the production. You can't imagine how much. Thank you.'

They stood close together for a moment. A sort of sigh of recognition flowed between them and then Mike stood away from her.

'I suppose I ought to get back to the fray,' he said, regret staining his voice. He took off his hat, ran a hand through his unruly curls and then crammed the trilby back on.

Dora took the hint. 'And I have no idea why I'm standing outside in the midday sun,' she said, a little too tartly. 'I'll be burned to a crisp.'

'You will indeed.' Mike sounded confused by the change in tone. 'You always burned easily. And your white skin is a trademark, isn't it? Back in the States?' The last part was bitter.

'Certainly is.' Dora turned away and scanned the bay, her eyes hot and unseeing with unshed tears. She loved this man. No matter what happened and, worse, however he decided to treat her, she loved him. She'd loved him all those years ago and loved him now. And always would. 'I just wish I didn't,' she muttered.

'Yes, must be a pain to always have to cover up.'

Dora fumbled in her pocket for her sunglasses. Putting them on, she turned back and regarded him. 'You have no idea of how much I have to hide,' she said, levelly. 'No idea at all.'

There was a beat and then he answered, 'We'd better get back into the theatre, then.' As Dora went to walk away, Mike caught her by the arm. 'Come to the house later,' he said urgently.

She met his gaze, inscrutable behind the sunglasses. She knew precisely what it meant. And simply nodded.

Chapter 31

It was late when she drove the Mini along the drive to his house. The light was just going, but the evening air remained hot and heavy. The storm had done little to clear the heat, after all. The heady scent of Nicotiana plants embraced her as she got out of the car. With the palms framing either side of the bungalow, she could have been in the south of France.

She'd managed a quick shower after the rehearsal had finally ground to a halt, had warned her parents she wouldn't be back – and fled before they asked too many questions. She hoped they'd assume she was staying at Millie's again.

She stood for a moment, leaning against the car and enjoying the feel of the silky evening air stroke her bare arms. Her parents knew it was Mike who was directing *Persuasion* but had remained silent on the subject. The channel of communication between her and her parents was twisty and blocked by all kinds of historic rubble. They were expert at ignoring anything they considered unpleasant and, for them, Michael Love definitely fitted into that category.

When her parents had discovered their affair, they'd banned

her from seeing Mike and attending drama club. Dora wasn't sure which hurt the most. Mike and the drama club had been entwined. They'd been Romeo and Juliet to each other, Benedict and Beatrice, Tristan and Isolde. Joe Latham had been nothing if not ambitious in his choice of texts.

Applying to go to drama school had been an escape from the gilded cage her parents had trapped her in. Maybe part of her had thought she'd find Mike in London, but he'd only reappeared on the acting scene when she was in the States and then in a very different sphere to her. Whatever their motives, the various adults in their lives had been very successful in driving – and keeping – them apart.

She looked up as the front door opened. Mike stood, in the inevitable scruffy jeans and loose shirt, with a guarded smile on his face. Whatever anyone had tried to do to keep them apart had, in the strangest way possible, led to this moment. And, even if it was the only time she'd ever have with Mike again, she was determined it would happen. It had been too long.

'Hello Mike,' she said softly and went in, trailing the hot flower scent of the night in her wake.

Chapter 32

The sex was amazing. Of course it was amazing. They'd always known exactly what gave each other the most intense pleasure. When seventeen, stamina, enthusiasm and a willingness to explore had led the way. Now base instinct was layered with experience. It made it a heady delight. Otherworldly; almost transcendental.

They made love throughout the night, their bodies becoming slick with sweat from the heat of their passion. The slid over and around one another, their bodies slippery like seals, until eventually they lay exhausted as the sun hit the sea and shot hazy pink rays across the bed. The cool tones of dawn found them sleepless and wide-eyed at what they'd just created.

It also brought the reality of the moment into sharp focus.

'I ought to go,' Dora said. She swung her legs out of the bed, but paused and turned back to him. 'Long day ahead. And, don't worry, *Persuasion* will be perfect, Mike.' A horrible sort of politeness was strangling her words.

He rolled over, watching her dress. 'Thank you. I want it to be perfect.' There was a long pause and then his tone changed. 'I expect you'll go back to the States afterwards.'

Dora used every ounce of acting skill to answer. 'I expect I will.' She slid her t-shirt over her head and hid her burning face. 'That's where my career is, after all. And I expect you and Kirstie will go back to London.' She concentrated on buttoning her linen trousers. For some reason her fingers had become fumbling and useless.

'I suppose. We've got *The Shrew* on hold. They agreed to delay it until we'd done *Persuasion*.'

'That's great.' She grabbed her bag and hunted inside for her car keys.

'Dora —'

'I need to go,' she said in an over-bright voice. 'It was,' her voice softened, 'It was perfect, Mike. The perfect one-night stand.'

And it had been. It had also been the worst mistake she'd ever made. For now she'd had him again, there was no chance she would ever get him out of her system. 'For old times' sake, eh?' She swung her bag onto her arm.

'Yeah. For old times' sake.' His voice held bitterness.

She'd left before he'd finished the sentence and missed the desolation etched onto his face.

Chapter 33

As rehearsals continued in ragged style, Dora kept her distance from Mike, keeping any interaction with him professional. She couldn't help herself watch avidly as Kirstie pawed at his arm or stood too close. Mike didn't seem to react, but it still created a jealous murder in Dora's heart.

She thought she'd been pretty good at hiding her despair, but a conversation with Ellie suggested otherwise.

'You okay, Dora?' the younger woman asked during a break.

She'd found Dora sitting on a bench in the cobbled square at the front of the theatre. From here you could see both sides of the bay. There was a yacht race in progress and crowds of onlookers were strung along the promenade. Their cheers could be heard against a background of traffic noise from cars squeezing up the narrow lane past the theatre and into town. Berecombe had been getting steadily busier throughout June and was gearing itself up for the season proper when the school holidays began. The hot weather helped. It was turning out to be a record-breaking summer.

Dora looked up and stifled her irritation. She'd hoped for five minutes' peace before the next part of the rehearsal ground on.

'Can I join you?'

Reluctantly, Dora nodded and shifted her bag off the seat next to her.

Ellie spread a hand to the boats curving and surging with the frothy waves out in the bay. 'Isn't it glorious? A perfect seaside day. I expect your friend Millie is busy in her café, isn't she?'

Dora nodded again. For the first time in weeks she longed for a cigarette. She hadn't seen much of Millie in the last few days. The café had been busier and Millie had been seeing a lot of Jed. Besides, Dora hadn't felt like company. Millie was too happy with Jed to have to suffer Dora's angst over Mike.

Ellie dug into her bag and found a plastic lunch box. Fishing out a knife she concentrated on cutting an apple into slices. 'Would you like a bit? I get them from the greengrocer's in the high street. Organic and luscious.'

Dora's mouth watered. She'd been too stressed to eat much recently and was getting painfully thin. 'It looks good,' she admitted and accepted a slice. 'Thank you.' She relented a little. Ellie was too nice a person to bear the brunt of her foul mood. 'And yes, thank you for asking, I'm fine. Just pre-publicity jitters.'

Ellie nodded vigorously and chewed before answering. 'I hear Mike has quite a junket lined up for tomorrow and Friday. You must be used to it, though.'

'I am. I just haven't done any for anything other than *The English Woman* for a while. And,' Dora shrugged her shoulders, 'This all means so much to Mike; I want to get it just right for him.' She accepted another slice of apple. 'Well, for everyone.'

'Know what you mean. Can't believe we're on in a week. It's gone so quickly. Doesn't seem five minutes since that awful read-through.' Ellie shuddered. 'God, I was bad.'

Dora managed a laugh. She relaxed a little. She'd forgotten what good company Ellie could be. 'Tickets have sold well and most of the kids have their entire families coming, so we'll have sympathetic audiences willing us on, at least.'

'Just as well for some of us,' Ellie said through a mouthful of apple. 'Mike says he's directing *The Shrew* next. In London, apparently.'

'So I understand.'

'Talk about going from the sublime to the ridiculous,' Ellie giggled. 'Or I suppose that should be the other way round. I've asked if I can audition for the younger sister. What do you think?'

'Bianca?' Dora turned to her. 'You'd be marvellous,' she said warmly. 'You're made for that part. Go for it.'

'I will, then. I've loved working with Mike. What about you?'

'It's certainly had its moments.'

'Wasn't what I meant. What are you going onto next?'

The urge for nicotine became stronger. Dora took another apple slice instead. 'Oh, you know, back to the States.'

'Thought you might be. *The English Woman* is such a big hit.' Ellie sounded disappointed. 'It's a shame, though. I've loved working with you too. I've learned so much.' She nudged Dora's arm. 'Wish you could stay in the UK, though. You could try for Katherina. Think how much fun we could have.

I can just see you and me as sisters.'

Dora looked resentfully over to where Mike and Kirstie had appeared in the entrance to the theatre. They looked to be in a deep discussion, possibly over the posters advertising the play and which were plastered all over the boards on either side of the door. 'I suppose Kirstie will be AD.'

'Suppose so. They seem a bit of a permanent team, do Mike and Kirstie.'

'That's what I heard.'

'And I'd imagine Kirstie is gagging to get back to the Smoke.' Ellie bit into the last piece of apple with her strong, white teeth. 'Her boyfriend lives there. She must miss him.'

'Boyfriend?' The heat shimmering off the sea dazzled Dora for a second. She shoved her sunglasses further up her nose. 'You mean Mike?'

Ellie stared at her. 'Mike? You're way off the mark there.' She leaned closer and Dora could smell the suntan lotion on her hot skin. 'Don't say a word but our Kirstie has been seeing Phil. The very-married Phil. The very-married-to-someone-else Phil. Mike, much to the disappointment of the single members of the cast, male *and* female, has resisted all known advances. Including mine.'

Dora began to laugh weakly.

'Oi! What's so funny? The idea of me and Mike?'

'I'm sorry, Ellie. Not at all. If anything, I think you're far too nice for him.'

'That's what I think too,' Ellie said, a wicked gleam in her eye. 'So I'm going out with Albie instead. You told me I should be nice to the lighting director.'

'Did I? I'm sure I probably did.' Still laughing, Dora put an arm through Ellie's. 'And it's true, good lighting can make or break your career. And he is rather gorgeous. Lovely skin.' She gazed at Mike, where he was frowning down at Kirstie in much the same way as he would to an annoying but determined wasp. How had she got it so wrong? She felt a little sigh deflate some of the tension inside. However Mike felt about her, at least he hadn't been cheating on somebody else when they'd slept together. At least she knew that.

'Well, you seem more cheerful.' Ellie got up and gathered her things. 'I was beginning to think I'd upset you in some way. I meant what I said, Dora. I've really loved working with you.' Reaching down a hand, she added, 'Come on, time to get back at it.' She rolled her eyes. 'Let's hope Greg isn't too hopeless in the next act.'

Dora looked up, shading her eyes from the bright sun bouncing off the cobbles. 'And I've loved working with you too, Ellie. And thank you for being such a good friend.'

'Me?' Ellie blushed. 'I don't think I've done much, have I?'

'Oh hon, you have no idea.'

Chapter 34

Millie looked around the café terrace with pleasure. She loved an excuse to have a party, not that she really had a reason for this one. It was just that the wonderful weather was continuing, trade was picking up at the café with the summer season getting going. She was happy and wanted her friends around her to celebrate the fact.

Some of her favourite people were here. She still couldn't talk to Biddy and Arthur without grinning and blushing like an idiot. They'd never mentioned anything about any missing clothes, so she was doing her best to forget all about what had happened at the picnic. Tessa had brought Ken and their two younger boys and Zoe, chilling out from the stress of A levels, was holding onto boyfriend Sean as if she never wanted to let him go.

Millie had done the rounds with the first few bottles of wine and now, happy that everyone had something to drink, was content to let Clare take over with the trays of canapés.

Dora had brought some of the cast of *Persuasion* over too. Millie had warmed to Ellie immediately when introduced to her and new boyfriend Albie. She thought Greg was a big likeable bear of a man and even didn't mind Kirstie too much. Millie thought she could love the world now that she and Jed were back together.

Life, she'd decided, was definitely too short to hold a grudge – or to mistrust people. Jed had made a mistake, admittedly a big one, but it was time to move on.

Who was she kidding when she said there was no excuse for this party? Thinking back over the exquisite night she and Jed had spent together, Millie thought she had the very best of reasons to celebrate. She watched him talking to Dora. He had on his pink shirt and white jeans again and her heart swelled with love and tenderness for him. Dora was looking equally spectacular in a lime-green halter-neck sundress. They were flirting slightly in the way beautiful people do. Relaxed in the knowledge there was no chance of it ever developing into anything.

'Hi Millie.'

'It was Mike.'

'Hello Mikey, I mean Mike.' Millie beamed at him. Now she was happy she wanted everyone else to be so too. 'Have you got a drink? Something to eat? The teriyaki beef cups are very good.'

Mike laughed. 'Already had some and they were.' He held up his glass. 'And this is some of your punch. It's delicious. Homemade?'

'Of course.' Millie batted her eyelashes. 'Although I have to confess to it being Clare's idea. She thought a melon and cucumber punch with lots of mint would be just the thing on a hot summer's night.'

'And she'd be right.'

'There's something alcoholic if you prefer. Prosecco and wine, or a lager?'

'I'll stick to the punch thanks, seeing as it's so good.'

Millie followed Mike's gaze to where Jed and Dora were still chatting. 'They make a gorgeous couple, don't they?'

'Yup.'

'You've been making my friend work far too hard,' Millie complained. 'I've hardly seen her lately.'

Mike nodded. 'The press stuff took hours. I've a lot to thank Dora for. She brought in journalists from all over the place. International as well as local. We got some television coverage too.' He shook his head in disbelief. 'It was amazing. *She* was amazing. She did most of the interviews. On the second day she was at it for over nine hours solid. No break, except for a quick coffee. I've never seen anyone work so hard.'

'Dora always knew how to work hard,' Millie agreed. 'It's funny because if you didn't know her very well, you wouldn't think that of her at all. She gives off this flippant, don't-care attitude.' Millie gave Mike a sharp look. 'If you take her at face value, you'd think she doesn't care about anything or anyone at all. Just breezes through life. But when she commits, she really commits one hundred per cent.'

Mike didn't answer. Instead he turned to the sunset.

In the west a vivid patch of orange glowed as the sun nudged the sea. The sky lowered indigo over clouds streaked with crimson zig-zags. It had been yet another hot day.

'It's so beautiful here,' he said so softly that Millie hardly heard him. 'I expect Dora will miss it when she goes back to the States.'

His misery was so acute that Millie longed to tell him the truth. But she'd given Dora her word that she wouldn't reveal what had happened to *The English Woman*. Besides, she had no idea what Dora planned to do, she hadn't mentioned anything lately. Millie wondered if she'd go to Italy but, for all she knew, Dora might return to LA. Surely she'd still be in demand. And, however lovely, Millie certainly didn't think Berecombe would be enough for Dora, especially in the winter when the town hibernated. But she wanted to give Mike a crumb of comfort, some encouragement. Dora and Mike together had the air simmering with an unspoken and urgent passion. Dora had had a few casual boyfriends in the States but she'd never talked about anyone being serious. Had always batted off any teasing questions with the claim she worked too hard to have a relationship. Was it possible she'd only ever truly loved Mike? And looking at his face now, Millie was certain Mike was completely and utterly in love with Dora.

But she'd promised Dora she wouldn't say anything.

'Dora seems to be happy working on *Persuasion*,' she lied. 'I can't wait to see it.'

'Yeah.' Mike looked at his feet.

'Um. I expect it makes a difference to be on a stage when she's been used to working in television.' Millie hadn't the faintest idea what the differences were but she'd heard Dora mention the two types of acting involved slightly different skills.

Mike remained silent and concentrated on his punch.

'Help me out here, Mike.' Millie muttered through gritted

teeth. 'Oh Ellie,' she said brightly as the girl joined them. 'What can I get you?'

'I'd love another glass of punch. It's delicious, Millie.'

'Thank you. Here you go.' Millie topped up her glass.

'Fab. Lovely evening,' Ellie said. 'I'm getting a bit nervy about opening night,' she said to Mike, 'But can't wait to get it before a live audience. Always get that itchy-feet feeling when you know it's ready.'

'Glad you think it's ready,' he answered.

'Couldn't be anything else with you at the helm,' she replied loyally. 'And Dora is going to be the absolute star turn.'

All three watched as Dora laughed at something Jed said. She flipped her long hair over a bare shoulder and the dying rays of the sun turned it gold. She looked every inch the star.

Mille felt Mike shift beside her. 'I expect Dora is thinking about what to do next,' she blurted out, desperately. 'In her career, I mean.'

'Well, I know what I'm doing next, thanks to this gorgeous man.' Ellie slipped a hand through Mike's arm.

Mike nodded abruptly.

'And I know what Dora's plans are. She told me. She's off back to the States as soon as *Persuasion* is over. Can't blame her. Most of us dream of making it big in Hollywood. She'd be a fool not to go back.' Ellie sighed. 'Just wish I could have persuaded her to stay for a little longer.'

Mike's mouth tightened and a slight flush bloomed under his suntanned skin. Millie's heart sank. So Dora really was going back to America and not even this man was enough to make her stay. She watched as Dora turned to Mike and made eye contact then, to Millie's dismay and frustration, he turned on his heel and headed to the beach without saying a word.

Chapter 35

It was late and the party was in its dying embers. Most people had left, leaving a few sitting on the terrace drinking the last of the wine.

Dora sat with Millie, their chairs facing the low wall, which looked over the beach and the sea beyond. It was a still, humid night. Even the sea was quiet, with just a hazy moon decorating it with a tranquil silver path.

Dora swung her legs from out of their position propped on the wall and poured the rest of a bottle of Prosecco into their glasses.

'Lovely party, Mil.' She watched, amused, as her friend tore her eyes away from Jed and focussed on the conversation.

'Yes, it has been, hasn't it?'

'How's it going?'

Millie picked up her glass. 'How's what going?' she said, deliberately misunderstanding.

Dora put her feet back up onto the wall and nudged Millie's bare toes. 'Don't come the innocent with me. How's it going with you and Jed?'

Millie grinned and shifted back on her chair, stretching

her arms above her. 'Let's just say matters are developing in the most satisfying way.'

'Looks like it.' Dora's eyebrows rose. She glanced over to where Jed was chatting to Tessa and her husband. 'Can't say I blame you. I'm becoming very fond of him too. Mind you, when I chatted to him earlier all he could talk about was you. The man's obsessed.'

'Quite right too,' Millie said and sipped her fizz with a smug grin.

'And the business side of things?'

'We're just beginning talks. Arthur knows a solicitor who's going to draft up some details. I want to make sure I've got it absolutely right and I'm not rushing into anything.'

'Sounds sensible, hon. What's the plan, then?'

'Well, we'll see this season through. Close over the winter and get the refurb started then.'

'Emilia Fudge closing her beloved Millie Vanilla's? Never heard the like. How will Berecombe cope?'

'Ha ha. I suspect Berecombe will cope by flocking to Blue Elephant. Don't tease. It's a big gamble for us to close completely.' Millie sighed. 'Can't see how else we're going to get the work done, though. Jed's got some amazing ideas for the café and the only way we can do them is by closing down.'

Dora noticed the use of 'us' but didn't comment. 'Didn't mean to tease, Mil. Hey, I'm just glad things have worked out. For one of us, at least.' She clinked her glass against Millie's. 'You go, girlfriend. I'll make sure I'm back for the big launch.'

'You'd better be,' Millie said, warmly. 'Ah Dora, do you have to go back to the States?'

'It's where the work is, honeybun.'

Millie took a deep breath and then launched in. 'Couldn't you stay a while longer, though? Ellie was saying earlier that, um, Mike's doing *The Taming of the Shrew* next. There could be a part for you. And you did say *The English Woman* isn't going to made any more.' Millie trailed off. Dora had gone very still and tense.

'There could still be work for me,' she replied in a tight voice.

'But there could be work here for you too. Well, not here in Berecombe, obviously, but maybe in London. With Ellie and Mike. You've been saying how much you like working with Ellie. And Mike.'

'It's not that simple, Millie.'

'I can't see why,' Millie persisted.

'Will you leave it?' Dora hissed. 'Just fucking leave it.'

Millie stared at Dora in shock. She was ashen. Millie leaned closer. In the flickering light given off by the fat candles they'd placed along the wall she could see she was close to tears. 'Dora Bartlett, I've known you since we were four and a half. It's obvious you're unhappy. Deeply unhappy and, if I'm not very much mistaken, have been unhappy for ages. What's wrong?'

Dora dashed a hand across her eyes. She was silent for a long time. 'Everything,' she said eventually, in a strangled voice. 'Everything's wrong and the only way I can cope with it is by getting away. As far away as possible.'

Millie put a hand on her arm. 'Is it Mike?'

'Of course it's Mike.' It came out on a jagged, drawn-out

breath. 'It's always been Mike.'

Millie shunted her chair nearer and put her arm around Dora's shoulders. 'Oh, my lovely. Do you still love him?'

'Of course I do. I've never stopped,' Dora wailed.

Millie gathered her up in her arms and rocked her, soothed her as if she was a baby. Dora didn't cry. It was worse. She trembled in Millie's arms and whimpered quietly like a wounded animal. Millie didn't say anything, just held her until the storm passed.

After a while, Dora shook herself off, hunted in the pocket of her dress for a tissue and wiped her eyes. 'Sorry,' she mumbled.

'What for?'

'Going all soppy on you.' Dora blew her nose, becoming more Dora-like. 'It's just I've held it in for so long. I haven't told anyone.'

'Not even him?'

'Especially not him.'

'Why?'

'Because he's moved on, Millie. Like they do. Like men do. We love them and I don't think we ever stop. Not truly. Not even when the relationship's over. They still hold onto a little piece of our hearts, which we can't give to anyone else.' She shrugged. 'Men are different. They compartmentalise. They have work. They have sex. Then they're biologically programmed to move onto the next conquest.'

'You can't mean that?' Millie said, appalled. 'That's just not true, Dora.'

Dora screwed up the tissue into a ball. 'That's what it's

always seemed like to me,' she said mutinously.

'Is that how Mike's been? I can't believe it.'

'Well, he's been professional. Distant but professional.'

'Apart from when you two had sex, I presume?'

Another pause. 'How did you guess?' Dora concentrated very hard on the shifting blackness of the sea.

'Wasn't tricky,' Millie said, drily.

'We have slept together,' Dora admitted. 'But it was a one-night stand.' She gave a sigh that seemed to come from deep within. 'It was wonderful, but it was just a one-off.' She shook her head a little and lifted her chin. 'Won't happen again.'

Millie thought back to how she'd witnessed Mike look at Dora. Hungrily. Desperately. As if he was having what he most desired ripped away. He hadn't the face of a disinterested man. Anything but. 'Are you sure he doesn't feel the same?'

Dora nodded miserably. 'He's never given me any reason to think otherwise. So I think it's just best to cut my losses and go back to LA. I haven't got a future here,' she added in a hollow voice.

In a dark corner of the terrace, where the candles had long since sputtered out, came the harsh sound of a chair being scraped across concrete.

As Dora and Millie looked around, they could just make out the silhouette of a tall man get up and walk away in the direction of the promenade. As he neared the first of the streetlights, it picked up on his white linen shirt and dark, unruly hair.

Mike.

Dora and Millie stared at one another.

Millie reached out a comforting hand again. 'You okay? Think he heard anything?'

'I think it might be more a case of how *much* he heard.' Dora's eyes were wide with horror. 'How long has he been sitting there?'

'I don't know, my lovely.' Millie stared out to where Mike was striding along the prom. 'I don't know.'

Chapter 36

The day of the final dress rehearsal dawned predictably hot. The heatwave continued unabated. Grass had long since frizzled to a dull yellow, the media was hysterical about the threat of a water shortage and people had given up watching the weather forecast; they took it for granted it would be another hot and dry day. With the exception of the recent thunderstorm, no rain had fallen for weeks.

As Dora walked along the promenade, it was already getting warm. A sluggish breeze came in off the sea, but not enough to dispel the heat haze that hung low and heavy. Sea and sky merged into a blurred, blue-ish grey and it looked as if someone had tried to rub them out with a dirty eraser.

She and Millie had continued to drink after the party had wound up and she had, once again, slept over at Millie's flat. She was feeling rubbed out and blurry herself. Being hung over probably wasn't the ideal state in which to deal with such a crucial day at work but Dora consoled herself that it would dull the pain of seeing Mike.

She squeezed through the photographers hanging around the theatre entrance – since the publicity had gone out there had been a few dogging her steps – and went inside. The little theatre was alive with people. She stood for a minute, letting her eyes adjust to the lack of light. It was quite a contrast to the sunny, straightforwardly touristy day outside. Taking off her sunglasses she surveyed the scene, breathing in the adrenaline of the day before a show went on. Nowhere smelled quite like theatre, Dora thought. The close, almost dusty smell, underlain with a whiff of perspiration, panic and the legacy of productions past.

Hammering came from the stage as an adjustment was made to the proscenium. Albie was on a ladder, swearing volubly as he adjusted a gel on one of the lights. Marie, the wardrobe mistress, jogged past, her arms full of tailcoats, her mouth full of pins.

The realisation of how much she loved it all hit Dora with a blow straight to the solar plexus. How could she ever go back to the glitzy and hard-nosed world of American television? She had the unpretentious grime of theatre dust under her nails now. It was all she wanted. But, if she thought getting another TV role in the States was going to be hard, getting a stage role would be nigh-on impossible.

'Better get yourself into costume,' Kirstie called as she hurried past, the inevitable mobile in her hand. 'Beginners at literally nine-thirty sharp.'

'And so it begins,' Dora murmured. She had a broken heart. This might be the only time she acted in a theatre for the foreseeable future. She was sick with nerves and a residual craving for a cigarette. Despite all this, she gave Kirstie a huge grin and made her way to her dressing room.

Chapter 37

It was only after the interval that things began to unravel. Coming out of the dressing room she shared with Ellie, Dora overheard a raised voice coming from the room next door. It was Greg.

'Mike, I can't do it.'

There was a muffled answer.

'No! God Mike, I know you've tried every which way but look at me. Look at me! I'm a wreck. If I go on, I'll just let everyone down. I'll let you down.'

There came another quiet response, she assumed from Mike.

Dora hesitated, wondering how she could help. Just as she was about to knock on the door to say how good she thought Greg had been in the first act, the door flew open and he strode out.

He barged past her and disappeared along the dimly lit corridor. Mike appeared at the doorway and stopped when he saw Dora.

She caught his gaze. His face was pinched with tension. 'Who's his understudy?'

'Josh,' Mike said, without preamble.

'Shit.' Josh was one of the amateurs. Talented and keen but inexperienced. 'Do you think he's up to it?'

Mike shrugged. He sagged against the wall suddenly and put his face in his hands. 'I've let everyone down, haven't I?'

'You're not Greg.'

He looked at her, 'But I was the one who took a gamble on him. And I was the one who was stupid enough to put a beginner in as his understudy. How egotistical does that make me? Being so over-confident that there wouldn't be a problem. And no, to answer your question, I don't think Josh will be up to it and I don't want to force him into that position.'

'Well, there's only one thing for it.'

'And that is?'

'You know the words. You do it.'

Chapter 38

Some initial nervy mistakes apart, with Mike as Wentworth, the cast gelled better. To Dora's relief. She could sense them willing the production to be a success. Willing Mike to be a success. Their deep regard for their director was palpable. The faith and confidence went both ways, it seemed.

Acting with Mike again made Dora's heart sing with joy. It was like putting your aching foot into a comfortable slipper after suffering killer heels all day. She hadn't realised how insecure she'd been when acting opposite Greg. Her acting muscles relaxed and her performance began to sing too.

The second half flew by and, almost too soon, they came to the other crucial scene in the play: the one with Wentworth's letter. It had been directed so that Anne was stage front, holding the letter and staring into the auditorium. Mike said he wanted every reaction nuanced on her face and signposted to the audience. 'It's where Anne gets her reward for being faithful and good,' he'd explained. The small party at the apartment in the White Hart, Mrs Musgrove, Mrs Croft and Harville were in freeze-frame behind her. Wentworth stood, slightly off-centre and spotlit.

When Mike began to speak, Dora thought her heart would wrench itself in two.

'You pierce my soul. I am half agony, half hope. Tell me not that I am too late ...'

With difficulty, Dora controlled her breathing. A sob erupted and she stifled it. Do not lose control, she implored herself, silently. It was the hardest thing she'd ever done. The words were Wentworth's, via the genius pen of Jane Austen, but the raw emotion was Mike's alone.

'I offer myself to you again with a heart even more your own, than when you almost broke it eight years and a half ago.' Mike's voice splintered with emotion. 'I have loved none but you ...'

Dora squeezed shut her eyes. Tears streamed down her face and every particle of her being wanted to turn around and take him in her arms. She'd always known Mike to be a consummate actor, but it was almost as if he really meant the words. The rawness in his voice was too much to bear.

She was desperate to stop, to take time to collect her thoughts, get her performance back on track. There was no way she could interrupt the rehearsal. She owed it to the rest of them to keep going. So she did.

When it was finally all over, there was no opportunity to speak to Mike. After the briefest of a curtain call practice, he'd immediately been mugged by a fretful Kirstie.

Ellie approached her, an anxious look on her face. 'Do you think Greg will be back for the first night?'

Dora watched from the stage as Mike, still in his Regency sea captain's uniform, disappeared upstairs to the offices,

Kirstie hot on his heels.

'I don't know, Ellie.' She glanced at her and put a comforting arm around her shoulders. 'In some ways it would be better if he didn't.'

Chapter 39

'Poor Greg,' Millie said. 'He must really have been going through hell.'

Dora, fractious with first-night nerves, had risen after a sleepless night and was sitting with Millie and Jed on the café's terrace. It promised to be another sticky, overcast day and Dora could feel a film of sweat forming on the back of her neck already.

'Yeah, Mike sent a text round last night to say Greg had officially pulled out of the show. He's gone home to be with his wife.'

Millie tutted. 'Poor man. He's so nice too.'

Dora nodded. 'He is. And, even though I sound like a queen bitch for saying it, it's a much better play with Mike as Wentworth. I think we're all quite relieved, to be honest.'

'No team can operate properly knowing there's a weak link at its core,' Jed put in.

'You're absolutely right,' Dora agreed. 'Think that's been the problem all along. It's been such a difficult rehearsal period.'

'And how did, Josh, is it, take the news that he wouldn't

be getting his big break and step in as Greg's understudy?' asked Millie.

Dora grinned. 'More relief. Turned out he hadn't learned all the lines.'

'Ouch.' Millie winced. 'Mistake.'

'Big mistake, but if he wants to get anywhere in the theatre, it's one he'll learn from.'

'What about the funding? Phil isn't really going to pull out, is he?' Jed asked. 'You mentioned the other night it was dependent on Greg being in it.'

'No.' Dora shook her head and grinned. 'He had, shall we say, someone very persuasive who had a word.'

'Thank goodness for that.' Millie breathed out a sigh. 'So, you're all set up for the first night? I can't wait to see Mike as Wentworth. I bet he looks a dream in a pair of breeches.'

'You're not wrong there, Mil.' Despite all the uncertainties of the last few hours, Dora couldn't help but agree.

'Oh and I can't wait to see you too, of course,' Millie added hastily, catching sight of Jed's jealous face. 'From everything I've heard, it's going to be a hit. A palpable hit.'

'Wrong play, honeybun.'

'What do you mean?' Millie flapped her hands at Dora. 'Oh, get on with you, as Biddy might say.' She stood up. 'Seeing as my literary pretensions are being scoffed, I shall stick to what I'm good at and get us something to drink. Tea or lemonade, people?'

'Lemonade please,' Jed and Dora chorused.

'Lots of ice?'

'God, yes please,' Jed said with feeling.

'Consider it done.' Millie turned on her heel. 'I shall exit pursued by a bear. I know, I know,' she put up her hands as she went. 'Another wrong play.'

Dora regarded her friend fondly. 'Love you, Mil,' she called. 'Even if you don't know your Shakespeare from your Austen.'

'Think you'll find my Emilia has other skills, and many of them,' Jed defended stoutly and then grimaced as he tugged at the collar of his polo shirt. 'Why, when it's hot in the UK does it always get so humid?'

'They've warned it could get to the high eighties today, although you never notice how hot it is when you're inside the theatre.' Dora smiled. 'I know what you mean, though, just wish it would break. And that's coming from someone who hates thunderstorms! Still, I suppose it's good for business.' Shading her eyes, she looked out to the beach, where, even at this early hour, families were setting up camp. 'What's with this new trend for tents on the beach?'

Jed shrugged. 'Beats me,' he said on a laugh. 'Maybe it's somewhere to get out of the sun.'

'Here we go,' Millie brought back a tray of glasses and a jug rattling with chunks of ice. 'Oh hello,' she said brightly as a man and a woman walked onto the terrace. 'I'm terribly sorry but we're not open for another hour.'

Jed shot to his feet. 'Alex,' he cried. 'You got here okay. And Ma!'

The tall, elegantly lean man grinned. 'Hi, little bro. Thought we'd come over and see what all the fuss is about Berecombe.' He pushed up his horn-rimmed specs. 'After all, you seem to spend an inordinate amount of time here. I can't begin to imagine what the attraction is.'

The brothers man-hugged and then Jed took the woman's hand and led her forward. 'Dora, Millie, that streak of skinny bacon is my brother Alexander and this,' he paused for unnecessary dramatic effect and seemed nervous, 'Is my mother, Vanessa. Ma, this is Millie.'

The woman nodded coolly at Millie then did a double-take. 'Oh, but surely you're Theodora Bart?'

'I am.' Dora got to her feet. 'Delighted to meet you.' She held out a hand and the older woman took the very tips of her fingers in the barest gesture of a social handshake. 'I'm afraid I ought to go.' She looked from Jed to his mother and then to Millie and felt uncomfortable. Meeting the parents for the first time and especially meeting the *mother* of the man you were in love with, should be a private affair. 'We open *Persuasion* tonight. Lots of last minute things to do,' she lied.

'Of course. Alex and I passed the theatre on our drive through town. Jed told me about your little production.'

'Determined not to rise to the bait, Dora gave a show-biz smile instead. 'I'd say do come and see it but we're sold out tonight.'

'Oh, I'm sure I can pull a few strings.' Vanessa smiled glacially. 'And, after all, it's hardly the West End, is it?'

This was too much. Dora felt a twinge of concern for Millie. Jed's mother was a bitch. 'Hardly.' She matched the woman's icy expression. 'It's *so* much more important than that. I do hope you manage to get a ticket.' She turned to Alexander. 'Sorry to say hi and bye. I'm sure we'll be seeing more of you if you're staying in the area.'

'That would be delightful.' He gave an old-fashioned bow.

'Sorry to have to go, Mil. Jed. Laters, honeybuns.'

As Dora left, she could hear Millie offering everyone lemonade or some cinnamon toast and relaxed a little. She'd felt guilty leaving her alone with Jed's mother; the woman was obviously difficult. But still, Millie would win her over. There was no one alive who didn't love Millie, was there?

Chapter 40

Millie hopped from foot to foot and wished she'd remembered to put a brush through her hair that morning. She lifted it off her neck in a nervous gesture. 'Are you sure I can't get any of you anything?'

'I'd love some of that lemonade,' Alex said. 'It looks just the thing for a hot day like today.'

Grateful to be given something to do, Millie beamed at him, only to see him blink shyly behind the heavily framed glasses in return.

'Oh do sit down, Alexander, for heaven's sake. You're making me even hotter by hovering there,' Vanessa snapped.

'Yes mother.' Deflated, Alex sat, his long frame bent almost double on one of Millie's outside chairs.

'We can't tempt you to some, Ma?' Jed asked. 'Millie makes it herself.'

Vanessa eyed the jug and its creamy yellow contents with distaste. 'I'm avoiding sugar at the moment, as you well know, Jeremy.'

'Well, I'll have some as it's completely delicious.' He poured himself a generous glassful and winked at Millie as she slid into a chair next to Alex.

'Actually, I'm very careful to add only the minimum of sugar,' she began.

'So this is where you've been spending all your time, Jeremy?' His mother interrupted and regarded the café with a baleful glare.

Millie wished, not for the first time, that the full refurbishment had already gone ahead.

'I must say, I rather hoped it would be more like Hix or at least along the lines of that charming place at Burton Bradstock. That's so chic.' She smiled at Millie, but it didn't reach her glacially blue eyes. Like a predator sensing the weakest member of the herd, she turned on Jed. 'And *this* is what you hope to invest in?'

Jed tried to look unfazed. 'Yes, Ma.'

'*This* is what you've given up your consultancy work for?'

'I thought you'd be pleased I'd finally found what I want to do. And this *is* what I want to spend the rest of my life doing.' Jed sounded mystified. 'I don't understand. You thought it was a good idea when we talked on the phone.'

'But really, Jeremy. This place? It's hardly more than a greasy spoon.'

Millie jumped up. No one, *no one* insulted her café. 'Excuse me, Millie Vanilla's is a lot more than a greasy spoon. Not that there's anything wrong in that,' she added hotly. 'I cook all my food myself and use the best, locally sourced organic produce.' She drew herself up. 'And I'd be happy to prove how good my food is.' She held out one of the laminated cards that served as a menu and wished it wasn't so dog-eared. 'If you'd like to choose something? Specials are changed daily and are on the blackboard. Feel free to go inside and have a look.'

Alex stood too. 'I'm sure Mother didn't mean any offence.' He glared down at her, the dull light glinting on his glasses. 'Did you, Ma?'

It seemed to check Vanessa. She got up. 'Of course I didn't, Millie,' she trilled. 'Please don't think that. It's just that it's so very different to what Jeremy had led me to expect. And, if he's planning on investing rather a large sum of money, I felt it best to check it out beforehand.' She gave a tight smile. 'And I have. So lovely meeting you, Millie, my dear.' She took her eldest son's arm. 'Alexander, I'm very warm. Could you take me back to Lyme Regis now please? I think I'd like to have a cold drink before we go out to lunch.' She twisted her mouth at the jug of lemonade. 'One without quite so much sugar.'

Alex gave Millie an apologetic look. She had the strong impression he often stepped in as peace-maker. He pulled a face at Jed and led his mother away.

Millie collapsed onto the chair opposite Jed. She was too furious to remain standing.

Jed stared out to where a row had broken out between two families vying for the same tiny patch of beach. A pulse was beating in his cheek.

'Well?' Millie demanded.

He scuffed his deck shoes on the sandy concrete. 'She's a bitch.'

Millie relaxed a little. 'I'm glad you said it. I couldn't really insult your mother, having only just met her.'

Jed traced a trail of lemonade down the outside of his glass. Staring at his sticky finger he licked it moodily and then blew out a long breath. 'She isn't always like that. It's just she's a bit prickly about me giving up my job and,' he hesitated and then looked Millie straight in the eyes, 'She's obviously not very happy about me investing in the café.'

'I rather gathered that.' Millie's mouth twitched. 'It's almost funny, when you think about it, isn't it? I don't think I've ever met anyone who was such a blatant snob. Sorry,' she added, 'I know she's your mum, but she really is.'

'I know.' Jed stared morosely at the pattern his shoes had made on the floor.

'Still, if I agree to you investing, although it would be nice to have your mother's approval, it's not the end of the world if she doesn't.'

Jed shifted uncomfortably again. 'The thing is, Mil. That's the problem.' He glanced up out of troubled eyes.

'What do you mean?' Millie had a horrible feeling what he was about to say wasn't going to be good news. She edged onto the rim of her chair, her heart thumping. 'Is there something you haven't told me, Jed?' Her voice went very hard. 'Is there something else you've lied to me about?'

Chapter 41

'What?'

Millie jumped up and began pacing back and forth across the terrace. She put her hands to her ears, as if to massage in what she'd just heard. 'No,' she said, shaking her head. 'Tell me again.'

Jed dropped his chin to his chest in frustration. 'I only have a little spare cash at the moment,' he began. 'What with Blue Elephant not paying me the full fee as I didn't complete the contract and, oh, I don't know, it's quite expensive living down here.'

Millie stopped pacing and glared down at him. She thought about the expensive dates he'd taken her on and felt a twinge of guilt. She'd be happy with just a bag of chips on the beach. As long as they were together. 'Well, it's only expensive if you let it be. What about your car?'

'Well, I took over the lease on that.' He shrugged. 'I needed something to get around in.'

'And it didn't occur to you to buy something older? Cheaper?'

'False economy. I need something reliable.'

Millie sat down again. 'And this money, the money you planned on investing in Millie Vanilla's, it's held in an account?'

'Yes.'

'And what, you get an allowance from it or something?'

Jed shook his head. 'It's not quite an allowance. The money was from Dad's family. It went into a trust for us. We've been getting a smallish sum every year and get the remainder when we're thirty-five.'

'Sounds like an allowance to me,' Millie said drily. 'But what has your mother got to do with it? I still don't understand.' Millie screwed up her face. 'Funnily enough, it's not a problem I've ever had to deal with.'

Jed sighed and then went on patiently. 'I have to go to Ma's accountant and give him an idea of what I plan to spend the money on. That is, the money you're calling an allowance. I can't access the lump sum at all until I'm of age.'

'Okay,' Millie said, slowly.

'The problem is, if he thinks I'm being too extravagant or splashing out on something he thinks Ma wouldn't approve of, he passes it to her. She gets the final say and she won't agree the bank transfer if it's something she doesn't approve of.'

'So that's why she came today. To see whether I'm a good investment?' Millie gave a harsh laugh. 'I think we know the answer. She spread her hands helplessly. 'I thought all your wealth came from your job?'

Jed had the grace to look embarrassed. 'It does. It did. But, you know what they say, you spend up to what you earn. The job gave me spending money, but I knew I could always back it up with some from the trust. As long as Ma approved.'

'Oh my God!' Millie sat back, her palms to her cheeks, a horrified expression on her face. 'I've just realised what you are.'

'What do you mean, *what I am?*' said Jed, irritably.

'You're a trust-fund kid.'

'And you wonder why I was reluctant to tell you, Millie? You made your feelings very clear about this sort of thing when we were on the beach that day.'

'I did. And you could have told me then, couldn't you?' Jed didn't answer. 'You've never really had to work for anything, have you?'

'I worked, Millie,' he said tightly. 'I worked damn hard and I was good at it.'

'But you didn't have to. You could have lived off this trust, couldn't you?'

He blew out an exasperated breath. 'But I didn't. Both Alex and I work.'

'But you didn't really *need* to,' Millie persisted. 'You've never really known what it's like not to have money, have you? Or to live under the threat of not having any.' She paused and then went on, 'There have been times I didn't know how I was going to pay the electricity bill, the business rates, or whether I had enough to pay my suppliers at the end of the month. You've never known what that feels like, have you?'

'No. Not exactly.' Jed kicked at a pebble. 'Of course I haven't, Millie! But what's this got to do with anything?'

'It's the whole point. Whatever you've wanted you've bought. Be it a holiday or the latest fashionably expensive watch.'

'Jeez, we're not back to that argument, are we?'

'Yes, maybe we are.' Millie sat back and gazed at him sadly. 'I nearly let you into my life completely. I nearly let you invest in my business. My livelihood.'

Jed reached out and took her hands in his. 'And I still can, Millie. We could do marvellous, wonderful things with the café. It could be the next Hive Beach Café, if that's what you want it to be.'

Millie eased her hands from his. 'And what would happen when we hit a rough patch, Jed?' she said gently. 'When trade isn't so good. When the profit margins are down. Blue Elephant is still a threat. It could wipe me out completely. What would you do then? When you couldn't buy that four hundred-pound jacket you'd set your heart on, or when you told yourself you needed a newer car? I couldn't run my life, or my business, knowing you were running to your mother and asking for the next allowance.'

'Do you really still think me so shallow?'

Millie was silent for a moment. Then she said, 'I don't know, Jed. Maybe that's the problem. We still don't know one another well enough. Maybe we're rushing into something too quickly.'

'I love you.'

Millie felt tears threaten. 'I know you do.' In a strangled voice she added, 'And I love you, but I'm not sure it's enough.'

'I can't believe you're saying this. How can I prove myself to you? What can I do to make myself worthy of you?' He blew out a frustrated breath. 'Am I ever going to be good enough for you? Am I ever going to reach your sky-high standards?'

Millie felt a pang of guilt. He looked so desperately unhappy. But how could she trust her business to someone who had never fought as hard as she'd had to? How could she trust *herself* to him? And then there was his mother.

She took his hands back into hers. 'Everything inside me, every pore of my being wants to be with you. Believe that, Jed. But every time I let myself, something seems to get in the way. Your mother turning up today, for instance.'

'I'll get a business plan together to show Ma. I'll convince her it's a sound investment.'

Millie shook her head. 'But she'd never really accept me, would she? To her I'd always be the reason you threw away a promising career. In her eyes the café would be the thing you'd squandered your inheritance on. And if it made a loss or closed down – and those are very real dangers, Jed, then she really would never forgive me. Or, more importantly, you. And I could never come between you and your mother.' She swallowed, her throat aching with unshed tears. 'You only get one of those in a lifetime.'

Jed stood up. He pushed a frustrated hand through his hair. 'You are the most stubborn, pig-headed woman I've ever met.' He softened the words with a short laugh. 'Most of the girls I've dated actually see my money as a bit of a bonus. I dare say a lot of them have only gone out with me because I was wealthy. But you, *you* Emilia Fudge, can only see it as this insurmountable barrier. That it makes me some feckless youth who can't budget and has no idea of the cost of anything, or even what hard work is.' He sat down, deflated and took her hands again. 'And you know what? I'm not going to give up on you. On us. I'm going to prove I'm worthy of you. I have absolutely no idea what I'm going to do but I'll bloody well do it. You'll see.' He gave an impish grin. 'And now seems the best time to start.'

Millie sat and watched as Jed's tall figure dipped in and out of the crowds as he strode along the promenade. Had she done the right thing? Was Jed really capable of working alongside her, or would he blow the first month's takings on some luxury, some frippery? Her heart shifted. So this is what happened when you dared open your heart. She wished she could just run away. From everything. She put her head in her hands. 'Why couldn't it all be simple?' she moaned.

She was still there when Clare arrived for her shift.

Chapter 42

Dora clutched Mike and Ellie's hands as they took yet another curtain call. It was the third time the cast had been brought back onto the stage. The dusty little theatre was alive with excited pleasure. Dora was shaking and delirious with adrenaline. There was nothing like the magic of theatre and the first night had gone better than any of them had expected.

She blinked hard as flash bulbs popped as the press photographers went into a frenzy. The audience rose to their feet, clapping and cheering. Before she knew it, the other actors backed away and left her and Mike to take a bow on their own. Mike raised Dora's hand to his mouth and kissed it, sending the audience into raptures.

'Kiss her', someone shouted from the front stalls. 'Kiss her properly!'

Mike, high on the night's success and a wicked look lighting his blue eyes, drew her to him. 'Thank you,' he mouthed. 'Thank you so much.'

Dora shook her head a little. She began to reply, but his lips crushed hers and the noise hit the roof as the crowd roared its approval.

He set her down again and they grinned inanely at one another.

'Don't think this is quite Regency etiquette, Captain Wentworth.'

'Do you think I give a bugger?' he replied and kissed her again. When he released her this time, he whispered against her ear, 'I need to talk to you. Catch you at Millie's party?'

She nodded, too fizzy with relief that the play had gone well to wonder what he wanted.

Then the moment was broken as her hand was grasped by Ellie as the others joined them for one final curtain call.

Chapter 43

Dora cornered Millie on the café's crowded terrace. It was the first time she'd had the chance to speak to her.

The cast had been greeted with cheers from the other guests, who had formed a rowdy arch in their honour. The champagne flowed freely and Dora had drunk just enough to begin to wind down from the whole giddy experience of the first night.

'What's wrong?' she demanded of Millie. 'You've been looking miserable all evening. Is it that bitch? Jed's mother?'

Millie shook her head quickly. And then grimaced. 'No and yes, I suppose.'

Dora sipped her fizz. 'Well, that's as clear as mud, then. Spill.'

Millie filled her in. 'So, I just don't know if Jed and I can have a future together,' she finished.

'Oh hon.' Dora put an arm around her. 'I'm sure you can work something out. You'll teach him the art of money appreciation. So what if he's a trust-fund kid?' When Millie looked unimpressed by the comment, she added, 'Look, you two are meant to be, I just know it. I've never seen a couple more in love.'

'Yeah well, it's not looking good at the moment. Give me that glass.' Millie took the flute off Dora and drained it.

'Slow down, girlfriend. You know you've no head for alcohol.'

'After slaving over you lot for this party, I think I deserve one,' Millie said bitterly. 'And maybe another.'

'You okay, Mil? You don't seem yourself.'

'Lot on my mind. Big decisions to make.' She began to head off inside the café where, courtesy of Phil, a table groaned with food and champagne. She had to come to a halt when Biddy forced her way through the crowd to stand in the middle of the terrace. The woman tapped a teaspoon against her glass, swaying slightly.

'Someone else who's been at the champers,' Dora observed and went to stand with Millie.

'Ladies and gentlemen,' she began, 'I'd like to congratulate you all on a wonderful night.' She turned to Mike and beamed at him, but this being Biddy it was more of a glare. He looked distinctly uncomfortable. 'The Regent Theatre will have a secure future from now on.'

'Did you put her up to this?' Dora hissed to Millie.

Millie shook her head.

'And, my dear friend Joseph Latham would have been very proud of you all.'

Millie turned to Dora in horror. 'You don't think –'

'That old Joe was a client?' Dora giggled. 'Why not!'

'So I'd like to propose a toast. Let us raise our glasses to the Regent Theatre!'

'The Regent Theatre!' everyone chorused, more than a little

drunk and too wary of Biddy not to comply.

The cheers subsided but Biddy hadn't finished with them. A peculiar and very alien expression came over her.

'Don't know about you,' Dora gasped, 'But that coy look doesn't sit well on Biddy's face.' She took Millie's arm for strength.

'As some of you know, Mr Arthur Roulestone and I have become extremely good friends of late. So good, in fact, that he has just made me an offer of marriage.' Biddy paused.

'Did she just simper?' Millie marvelled.

'Did she really think this was the appropriate time and place?' asked Dora.

Biddy apparently did. 'And I accepted!' she continued, on a hiccough. 'So could I propose another toast? To Arthur and Biddy!'

There was a bemused murmur of 'To Arthur and Biddy' and a gentle ripple of applause.

'I'm feeling distinctly queasy,' Millie muttered.

'Too much champagne, hon?'

'Not enough, more like. The image of a nude Biddy and Arthur keeps invading my head. Oh, and she still hasn't finished. How much has she drunk?'

'And,' at this Biddy turned her lighthouse gaze on Millie. 'As no church would probably have me under its roof, I'd like to ask my dear friend Emilia if she would host the wedding party here. We'd like to get married on the beach.'

'She's going to have the dogs as bridesmaids,' Millie said in awe. 'I just know it.'

'And I'd like to have the dogs as attendants,' Biddy rambled on. 'Arthur and I, or should I say my *fiancé* and I,' at this she giggled, 'Are thinking a Christmas wedding would be the thing. So, stir your stumps everyone, now we can get this party really started!'

She was about to say more when Mike materialised at her side. 'Can I be the first to congratulate you and Arthur,' he looked around, 'Wherever he is.'

'If he's got any sense he'll have made his getaway,' snorted Dora. 'In a very fast car. A Christmas wedding? On the beach? With doggy bridesmaids? And here's me thinking I'd left the LA lunacy behind.'

Mike was still speaking and trying to usher Biddy to one side. 'And thank you for those kind words about the theatre. Joe would indeed be proud.' He looked over to Millie. 'Could I add my thanks to Millie for hosting our first night party here.' He grinned when he saw her exhausted face. 'I know there's a one a.m. curfew for parties on the beach, so maybe we should begin to get to our beds. It's been a long day and I, for one, am very weary.'

'He's so lovely,' Millie sighed.

Dora gazed at Mike. She was sure her heart was visible on the outside of her breast and was pulsing red with love, cartoon-like.

He began to encourage guests gently off the terrace and looked back at her. He smiled and the cartoon heart swelled, threatened to pop off and head skywards. 'He certainly is,' she whispered, smiling back at him. 'He certainly is.'

As they moved towards each other, the first fat, hot drops of rain fell.

Chapter 44

The rain and thunderstorm dispersed the party-goers. Even Biddy took herself off, muttering darkly that no one in the town knew how to party properly. Soon the only people left in the café were Millie, Mike and Dora.

Millie took one look at the expression on Mike and Dora's faces, made her excuses and disappeared into the kitchen. She was sure neither had heard her plea that she needed to begin doing the washing up.

Dora sat at the table in the window and watched the rain chase wild dusty patterns in the glass. She flinched as thunder hit hard.

'You never liked thunderstorms, I remember.' Mike joined her and took her hand in his.

'True.' She could hardly breathe at his nearness. Or maybe it was just the stormy atmosphere.

'Dora, can I ask you something?'

She turned to him. The rain had teased his hair into curls. With his sun-darkened skin he looked more the rogue than ever.

He took her chin between tender fingers. 'Will this take your mind off the storm?' he whispered and kissed her.

'Is that what you wanted to ask me?' She said when it was over. She'd hardly noticed the flash of lightning and the thunder that followed. Maybe it had actually happened, or maybe it was the sparkling lights and roar in the blood that invaded her when he kissed her.

He shook his head and smiled. 'Not quite.' He pursed his lips. 'I realise I wasn't meant to hear, that night out on the terrace when you and Millie were talking, but I just have to know.' He gave her the full force of his penetrating gaze. 'I want to know. No,' he corrected himself, 'I *need* to know, if there's a tiny piece of your heart that's still mine?' He took a breath. 'I need to know if you still love me, Dora.'

Dora gasped. He had heard that night, then. She went rigid. 'Why, so you can have a good laugh at my expense when you go back to all your women in London?'

'Dora,' he laughed quietly. 'Dora, my love. Always so prickly. I need to know because I've never stopped loving you.'

The storm began in earnest. Wind hurled rain at the café's windows and a smattering of pebbles whip-cracked against the glass.

Dora didn't move. She focussed on Mike's face. On his blue eyes, so warm and loving. On the mouth she longed to kiss again.

'Those words I say as Wentworth,' he continued, 'They may have been Austen's, but they could be mine. I meant every last one of them. I loved you ten years ago; I love you now. I'll never stop loving you, Dora. Although,' at this, he sat back and rubbed a frustrated hand over his face, 'Sometimes you make it extremely difficult.'

'You never came after me. You must have known where I

was. You never came looking.' It was a croak. It came out of a throat constricted with emotion, swollen with too many unshed tears. Tears she held for him.

Mike gave her an old-fashioned look. 'Your father made it very clear what would be done to me if I ever wanted to see you again. Joe got me out of Berecombe as soon as he could and helped me get into theatre school. I don't know what would have happened if he hadn't.'

A flash of lightning daggered across the café and lit him up. It revealed the lines put around his eyes by laughter, the creases from mouth to nose exaggerated by tiredness, the silver threads in his dark hair. Was it possible he really did love her?

He shrugged wearily. 'Booze took over for a while once I'd got to London.' He glanced at her from under dark lashes. 'I knew you were in the city, I just didn't have the guts to look you up. And, after all, I'd been told you weren't interested any more.' To answer the query in her eyes, he added, 'Your wonderful father again. I rang your home number. Once I'd got myself sober, you'd gone to the States and your dad proved himself right.' He laughed. 'You were definitely out of my league then.'

'I had no idea.'

'I tried your mobile too. No answer.'

'Oh my God,' Dora said slowly. 'Mum and Dad gave me a new one just before I left for Central. They boasted it was top of the range, all set up with the numbers I'd need.'

'Have to hand it to your father, if he's determined to do something, he certainly succeeds.'

'Oh Mike, I didn't know all this, I swear.'

'Why should you know?' Mike shoved a hand through his hair again as a clap of thunder hit the building. 'God Dora, I tried to forget you, I really did. Alcohol, hard work, other women. Nothing did it. When the job came up in Berecombe I could hardly believe it. And when you walked past me in the pub, dressed as a duck, I really thought I was hallucinating, even though I was stone-cold sober.'

Dora winced at the memory. 'You haven't always been very nice to me.'

Mike edged his chair nearer her. Placed a gentle hand on her neck to bring her closer. To kiss again. His eyes were focussed on her lips as if he couldn't look away. 'Self-preservation, my lovely. You haven't exactly been forthcoming with your feelings about me.'

As they kissed again, the storm raged around them, through them, in them. And then quietened into acceptance.

Mike rested his forehead against hers. In the distance, piercing through the sound of the rain, which was still hammering down, a telephone could be heard.

Millie peered around the kitchen door. 'Sorry, you two. I hate to interrupt, but it's Kirstie on the phone for you, Mike. She said she'd tried your mobile but it's dead.'

Dora felt laughter ripple through Mike.

'One day,' he said, 'I'll explain all about Kirstie.'

'Mike, I really hate to do this,' insisted Millie, as they hadn't moved. 'But she said it was urgent. There's something going on at the theatre.' As he shot up, alarmed, she added, 'And don't go along the prom. It's flooded. The local radio's just said we've had a month's rain in an hour.'

Chapter 45

'Oh shit.'

'For once, my darling Dora, I happen to think your language is appropriate.'

Dora went to where Mike was standing in the middle of the theatre, surveying the damage. She put her arms around his waist and willed him some strength. 'I thought the roof had been fixed.'

Mike gave a gutsy sigh. 'Turns out it wasn't only a heating pipe. According to the loss adjustor over there,' he nodded to where a man in a gilet and corduroys was talking into a mobile, 'There was a problem with a gully on the roof. Looks like it's been dodgy for a while. Last night's rain finished it off. And, with the place being right on the seafront, it's been bearing the brunt of every storm for a long time.'

Dora looked around. She could hardly recognise the place from last night. All traces of their triumphant first night had been obliterated. The stage and kitchen had escaped any damage but nearly all the stalls area was completely ruined. Water still dripped despondently from the roof and the smell of wet plaster made her nose itch and her throat close. The

354

first ten or so rows of red velour seats were soaked through and unusable, certainly in the short term. Most were also under heaps of sodden, broken ceiling tiles.

Mike had gone straight to the theatre when he'd left her. He'd insisted he could cope with Kirstie's latest crisis and that she should go home to her parents.

His call that morning had come halfway through her bitter recriminations with them over breakfast. Their reaction to it being Mike on the phone had decided her. Having packed her bag in the night, she'd called Millie and had taken refuge in the flat. Dora wasn't sure if she would ever be able to have any kind of relationship with her parents again.

The horror of the conversation with her parents, though, fled in the face of this. 'Oh Mike,' she said. 'It's awful.' She felt tears threaten. 'All our hard work!'

Some of the others were beginning to trickle in. Maria stood, her mouth open at what she was seeing. Albie was consoling a weeping Ellie and Josh had his arms around Lily. Their shock was palpable.

'Well, there's literally no way we can put a show on tonight.' It was Kirstie, as crisply efficient as ever. 'The place is ruined.'

Mike toed away a wet piece of plaster and agreed. 'Can you get the box office to organise refunds as soon as possible. Oh and try to keep the press out, will you? They love a disaster.'

Dora gazed at them. They had all worked so hard for this. Had endured nerves and tantrums, Greg's departure. She thought of old Joe Latham. Of the blood, sweat and tears Mike had poured into it. Of how much she, despite everything, had loved working with them all. So much was riding on

Persuasion being a success. Surely, there was something they could do to save it? An image of the gorgeous cobbled square in front of the theatre rose in her mind. With its backdrop of the sea, it could be perfect. The beginnings of an idea formed. It might, *might*, just work.

'Actually, maybe we could let them in. You're right, they do love a disaster,' Dora said suddenly, detaching herself from Mike's embrace. 'And it might work in our favour. I think I've got an idea.'

Mike looked at her with interest. 'What?'

Dora turned to Kirstie. 'What's the weather forecast like?'

'The weather forecast? How should I know?' Kirstie muttered, looking startled. 'Hang on, bear with,' she tapped her phone with her French-manicured nails. 'Returning to warm, dry and sunny, but less humid,' she recited. 'Does that answer your question?'

'Wonderful. That should do. Maria, are the costumes all okay?'

'Yes, fine. Might smell a bit but everything at the back of the theatre is still dry. I'd have to air them out, though.'

'Albie, could you run some lighting cables outside?'

'Don't see why not,' he shrugged. 'The main rig is unaffected. Trust me, that's a good thing. You don't want to mix water and electricity.'

'Quite.'

'And if I can't get them to reach, I know a bloke over at the Northcott. He might be able to help.'

'Fab.' Dora eyed the stage. It was dry and still in one piece. The set was simple: just a few pieces painted blue and gold and carefully chosen to hint at a Regency drawing room. The whole stage set wouldn't take much to move. If what she had in mind worked, they wouldn't even need the heavy velour stage curtains.

But what would people sit on? She looked at the ruined seats in despair. An audience couldn't sit on cold cobbles. 'Have we any spare seating? she asked.

Josh, forgetting he wasn't still at school, put up his hand. 'Yes,' he said enthusiastically. 'There are a whole load of wooden fold-up chairs in the underground store.'

'Usable?'

'Yes, Miss Bart. Not very comfortable,' he admitted, 'But you can sit on them. Just need a bit of muscle power to haul them all out and give them a good clean.'

'Okay.'

'Dora, what's going on?' Mike came nearer. He gave a tired grin. 'You're all fired up.'

Dora swept the little group with a wide smile. 'All may not be lost, my little band of not-so-merry players. We may not be able to put on a show tonight but, with a wing and a prayer and a minor miracle, we'll be able to perform tomorrow.'

'How the hell are we going to do that?' Kirstie asked.

'Yup, my lovely. How do you propose to put on the play in this mess?' Mike spread his hands to the ruined theatre.

'Ah. We won't perform inside, Michael,' Dora said, with a slightly manic gleam in her eye. 'We'll put it on outside. Haven't you always wanted to do open-air theatre?'

Chapter 46

They did it.

Somehow.

Dora dragged in everyone she could think of to help and, with her star pulling power, most were willing. A hung-over Biddy helped Maria out with airing and ironing the costumes. Josh got together a band of schoolmates and, along with Sean Tizzard, retrieved the haul of chairs from the dungeon-like store. Albie made repeated trips to his pal at the Northcott to borrow some longer cabling and then began assembling a new lighting rig, suitable for an outside space. Kirstie organised the box office and then master-minded the publicity. Even Millie, with a busy café to run, found time to provide sandwiches and cold drinks.

Everyone worked until they dropped, but the real revelation was Jed. He drove Albie into Exeter, sourced a jet-washer to wash down the chairs and collected the food from Millie Vanilla's. If this wasn't enough, he began to build the rough wooden platform that would become their stage. Dora wondered what he was trying to prove. Or to whom. She also wondered if Millie really knew what she had in him.

But she didn't have time to think about Jed and Millie's relationship. She didn't have time to even think about her own. Mike had drawn up a punishing rehearsal schedule.

Ken Tizzard offered them the Arts Workshop to rehearse in peace and the cast battled to make the play work in a different way. They rehearsed into the early hours and Dora and Mike collapsed on Millie's sofas, too exhausted to even speak. It would be a completely different, pared-down production but, with Lyme Bay as an inky background, it might just work.

And it did. It was a triumph. Everyone said so. As the sun bled from the sky and darkness gathered around them, the audience magically hushed and hung on every word the actors uttered. It gave the play an intimate feel it lacked before. Even the seabirds knew their cue. When Ellie, as Mary Musgrove, announced 'Oh I am wild to see Lyme!' a gull sounded its mournful cry in response.

The press had gone wild as well. After the seventh curtain call and when the audience had finally dispersed, Millie hosted an impromptu press conference at the café. The journalists were desperate for interviews. The phoenix-from-the-ashes quality of it had them excited. National and international television had been at the performance and Kirstie reported that two well-known US show-biz vloggers had featured the story too. She'd nagged Phil into providing yet more champagne and the fizz added to the intoxicating atmosphere.

When Dora had batted off the last of the reporters – she'd been the one most in demand – she looked around for Mike.

He was talking to Millie at the other side of the terrace.

'Can I borrow him for a moment, Millie?' she said, without taking her eyes from his face. 'We have something very important to discuss. In private.'

Millie, looking from one friend to another, smiled and melted away.

'You've made your feelings clear, Mike,' Dora said, hardly believing she was about to say the words, 'But I don't think I have. As she reached up to kiss him, her mobile shrilled.

Mike's mouth quirked. 'We seem doomed to be interrupted by phone calls.' He nodded over to where Kirstie and Phil were bickering. 'At least it can't be Kirstie this time. You do know there's nothing going on between her and me, don't you?'

Dora touched her fingertip to her lips and then to his. 'I've known about her and Phil for a while,' she said as she answered the call. 'I'm really sorry, I've got to take this, it's my US agent.' She made an apologetic face, which changed to shock as she listened. 'They've offered me what? Back in the States?'

When she'd clicked off the phone and looked up to share the news with Mike, he'd vanished.

Chapter 47

She found him sitting on an abandoned deckchair on the beach. He'd dragged it to the water's edge. After hunting along the promenade, she'd only spotted him because of his white shirt glowing dully in the dark. As she took off her shoes to walk barefoot across the sand, a firework shot across the sky and soared out to sea.

'Hi Mike,' she said softly.

'You're going back to the States, then?' he asked, without preamble.

She sat down on the sand next to him. Another firework blew the night sky into a thousand yellow and red stars.

'Nice fireworks,' she said evenly. 'Sea cadets are having a party, apparently. Putting on quite a show.' When he didn't answer, she added, 'Why did you disappear?'

'Thought I'd leave you to your phone call.'

'I'm sorry. It was rude of me to take it, but I hadn't spoken to Cassie for months.' Dora squeezed some sand between her fingers, enjoying its cool silkiness.

'Has she got some work for you?' Mike's voice was strained.

'She has, actually. The same studio that made *The English*

Woman has a pilot they'd like me to try for. Sure-fire hit, they said. News of our success in Berecombe has even found its way over the pond, it seems, and I'm in demand.'

'Naturally.'

'And yes, it would take me back to the States, of course.'

'Of course.'

'Except there's a problem.'

She felt Mike shift. 'What's that? Not enough money?'

'Oh, they're offering plenty of that,' she answered, deliberately not rising to the bait. 'It's just that I think I've decided I don't want to work in American television any more. Well, to be honest, American TV had rather decided it didn't want me. They pulled *The English Woman*, did you know?'

Mike turned to her. In the light given out by a rocket shooting orange into the sky she could just about make out his wary expression. 'Why didn't you tell me?'

Dora shrugged. 'And admit my failures to you? No chance. And then I found out I quite liked working in the theatre. Think I've decided that's what I want to do.'

'Oh.' Mike said it on a long breath, as if realising what she was saying. He stood up, reached a hand down to her and pulled her to him. 'Always so proud.' As she shivered against him, he added, 'You're cold.'

'Well, if you were more of a gentleman, you'd have offered me your deckchair,' Dora complained. 'I've been sitting on the damp sand.'

Mike stepped away, took off his shirt and wrapped it around her. He pulled the sleeves together in a knot, imprisoning her. 'Better?'

'Slightly.'

'There's something about you that makes me behave in a very ungentlemanly fashion, Dora.'

'I'm very glad to hear it,' she replied primly.

He gave a slight laugh and kissed her.

When she surfaced, she said, 'You always kiss me as if it's the last time you ever will.'

'Another complaint, Dora?'

'Not at all. I think you'd better kiss me again.'

'Truth is, I never know whether it will be the last time I kiss you.'

'Well, I'd better put you out of your misery, then,' she said softly. 'I'm definitely not going back to the States, Mike.' She felt relief drain through him. 'Was that what you were worried about?'

He nodded. 'Wasn't sure if there was anything to keep you here.'

'There's you.'

'What, a washed-up alcoholic theatre director? Am I good enough for you, Dora?'

Dora nuzzled his stubbled chin. 'A very talented theatre director and the only one I've ever wanted.'

'I'm not easy to be with,' he warned.

'I don't think I am either. But we'll muddle through somehow. I hope your house in London is big enough,' she added. 'I appear to be homeless.'

'Think we'll muddle through somehow.' Another firework shot over their heads. 'How are you going to pay your rent, though?' He grinned wickedly. 'As well as being homeless, you appear to be unemployed too.'

'Ah. Thought I'd sleep with a director I happen to know. I hear he's putting on *The Taming of the Shrew*. Quite fancy myself as Katherina.'

Mike pulled his arms around her more tightly. 'Thought I might try out for Petruchio. I hear the leading lady is a right diva, but I reckon it would be fun sparring with her.'

'Are you going to take me to London, then, Mike?' Dora sighed as she snuggled into him.

'Well, there's one condition.'

'What's that?'

'That you tell me you love me.'

Dora sighed happily, the glow from a thousand shimmery firework stars illuminating her love. 'Release me from this ridiculous shirt,' she said, 'And I'll not only tell you but I'll show you as well.'

As they kissed, the fireworks soared above and beyond them and Dora was sure some shot right through her very being. She was lit up with love.

'I love you, Mikey, Mike, Michael Love. And this is definitely not the last time you'll ever kiss me. Not any more.'

'Not any more, Dora,' he said as he kissed her again. 'Definitely not any more.'

Chapter 48

Millie stood on the edge of the terrace watching Mike and Dora kiss in the light of the fireworks. She was happy for them. A chill wind scurried around her bare legs. Shivering, she hugged her arms around her, determined not to feel lonely. Everyone else was coupled up. Arthur and Biddy, Albie and Ellie. Even Kirstie and Phil seemed to have forgotten their differences and were sitting in a dark corner, kissing.

She wondered if she was in shock. She'd been functioning on auto-pilot ever since the phone call the other night. Ever since she'd made her decision.

'Hello, Millie.' It was Jed.

Turning to his familiar form, she couldn't help but reach out and wrap her arms around him. Although when he heard what she had to say it might be the last time she ever held him.

'You're freezing. Here, have this.' He took off his jacket and placed it around her shoulders. 'Good party. As always.'

She nodded. 'Thanks. Dora and Mike are really appreciative of all you've done. They said you haven't stopped.'

He gave her a sharp glance. 'Not bad for someone who

doesn't know the meaning of hard work.' Then he softened. 'Sorry. Don't want to pick an argument. Loved it all, to be honest. Think I might look into fund-raising for the new theatre. The Arts Centre too.'

'Sounds great.'

'Maybe we can join forces? Hold some events at the café?'

'Maybe.' Millie backed away from him a little to give her space. 'Um. The thing is, I'm not sure I'll be around.'

'Why, where are you going?' Then he saw her expression. 'Jeez, Millie, what's going on?'

Millie took an enormous breath and said in a rush, 'Look, there's no easy way to say this, so I might as well come straight out with it. Clare's parents have offered to buy Millie Vanilla's off me.'

Jed collapsed onto the wall. He was silent for a long time. Then, shaking his head in disbelief, he added, 'When did all this happen?'

'They rang me the other night. I've been thinking about what to do ever since.'

'Is this anything to do with our argument? Christ, Millie, this has come out of the blue.'

A rocket shot over the bay, screaming maniacally. Millie was beginning to hate fireworks. They seemed to be the back-drop to every emotional scene in her life.

'It's nothing to do with us, Jed.'

'Then why didn't you talk it over with me?'

'I don't know, really.' Millie sighed. 'We've all been so busy rescuing *Persuasion* that there hasn't been the time and I suppose it *is* my business.'

'I've never thought otherwise, Millie.'

Was there an edge to his voice? Millie couldn't blame him. 'No, I know.' She sat next to him and took his hand. 'The thing is, it could be my chance to get away from Berecombe for a bit. I've been thinking it over a lot recently.' She leaned against him, relishing his solidity. 'I'll try to explain, although it doesn't make sense to me either. For years I thought my parents would want me to carry on the business in their memory. I thought it would have made them happy, but now I'm not so sure.' Millie frowned out into the night. 'I'm not happy, Jed. I don't think I've been happy for a long time. And I'm sure my parents wouldn't want that.'

'What are you going to do?' Jed's voice was strained.

Millie straightened her shoulders. 'I'm going to travel. Do all those things everyone else I know has done. I'm going to ask Dora if I can borrow her villa in Siena so, to start with, I thought I'd have a holiday.'

'I could have come with you, Millie.'

'I know.' She tightened her hold on his hand. 'But I think I need to do this myself. For myself.' She willed him to say the right thing. If he begged her to stay, she just might.

After a long pause Jed nodded. 'I understand.'

'Thank you, Jed.'

'What are you going to do with Trevor?'

'Biddy and Arthur are going to look after him. He loves Arthur.'

'Let me take him, Millie. He loves me too.'

Millie turned to him. 'Would you do that?'

'For you? Of course. I'm staying around, Millie. I'll be here when you come back.'

Millie felt the tears begin. 'I can't promise I'll know what I'll want when I come back.'

'Then we'll work it out,' he said simply. Lifting her hand he kissed her wrist. 'We'll work it out together.'

Above them a shower of red fired up the sky and then died to black.

Christmas Weddings

Chapter 1

It was weird coming back. Weird and cold.

Berecombe looked at once comfortingly familiar and slightly distorted, as if seen through a special-effects lens. Alf the Taxi dropped Millie off on the promenade outside the café, helped her with her rucksack and drove off with a cheery wave.

Feeling desolate, she looked around her. The sea was churning a dull grey in Lyme Bay and the sky was threateningly low and of a similar hue. In fact, Millie decided, everywhere was grey. The town had lost its bright bunting and bedding plants and was shuttered up for the winter. It was home, but it all looked smaller, inward-looking. After the vibrant noise and colour of Thailand, Berecombe, in the first week of November, was depressing.

She shivered violently. She was freezing and bone-weary. Heaving her rucksack onto her back, she made her way to the flat. All she wanted to do was to crawl under a duvet.

Chapter 2

'The wanderer returns!' Tessa threw her arms around her friend and ushered her inside. 'Come inside, pet, it's brass monkeys out there.'

As usual, the Tizzard family home was in a state of chaos. Several very male-smelling pairs of trainers littered the hall and Millie had to navigate around an airer over which hung a pile of school uniform. She followed Tessa into the kitchen, which was an oasis of calm in comparison and smelled comfortingly of freshly made bread.

'Cup of tea and then you can tell me all about it. Oh bab, it's so good to have you back.'

Before Millie could answer there was a frantic scrabbling at the kitchen door. 'Think there's someone a bit desperate to see you,' Tessa said, as she grinned and opened it. A barking woolly blur hurled itself onto Millie's lap.

'Trevor!' Millie surrendered to his ecstatic welcome. 'Oh, how much have I missed you.'

While dog and mistress became reacquainted, Tessa made tea and, once everything had calmed down, perched herself on a stool. She shoved a mug across. 'First English cup of tea since you've been back?'

Millie nodded and reached over Trevor's head to pick it up. After the first sip, she sighed in ecstasy. 'Heaven!'

'Digestive biccies there. Just don't let Trev get hold of them. He's a devil for them. Worse than the kids.'

Millie dunked half and crammed it into her mouth, ravenous. She gave Trevor a sneaky fragment while Tessa's back was turned. 'I still don't understand why you ended up taking him,' she said, with a full mouth. 'Back in the summer Jed said he was happy to look after him until I got back. So, he and his brother are living at The Lord of the Manor now? What's the deal with that?'

'Alex has bought it. Taking a sabbatical or something from hedge-fund managing, or whatever he does in the city.' Tessa made a face.

'Blimey,' Millie said, impressed. 'How much money must he have? What are the plans for it?'

'Don't know, kiddo. He and Jed are living there while he decides what to do. Reckon it'll be another swanky-wanky place with scraps of food and hot and cold running helipads.'

'Plenty of room for a dog, though,' Millie said thoughtfully. 'Not that I'm not very grateful that you took Trevor in,' she added hastily. She hid her nose in the dog's fur and received rapturous licks in return. 'I know he adores it here.'

'The boys have loved having him. It was no bother. In fact, Trevor can stay and I'll boot Roland out. Trev makes a lot less mess than my youngest.'

'I hope you weren't put out that Jed had him. It's just that he offered and it all happened so quickly.'

373

'We've loved having him, Millie.' Tessa's voice was firm.

'So, why did Jed not keep him all autumn? Poor Trev, he must have been so confused,' Millie said indignantly.

'Think he's working long hours. Didn't want to leave the dog on his own.'

'I suppose that makes sense. What's this new job of Jed's, then? You mentioned something when I rang but I was too knackered to take anything in.'

Tessa concentrated on drinking her tea. 'Dunno. I'm sure he'll tell you all about it when he sees you.' She put the mug down. 'Now come on, I don't want to talk about Jed, I need to hear what you've been up to. It's been a miserable, wet autumn in Berecombe and I need to hear about sunshine and hot men.'

Millie could tell that Tessa was holding back, but there was no point pressing her. She took another life-affirming slug of tea and launched in.

Chapter 3

'So you stayed at Dora's villa? What was that like?'

'Oh, Tes, it was amazing. In the hills just outside Siena, swimming pool and everything. The most wonderful views across the olive orchards. I had the use of a tiny Fiat and there was a family-run trattoria nearby that did the most gorgeous food. I've come back with a notebook stuffed full of recipes. You'll have to try the lemon polenta cake, it's heaven on a plate.'

'Can't wait. No equally heavenly men?'

'Well, there was Savio. He took me out and about a few times.' Millie got out her phone and flicked through some pictures. 'Here he is.'

Tessa's eyes widened. 'Well, he's a spunk on a stick, isn't he?'

Millie took the phone back. 'Not bad,' she said airily. 'Very charming and quite wealthy too.' She caught Tessa's look and giggled. 'Purely platonic, Tes, at least on my part.'

'Whatevs, bab. And you left all that and came back to *Berecombe*?' Tessa pulled a disbelieving face.

Millie hugged Trevor. 'Well, I had one or two things to

come back for.'

'Fair enough. So why did you go onto Thailand?'

'Eleri got in touch with me.'

'Elle-Lairi,' said Tessa, pronouncing it with difficulty. 'Who's she, when she's at home?'

'Maybe you don't know her? Old Davey's granddaughter? She hasn't been to see him since she was a kid. She's changed a lot since then. She'd heard from Davey that I was doing a bit of travelling and said she was on this fantastic island in Thailand. Koh Phangan. Would I like to go over and join her?' Millie put Trevor down as he was wriggling and obviously wanted a drink. She watched as he slurped noisily from his bowl. 'I've always wanted to go to Thailand.' She made a face. 'To be honest, Savio was getting a bit keen so I needed an escape. It was cooling down, too, so I thought I might as well head for some sun.'

'Yeah well,' Tessa put in drily. 'That's the problem with gorgeous Italian millionaires. You just have to get away from them.'

'He wasn't a millionaire, Tes.' She reconsidered. 'Actually, he might have been, he did have a Maserati.'

'Oh well, in that case, you did the right thing, bab. Run. Run away as fast as you can.' Trevor put a nose on Tessa's knee, soaking her jeans with his wet whiskers. She pulled a face at him. 'Your Millie needs her head examined, Trev, my boy. So what did you do in Thailand once you'd got away from this Maserati-driving monster of an Italian hunk?'

'Had a good time. Sunbathed, swam in the sea, helped out in the bar that Ri, that's what Eleri likes to be called, was working in. I played with the baby monkey that the bar owners had as a pet, went to some pretty wild beach parties. It was cool.'

Tessa stared at her friend. 'It's done you good too. You've changed, Mil. The suntan suits you.'

'I've got some incredible Thai recipes.'

'Not changed that much, then.'

Millie laughed and finished her tea. 'Maybe not. And I don't think I'll try out the chicken-feet stew on Arthur and Biddy.'

'Has it got something out of your system?' Tessa asked curiously.

'Ah Tes, that I'm not too sure about.' Millie traced a finger over the pattern on her mug. 'Now I've seen what the world outside Berecombe can offer,' she added. 'I'd quite like to see some more.'

'What's the plan now, then?'

Millie broke off another bit of biscuit and crunched thoughtfully. 'I suppose the first call has to be to Jed,' she answered eventually.

'And what you going to say to him, kiddo?'

'Ah. That's the problem, Tes. I have absolutely no idea.'

Chapter 4

Millie strode into the hall of The Lord of the Manor hotel two days later. She hadn't been for years. There had been no need. Nothing, as far as she could see, had changed. The massive mahogany desk was still dominating the space, with the moth-eaten stag's head above. The ancient Persian rug remained to trip you up as you entered and there was still an enormous chipped blue and white vase acting as an impromptu umbrella stand by the door.

There was no one around. And it was freezing cold. Millie, in four layers and her father's overcoat, shivered. She knew Jed was here as his Golf was parked up outside. Spying an old-fashioned brass bell on the desk, she rang it.

Somewhere high above her a door slammed and there came the sound of feet running down the stairs. Jed came into view. He stopped dead when he saw her.

Millie stared back, her heart thumping uncomfortably under all the layers. He looked paler than she remembered, but that could be in comparison to Savio. He also looked thin and tired and far less glamorous.

He came to her, his hands stretched out to take hers. 'Millie,' he said, on a long breath. He held her at arm's length. 'Jeez, you look good. So brown!'

'Hello Jed.' It came out on a whisper. She didn't know what to say or how to react to the man. He looked so unfamiliar. Had she been away for only three months?

He pulled her to him and enveloped her in a hug. This was slightly better. Jed smelled as he always had, of some expensive cologne.

'Oh, it's so good to have you back.'

Millie let herself be held, relishing the feel of his strong arms around her.

He released her, perhaps sensing her reserve. 'Got time for a coffee? Can't say it'll be anywhere near as good as yours, but it'll be hot. You need something to keep yourself warm in this barn of a place. Come into the office.' Taking her by the hand, he led her through a door behind the desk. It opened out into a crowded and shabby room. Its only redeeming feature, a floor-to-ceiling window, which gave views onto the gardens.

Jed swept a pile of papers off an ancient chesterfield. 'Won't be a moment. I'll put the kettle on.' He disappeared through another door and shouted back, 'It's a shocker, this place, isn't it? Alex's really taken on a mammoth task. I'm not entirely sure he's sane.'

He came back bearing two steaming mugs and a packet of custard creams. 'I've been missing your cakes. These are a very poor substitute.' He put everything down on top of a desk groaning under the weight of yet more paper.

Millie picked up her mug of instant, wrapping her frozen

fingers around its warmth. 'I can understand why the Simpsons sold up, but why on earth has your brother bought it?'

'God knows,' Jed said cheerfully. He slid into the chesterfield's twin. 'More money than sense, I've always said. Had enough of the city and got money to burn. He's got friends who run hotels; you remember that one we went to in Poole? Chap that owns that has a chain. Alex has been taking advice from him. Fancies setting this up as some kind of retreat for burned-out execs. The only thing that's burning is money at the moment. It's cost Alex a packet already and he's only got as far as building repairs. He wants to do a complete refurb eventually.'

There was a silence as they drank their coffee. Jed offered Millie a biscuit and took one himself when she refused, crunching it loudly with his white teeth.

'It's so good to see you again, Millie.' He smiled at her, his dark eyes warm. 'I only wish there was time to catch up properly. We'll have to do dinner. I want to hear all about your adventures.' He took his phone out of his breast pocket and grimaced. 'No time now, though, I have to get to work.'

'Yes, that's what I was going to ask you about.'

He double-guessed. 'Is Trevor okay? I loved having him. There's so much space for him here, but when I got this new job the hours were just killers. I couldn't leave him on his own and Alex is up to his proverbials with all the repairs. Tessa didn't mind and I knew you'd be happy he was with the Tizzards.'

'He loved it with them, but it would have been nice if you had told me what you had planned for my dog,' she said crisply.

Jed looked shamefaced. 'I'm sorry about that, Millie. Didn't want you to worry about him.'

'Not the point, Jed. The first I knew was when I rang Tessa when I got back.' She blew out an exasperated breath. 'Whatever. He's fine. And it wasn't what I was going to ask, though. What's this new job?'

Jed's phone beeped. He leaped up. 'I'm late. I've got to go, Millie darling.' He dropped a kiss on her head. 'I'll give you a bell about dinner.' His phone beeped again. 'I'm so sorry. When the call comes through, I have to go.'

Millie twisted to watch Jed as he ran out. He deftly avoided his brother coming the other way.

'Ah, Millie,' Alex said. 'How very lovely to see you again. Has my errant brother been looking after you? He always seems to be in a tearing hurry these days.' They heard the sound of the Golf's engine gunning down the drive. Alex peered into Millie's mug. 'Instant,' he said with some disgust. 'He could have made time to make you some proper coffee.' He sat in the chair Jed had just vacated and took a custard cream.

'He seemed to be in a hurry to get to work.'

'They keep him on quite a tight rein, as I understand.' Alex picked up some papers, scanned them half-heartedly and then replaced them.

'What's he doing? More consultancy?'

'If only, Millie. If only. No, didn't you know? My little brother has got himself a job with Blue Elephant.'

Chapter 5

'Who's that?' Tessa asked.

Millie started. She'd been miles away. Wiping down a table, she concentrated on Tessa who was, unsubtly, trying to take her mind off Jed. 'Eleri? I told you about her. Davey Pascoe's granddaughter. Remember I said we hooked up in Thailand.' Millie reined in her irritation. She was sure she'd told Tessa about her. 'We travelled back together and I said she could help out every now and again. Need an extra pair of hands in the café now Zoe's in Durham and Clare's at catering college.'

Tessa stared at the willowy figure, dressed in a blue and green chiffon kaftan and bell-bottoms. Eleri sensed she was being discussed and turned around and smiled. Her light eyes rooted Tessa to the spot. 'She's gorgeous.'

'Certainly is and a hard worker too.' Millie took a loaded tray into the kitchen and Tessa followed at her heels.

'Get you, hooking up with folk like a seasoned traveller. Remind me how you two met up, then?'

'Well, I got myself to the same island she was living on and one morning she just appeared out of the sea. Keen swimmer, apparently. Used to do it competitively.'

'And you offered her a job. Just like that?'

Millie plunged a stack of plates into hot water. 'Yup.'

'No references?'

Millie shrugged. 'None needed really. If she hadn't worked out, I wouldn't keep her on. But she's been great.'

'Ken would die to paint her.' Tessa peered through the porthole window in the kitchen door. 'With those amazing eyes and all that hair.'

Eleri, her golden-brown hair tamed into a waist-length plait, was chatting to an obviously smitten Arthur.

'Well, if she hangs around long enough, he can. She's staying with Old Davey for the time being. You know him, lives in the last bungalow before the cliff?'

Tessa nodded. 'Yeah. He took us all out mackerel fishing years ago, when the kids were small. Forgotten he had family, though.' She picked up a tea towel and began to dry the plates Millie had washed. 'If you keep getting busy like this, you're going to have to invest in a dishwasher, bab. And you haven't got enough crockery to turn around quickly.'

Millie brushed back her fringe from a steamy face. 'You could be right there. I'll add it to the list of suggestions for Clare. It was her mum's networking group that was in today.' Returning to the subject, she added, 'Think Ri's parents moved to Wales years ago. If Ken wants to paint her, he'd better be quick. She doesn't seem to stay in one place for long.'

'I'll tell him.' Tessa once again looked through to the café. 'She looks so free.' She sighed the sigh of a woman with a husband and three demanding sons at home. 'Must be great to flit about the world, without a care. And there's something mesmerising about her, isn't there?'

'Agreed. She's amazingly calm. Nothing seems to faze her. She's a bit fey too.' Millie wrinkled up her nose. 'Think that's the word.' She rinsed a couple of plates. 'Haven't you heard the story? Rumour is, someone in her family long ago married a mermaid and made her live on the shore with him. Apparently all the female members of the family have that spectacular hair and pale eyes.'

Tessa turned around and stared at Millie, round-eyed. 'No way! What a story. Oh Ken has to paint her now.'

'He might have to pay. Think she's strapped for cash at the moment.' Millie bit her lip. 'And she's not alone.'

'How's the sale going?'

Millie winced. 'Slowly. I'd hoped to exchange by now, but Clare's parents are checking out yet more things. They're having another survey done and a feasibility report on top.'

'Do they want to buy this place or not?'

Millie sank against the prep table. Everything threatened to overwhelm her. 'Suppose it's only sensible to be cautious. It's a big thing to take on. It's just that, oh Tes, I only went travelling on the understanding the café was sold. And now I'm so broke I don't know what to do.'

Tessa wrapped her in a hug. She knew there was more to this than just moving stress. 'I'm sure it'll all go through soon. You know what they say, solicitors love making everyone panic until the last minute and then it all goes through without a hitch. And once it's sold, think of all the lovely lolly you'll have. You'll be able to do anything you want. Wherever you want. Just like Eleri. Maybe even get back in touch with that Italian bloke.' Tessa tightened her hold. 'Berecombe won't be the same without a Millie Vanilla's, though.'

Millie's answer was muffled and unintelligible.

'And I'm sorry I didn't tell you about Jed's job. Thought it was his news, really.'

'Why has he gone and got a job with Blue Elephant?' Millie wailed. 'I just don't understand, Tes. How could he do it to me again? It's such a betrayal.'

'I don't know, bab. I just don't know.' Tessa held her until the sobs subsided.

'And I want the café to do well for Clare.' Millie sniffed. 'Jed working for Blue Elephant is going to put a dent in the profits. I just know it.'

'What are you going to do about it?'

Millie stepped away from her hold, wiped her face with her pinny and said bleakly, 'Have it out with him. That's if I can ever get hold of him. He seems to be working all the time.'

'Avoiding you?'

'Well, he won't do that for long. Not in a town the size of Berecombe. He owes me an explanation. And he's bloody well going to give it to me.'

Chapter 6

Eleri twisted over. The water caressed her wet-suited body like silk. Lying on her back and floating, she stared up at the moonless night. As she'd done as a child, she located the familiar shape of the Plough and then traced the route to Cassiopeia. It gave her satisfaction to see them still there. The stars were often the only constant in her ever-changing life.

The only sound was the quiet wash of the sea around her. The only colours black and silver. Closing her eyes, she surrendered herself to how alive her senses felt. She was more at home in the sea than anywhere. A tremor ran through her. She was getting cold. The sea temperature on a Devon November night didn't compare to the tropical seas she was more used to. She needed to get moving again. Besides, if Davey found out she was swimming at night, alone, he'd be furious. Reluctantly, she twisted again and power-crawled to shore.

Chapter 7

Millie sat at the table in the window. A grey pall of fog hung over the promenade. It blanketed out the sea and all was peculiarly hushed. Ever since she'd returned from Thailand nothing had seemed to go right. Even the weather had been unremittingly grim. Usually she didn't mind. In fact, she used to take pleasure in the quiet, out-of-season days when she had the place to herself. It was a time to catch your breath before everything revved up again.

She stirred her hot chocolate without interest and glared at her mobile, willing Jed to return her call. It remained stubbornly quiet. She'd rung him several times and he hadn't bothered to get back to her. The one bright thing in this sea of grey was Ri. The girl floated in and out of the café, working without seeming to put any obvious effort in, getting things done and spreading a palpable calm in her wake. Millie couldn't afford help, but she found she lacked the enthusiasm or the stamina to do everything herself any more. Not for the first time, she wished the café sale had gone through and she was free of it. It had become a burden she no longer wanted.

The bell on the café door had her looking up in the vain

hope it was Jed.

'Hello Millie,' Alex said. 'I wonder if I might have a word?'

Too disappointed to speak, Millie gestured to the empty chair beside her. Behind, she heard the sudden silence as Arthur and Biddy stopped bickering. Whatever Alex's business, it would be all over Berecombe by tomorrow.

'Hi *bach*, I'm Eleri. What can I get you?' Ri appeared from nowhere, with order pad in hand. She smiled down at Alex.

'Oh. Um. Ah.'

The tops of his ears turned pink. Millie took pity on him. Eleri had this alarming effect on most of her male customers. It was making for good repeat custom. 'Why don't you have one of Ri's special hot chocolates?' she suggested. ' Just the thing for a foggy day like today.'

'Thank you. I will.' Alex eyed Millie's mug. 'But without the marshmallows, if I may.'

Eleri made a face. 'It's not my special hot chocolate without them. See, I make them into little white chocolate and marshmallow flowers. They're magic. Go on. Have the marshmallows. Live a little.'

'Right.' Alex gulped in the face of all her gorgeousness. 'Okay. Whatever you say.'

'Wonderful. Can I get you another, Millie?'

'No, I'm fine, Ri. Thank you.'

Alex twisted to watch her as she made her way back to the kitchen. 'My word.' He unwound his scarf and unbuttoned his coat. 'Eleri. What a pretty name.'

Millie smiled. 'Welsh, apparently. And yes, it is pretty, but she prefers Ri.'

'What a shame to abbreviate it. Eleri.' He sounded it out with relish and shook his head. 'Never encountered an Eleri before.'

'I think she's one in a million. Alex, it's lovely to see you, but I can't imagine you came to discuss my staff.'

'Ah. No I didn't.' He took off his specs, de-misted them and popped them back on his nose, clearing his throat slightly as he did. 'Bit awkward this. I've come to apologise, actually.'

'Whatever for?' Millie was taken aback.

'For blurting out that Jed is working for Blue Elephant. I had no idea he hadn't told you.' Alex tugged at the collar of his crew-necked sweater. 'I feel awful. I had no right. It was Jed's news and I understand Blue Elephant has caused some, shall we say, friction between you.'

'Just a little.'

'I really thought he'd mentioned it.'

'Strangely enough, Jed forgot to email me the news that he is working for my biggest rival.'

'Ah yes.' Alex paused to take off his coat. He folded it neatly, put it on a chair and then remained standing as Eleri returned with his chocolate. 'Wonderful. Thank you.' Pushing his glasses back up his nose, he added, 'Marvellous.'

'Just pop the flowers in the hot chocolate when you're ready,' she said, in her soft Welsh accent.

She and Alex gazed at one another. Even through her fugged-up state Millie could feel the attraction zinging between them. Goodness me, she thought. Now, that's a match I wouldn't have predicted. Opposites must attract.

'If there's anything else you need,' Eleri added, staring

wide-eyed at Alex. 'Just let me know.'

'Eleri, I need another coffee.' Biddy's overloud voice broke the moment.

'Coming right up,' Eleri murmured, her eyes not leaving Alex's face.

'And I'd like it now, please!'

When Eleri had gone, Alex subsided into his chair. 'I say,' he breathed. As instructed, he put the white marshmallow flowers into his hot drink and was taken aback to see them open up. 'Now, how does that happen?' he murmured in astonishment.

'Some of Ri's magic, I think. Actually, I think she got the recipe off the net. Fun, though.' Millie watched him sip his drink, fascinated to see him approach it as if it were something alien. 'Alex, thank you for your apology, but I don't really think it was yours to make. What I'd really like, what I really *need*, is an explanation as to why Jed feels he can do this to me.'

Alex fidgeted with his serviette, nervously. He cleared his throat again. 'Millie, my dear, I'm afraid I can't add much to what you already know.'

'But that's it,' Millie burst out. 'I don't know anything at all. Jed was pretty good at keeping in touch when I was in Italy but it all tapered off a bit last month.'

Alex nodded. 'That's about when he got the job.'

'Figures,' Millie said acidly. 'What exactly is he doing?'

'He's in charge of buying, from what I can gather.' Alex shrugged. 'If I'm honest, he hasn't said all that more to me, but then I've been busy.'

'I just don't understand why he's working for that company

again, of all people.'

'Well, he had to get some kind of employment. He'd been fund-raising for the theatre and the Arts Workshop, but that wasn't paid.'

'Isn't his trust fund enough?' Millie tried not to sound bitter.

'Ah.' Alex stared into his mug. 'Oh dear. You haven't heard about that either?'

'What? Oh what now, Alex?'

'Jed hasn't been taking his allowance. I understand it has something to do with how you feel about trust funds? Something to do with proving he can manage without it?'

Millie let out a breath. One she hadn't known she'd been holding. She felt very tired. 'We had a conversation, an argument, I suppose.' She shot Alex a rueful look. 'I made it quite clear I don't approve of those who don't have to work for a living.'

'Yes, he mentioned that.' Alex spooned out a marshmallow flower and ate it cautiously. 'I would imagine, by taking on this job, that Jed is trying to prove to you that he can work his keep.'

'But why Blue Elephant, of all places?'

Alex shook his head. 'I've no idea. He was rather keen to stay in Berecombe for when you came home. And from what I've gathered since I've been here, there are not many employment opportunities, and especially at this time of year. Maybe he had little choice?'

'True,' Millie said slowly. A thought struck. 'Your mother can't be very happy about it.'

Alex gave a short laugh. 'I think that might be the understatement of the year. She's apoplectic.' He sighed. 'Jed's never really found what he wanted to do with his life. Or hadn't until recently.' He smiled kindly. 'I've never known him so enthusiastic over anything as he was about your café. Your lifestyle. It really speaks to him. And this,' he spread his hands to include the town. 'Having spent some time in this part of the world I'm beginning to see the appeal.'

'Then why hasn't he said all this to me? Explained himself?'

'Ah. May I tell you something about Jed?'

Millie nodded. 'Please do. I feel as if I've never really understood him. Never really go to know him properly.'

'I understand.' Alex took a deep breath.

Chapter 8

'Jed has always had, shall we say, a difficult relationship with our mother. I seemed to fulfil her expectations as a son. Did what I was told, did well at school, university, went into a career of which she approved. Jed, on the other hand, was rebellious, even as a baby. Fought her on everything and anything.'

'I can well believe it.'

Alex gave Millie an old-fashioned look and pushed up his glasses. 'I'm not sure mother knew how to handle him after sailing though motherhood with me. But, even though Jed can be rebellious and doesn't take orders very well, underneath it all what he most likes to do, especially for those he loves, is please them. Make them happy. The more pressure mother put on him to settle down to something, the more frustrated he became that he couldn't find a career that both he and mother wanted. And I'm afraid, when Jed is in that position, he simply clams up. Keeps his secrets very secret.' Alex leaned back and pursed his lips. 'We all thought he'd settled to his management consultancy, he was certainly very good at it and then he met you and went in another direction altogether.'

Georgia Hill

Millie was silent for a moment, digesting this new information. It made a mad kind of sense. Whenever Jed had done something he thought she disapproved of, he'd simply avoided telling her.

'It still doesn't explain why he felt he needed to work for my biggest rival.'

'No,' Alex agreed. 'It certainly doesn't explain that.' He stood up. 'I'm sorry I can't shed any light on that, my dear. But there must be a good reason. Jed doesn't do anything to hurt people in such a blatant way. It's simply not in him. He's a loving man.' Alex coughed again, embarrassed at all this talk of emotional matters. 'And I think he loves you very much.'

Millie stood too. 'He's got a funny way of showing it.'

Alex's eyes twinkled. 'That, I can't argue with.'

Eleri came to collect their empties. 'Was everything alright?'

'It was delicious,' Alex said. 'Especially the marshmallow flower things.' He reached into his pocket. 'I nearly forget to pay. That wouldn't do at all, would it?'

Millie stayed his arm. 'On the house. I appreciate you coming and trying to put things right.'

'Just trying to help.' He shrugged back into his coat and wound his scarf around his neck. He reminded Millie of a well-meaning giraffe.

'Good morning, ladies,' he said and went.

Eleri picked up their mugs. 'What a lovely man,' she said. 'Such a kind face.'

'He was very taken with you.'

'Was he?' She concentrated on clearing the table, but Millie detected a quickening of interest.

394

'Absolutely. Wound up tighter than that cashmere scarf he was wearing, though.'

'Yes, I got that impression too.' Eleri laughed. 'I'll just have to try and do something about that then, won't I, *cariad*?' Then she rolled her eyes as Biddy shouted another demand from behind them.

Chapter 9

Eleri was delighted when, only a few days later, Alex made a return visit to the café.

'Um. Ah. Hello Eleri. Message for Millie.'

'I'm so sorry, I'm afraid she's not here this morning but she'll be back in later, mind. Can I pass it on?' Eleri was aware Alex was staring.

'What?'

'The message. Shall I pass your message on?'

'That would be wonderful.' He gave a heartfelt sigh.

Eleri put her head on one side. 'If you don't mind me saying, you look exhausted.'

Alex gave her a weak smile. 'Knackered, actually. Bloody roofers.'

'Ah. Having work done on the hotel, aren't you? Millie mentioned something. Look, sit yourself down, lovely, and I'll get you a coffee. We're quiet at the moment, so I can join you and you can tell me all about it.' As she went to go into the kitchen, she stopped and turned. 'How about a bacon roll too? One left over from breakfast.'

Alex gave her a painfully grateful look before sinking into the same chair he'd sat in the other day.

Once he'd eaten and Eleri had served a couple clad in cagoules and walking boots, she joined him with two more Americanos.

Alex sat back in his seat and sighed again, this time happily.

'Now then, you look a much happier man.'

'I am. That was just what I needed.'

'Can't go wrong with a bit of bacon and some caffeine. Sure to hit the spot. Whatever the spot is that's in need.' She nudged his coffee nearer. 'Got some orange marmalade cake as well, if you've room.'

'Thanks, but no thanks. Haven't got a terribly sweet tooth.'

Eleri gasped. 'That's the most shocking thing I've ever heard. Please don't let Millie hear you say that.'

Alex grinned, appreciating the joke. 'I won't.'

'So, what's got you all tense and stressed?'

'How did you know I was stressed?'

'Not difficult to guess, lovely.'

Alex pushed up his specs and blew out a breath. 'The hotel. It's a nightmare. It's been a nightmare ever since I bought it.' He stopped and a rueful expression overcame his thin face. 'I don't usually talk about my problems, especially not to a stranger.'

'Well, no one's a stranger in Millie Vanilla's. And it can be good to share problems.' Eleri picked up her coffee. Holding it between her hands, she closed her eyes and breathed in the aroma. 'Got to be one of the world's great pleasures.' She drank, aware Alex was watching her avidly.

Putting her cup down she said, 'Now, come on, why are the hotel repairs causing you so much hassle? Money?'

'You're very direct, aren't you? Funnily enough, no.' Alex

took off his coat and scarf. He seemed flustered. 'Got rather warm in here, hasn't it?'

'Millie likes to keep her customers cosy.'

'Yes, it's jolly cold today. Somehow hadn't thought it would be by the coast.'

'Arthur thinks we're in for a harsh winter.' Eleri smiled kindly. 'I suspect he says that every winter, mind.' She watched as Alex drank his second coffee. He ate and drank as if it was purely fuel, she observed. There was little sensual pleasure in it. A closed-up man, she decided. 'It's usually money that causes the renovation stress, but not with you, so what is it?'

'Oh, it's the untidiness of it all,' he blurted out. 'The men seem to turn up when they like, leave their stuff all over the place, don't finish one job before going onto the next.' He wrinkled his nose in such disgust, Eleri wondered what he was about to say. 'And have Radio Two blasting out at all hours.'

'Shocker. I'm guessing you're a Radio Four man?'

'Three, actually.'

Eleri sat back and laughed out loud. 'They sound like fairly typical builders to me.'

'Do they?'

'Are they doing a good job? Are you pleased with the results?'

'Well, yes, I suppose.'

'And are you providing them with tea and biscuits?'

Alex looked at her in horror. 'Should I be doing?'

Eleri shrugged. 'Can't hurt. How about you set up a drinks station with a kettle and teabags and coffee and such? Even Kit Kats maybe? Might oil the works when you ask for the

398

radio to be turned down.' She laughed. 'Have you never lived with builders before?'

'Never.'

'I think they run on tea and Radio Two. Chocolate digestives help too.'

'I'll try that. Thank you.'

'You're welcome. My Da runs a building firm back in Wales, so call it insider knowledge. Or a plea on behalf of good will to the building trade.' Alex didn't comment, so she added, 'What are your plans when the building work is done, then?' She was dismayed to see his face crumple and his shoulders sag.

'That's the other, enormous black hole of a problem. I don't know.'

'Surely you've got a design consultant or an interior designer on the go?'

He shook his head. 'Thought I'd get one on board when I'd decided what sort of place to go for. And, apart from an outline plan, I have absolutely no idea. The hotel is a bit of a gamble for me.' He shrugged. 'Oh I'm used to gambling with money. That's what I did in the city, I suppose. But this,' he spread his long-fingered hands, 'This is something else. I'm rather out of my depth.'

He looked so forlorn, Eleri wanted to hug his too-thin shoulders. She contented herself by putting a comforting hand on one of his. 'Oh *cariad*. I think you were meant to walk into Millie Vanilla's. You were meant to meet me. You lucky, lucky man. I just happen to have a degree in interior design and I'm dying to have a look at your hotel!'

Chapter 10

They were so engrossed in discussing ideas that they didn't see Millie burst into the café. She brought with her a snarl of vicious sea wind and had trouble closing the door against it. A shivering Trevor headed to his basket against the radiator.

'Bugger, it's cold out there.' She rubbed her hands together before unwrapping her many layers and hanging them on the pink and blue hat stand. 'Oh hi, Alex,' she said, spotting him. 'I've been trying to get hold of your brother. Again. I'm beginning to think he's avoiding me.'

Alex blinked owlishly at her. 'Message. Ah yes, I have a message. Jed told me to say he's had to go abroad on a buying trip.'

Millie stood before them, hands on hips, expression mutinous. 'How convenient.'

'No really, it's not, actually.' A lock of dark blonde hair flopped forward and Alex flicked it away nervously. 'He's had to go to Bogota. I could have done with him being here.'

'We could both do with him being here,' Millie snapped. 'He still owes me an explanation as to why he's working for

Blue Elephant, remember? And Bogota?' She wrinkled her nose. 'Where's that?'

Eleri stood up gracefully. 'Colombia. South America,' she added, as Millie still looked puzzled. She turned to Alex in concern. 'Not the safest of countries to travel in.'

'I assume, as it's work, he'll be well-protected. But, as it happens, I agree with you, Eleri. I voiced my concerns at him having to go there.' Alex shrugged. 'He's a seasoned traveller, though, he knows how to look after himself.'

Irritation battled with worry within Millie. She tried not to pout. 'I just wish I knew what was going on in his mind.'

Eleri began to pick up the cups and plates littering the table. 'All will be well, don't you worry. Jed would never do anything to hurt you. Either of you. He loves you both very much. I'm positive he has a very good reason for working for them.' She smiled enigmatically and drifted to the kitchen, bestowing a serene glance on the cagoule couple, who blinked back, startled by the vision of calm and beauty.

Millie stared after her in exasperation. 'Much as I admire Ri, and I do very much, I sometimes think she comes from a different planet. How is she so certain about these things? I think she's off her rocker most of the time.'

'Do you?' Alex murmured, also staring. 'I think she's the most marvellous creation I've ever met.'

Chapter 11

Eleri accepted Millie's offer of a lift up to The Lord of the Manor on the following Sunday. She couldn't wait to look around. Alex had rung during the week and they'd had long conversations over some of the things he hoped for the hotel. It was an exciting project and, for the first time ever, since graduating, she was itching to put the skills she'd learned into practice.

They trundled along the pot-holed drive in Millie's Fiesta. She changed gear to slow down and swore when the car resented her clumsy driving.

Eleri knew Millie still hadn't heard anything from Jed. More worrying was his lack of communication with his brother. Jed had been gone for the best part of two weeks and Alex hadn't heard from him either. From experience, she knew parts of South America could be dangerous. She'd asked her Tarot cards on the previous evening. Relieved when the star came up – her favourite – she knew Jed was okay. She'd been slightly more troubled by the moon card. His way forward, although eventually having a positive outcome, was clouded with uncertainty. She just wished he'd get in touch with those who loved him. She heard Millie swear again as she braked harshly, scattering gravel, and sensed her pain.

Alex greeted them at the main door. He wore a bulky overcoat, a beanie and woollen gloves. He clapped his hands together, causing some crows to fly up from out of the trees lining the driveway. He glanced up, following their flight into a cloudlessly blue sky. 'Think it might be warmer out here than inside. Hope you've got something cosy to wear.'

Eleri reached into the back of the car for the thick woollen poncho she used as a coat. 'We'll be fine,' she said. 'Can't wait for the tour.' Once she'd tugged the poncho over her head, she examined the front of the hotel. An elegant building, it had a symmetrical Georgian facade. The roofers' scaffolding was shrouding its beauty, but she could see it would be stunning once repaired.

'Any news?' Millie asked Alex as she locked the car.

Alex didn't need to ask about what. 'Nothing, I'm afraid. Not a sausage.'

Eleri watched the hope drain out of Millie. 'It'll be fine, Millie. Colombia is a lot safer than it used to be for Western travellers.'

'Great,' Millie mumbled, not looking convinced.

Alex shivered. 'Shall we begin? It's a little cold to be standing around too long. Thought we'd go over to where I hope to put the spa.'

He led them behind the main building of the hotel to what must have been the old covered swimming pool. The water had been drained from the pool and it lay forlorn and lonely in the echoing space under the shabby glass dome. The sharp winter sunlight only emphasised the neglect.

'Hoping to get the glass replaced,' Alex said. 'I rather like the shape of the roof, although the glass has seen better days.' He nodded to the wall of white-painted breeze blocks. 'That's all coming out. It'll be bi-fold doors that can be opened in warm weather. Not like today, eh?' He smiled kindly at Millie.

He was so obviously trying to be extra nice to her that Eleri's heart melted.

'We'll have treatment rooms behind and maybe a small café. I'd like some advice from you, Millie, about what to serve.' He grimaced. 'I'd like to think the fad for green smoothies is over now but I'd like healthy stuff on the menu. That will fit into the whole ethos.'

'So you're still going with some kind of chill zone for burned-out executives?' Eleri asked.

Alex nodded. 'That was always my intention but I was never sure quite how to achieve it.'

'Well, there's lots of things we can do. Water features, soft lighting, the right sort of music,' Eleri said. She turned to Millie. 'Do you remember that place we went to in Panburi?' Millie nodded, but didn't answer, she was obviously miles away, so Eleri went on. 'It was this fabulous spa and hotel right on the beach in Thailand. Lots of tropical dark wood and silks. You could try that sort of thing here. Not those colours,' she added, hastily. 'Not in the UK, it wouldn't feel right, but maybe stick with natural materials, local woods and fabrics, to aim for a really tranquil atmosphere.' She scanned the sad and defeated room, visualising how it could be. 'Beech, pale blues, creams and whites. They would look great in here and would reflect that you're not far from the sea. You could carry them through to the main building, if you like, but warm them up slightly. Add some red and more vibrant blues.'

'I like the colours used at Millie Vanilla's,' Alex put in, clearly out of his depth.

'They look good, don't they?' Eleri answered, as Millie still wasn't listening. 'I hate to say this, Alex, but you're right, you know. It is colder in here than outside.' She shivered violently. 'Could we go inside the hotel now, do you think?'

Alex led them on a quick tour of the rest of the hotel and they ended up in the shabby and cluttered office behind the desk in the foyer. He brought over a tray of coffee and sandwiches and toed an ancient electric fire closer to them.

'Coffee, I think, to warm us up, and then maybe you can both have a look over –'

He didn't finish, as a familiar voice sounded from the door. 'Coffee. Just what the weary traveller needs.' Jed dropped his case and grinned. 'Actually, having just drunk nothing but the stuff for two weeks, I'd rather have a big mug of tea. Hello everyone.'

Chapter 12

Pandemonium ensued. Millie ran over and hugged him to her, Eleri grinned and introduced herself and Alex busied himself by making tea and shuffling another chair next to the fire.

Once everything had calmed down, Jed took a seat nearest the fire and looked about him. 'It's so good to be home, although it's funny to think of the Lord as home.' He unzipped his jacket. 'And I know it hasn't been long but at times it seemed I was away forever.'

'You look tired,' Alex said, with concern.

'Yes well, at times it wasn't much of a picnic. And I'm sorry I've been out of contact. Communications were a little ropey where I was.' He blew out a breath so that it made his over-long fringe shoot up. 'It's been quite the trip.'

'Trouble?'

Jed pulled a face at his brother. 'You could say so. Once or twice.'

'The gang culture still not sorted, then?' Eleri put in. 'They're called the *bandas criminales,* I believe,' she added.

Jed took a swig of tea and shrugged. 'Looked to be still

active where I was travelling.'

'Why were you there, then?' Millie asked, with an edge to her voice.

'Work. Trying to source coffee growers.'

'For Blue Elephant.'

'Yes, Millie. For Blue Elephant.'

Eleri gave Alex a sharp glance. 'Alex *bach*, did you say you were going to show me the old stable block?'

'Did I?' Alex looked surprised and then caught on. 'Oh yes.' Untangling his long legs, he got up and held out a courteous hand. 'You said you had some ideas to turn them into self-catering accommodation. I'd love to hear about them.'

They left without Jed and Millie noticing.

'I can't believe you're working for them.' Millie hurled the words across the room.

Jed pushed a weary hand through his hair. 'There are times when I can't quite believe it myself.' There was a heavy silence, then he added, 'Do we have to do this now, Millie?'

'Yes, we have to do this now, Jed! You know how I feel about that company. You know what they might do to my business. How could you get a job with them, of all people?' Millie bit down on her anger.

Another silence. Jed dropped his empty mug onto the desk with a thud. There was a beat going in his cheek. He rose and went to the window, looking out into the grounds, as if longing to escape. He was still wearing his orange puffa and it glowed against the silvery-blue sky. 'This place is going to be great when it's finished. Must be Georgian. Or older. What do you think?'

'Jed. Answer the question. I deserve that much, at least.'

He turned and leaned against the sash window frame. 'You do, of course you do.' He folded his arms and gave an empty sigh. 'And I'm so very sorry, sorrier than you'll ever imagine, but I can't answer you.'

Millie stood up, her hands clenched to white knuckles. 'If you don't give me a reasonable explanation why you're working for Blue Elephant then I can't ...' she choked a little. 'Jed, I can't see how we can move forward. Everything between us will be over.' She sucked in a shuddering breath. 'Once and for all.'

'Don't say that, Millie. Please don't say that.' Jed came nearer and took her hands in his. 'I wish I could tell you, I really do.' His face was anguished. 'But I'm not able to explain. I daren't.'

Millie's lip quivered. His touch had broken through the anger into her concern. 'We've been really worried about you, you know. *I've* been really worried about you.' Furious tears began to rise. She shook off his hold and distanced herself. She couldn't decide whether to hug him safe, or shake him. 'I can't understand why you can't tell me.' She just about stopped herself stamping her foot in frustration. 'Jed, anyone would think you're a secret agent or something.' A flicker in his expression had her gasp. 'You can't be serious?'

He shrugged, deadly solemn. 'You're going to have to go with me on this. You're going to have to trust me.'

'What again?' Millie burst out bitterly. 'How many times have you asked me to do that? And each time you've held something back from me, something really important.

Something I should have known.' She shook her head, tears falling. 'Oh Jed, I just can't do this any more. I'm tired of it. It's over.'

'Millie, don't say that,' Jed's voice was hoarse with emotion. 'Please give me this one last chance. Just give me a few months and I can prove I'm worthy of you.'

The cold air stilled. A dust mote spiralled down. Millie watched it, trying to decide what to do. She contemplated going to him, holding him close, kissing him until their breath was spent. She longed to forget all this was happening. To pretend the only thing that mattered was her and Jed. Then the image of the opening day at Blue Elephant swam into her vision. Of its slick wooden tables and top of the range coffee machines. If she didn't fight for her business, it would be worth nothing and she certainly wouldn't succeed in selling it. And if she had to fight Blue Elephant then she would have to fight Jed too. Hardening her resolve, she reached for her coat.

As he went to her she held out her hand to ward him off. 'Don't touch me. Don't ring me. I don't want anything more to do with you.'

Tears pouring, she stumbled out, ignoring his protests.

Chapter 13

'I'm really worried about Millie,' Eleri said, as she put down one of the building plans she and Alex had been poring over.

Once again they were sitting in the shabby little study at the Lord. Alex had collected her and they'd spent all morning discussing ideas for the hotel.

'I tried talking to her yesterday but she refuses to discuss it. I know he's doing all this for the best but she won't even have his name mentioned.' She sighed, a look of concern flickering across her eyes. She shook a heavy lock of hair off her face, heedless of the effect this had on Alex.

He turned down the radio, which had begun to blast out Slade's Merry Christmas Everybody. 'It's completely unlike him to deliberately hurt someone,' he agreed. 'And I know he loves Millie very much. I just don't understand any of it.'

Eleri wasn't about to give up on the conversation so easily. 'There must be a way we can help them find each other again, Alex. Everything will sort itself out in the end, but can't we nudge them in the right direction? Millie's so sad. Has Jed said anything to you?'

'Not a dickie bird.' Alex pursed his lips. 'And it's not like him. We're awfully close, he usually tells me everything, sometimes more than I want to hear.' He gave a short laugh. 'But this time he's not said a word. Not that he's been around very much. Whatever he's doing for Blue Elephant, they're getting their money's worth. I hardly see him. He's off on another buying trip soon too. Back to South America.' He shook his head. 'I really don't know what we can do, Ri.'

Eleri bit her lip. 'Nothing at the moment, I suppose. We just have to trust to what fate has in store for them. I hate seeing Millie so unhappy, mind.' She blew out a frustrated breath. 'It'll all work out for the best in the end, *cariad,*' she added, more confidently. 'I'm positive. I'm just getting impatient.' Reaching for her mug, she drank her remaining coffee.

Alex gave her a curious look. 'How are so sure of everything? I've got to be honest, with Jed showing no signs of giving up working for Millie's rival business, their situation isn't looking terribly peachy to me.'

'I read my cards. They told me.'

'Cards. What cards?'

'Tarot cards. I asked them if all will be well between Millie and Jed and it will. Eventually.' Eleri wrinkled her nose. 'It just takes time sometimes. And patience. Can be frustrating to watch from the sidelines, mind.'

'Tarot cards?' Alex drew himself up. 'I don't hold with that nonsense.'

Eleri smiled at him, fondly. 'Now then, of course you wouldn't. Virgo aren't you?' At his blank look, she added, 'Birthday in September?'

'Yes. How on earth did you know?'

'The most logical of astrological signs. Scorpio rising too, I would imagine.'

Alex laughed and stood up. He collected their empty mugs. 'Astrology as well? I don't believe in that either.'

'Well, of course you don't, *bach*,' Eleri said serenely. She gazed at him, unblinking. 'What about you take me to lunch and we can discuss it?'

'Ah. Yes.' Alex cleared his throat nervously. 'Actually, I was about to suggest that. Not to talk about astrology or anything, but we could discuss a plan of action for Jed and Millie.'

'Of course. And maybe we could use the time to get to know one another better too?'

The top of Alex's ears turned pink. 'Um. Yes. That would be splendid.'

Chapter 14

'Zoe!' Millie ran across the café and hugged the thin girl who had just come in.

Eleri looked up with interest. It was the first time in weeks that Millie had been so animated. She was curious to see who had sparked it.

'Come and meet Eleri.' Millie brought Zoe over and introduced her. 'You've just missed the rush. We've had another women's networking event in here this morning.'

Zoe's pierced eyebrow rose. 'Can't see Granddad enjoying that.'

Millie laughed. It was a croaky sound, as if she was out of practice. 'He doesn't. Avoids the place until the coast is clear. He'll be in later, though. He's taken Daisy and Trev for a walk while the place was seething with dolled-up women. Turns out they're not too keen on dog hairs on their business suits. Come on, let's all sit down while we've got a minute. Chocolate brownie? Or a slice of Ri's *Bara Brith* with salty butter. It's really good.'

Zoe groaned and collapsed onto a chair. 'Oh, it's good to be home. Can I have both, please? I'm starving. Dying to hear all about your travels, by the way. Dead jel.'

'You can have anything you like, my lovely, including a potted history of the last three months. Large latte to go with them?' At Zoe's nod, Millie began to go into the kitchen. 'No, you sit down too, Ri. You haven't stopped all morning. I'll get the food together. Cold outside, isn't it? It's made your nose go all pink, Zo.'

Eleri sat opposite Zoe and smiled at her. 'It's good to see Millie cheerful again.'

'What's happened?' Zoe started in concern. 'Last time I heard everything was sweet.'

As Eleri gave a brief explanation, Zoe's frown deepened. 'It's all been going on here, hasn't it? Had no idea. Been a bit wrapped up in uni life, I suppose. Sean hasn't said anything either. My boyfriend,' she added, at Eleri's questioning look. 'Not that he might be my boyfriend for much longer.'

'What's all this about the silent but otherwise delightful Sean?' Millie asked as she nudged the kitchen door open with a foot. She carried a laden tray over to their table. 'Got some left-over finger sandwiches here too. The networkers don't eat very much. Egg and cress and smoked salmon with cream cheese. Oh and some honey-glazed mini sausages.'

'Perfect,' Zoe sighed, as she eyed the food greedily. She pulled off her over-sized beret. 'Picky eaters don't sound like your sort of customer, Mil.'

'They're not really,' Millie answered, as she sat down. 'But it's business.'

'Place busy?'

'Ish.'

414

'Can't believe you're selling up,' Zoe said, through a mouthful of food. 'Clare's parents still buying?'

'Allegedly.' Millie sipped her coffee moodily. 'It's taking forever to go through, though.' Putting her mug down she sighed.

'You've just missed the Christmas lights switch-on, Zoe,' Eleri said, in an attempt to lighten the mood. 'They look so pretty in the high street. All white, they are. And there are mini trees up on every shop too. Looks really festive in town now. We had quite a crowd in here that night, didn't we, Mil? Stayed open late. Served soup.'

'Curried parsnip and Tessa's walnut bread,' Millie added. 'And it's carols around the big tree on the prom next week. You're back early, Zo,' she said, changing the subject. 'Term hasn't finished already, has it?'

'Got ill. Iller than a very ill thing. Chest infection that wouldn't go away. Campus doc was worried it might turn glandular so she sent me home two weeks early. I'll miss all the parties,' Zoe said gloomily. 'Just my luck. Might be the universe punishing me, though.'

'What for, *bach?*' said Eleri.

Zoe pushed away her plate with a cavernous sigh. I two-timed Sean.

Chapter 15

'Oh,' Millie said, obviously trying to sound neutral.

'Who with?' Eleri asked. She was beginning to like Zoe. She watched as the girl divested herself of coat, scarf and fingerless gloves.

'Jason. A boy in my nineteenth-century literature class. We bonded over *Jane Eyre*,' Zoe said, dreamily. She nibbled a sausage. 'These are yummy, Mil.'

'Ah, Bronte will do it every time.' Eleri broke off a piece of *Bara Brith* and ate delicately.

'I'll say it did. It's even worse than that, though. Jason loves Mrs Gaskell too.'

'I got round to reading *North and South*,' Millie said. 'Eventually. That John Thornton. I completely fell for him. The moody mill owner. So hopelessly in love.'

'Jason is like Mr Thornton. Proud. Intelligent.' Zoe gave a sigh.

'Drop-dead gorgeous?' Eleri put in, a twinkle in her eye.

Zoe nodded. 'Obvs. More gorgeous than a very gorgeous thing.' She sighed again. 'And so principled.'

'Not all that principled if he's going out with someone

who's already got a boyfriend.' Millie's voice was sharp.

Zoe looked shamefaced. 'It wasn't like that, Mil. He knew I had Sean at home.' She traced a brownie crumb around her plate. 'It was me. I seduced him. Over *Wuthering Heights* and too many vodka shots.'

Eleri caught Millie's eye and managed to keep a straight face. 'Vodka will do it as well,' she said. 'What are you going to do then, lovely?'

'Do I have to do anything?' Zoe had a hopeful note in her voice.

'No –' Eleri began.

'Yes you do.' Millie rose abruptly. 'Of course you have to do something. You have to decide who you want. Sean or this Jason bloke.' She glowered down. 'You have to decide what you want in life and then stick by those decisions, however hard that might be. I expected better of you, Zoe, I really did. Poor Sean. He's been like a lost soul without you. He really misses you and you had to do this to him. Tessa's one of my best friends and Sean is very dear to me too. I'm ashamed of you. I really am.' She turned on her heel.

Zoe stared open-mouthed as Millie stomped into the kitchen. Her face crumpled.

Eleri put a hand out. 'Take no heed, *cariad*.'

'I've never seen her so angry,' she said, on a hiccough. 'I thought she'd be more understanding.'

'Now then, don't take on so. It's herself she's angry at, not you. You just happened to be in the firing line today. Drink your coffee, I'll go and see if she's okay a little later.'

'She's changed. Millie never used to be like that.'

Eleri stared at the resolutely shut kitchen door. 'She's just going through some stuff, that's all.'

'Well, she doesn't have to take it out on me.' Zoe got up. Taking a holly-patterned serviette, she wrapped her uneaten cake into it. 'Tell her I won't bother her again.'

She slammed the café door shut with such emphasis it shook the entire building. It broke the bell, which dropped off and landed on the wooden floor with a discordant jangle.

Eleri stared at it, feeling the waves of anger revolve around the room. 'This won't do,' she muttered. 'This won't do at all.'

Chapter 16

'Millie!'

Millie turned around. It was gloomy on the beach this early in the day. The winter damp seemed to get right into your bones. If she didn't have to walk Trevor, she wouldn't be here at all.

It was Jed. She nodded at him. 'I thought I'd told you to keep away from me.' She wrapped her overcoat around her defensively.

He jogged up to her, his face pinched with cold. 'You did.' He thrust his hands into his puffa. 'Jeez, it's cold.' He glared up at the just-lightening sky. 'Arthur thinks it's going to snow.'

Despite herself, Millie laughed. She followed his gaze to the east and to the star-shaped light that had just burst through the grey clouds. 'Arthur says that every winter.'

Jed smiled into her eyes. 'So he does.'

'When were you talking to him?'

'Oh, you know, we have a chat every now and again. I pop in to see how Daisy's getting on after her operation.' He bent to acknowledge Trevor's ecstatic welcome.

'That was ages ago.' Millie staggered as a great gust of icy wind whipped off the surf and caught her unexpectedly.

Jed gave Trevor's ears a thorough rub and straightened. He shrugged, 'I've become very fond of them both. Biddy too.'

'Biddy?'

'Yeah.' He clapped his hands together to rid them of the sand from Trevor's coat and put them back into his pockets. 'Biddy's had an amazing life. Dined with kings.'

Millie snorted. 'So Biddy says.' She pulled her pink woolly hat down over her frozen ears.

He gave her a keen look. 'It's not like you to be cynical.'

'No? Well, maybe lately things have happened to change that.'

'You're organising their wedding, aren't you? On the beach? I can't think of a better place to get married.' He came close and followed as Millie, too cold to stand still, began to walk back to the promenade.

'Well, they'll have to get married properly in a register office as well. I can't do the legal bit at the café.'

'Oh,' Jed said. 'That's interesting. I hadn't realised.'

'Yes, it's not legally binding unless –' she stopped and shook her head. 'Why am I standing on the beach at eight in the morning discussing Biddy and Arthur's wedding plans with someone I told to stay away from me?'

'Maybe it's my inherent charm?' Jed tried a winning smile but his teeth were chattering too much from the cold.

'Maybe it's your middle-class over-confidence?' Millie retorted.

He winced. Putting out a hand to stop her as she tried to go, he added, 'I've come to say goodbye.'

That checked her. She wheeled around. 'Goodbye? Why, where are you going?' She took two steps nearer. 'Jed, are you leaving Berecombe?'

'Only temporarily. Hopefully. I've got to go on another buying trip.' He bit his lip. 'It might get a bit hairy.'

'What? A coffee buying trip? For Blue Elephant?' Millie didn't bother to hide her disdain. 'The only hairy thing that might happen is you having to put up with economy instead of business class.' She tried to go. 'Take your hand off me, Jed. I thought I'd made myself clear, I don't want anything more to do with you.'

'I just wanted to see you to say goodbye, Mil. Just in case –'

'What? That you have a hissy fit and get thrown off the plane because they've run out of champagne?' She turned again and stomped, as best she could, through the soft sand, whistling to Trevor to follow.

The dog stayed at Jed's knees and whimpered, staring up with troubled eyes. Jed blew out a breath. 'Tell your mistress I just wanted to say goodbye in case, well, in case something happens. Will you do that, Trev?' He bent to caress the dog one last time. 'Oh and tell her I love her, won't you?'

Trevor's only response was a short bark and then he scamp-ered after Millie.

'I really love you, Millie,' Jed added, forlornly, as they disap-peared. 'That's all I wanted to say.'

Chapter 17

Eleri found Zoe in the shelter along the prom a few days later. The girl was huddled up in a parka, her nose hidden by a multi-coloured scarf and she was staring at her phone.

'Hey Zoe. We haven't seen you in the café recently.' She sat down next to her. 'It's freezing out here, girl. Why don't you come to the café for a hot chocolate? We've got some old-fashioned jam roly-poly on the go too. It's lush with Millie's homemade custard.'

Zoe huffed and buried herself deeper into her scarf. 'I don't think I'd be welcome. What with me and my two boyfriends.'

'Now then, don't take on so. You know Millie's unhappy. She's really sorry she snapped at you.'

'She could apologise herself.'

'Yeah, she could. She's been a bit preoccupied, though.'

Zoe shuffled a bit, but Eleri could sense her softening.

'What's happened?'

'Jed's had to go back to South America and Millie worries about him being over there.'

'Thought they'd had a bust-up?'

'Ah come on, Zoe. You know that just because you split

with someone, doesn't mean you stop caring about them.'

'No. Suppose.' Zoe stared gloomily at an elderly couple walking their terrier along the prom. Even though it wore a cheery red jacket, the poor thing looked frozen. She said as much to Eleri.

'Maybe it needs somewhere to warm up? If only this town had, oh I don't know, a dog-friendly café doing really great organic food and specially made dog biscuits ...'

'Come off it, Eleri.'

Eleri chuckled. 'I will if you come and talk to Millie. She wants to see you. Tell you what – the café's missing a Christmas tree. If you come and get one with me, the hot chocolate's on the house. Oh and it's Ri to my friends.'

Zoe's mouth emerged from her scarf. 'Can I decorate it?'

'With the work me and Mil have on, you'll have to. And we've got all these Christmas cards to go up somewhere.' Eleri sighed dramatically. 'Just haven't had a chance to do anything Christmassy at all. Needs an expert touch, mind.'

'Oh, I'm really good at that sort of thing.' Zoe sat up. 'I did the lights last year.'

Eleri stood up. She reached out a hand. 'We'd better go and get this tree, then, *cariad*.'

As they walked along the prom, heads down against the wind, Zoe tucked her arm into Eleri's and pulled her closer for warmth. 'Ri,' she asked. 'Is it true what they say? Are you really a mermaid?'

Eleri's giggle skittered into the air and drifted up into the silvered sky.

Chapter 18

Somehow, they managed to carry the tree back along the prom from town, with Zoe at the front and Eleri taking the bulk of the weight at the trunk end.

'Oh my goodness,' Millie said, as they barged their way through the door of the café. 'I haven't had a real tree in here for years. It's enormous!'

Zoe puffed. 'Think there really is something magical about Ri. She got the price down by twenty quid.'

Millie shunted a table and some chairs out of the way. 'Here, shall we put it against this wall?'

They levered it into place, hampered by a very excited Trevor, who scampered around sniffing and playing with the bits of branch that had fallen off. Millie cut away the netting and all three women studied it. It was so tall its top nearly reached the café's ceiling.

Eleri, hands on hips, frowned. 'I don't think magic had anything to do with getting the price down. I reckon we've been sold a dud.' She put her head on one side. This tree has got a definite kink.'

Zoe hopped from one side of the tree to the other. 'Ri's got a point. It's bent halfway up.' She giggled.

Millie came to her and pulled her into a hug. 'Well, I think it's perfect. Just smell the scent of pine. There's nothing like a real tree. Thank you both. And Zoe, I'm so sorry for biting your head off the other day, my lovely. Will you forgive me?'

'Yeah. Course.' Zoe gave an embarrassed shrug.

'More forgiven than a very forgiven thing?'

'Aw Mil.' Zoe screwed up her face. 'Where'd you get talking like that?'

'I've absolutely no idea.'

The newly restored doorbell jangled and alerted them to customers. It was the couple with the shivering terrier.

'Basket Trevor,' Millie said, automatically, and he padded away.

'Excuse me,' the woman said. 'I don't suppose you're open, are you? We tried that elephant place on the high street but they don't allow dogs in.'

Millie went into professional mode. 'Come in, come in. It's too cold to be out there for long. Come and sit yourself down over here at the window.' She smiled. 'Best table in the place.'

As they took off coats and scarves their dog wandered over to say hello to Trevor and then sniffed the Christmas tree with interest.

Millie handed over a couple of menus and followed Eleri and Zoe into the kitchen. She peered into the pot of potato and leek soup bubbling away to itself on the stove and flicked the switch on the kettle. Eleri disappeared to find a broom to sweep up pine needles and Zoe stared through the porthole window.

'That tree definitely needs lots of lights,' she said, happily. 'I'll see what Granddad has going spare. Oh no!' she gasped.

'What is it?' Millie asked, busy getting a tray ready.

'There might be a reason not to have a real tree in a dog-friendly café.'

'What's that then, my lovely?' Millie looked up to see Zoe's face creased with laughter.

'That little terrier? He's just cocked his leg on the trunk!'

Chapter 19

Eleri sat on the stool in the Arts Workshop and smiled at Ken. 'At least you've got it nice and warm in here.'

Ken grunted. He was peering into the viewfinder of an impressive-looking camera. 'Yeah well, if you're sitting for any length of time, you get cold, my friend. And I can't work if my hands are stiff. Is it okay if I take some shots? I use them with the preliminary sketches. Builds up the ideas.'

'That's fine.' Eleri rocked her head from side to side to loosen a kink in her neck. Too much time on land, she decided. I need a swim, I'm getting stiff. 'Do you want me to sit in any particular position?' She flicked her plait off a shoulder.

'No, no. Just try and relax, if you can. For this first session I just want to see how the light falls on your face. Get a few ideas going. I'll probably just talk a lot and get you to talk back. Don't feel you have to sit still. Try to react naturally.'

'Great-looking camera.'

'Can't beat a Leica lens.' Ken began rattling off a few shots. 'I'll have you back and do some sketches and then I can start the painting proper.'

'I had no idea you had to do so much prep.' Eleri stretched

her back and lifted her hair off her neck.

'Yeah well, the more notes I have, the less time you have to spend sitting for me. I'm sure you've got better things to do.' Ken came close. 'Can you loosen your hair for me?' He took a photo of Eleri's hair as it tumbled, in a golden-brown waterfall, down her back. 'There is one thing, though. I wanted to ask how you felt about –'

'Posing naked?' Eleri shrugged. 'I don't see why it would be a problem.'

'Fantastic. It might be an option. Might not. You can always have Tes as chaperone, if it helps.' He emerged from behind the camera and grinned. 'Haven't decided how to go with this portrait yet. But we'll keep it in mind.' He took another photograph. 'Yes,' he yelled. 'That look into the distance, that works really well.'

Chapter 20

'No, that's fine.' Millie nodded into the phone, feeling sick. It wasn't fine at all. 'I completely understand. Of course the feasibility study shows little potential profit. But if I could just explain some of the ideas I've had and some of the new customers we've attracted to the café recently.' She listened as Clare's father interrupted. And quashed all hopes of a sale.

'Well, that's it, then,' she said to Trevor as she replaced the receiver. 'That's the end of that particular adventure.' She gathered his warm little body to her and went to stand at the sitting-room window. It was foggy again tonight, hushing the sea. Even the Christmas lights strung along the harbour buildings were barely visible. The flat could feel very remote on nights like tonight. Few people lived nearby when it was out of season and Millie had never felt more alone. Holding Trevor closer, she whispered into his fur. 'What are we going to do about paying the bills? I'll have to let Eleri go. And I knew I shouldn't have bought that extravagant tree. Oh Trev and what about that threatened hike in business rates. What are we going to do?'

The envelope, with its strident Blue Elephant logo, sat on

the arm of the sofa. It had arrived that morning. At the time it had made her laugh and she'd nearly ripped it up. But this morning she'd still thought Clare's parents were pursuing the purchase of the café.

Trevor, wriggling in her tight hold, protested, so she put him down. He found his squeaky toy and began to play with it noisily, oblivious to her distress and the fact that he might not have a roof over his head for much longer.

'Well, that's it then,' Millie murmured, a solitary tear rolling down her cold cheek. 'Blue Elephant you've won.'

Chapter 21

Eleri spread the lifestyle magazines out on the table in front of her. The café had been quiet all morning and she thought she could sneak in some work. They'd been due another networking group but Clare's mother had just rung and cancelled all bookings for the foreseeable future. Millie was nowhere to be seen, having muttered something about having to make some important phone calls.

As she drank her coffee, Eleri took time to enjoy Zoe's Christmas decorations. The endearingly wonky tree was now festooned in pink and silver tinsel and glowed with a mass of white lights. Zoe had spent an entire weekend making pink cupcake Christmas decorations out of painted cardboard. They were so effective they'd had several customers ask where they could be bought. The fairy lights, with their fluffy trim, weren't to Eleri's taste, but she had to admit Zoe had natural artistic talent. She'd learned that the girl had given up her painting and thought it a mistake. Zoe had potential; she was wasted doing English Lit.

The café looked much improved with a few singing snowmen around, not to mention the blow-up Father

Christmas in the corner, where Trevor guarded it jealously. The decorations hid the inevitable chipped paint and hard knocks of a season's wear and tear. The quick-fix overhaul of last year had done its job but was only temporary. The long-planned refurbishment, Millie had explained, was having to be postponed.

The Christmas decorations were fun, Eleri decided, and fun was in short supply in Millie Vanilla's at the moment. And the customers seemed to notice. There had been a notice-able lack of business in recent days. The cancellation of the networking groups might just be the death knell.

Trying not to worry about Millie and her café, Eleri flicked through a magazine. She paused at a page. Liking a picture of a tented ceiling and enormous chandeliers, she reached for her scissors and cut it out. 'Would be a marvellous look for the restaurant at the Lord,' she murmured to herself. She loved creating mood boards. It took her back to cutting and sticking sessions on wet Sunday afternoons when she was a child. Glancing up, she saw it was beginning to rain. It was the sort of light but persistent seaside rain that made you wetter than expected. No wonder there were no customers venturing as far along the prom as Millie Vanilla's. They'd all be shopping in town and diving into Blue Elephant.

Eleri shivered. It was cold in the café. Millie had turned the thermostat down and snapped at her when she'd mentioned it. She picked up her mug and drank, thoughtfully. Millie had looked ashen when she'd slammed out. Something was wrong. Deeply wrong. You didn't have to be a 'sensitive' to guess that. Eleri wondered how long things would take to work themselves out. At the moment it didn't look good for any of them. Sighing and wishing fate would hurry up and sort it out, she turned another page and stroked an image of some chairs. The deep-blue velvet was a great look. Not with the cheap gilt trim, though. She continued to work through the magazines methodically. She'd already begun a list of possible therapies that the hotel could offer; she had enough contacts to pull in favours. She allowed herself a little wiggle of excitement. It was so good to be working on something that she had been trained for. For the first time in a long while, maybe ever, she felt the tug of roots. Of wanting to stay in one place for good. She and Alex had got on brilliantly when he'd taken her to lunch. She'd be happy to work for him. And, when the love between them happened, as she knew it would, she'd welcome it.

A shadow, dark and foreboding, misted into the room. Its tendrils gripped at her, clouding her vision. Dropping the scissors with a clatter, she put a hand to her temple as the pain struck. Something terrible was happening. It was happening right now and there wasn't a damn thing she could do about it.

Chapter 22

Millie parked outside the front door of the Lord to let Eleri get out. She had no intention of lingering. There was nothing for her at the hotel and she had Christmas shopping to do. She and Tessa planned on going into Lyme later. If what she'd put into motion ten days ago happened, she might actually have more than a fiver to spend on present-buying this year. Besides, she had no desire to play gooseberry to the affair quietly blossoming between Alex and Eleri.

Alex appeared at the door, looking anxious. 'Good morning, both.' His breath puffed out in the cold air. 'Jed's back. His trip was curtailed somewhat. Come in, come in.' He sprinted around to the driver's door before Millie could change her mind. Opening it for her, he whispered, 'Do come in. I'm rather worried about the old boy.'

Alex led them, this time, into a recently refurbished sitting room. By the hotel's standards it was probably considered small, but Millie thought the café would fit in twice over. She glanced around, appreciating the subtle blues and creams, her attention caught by an enormous abstract hanging on one wall.

'One of Ken's,' Eleri explained. 'Alex and I thought it would be lush to display some local artists in the hotel.'

'And, of course the main advantage is, as it's a free advertisement for them, I haven't had to pay a penny for it.'

'Alex!' Eleri nudged his arm playfully. 'You don't mean that, *bach*.'

Alex regarded her with affection. 'Don't I? The other advantage is if I absolutely hate the piece, I can change it at will.' He pulled a comical face at Millie.

Eleri put an arm through his and looked up at him, laughing. 'You don't mean that either. Ken paints genius stuff.'

Jealousy shot through Millie. They looked so relaxed with each other. Had already got to the tender, bantering stage of their relationship. She wondered if they'd slept with each yet and guessed not. Eleri might have to work a little harder at piercing Alex's closed-up shell. Although he was a lot more relaxed these days, he was nothing like his brother. At the thought of Jed another tumult of emotions flooded her. Not jealousy this time. Love, loss, longing. Anger. All far more complex than she imagined Eleri and Alex were experiencing. Fear prickled. She wondered why his brother was worried about him.

'Hello Millie.' A soft voice had her wheeling around. For a moment Millie didn't recognise him. In place of the glossy Boden boy was a shadow, a wraith. He wore an over-sized navy and claret striped dressing gown. Alex's at a guess.

'Jed.' She went to him and took his hands, any antipathy forgotten. 'You look terrible.'

'Thanks.' He managed a grin. 'Can we all sit down, do you

435

think?' He sank onto the nearest sofa. Millie thought he winced in pain.

She sat next to him. 'Have you been ill?'

'You could say that.' His attempt at joviality was pitiful. 'Picked up some kind of bug and couldn't shake it off.'

Alex busied himself pouring coffee for them all. 'Jed had to cut his trip short and get home.'

'Didn't get much work done,' Jed added. 'I had to get an earlier flight back.'

Millie looked from one brother to another. 'And neither of you thought to tell me?'

'Sorry, Millie. I only found out when I had the call from Heathrow to pick him up.' Alex handed her a cup. 'I collected him the day before yesterday. Since then it's been a bit hectic. Getting him to see a doc and sort out someone to look after him.'

'Would you care, Millie?' Jed asked, quietly.

'Of course I care! I love –' Millie stopped short and looked down, confused. 'We may not still be together but I still care about you. A lot.' She sucked in a breath to regain control. 'And you really do look awful.'

Jed slumped back. 'Yeah well. To be honest, I feel it.' He shook his head at Alex's offer of coffee. 'I'll stick with water, thanks, bro.'

'Are you eating? Is there anything I can make for you?'

'Oh, Millie my love. I wish I could have you as my nurse.'

Before Millie could answer, Alex butted in. 'You've got the inestimable Coral meeting your every need, Jed. At vast expense, I might add. And Millie hasn't time to play nursemaid.'

Jed met her eyes. 'Alex hired an agency nurse.' He pulled a gloomy face. 'She's terribly bossy. I don't like being told what to do, you see.'

'When did you ever?' Alex put in, drily. 'And may I remind you the alternative was Mother. Ma's brand of nursing is rather robust,' he added, as explanation.

Millie could well imagine.

'She's threatened to come down to see you, as it is.' Alex sat on an opulent blue-velvet chaise and grinned.

Jed let his head flop back as if the effort of the conversation was too much.

'What does the doctor think it is?' Eleri asked.

Alex answered, as Jed had his eyes closed. 'Some kind of infection. Should go in a week or so. As long as he rests. Which, of course, he won't.'

'Dengue fever, maybe? It's common in South America.' Eleri nodded at him. She seemed to know all about tropical disease. Draining her coffee, she stood up. 'Come on Alex, we need to go and fry our brains over a new name for the hotel. This room is looking fab, by the way. I can't believe how quickly you pulled it together.' She drifted out of the room.

Alex gave his brother a concerned glance. 'Don't let him do anything strenuous, please, Millie. If either of you need anything we'll be in the office. Or you can ring for Coral, of course.'

Chapter 23

Millie took Jed's hand, shocked to feel it so hot. He'd fallen into a doze. Gazing, she drank him in, greedily. She smoothed back his fringe, which had grown long and sun-tinted from the South American climate. The luxurious hair mocked his complexion, which although sun-tanned was worryingly dry and papery. Resting her head on his shoulder, she let time pass, content to be with him.

'You still here?' Jed asked. His voice seemed to come from a long way off.

Millie sat up, embarrassed. 'I think you should be in bed.'

'Is that a proposition?' He yawned hugely and grinned.

'Even if it was, which it isn't, I don't think you're in any fit state to act on it.'

Jed tried to slide himself up the sofa and stopped short, as if something hurt badly. He gave up. 'You could be right there,' he admitted. 'Jeez. It's so bloody frustrating. I'm never ill.'

'Is there anything I can get you?'

'Only yourself.'

Millie froze. 'Ah.' She slid her hand out of his.

Jed closed his eyes. He seemed to be drifting off again. 'And that's not going to happen, is it, Millie?'

Millie squeezed shut her own eyes. The tears were threatening. 'I don't think so, Jed. No.'

Jed sighed. The sound came from deep within his soul. 'Such a damn shame,' he whispered, his voice slurring slightly. 'We could have had such a good thing. But you're right. There's no hope of anything now.'

Millie, blinded by tears, searched out his hand again and they sat for a while in silence.

A woman in a blue top and matching trousers strode in. 'So there you are,' she said in a soft Irish accent. She stood above them, glaring down. 'Did I or did I not tell you, Jeremy Henville, that you were to stay in bed, now?'

This must be Coral, the nurse. She was at once terrifying and beautiful. Young, red-haired and curvy underneath the uniform. Millie stood up and glanced down at Jed. 'My fault,' she said. 'I should have called for you when I realised how weak he was.'

'My hero,' Jed said faintly. 'Is that mummy?' He opened one eye and it gleamed mischievously.

Maybe he was feeling a little better.

'Oh no,' he continued. 'How marvellous. It's Matron.'

Coming around to the same side Millie was on, Coral began to lever him up. Lifting him by his left arm, she winked, 'You're a whole heap of trouble, aren't you just? Come on, off with you now. Bed it is.'

Millie glanced from one to the other. Jed would be well looked after. There was nothing she could do. There was no place for her here. She turned away. The loss of him was too much to bear. It was over. Everything between Jed and her was finally, irrevocably, over. He hadn't fought for her. Had taken at face value when she'd said it was finished between them. She knew she was being contrary but hearing the same words she had fired at him come back at her made it seem so very final. Strangely, there was no pain. No sadness. Just a solid, lumpen ball of hideous regret at what might have been. Numbly, she reached into her pocket for her car keys and left.

Chapter 24

Alex parked Jed's Golf behind the scruffy building that was the Arts Workshop. A lager can skittered over his foot and came to rest against a mesh fence. Glancing around at the pot holes in the tarmac and the graffiti-covered walls he doublechecked he'd locked the car. Even on a crisp sunny day like today, the place was grim.

Ken stood next to a Christmas tree in the entrance hall. He was wearing a Santa hat. 'Alex, my man,' he said as they shook hands. 'There you are. Come on in. I've got a few paintings I think would look great at the hotel. This way.'

The building was much better inside. There was a smell of freshly painted walls and the corridor had photographs displayed all along it. Someone had put festive red tinsel around each one. From his quick glance, Alex saw the photos were of the various workshops that had taken place. It all looked to be far more thriving than it appeared from first impressions. He followed Ken into his studio. There was no hint of the season here. Instead, the bare room was painted a blinding white and flooded with light from a series of velux windows. It smelled alluringly of oil paint and linseed oil.

Ken caught Alex staring up at the windows. 'Your brother's handywork. Not that he put them in himself, like, but he got us the funding. Sweet, aren't they?' He shrugged. 'Loads of work still to, do but we're getting there.'

Alex admired his enthusiasm. 'I had no idea Jed had been so involved in fund-raising for the place.'

'Jed? Yeah, boy's done great. Still doing a bit, but he's been too busy with that coffee joint lately.' He went over to an easel and slid off its protective sheet. 'Never understood why he's got himself mixed up in that nonsense, but I suppose a bloke has to make a living.' He stood back. 'There. What do you think? Think it's finished? Always hard not to keep going back to stuff. That's why I'd like you to have it at the hotel. Can't keep fidgeting with it if it's up there.'

Alex crossed his arms and stared. He knew next to nothing about art. He'd never allowed himself the time off from the city to find out. But he knew what he liked and he liked Ken's work.

The painting before him was an abstract. He couldn't even begin to understand what the subject might be, but something about the cool green, grey and blue palette suggested a stormy sea, with an equally turbulent sky above it. He was reminded of the Turners his mother had taken him to see in the National Gallery when she'd had a brief but fervent fascination with art.

'You like it?' Ken's voice was eager.

'I love it.'

'But?'

Alex shot Ken a grateful smile for understanding. '*I* love

442

it, but it might be a tad riotous for a hotel designed to soothe the fevered brows of executives.'

Ken gave a short laugh. 'Okey-dokey, my friend. What about something more figurative? She's not ready yet but it won't be long before I've completed her. You might recognise the subject. She made my paintbrushes fly. Think I've aced this girl.' He strode to a corner of the studio and flicked off the stained sheet with a flourish. 'Ta da!'

Alex stared. It wasn't a completely realistic portrait, Ken's work never was, but Eleri's glorious hair and startling eyes were unmistakeable. Somehow his feet let him walk nearer. Ken had painted her against another vague seascape and he'd used the same cool tones as in the landscape. Here, though, the effect was languorous. Sensual.

Eleri sat half-turned away, the long lines of her back fading into a swirling green pattern. Her arms were raised, with one hand lifting her heavy hair away from the nape of her neck. The only point of sharp focus was her eyes. They looked straight at the viewer. Challenging and deeply sexy. Knowing. Something deep in Alex reacted. Tracing the lines of Eleri's s-shaped pose, he took in the generous breasts with the hint of nipple, the toned body, the wide hips, before they dissolved into the abstract pattern.

Apart from the collection of bangles she always wore, it was perfectly clear Eleri had sat for Ken completely and utterly naked.

Arousal churned uneasily within him with something else. Disapproval? Surely not. He'd never known anyone like Eleri. All his other girlfriends had been Sloaney blondes. Home

Counties, public-schooled and boring in comparison. They'd all drifted away when it became apparent he couldn't give them the attention they thought they deserved. Eleri's serenity and independence attracted him. Her alternative way of life and free spirit only added to her peculiar brand of glamour. But he wasn't sure he could cope with this.

'You alright, my friend? You've gone pale. This not right for you either?' Ken was disappointed. 'Magnificent though, ain't she?'

'Um.' Alex cleared his throat, forcing himself to get a grip. Seeing Eleri like this had completely unnerved him. Her portrait was somehow both unearthly and provocative. And deeply disturbing.

He found his voice. 'It's an incredible painting, Ken.'

'Still not right for the hotel, though?'

'Maybe I'll ... maybe I'll take the abstract after all.'

'You do that, mate.' Ken was delighted. 'Give me a tick and I'll get some bubble wrap round it.'

Alex slotted the canvas in behind the passenger seat of the Golf. His hands shook as he started the car's engine. 'Get a grip,' he rebuked himself. 'It's art. Beautiful art.'

But in the far reaches of his mind lurked the unworthy thought: what sort of woman would so easily take off her clothes in front of a complete stranger?

Chapter 25

Millie lay staring at the darkness beyond her bedroom window. She'd long given up on sleep. It was a clear night and there were one or two stars twinkling. She could hear the rush of the sea as it sucked at the shingle, but there was no wind. It was eerily calm.

Picking up her phone, she groaned as she saw it was getting on for three in the morning. Flinging back the duvet, she padded into the kitchen and to a startled Trevor.

Ignoring the Blue Elephant letter, which screamed at her from the kitchen table, she flicked on the kettle. She opened the cupboard and scanned its contents. What would a convalescent be tempted by?

Three hours, a Victoria sponge, an iced carrot cake and a batch of chocolate brownies later, Millie hung up her apron and whistled to the dog. 'Fancy a really early walk on the beach, Trev?'

As she stomped along by torchlight and Trevor ran about excitedly sniffing out the damp, seaweedy smells, Millie's thoughts returned to Jed.

The cooking, as always, had soothed her for a while, but

now her mood lowered again. The questions rolled around in an endless loop. Why had Jed taken a job with Blue Elephant? Had he deliberately wanted to hurt her again? Why couldn't she trust him? Was he going to get better? More questions battered at her like the sea spray foaming off the tide. What was she going to do about her bills? Could she muster enough energy for the wedding planning meeting with Biddy? Millie stopped and looked up to the sky. It was a tiny bit lighter and the stars had faded away. She whispered a fevered plea for help. She wasn't sure who she directed it at. God. The gods of the sea, or maybe Eleri's eternal universe? Millie didn't particularly care. She just knew she needed help from somewhere. She wanted to be happy again but, at this moment, she couldn't imagine ever being so again.

Chapter 26

An hour later, on the same beach, Eleri waded into the sea and dived under the water without hesitating. It was the only way when swimming in winter. Too cold to swim at night now, she'd reluctantly swapped to early mornings. There were one or two other hardy souls who joined her sometimes, but today she was alone.

She surfaced, gasping, relishing the surge of blood coursing around her body. Swimming in such cold water made her feel fiercely alive, especially now that she swam for the sheer pleasure alone. Her days of competitive training were long gone. She didn't miss the five a.m. starts at the pool in Cardiff. Had never really had the killer competitive instinct to do well in events. It was all about the water for her. She rolled onto her back and watched the clouds scud across the dawn sky. A stiff breeze whipped up the foamy waves and she laughed out loud at the glorious December day. She began a swift and even crawl.

Living in Berecombe was great. She enjoyed working with Millie. Loved working with Alex on the hotel. It would be Christmas soon. Saturnalia. Yulefest. Whatever you chose to call it, she loved it. Bringing in the evergreens to decorate, the rich food, the lights defying the darkest days. She was happier and more settled than ever before. Life was good. With Alex, it might even get better. The cards had told her so.

A strand of seaweed tangled around her foot. Stopping to shake it off, she missed the angry storm clouds on the early morning horizon.

Chapter 27

Once again Millie parked the Fiesta in front of The Lord of the Manor hotel. A slew of white Transits littered the carriage drive, so she imagined work was progressing on the refurb. She stifled a pang of jealousy. She'd hoped to refurbish Millie Vanilla's. At one point she hoped to do so in partnership with Jed. It all seemed a lifetime ago.

'This is the last time I'm going to allow myself to see him,' she promised herself, as she balanced the pile of cake boxes on top of one another. 'I can't let myself do this any more. Not after he said there was no longer any future between us.' Biting her lip to stop the sudden tears, she lifted the enormous lion's head door knocker.

'Ah, so it's Millie, isn't it?' It was Coral. 'Have you come to see the patient? Oh, he'll be that delighted. Come on in.' She led the way to the blue sitting room, chattering as she went. 'Between you and me, I think our friend is getting a wee bit bored. I'm taking it as a sign he's on the mend.' She opened the door with a flourish. 'He's moping in here again this morning. Mind you, it's the only room worth sitting in. I'll leave you to it unless you'd like coffee, that is?'

Millie shook her head and forced a smile. 'I'm fine thanks, but Coral, do you think you can do something with these? I've done a bit of baking for everyone.'

Coral's eyes widened as she took the boxes off her. 'Well now, I'd hoped that sugary smell was coming my way.' She grinned, lifting her freckled cheeks. 'Aren't you just the gorgeous one? I'll stow them in the kitchen. Are you sure I can't get you anything, now?'

'Coral, can you let Millie get a word in edgeways?' Jed yelled from the furthest corner in the room.

Coral rolled her eyes. 'See what I mean? I'll leave you to him. Shout if you want anything, or if His Nibs gets any more testy.'

Jed was sitting in a winged armchair in front of a floor-length window. A tartan blanket was over his knees, but apart from that there was nothing of the invalid about him.

'You look a lot better. More colour in your cheeks.'

He laughed without humour. 'Fever's gone. Forcing myself well before Ma gets here.'

Millie sank down on a neighbouring chair. 'Oh. She's coming after all, is she?'

'Apparently joining us for Christmas. I don't know who is worse. Ma and her *Country Life* ideas of what makes a perfect Christmas or Coral and her cod Oirishness.'

'My, we are in a bad mood today. Coral seems lovely.'

Jed shook a reproving finger. 'Don't you start.' He lay back against the chair, hands gripping with white knuckles. 'It's just bloody frustrating. I feel so much better as long as I'm sitting down, but it takes me an hour just to have a shower

450

and a shave.' He thumped the arm of the chair and then winced. 'And I've got so much to do.'

'Is this Blue Elephant stuff?' Millie tried not to say it stiffly and failed.

Jed gave her a shifty glance. 'You could say that.'

'I see.'

'Millie –'

'I've got some news, actually. I wasn't sure if you'd be well enough to hear it but thought you might like to be the first to know. Actually, you might know already, I suppose, seeing as you work for them.' Millie stopped, feeling Jed's glare hot on her face and aware she was rambling.

'Know what, Millie?' Jed's voice was dangerous.

'As Clare's parents have backed out of buying the café, I've accepted another offer.' Millie took a deep breath. If she said it out loud it would make it true. 'From Blue Elephant.'

'Millie no!'

She folded her hands demurely in her lap. 'It's not nearly as good an offer, but I'll be able to move away from Berecombe, maybe go travelling again. It'll give me some time to think about what I want to do. Put some plans in place for the rest of my life.'

Jed scrubbed his hands over his face. He didn't speak for a while, seeming to be struggling over a decision. 'I don't want you to do that,' he said eventually. He leaned forward cautiously. 'Stick it out a bit longer, please Millie.'

'You don't want me to do it?' Millie pulled herself up. 'It's not your decision to make, Jed.'

'Jeez, Mil. I'm fully aware it's not up to me. But listen, if you can carry on without making a decision one way or the other for just a few more weeks, I think things could change in Berecombe. Drastically. Please don't rush into anything.' Jed's voice was urgent.

Millie stared out at the landscaped grounds. A sea mist had come in with the tide and it was a depressing, drizzly day but, despite this, there was a team of gardeners working on the long-neglected lake. Once finished, the hotel was going to be spectacular. Tessa had been right after all. Alex had been talking through plans for a helipad. Millie couldn't comprehend the finances involved in setting up the place. Eleri had mentioned she knew money wasn't an issue. How wonderful. Millie tried not to be bitter or envious, but it was hard when she could see someone else's dream becoming a reality when all she wanted was to keep her little café going. How could Alex, and more importantly, Jed, understand her problems when they lived in a world where multi-million-pound hotels were created without worry over finance?

Glancing at Jed, with his monied gloss evident even in illness, she realised she'd been right all along. They came from different worlds and the gulf was too vast to broach. This Cinderella was going to have to back off from her Prince Charming one final time. Taking in his blonde hair and broad shoulders, remembering his skilled hands in bed, his many kindnesses and his generous nature, she wished, with all her heart, that it could have been different.

She began to speak, but her voice cracked with emotion. She took a deep breath and launched in. 'I'm not sure I have an option, Jed. I would have thought that was obvious. I'm running deeper and deeper into debt.' She made direct eye contact and wasn't surprised to see Jed look discomforted. 'I have to sell up and Blue Elephant is my only viable option.'

'You haven't signed anything?'

'Not that it's anything to do with you, but no,' Millie admitted. 'I haven't got that far yet.'

Jed slumped back in his chair. 'Well, that's one thing, at least.' Once again, he scowled out at the gardens.

Millie could see him thinking hard and furiously. Or maybe he was simply fascinated by the digging that had begun at the lake's edge. She couldn't, for the life of her, understand why what she did with the café meant so much to him. Their relationship was over. He'd said as much the last time she'd seen him.

'Jed,' she began, hesitantly. 'Can you give me one reason why I shouldn't go ahead with the sale?'

Jed turned to her, a muscle beating in his cheek. He opened his mouth to speak, then shut it again. He shoved a frustrated hand through his hair. 'I wish I could. You don't know how much, Millie.' He met her eyes, 'But I can't. Not at this precise moment.'

'I see.'

'No you don't.' He threw off his blanket. 'I just wish I wasn't so incapacitated. God, it's frustrating. I've got so much to do.' He reached forward and took her hands in one of his. 'Just promise me you'll hold off signing anything which commits you fully. Promise me, Millie!'

'Yes, okay. I promise.' Millie shook him off, wondering if he was still feverish. 'Not long until Christmas now, anyway.

Not a lot I can do until the New Year.'

'Good.' He sank back, looking relieved but pale. Their encounter seemed to have exhausted him.

There was another silence. An uncomfortable one, as if neither knew quite how to move forward. Both jumped as the door opened.

'That'll be Coral trying to force-feed me drugs again,' Jed said, irritably.

It was Coral, but she wasn't her usual cheerfully bustling self. She looked flushed and slightly dazed.

'Millie. You've got a visitor, so you have.'

A stocky, dark-haired man bearing an enormous bouquet of lilies strode into the room.

'Tesoro mio!' he proclaimed and presented the flowers to Millie. 'I find you!'

Chapter 28

'Savio?' Millie stared at him in shock.

'*Buongiorno, buongiorno*. I find you. Ah, *sei bella*.' He stepped forward, lifted her bodily from the chair and kissed her resoundingly on both cheeks. 'How I miss you, my little one.'

Millie teetered from his enthusiastic greeting, only too aware of Jed's penetrating gaze. 'How ... where ... how did you find me?'

'Ah, *cara mia*, I hunt all over Devon. I drive the car, she come all this way and find you.'

'In other words, you used a sat-nav?' Jed put in.

'*Si, si*, I use sat-nav,' Savio replied, ignoring the sarcasm. 'All to find my *bella* Millie.'

'But how did you know I was here, at the hotel?' Millie couldn't get over the fact he was in front of her. He looked every inch the wealthy Italian, with his mustard-leather coat and maroon silk scarf knotted oh-so casually around his neck. At once foreign and very much at home in the opulent surroundings.

'I see the *trattoria*. Millie Vanilla. I knock.' He shrugged.

'No one there. I see a *bella donna,* her name is Biddy, *si?*' He clapped his hands together. 'Oh so beautiful! All these English women are so beautiful. I ask her, where is my Millie? She send me here.'

'Oh bugger, Biddy! I was supposed to meet her for the wedding planning.' Millie clapped her hands to her burning cheeks. 'I completely forgot.'

'She has husband? No!' Savio made an eloquent noise of regret and then looked about him. 'A hotel, eh? *Bene.* I book room.'

'We're not open for business yet.' Jed's voice was acid.

'Oh, I'm sure we can find a room for one of Millie's friends.' Alex walked in. 'As long as he understands we're still rather a work in progress.'

'Say again?' Savio looked confused.

'The hotel is being re-built.'

'Ah. *Restaurato.*' Savio nodded solemnly. 'In *Italia* too, this happens. So I stay?'

'I don't see that will be a problem. Will it, Jed?'

'It's your hotel, bro. Do with it what you like.'

'Exactly.' Alex shoved his glasses further up his nose and held out a hand. 'May I introduce myself? I'm Alex Henville, the owner. Welcome to the Lord.'

'You are a lord, *vero?*' Savio was impressed.

Alex's ears pinked. 'Oh my goodness, no. That's the name of the hotel. If you come this way, I'll show you to one of the rooms we've actually managed to get finished. Is that your Maserati parked at the front? Wonderful bit of kit.'

'*Si si.* My car. All the way from *Italia* to see *mia bella* Millie.

I drive her.' Savio began to follow Alex but changed his mind and returned to Millie. Launching himself at her, he grasped her shoulders and said in an urgent undertone, 'We have much to catch up on, *cara mia*. Oh, that night in Siena, eh? *Fantastico!*' He kissed her thoroughly on the lips and then went with Alex, a stunned Coral tripping behind.

The room hummed with a potent silence. Then Jed said, 'So, Millie, are you going to explain your Italian friend, Savio? I'm all ears.'

Chapter 29

'It's not what you think.'

'And what do I think?' Jed got up. He held his shoulder as if in pain.

Millie buried her nose in the lilies to give her time to compose herself. The last person she expected to see in Berecombe was Savio. 'You think I've had an affair with Savvy.'

'And did you?'

'Of course not,' she replied, hotly. 'You've just met him. Do you really think he's my type?'

'I thought I was your type once, Millie.'

Millie's cheeks burned anew. 'I did not have an affair, or anything else, with Savio.'

'He seems very keen on you. Drove across Europe to find you.'

'It's not quite that romantic,' Millie said crisply. 'He's got relatives in Padstow. He's probably on the way to see them.'

'But even so, it's a bit of a detour.'

'Hardly. Not if you've come all the way from Italy.'

'Okay,' Jed said grudgingly. 'I'll admit defeat on that one. But what was all this about a hot night in Siena?'

'He took me to dinner, Jed. We had fun. I can't help it if he read more into the situation than was actually there. And he's like –' Millie stopped, lost for words. 'He's like that. Flamboyant. Over the top, even for an Italian.'

'He seemed very eager to reacquaint himself with you.' Jed was sullen.

Millie had had enough. 'So what if he is, Jed?' She paused and then launched in. 'You know what? I liked it. I liked being taken for dinner. Driven about in a flash car. Being taken to see the towers at San Gimignano. It's hardly my fault he's keener on me than I am on him.' She thrust the lilies at him. 'And what's it got to do with you, anyway? We've split up, Jed. I can see anyone I like and do anything I want.' She was aware of sounding petulant, but couldn't stop now. 'And if I want to be taken out by a sophisticated, cultured man like Savio, then I will.'

She turned to go, but Jed caught her by the hand, his eyes dark with anguish. 'Millie, I'm sorry. I'm just jealous.'

'Jealous? What right have you got to be jealous?'

'None. I know that.' He blew out a gusty breath. 'But I still care about you, Millie. I'll never stop.'

Millie drew herself up. 'All the time I've known you, Jed, you've asked me to trust you and, despite everything, time after time, I have. Maybe this time, it's your turn. You'll have to learn to trust me.' She hesitated, then leaned forward and kissed him softly on the cheek. 'But maybe it's too late for that. Goodbye Jed. We've had, well, we've had quite a time. And now it really is over.'

Then she turned on her heel and left.

Chapter 30

'Those flapjacks will need another five minutes or so, I reckon.' Eleri came out of the café's kitchen and deposited two steaming mugs of coffee next to Millie's laptop. She peered over her shoulder, humming along to 'Two Thousand Miles', which was playing on the radio. 'Got to be the coolest Christmas song ever,' she said. 'The Pretenders did such lush stuff. My Da's fave band. What are you looking up?'

Millie clicked on Google and frowned. 'These criminal gangs in Colombia.'

'Oh right.' Eleri nodded and sat down. She shoved up her collection of bangles and continued with her task of folding green serviettes into Christmas tree shapes. 'These *bandas criminales* thingies. I thought the Colombian government was trying to control them. Supposed to be a safer place to travel in now. Or so they say. I never managed to get that far. Stopped in Costa Rica.' She blew on her coffee and sipped. 'Gorgeous country. So much wildlife. What does it say, lovely?'

'It mentions something called BACRIM.' Millie scanned the computer screen. 'General term for drug-trafficking gangs. I think. There's a lot about trying to eradicate them and the

460

political situation. Certainly sounds like they're trying to do something, but I'm not sure I'm really any the wiser. Nothing to do with coffee anyway.' She let out a relieved breath.

Eleri folded the last of the serviettes and put them neatly into a tinsel-lined basket. 'Why did you think they might have something to do with coffee?'

'Oh, I don't know, Ri. I can't stop thinking about Jed. Something doesn't gel. He goes off coffee buying, gets a fever, gets flown back, but he's moving as if his body hurts.' Millie thought back to how Jed had winced when trying to sit up. 'More specifically, as if his arm hurts.' She went silent, deep in thought.

'Maybe the fever is making his muscles ache? Or maybe he's just weakened by it. He looked a lot better the last time I saw him.'

'When did you see him? Was he okay?' Millie tried to sound casual. It had been three days since she'd seen Jed. Three difficult days.

Eleri shot her a look. 'On his feet, looking a lot more cheerful. Giving Coral hell for making him rest. Asking about your pal Savio.'

Millie ignored the Savio comment. The man had been hovering around constantly since he'd arrived. Genial and entertaining he might be, he was a distraction she could do without. She would have to let him down gently. 'Good,' she said, vaguely, and stifled a pang of jealousy. She ought to be the one looking after Jed. Then she remembered they'd split up.

'You know, whatever the reason Jed has for working for

Blue Elephant and being so mysterious, I'm sure it's a good one.'

'I'm glad you think so.'

'Perhaps you should trust him?'

'Ri, that's all I've ever done.' Millie snapped the laptop shut. 'And it's got me into a mess time and time again. No, I'm done with being asked to trust Jed Henville. I'm afraid we're finally over. Thanks for doing the serviettes, by the way. And the white lights in the glass vases look great. Very festive.' She picked up her mug and drank her coffee.

Eleri accepted the change of subject matter. 'Thought they'd be good centrepieces for the wedding tables. Has Biddy suggested anything else?'

'Once she'd calmed down after I'd missed the meeting, you mean?' Millie smiled tightly. 'What hasn't she asked for? Think we've compromised on rows of lanterns with tea lights creating the aisle and an arch covered in white silk camellias and ivy.'

'Nice. The vases will go well, then. I could add some fresh greenery, if you like? Is she still going with a green and white colour theme?'

'As far as I know.'

'Are they still getting married on the beach?'

'Yes. Just out there.' Millie nodded to the stretch of flat sand in front of the café's terrace.

Eleri shivered. 'Won't it be cold, though? Weather's set for a really chilly spell.'

'Arthur's sourced a load of cast-iron braziers, apparently. They'll be lit.' Millie shrugged. 'Suppose the guests will just have to wear coats.' She grinned, enthusiasm for Biddy's wedding beginning to break through her numb misery. 'Biddy has insisted on the guests wearing red or white.'

'That's never popular.' Eleri laughed. 'People hate being told what to wear.'

'She says it's to make the photos look Christmassy.'

'Suppose she's got a point. How are the hot chocolate recipes coming on?'

'Tried a rum and salted caramel one last night. That might be a winner. Thought it would warm everyone up when they come in after the ceremony. And Biddy mentioned a problem with the invitations, so I've customised a load of Christmas cards. Oh and I thought I could make a batch of teeny mince pies and ice them with B and A.'

'Cool.' Eleri gazed at Millie. 'It's all going to be fab. Considering you've never hosted a wedding before, you've got a real knack for it, you know.'

'Have I? Thanks, Ri.' Millie shrugged. 'I feel I'm winging it, to be honest, but I suppose it's just an extension of what I've been doing at the café all my life. Making people happy.' Her voice quivered. 'Just a shame I couldn't make myself happy, isn't it?' She concentrated fiercely on drinking the last of her coffee.

'Millie, all will be well. Everything will work out, you'll see.' Eleri stood up and went to the door. 'There's an end to our peaceful morning,' she laughed. 'Here come the happy couple and Zoe too. Ooh,' she added, as a thought struck. 'Flapjacks!'

Mille stared at Ri's long, elegant back as she headed to the kitchen. She wished she could be as certain. All would be well? Fat chance.

Chapter 31

The arrival of Arthur and Biddy, with Zoe and the dogs, heralded a rush of customers. Chilled by the biting wind whipping off the sea, people crowded in for an early lunch. Millie's carrot and coriander soup served piping hot with Tessa's walnut bread sold out. For the first time in a while, the café was back to its fugged-up, cosy winter best and Millie, too busy to think, was almost content.

Once everyone was served, she leaned against the counter, overcome by affection for the place. It was made all the more poignant by knowing that Millie Vanilla's days were numbered.

She watched as Eleri chatted to Zoe. How could the woman be so certain about everything? Experimenting, she mouthed Ri's words, 'All will be well.' How on earth could she know? She tried it again, attempting more conviction this time. Looking about her, everything appeared to be exactly the same. Biddy was still eating her scone and slipping morsels to Elvis waiting under the table. Arthur was still looking through council papers. Davey Pascoe and friends were still spooning up carrot soup and tearing into the granary bread. 'All will be well,' she repeated, one more time and gave up.

She shook her head and regarded her friend. If Eleri had magical powers, Emilia Fudge sadly lacked them. Nothing had changed. She still faced having to sell up.

Having chatted to Biddy who had wholeheartedly embracing her role as a bridezilla, Eleri was now having an equally calming effect on Zoe. The girl had trailed in behind her grandfather, looking pale and withdrawn, but was now talking animatedly.

Millie glanced up as the door's bell tinkled. It was Alex. He put up a quick hand to Eleri and then approached her.

'Good morning. Happened to be in town and wondered if you have any of those savoury scones left?' He took off his specs and blew on them to clear them. 'I've become rather partial.' Replacing them, he blinked at her, hopefully.

'Morning, Alex,' Millie answered, resisting the temptation to ask after Jed. 'I do, as a matter of fact. They're not universally popular. Stilton? Or cheddar and chive?'

'Either would be wonderful. And I don't suppose you have any soup?'

'I'll see what I can find.' Millie was sure she had one portion left. She'd been saving it for her own lunch, but didn't seem to have much appetite lately.

'Marvellous. I'll just squeeze in here, shall I?' Alex took off his overcoat and scarf and sat down at the only empty table, behind where Eleri and Zoe were so deep in discussion they didn't notice. Amused, Millie saw him pick up one of Eleri's narrow silver bangles, which must have slipped off. He held it in his hand and stared at it as if it were a talisman.

Millie checked on Trevor, who was snoozing in his bed by

the radiator and went into the kitchen. As she prepared Alex's lunch, she thought over what else Eleri had said.

'Could I really be a wedding organiser?' she questioned as she stirred the hot soup. She heated the scones, one of each flavour, and spread them with a good dollop of George Small's salty butter. 'I don't know the first thing about it.' As she plated up Alex's meal and pushed open the door with her behind, a voice in her head whispered, 'You can do anything you want. All will be well.'

Chapter 32

Alex didn't know if it was the cold sea air or hard work but, since coming to Berecombe, his appetite had been insatiable. He stared down at his thick soup with its dollop of cream on top and his mouth watered. He bit into a scone. It was warm and buttery. Good food made with simple ingredients. It couldn't be beaten. He took up his spoon and tasted. Hot and carroty with warming coriander. Delicious. And perfect for a winter's day. As he ate, he became aware of the conversation going on behind him, although he really hadn't meant to eavesdrop. Biddy, having a shouted conversation with Millie about the expense of fresh flowers, along with Wizzard blaring out that they wished it could be Christmas every day from the radio, meant Eleri and Zoe had had to raise their voices.

'I just don't know what to do, Ri,' he heard Zoe say. 'Whatever I decide, I'm going to end up hurting one of them.'

'What does your heart say?'

'My heart?' Zoe laughed shortly. 'That says keep one boyfriend for college and one for when I'm at home. But I can hardly do that, can I? Just wouldn't be fair.'

'No, it wouldn't be fair,' Alex heard Eleri reply, soothingly. 'To any of you.'

'Did this happen to you? When you were at uni? Were you ever in love with two men at the same time? I can imagine you had guys queuing at the door.'

Alex stiffened. He straightened so he could better hear Eleri's response. And hated himself for it.

She laughed. 'Not quite, lovely.' She paused, then went on. 'I don't know. Maybe it was different in my day.'

'Yeah, 'cos you're, like, well old.'

Eleri ignored the sarcasm. 'Older than you, Zoe, and I went to university at a different time. It all seemed much freer then. I didn't have one boyfriend as such. It was all more about grabbing your pleasure how and when you could, I suppose.'

'What, like free love, you mean?' Alex could hear the awe in Zoe's voice.

'You could call it that. It was probably more like promiscuity.' Eleri laughed again.

Her bangle lay on the table next to his soup bowl. He'd meant to return it to her before he left. Picking it up, he traced the intricate Celtic pattern with a thumbnail.

'I've never seen my body as a possession,' Eleri went on. 'More like a tool to give me, and those I choose to share it with, pleasure. I've never seen why there has to be a moral code ruling over something as natural and lovely as sex.'

'Wow,' Zoe said. 'That's so awesome. So you've slept with lots of men?'

'Now, what sort of question is that, *cariad?*' Eleri gave her silvered laugh. 'And here's me thinking we were talking about you. I'll ask you again, what does your heart tell you?'

Alex heard Zoe give a great sigh. 'That I want to be free to be by myself for a bit. That I want ... that I want to find out who I am before I share my life with someone else, no matter how much I love them.'

'Then that's your answer.'

'But it'll hurt them so much, Ri.'

'And that's where you have to be brave, lovely.'

The rest of their conversation was lost in the fuss that Biddy and Arthur made as they left. Alex couldn't hear anything over Biddy shouting her farewells. After they'd gone, Zoe and Eleri returned to quieter voices and all he heard was muted whispers.

His hand fisted around the bangle. Putting it down, he stared at it. It had been bent out of all recognition. So had his view of Eleri. How could he have fallen in love with someone who'd as good as admitted to promiscuity? The image of her portrait swam into his vision. She had sat proudly naked, flaunting her sexuality as a challenge. The queasy mix of electric arousal and horror he'd felt in Ken's studio flooded him again. Eleri had professed to not having a moral code about sex, but it was as far away from his own beliefs as it possibly could be.

Pocketing the crushed bangle, he stood abruptly. He grabbed his coat and scarf, threw down some money and left.

Millie came to clear his table, astonished, as Alex ran out. In his haste he left the door swinging open, letting in snarls of a vicious winter wind. She closed the door and leaned against it. 'I wonder what was all that about. Ri, what was wrong with Alex, do you think?'

Eleri looked up. She stared behind her, at the chair he'd hurriedly scraped back so that it was wedged against hers. 'Oh no, she gasped.' She stared up at Millie in horror. 'I think I may have just blown the best thing in my life.'

Chapter 33

Eleri ran out of the café and paused, scanning left and right. Alex was getting into the Golf, which he'd parked on the prom. She got to the road just as he edged the car out from the kerb. Half closing her eyes, she stood, with her arms outstretched, straddling the white lines. She heard his tyres slide on the greasy tarmac as he braked to avoid her.

'Eleri, I could have killed you. Get out of the road!'

She ran to the driver's side. Her breath misting out as she panted. 'Let me explain. Please Alex.'

'What is there to explain? I heard what you were saying to Zoe. I heard all of it.'

'Then let me tell you about it.'

Alex's face was ashen, pinched with fury. 'I don't want to hear. I don't want to hear the sordid details.'

Eleri let her hands slump against her sides. 'But that's just it. It wasn't sordid. It wasn't sordid at all. The men I shared my body with, well, we made something beautiful. But it was just something physical. Not like it could be with you.'

He revved the engine. 'I don't want to hear about you and all these other men. I thought I'd made myself clear.'

'It's who I am, Alex. Or rather it's who I was. It's in the past, but I can't change that.' When he still didn't answer, she added, 'Does it really make that much difference? Can't we talk this through? We've always been able to talk. Can't we get past this?'

A car came up behind Alex's and tooted. 'I think you've talked enough today. I don't want to hear any more. I don't know how many ways I can say it before you get the message. I don't want to have anything to do with someone so lacking in morals.' The car hooted again, this time more impatiently. 'So, if you'll be kind enough to get out of my way, that's an end to it.'

She stepped onto the pavement and watched in misery as Alex gunned the engine and disappeared.

'Lover's tiff, my darling?' called the bloke who had been hooting. 'Cheer up. It's not the end of the world.' He drove off, tyres squealing as he rounded the corner.

'Oh, but I think that's where you're wrong,' Eleri murmured, too numb to cry. 'I think it is the end of the world. My world, that is.'

The following day, Millie dropped her at Axminster to catch the London train.

'I wish you weren't rushing off like this,' she said, as she parked up.

There was a dismal sleety rain falling and, despite the cheerful Christmas lights, everywhere looked dank and grey. People lugged holiday luggage towards the ticket office, their shoulders shrugged up against the cold.

Eleri didn't answer. Her silence was only punctuated by

the windscreen washers thumping rhythmically to and fro, until they stopped when Millie killed the engine.

Unbuckling her seatbelt, Eleri eventually began speaking. It came out in a rush. 'Alex is never going to understand me. He's never going to stay with a woman he considers has slept around. He's too straight for that.' She blinked back tears. 'And what I told Zoe was only the half of it. I don't think he'll ever believe I'm good enough for him.'

'Is that what he said to you? I can't believe it. Alex is dotty about you – anyone can see that.'

'More or less. Let's just say he wasn't in a mood to discuss the matter.'

'Oh Eleri, that's awful, not to mention completely untrue. How dare he? I'm sure he was just angry and shocked, though. It's not like Alex to be so judgemental. Can you give him another chance?' Millie went to turn the car engine on. 'Come on,' she said, decisively. 'I'll take you up to the hotel now and you can thrash it out with him.'

Eleri stayed her arm. She shook her head. 'It would be no use, Mil.'

'It must be worth a go. You two are made for each other.'

'Ah, but that's just it, I don't think we are,' Eleri said softly. 'If I have to be someone else for him, it just wouldn't work, much as I want it to. And now, well, now he's discovered the truth of who I am ...' she trailed off. 'Let's just say for once I don't think I can trust the cards.'

Millie stared open-mouthed. She had no idea what Eleri was on about. As the woman got out, heaving her rucksack onto her back and striding purposefully to the ticket office, she called out, 'Keep in touch,' but was ignored. So much for all being well, she said bitterly, as she reversed the car out of its space. The way things are going, they couldn't be worse. Peering through the windscreen and at the rain now falling heavily, she groaned as she joined the queue at the traffic lights. She'd agreed to meet Savio tonight. If he really had driven across Europe to find her, he deserved to know that there was no future between them.

Chapter 34

'So what did he say, our kid?'

Millie was sitting in Tessa's kitchen, drinking tea and sampling a new variety of flat bread. She chewed thoughtfully, eyeing up the fibre-optic tree on the windowsill. It was changing colour every few seconds and was peculiarly hypnotic. At least it was cheerful. Outside it was another day of dark clouds and cold winds. The calendar might be hurtling towards Christmas but the weather hadn't noticed. So much for Arthur's promised snow.

Tessa watched anxiously. 'The bread. No good?'

'Oh Tes, it's gorgeous but I'm not sure fig and Serrano ham fits in with my ethos of locally sourced.'

'Suppose not. But hey, the caff isn't going to be yours for that much longer. Why do you care?'

Millie swallowed. It was true. The thought that her life in Berecombe would be over in a few short weeks was terrifying.

'And I thought you'd like the Italian connection. Speaking of which, you still haven't told me how he reacted.'

'Who? Savio?'

'Know lots of Italian millionaires, do you, pet?'

475

Millie stared into her tea. 'He took me to Samphyre, Dora's parents' place. It was great food.' She drifted off for a second, dreaming about what she'd eaten the evening before. 'I had the house fish pie with loads of juicy prawns and a chocolate mousse with real gold flakes on it. It was fabulous.'

'Concentrate, Mil. Back to Savio.' Tessa rapped a teaspoon on the kitchen counter, making Trevor bark.

Millie pulled a face. 'I felt really guilty about him. I mean, I'd never actually encouraged him. He didn't need much encouragement, to be honest. Savvy sort of steamrolls you into submission and I suppose I'd just gone along with it.' She blew out a breath. 'He was okay about it, in the end. Sighed in an extravagantly Italian way, declared his undying love for me and then spent the rest of the night chatting up the waitress.'

'Oh bab, that's priceless. Is he going back to Italy now?'

'No, he's driving on to Cornwall. Turns out I was right about me being a bit of a stopover, he was heading to stay with family for Christmas.'

'Nothing to feel guilty about there, then. More tea?'

'Thanks.' Millie held out her mug. 'Hopefully not.'

'And no regrets over missing out on a Maserati and a villa in Tuscany?'

'Not quite my style.' She reached down to fondle Trevor's ears.

Tessa stirred a generous spoonful of sugar into her own mug. 'Ought to give this up, but the weather's so cold I need all the calories I can get.' She nodded to the gunmetal sky outside. 'At least we've got rid of that freezing fog, but I'm not sure this is any better. I've never known it so cold down here. Temperature dropped to minus three last night.' She gave a dramatic shiver. 'I'm not sure I'd have given up on some Italian sunshine so easily.' As Millie didn't rise to the bait, she went on. 'How's the wedding panning going?'

'Good, thanks. All set.'

'Still on for next week?'

'Yup. A Christmas Eve wedding. I'm just agreeing the menu. Steak pie with a Stilton and leek crust, winter veg and Pavlova with a berry compote.'

Tessa grimaced. 'Sounds a bit heavy for a wedding breakfast.'

'Well, it's what they want and the ceremony is at five, so people will want something warming to eat after they've been sitting on a cold beach.'

'Fair enough. Are the dogs still going to be bridesmaids?'

'Yes.' Millie giggled. Biddy's wedding was the one bright spark in her life at the moment. 'It's so sweet, they each have green velvet waistcoats and Elvis is ring bearer. It's in a little sparkly box hung from his collar.'

'Get away. Gotta love our Biddy. Tessa shook her head, fondly. 'What about a honeymoon?'

'Think they're waiting until the New Year and then going to somewhere on the Gower. Biddy said the beaches there are great for the dogs.'

'Ace. Speaking of all things Welsh, has that Eleri left you in the lurch?'

'Oh I can manage. Not that busy and Zoe is feeling better, so she's holding the fort today.'

'Can't understand what happened.'

'Nor me.'

'Mind you, Ken said that Alex was a bit of a stick in the mud. Went all peculiar when he showed him Eleri's portrait.' Tessa sniffed. 'Seemed an odd couple to me.'

'Did you? I thought they were well suited.'

'Cold fish, I thought he was. Not like his brother.'

Millie winced at the mention of Jed. She shrugged. 'I don't agree. I think Alex is just very conformist. I agree they were complete opposites, but I thought it worked. It's such a shame Eleri didn't give him more of a chance. He's distraught.'

'Is he?'

'It's all quite romantic in a way,' Millie sighed. 'He's gone up to London to try to find her.'

Tessa gathered up their empty mugs. 'Well good luck to him with that. Fresh one?'

'Oh, go on then.' Millie nodded. 'I agree with you there, but Alex seems to have friends in high places. He might just find her.'

Tessa snorted derisively. 'If there's one place you can hide in, it's London. Maybe he shouldn't have been so quick to judge the girl. We've all got our pasts.' Flicking on the kettle, she huffed at the injustice.

'That's just it, though, Tes. He hasn't rejected her. Not to my knowledge, anyway. Eleri *assumed* he wouldn't want her. She doesn't actually know. She didn't bother to stay and talk it through.'

'Always said she was weird.'

Millie raised her eyebrows. 'You said no such thing.'

'Hmm. Thought it, though. All that mermaid crap, I ask you.' Tessa opened a cupboard and rootled around. 'If Roland has eaten all the biscuits again, I'll tan his hide. Ah, here we are, choccie Hobnobs.' She threw the packet to Millie, who caught it. 'Don't suppose you know where she is, then? Ri, I mean.'

'No idea whatsoever. Only have her mobile number.'

'And I don't suppose you've given it to Alex, have you?'

Millie caught Tessa's eye and grinned. 'No, I don't suppose I have.'

Chapter 35

'I'd better go.' Millie drained her mug. 'Promised Trevor a run on the beach while the tide is so low.'

'Stick the news on for me, bab. I'll watch the headlines then take Ken a flask over to the workshop.'

Millie checked her watch. It was later than either of them had thought. 'Think you might have missed the main news. It'll just be the local stuff.'

Tessa shrugged. 'That'll do.'

Millie unearthed the remote from under a pile of yet to be put up tinsel and switched on the television. 'Yes, I was right, it's just starting.'

'Good afternoon, the headlines in the South West today –'

As Tessa settled down to watch, Millie ran some hot water over their mugs and plates and wandered into the hall to find her coat and woolly hat.

'Mil!' It was Tessa screeching from the kitchen. 'Millie, get in here. You've got to see this. It's Jed!'

Millie ran back, tripping over an excitedly barking Trevor as she went. Hurtling over to where the television screen was crammed up behind a spaghetti jar, she saw Jed standing in

480

front of the Blue Elephant café in Berecombe. 'What's he doing on the telly? He's supposed to be recuperating. Turn it up, turn it up.' She flapped an arm at Tessa. 'I can't hear over Trevor's barking.'

'Where d'you put the remote?' Tessa snapped. 'Oh, here it is.' She turned the volume to maximum.

'These are very serious allegations you're making, Jed. Can you back up your claims with evidence?' The journalist batted her eyelashes at him and thrust the microphone suggestively in his face. She was wearing an over-sized fake fur hat and looked frozen.

Millie picked up Trevor, hushed him and watched, open-mouthed.

'Obviously I can't – and won't – go into details right now,' Jed was saying, But yes, I have comprehensive evidence that Blue Elephant is not what it claims.'

'And what exactly do you mean by that?'

'I mean that the company is not sourcing any of its stock from ethical and Fair Trade suppliers.'

Millie made a little shocked noise.

The journalist scaled up her flirting. 'And can you explain why that's such an issue?'

'Well, Chloe, it matters to Berecombe as we're currently trying to obtain Free Trade status. Having a prominent company in town not willing to trade within the Fair Trade agreement certainly isn't an asset to our campaign. And besides, it should matter to all of us that the coffee we drink is grown –'

'Thank you, Jed.' Chloe cut him off and turned to camera.

Her face filled the screen. 'We approached Blue Elephant's head office for a statement but have received nothing from them as yet. And, as you can see, although it was expected to be open today, the café here in Berecombe is closed. More news on this developing story in the late-night bulletin.' She looked up at the sky. 'And now, from a very chilly Berecombe, back to you in the studio and the weather forecast. Maybe you can tell us if we really have some Christmas snow on the way!'

'Oh, my God,' Millie finally breathed. She collapsed onto a stool. 'Blue Elephant not using Fair Trade suppliers.' She stared at Tessa, wide-eyed. 'And Jed is telling the press all about it. Oh!' she put a hand to her mouth. 'Do you think that's why he was in South America so much? He was scouting the coffee plantations?' A guilty blush stole over her face. 'I accused him once of playing James Bond. Looks like that's what he was actually doing.'

'But he's *working* for them.' Tessa crunched into a biscuit, scattering crumbs, to Trevor's delight.

'And what better way to discover exactly what's going on.' Millie clapped her hands as a thought struck. 'That's why he did it. That's why he got a job with them. Oh Tessa. He joined Blue Elephant in an attempt to uncover them!' She ran back out into the hall. 'Can you look after Trev for me? I've got something I really need to do.'

Chapter 36

Millie shoved the accelerator hard to the floor and cursed that her car was twelve years old and had a top speed of forty. Overtaking a tractor, she willed her little car wings so that it would fly up the hill, out of town and towards The Lord of the Manor.

Her mind was racing. Jed *must* have taken the job with Blue Elephant so he could investigate them. Had he suspicions before about their buying policy? Millie thought back to when Tessa was baking bread for them. She remembered her complaining that they'd wanted her to use less expensive ingredients. But it was a huge leap from cutting corners to maximise profit to deliberately sourcing from non Fair Trade coffee growers. Millie knew all about coffee worker exploitation. She had always bought from wholesalers who could certify that their supply was Fair Trade. It added to her outgoings but she thought it was worth it. That Blue Elephant were undercutting her through such means drove a glorious, white-hot fury through her. Changing down to turn onto the long drive leading to the hotel, she ignored the ominous groaning coming from her car. She gunned the engine towards the front door. Could it all be true? She had to know.

There were no white transit vans in evidence today. Millie did a tail-end skid and came to an abrupt halt next to a sleek grey limo. As she did so, the door of the hotel opened and Jed staggered out. He was flanked by two sinister-looking men in dark suits. They were gripping him by the arms.

Millie leaped out of the car and raced towards him. 'Jed! I've just seen you on the news.' She stopped. The men holding Jed didn't speak. Didn't stop. They propelled him to the limo.

'Mil, they're taking me to Exeter. To the Blue Elephant offices.' One of the men pushed him forward more roughly and he yelped in pain.

'Get your hands off him, he's been ill!' Millie got hold of one of the thugs and tried to prise him off. It was like tackling a gorilla. She was shoved away and stumbled to the ground. Sitting up, she rubbed at her bruised elbow. But Jed was coming off worse. To her horror, she could see blood seeping through the sleeve of his rugby shirt. Quite a lot of blood.

'Don't you dare fucking touch her!' he yelled, but was jostled into the back of the car. 'Get hold of Alex, Millie. Get Alex, he'll –.'

The limo's doors slammed shut on his words and the car spat gravel as it skidded away.

'But I don't have his number,' Millie shouted at the disappearing car, as she staggered to her feet. She considered getting into the Fiesta and giving chase. Looking at the speed at which the limo had hit the road, however, she knew she'd never catch it.

'Jed, I love you,' she whispered, but the sound drifted uselessly into the leaden sky. Two crows flew over the skeletal outline of the chestnut tree. Millie watched for a second, thinking hard, and then turned decisively into the hotel.

Chapter 37

The place was deserted. Maybe Coral had finally given up on her patient? More likely she was just having a day off. Millie tried Jed's mobile but it went straight to message. Hurrying into the little office behind the reception desk, she began to hunt for a list of telephone numbers.

'There must be one for Alex here,' she muttered as she sent a pile of papers cascading onto the floor. After a fruitless search, she sank onto the chesterfield. Thumping the arm in frustration, she thought hard. Then she had a brainwave; she knew who might have Alex's mobile number. Getting out her phone, she tapped on Eleri's name. 'Pick up,' Millie whispered, 'Please, Eleri, pick up.'

Ten minutes later, after explaining everything to Eleri, Millie had got through to Alex's phone. He didn't answer so, after much swearing, Millie composed herself and left a message.

She was aware of time slipping past. Jed needed her. He needed her help and she was failing him.

'Think, woman. Think. Who could help? I need someone legal. Arthur!' she cried suddenly. 'He knows a solicitor.' Punching in Arthur's number, she explained the situation as best she could. He returned her call a few minutes later. His solicitor friend thought it was way out of his league but had a son, Gavin, who was a barrister in London. Almost as soon as she clicked off the phone, it rang. It was Alex. He listened intently, grasped the seriousness of the situation instantly and demanded Gavin's number.

'Leave it with me, Millie,' he barked. 'Meet me at Exeter Airport's Pick Up and Drop Off. I'll be as quick as I can.'

Millie scribbled a hasty note for Coral and went.

Reversing into one of the only spaces left in the short stay car park, Millie wondered how long she'd have to wait. 'Can't be easy to get a flight from London that quickly,' she muttered. 'Especially at this time of the year. Everyone's on the move.' She rang Tessa and asked her to look after Trevor for a while longer and then tried Jed's mobile again. Once more, it went straight to message. Her stomach knotted with tension and she willed Alex speed.

She watched a couple in Santa hats and tinsel 'scarves' trundle a suitcase to the Volvo parked beside her. Christmas seemed a distant irrelevance. She felt very detached from all the festivities. The world had shrunk to sitting in the car, getting cold and fretting over whether Jed was alright.

'I don't think it is beginning to look a lot like Christmas at all,' she snapped at the radio, too on edge to be soothed by a crooning Michael Bublé. She stifled a nagging desire for the loo and regretting drinking so much tea at Tessa's. Switching off the radio, she jumped a foot as the passenger door opened. It was Alex.

'This is Gavin,' he explained as a chubby guy in a black

suit got into the back. 'Drive, Millie.'

He gave her the address of a nearby business park, clipped on his seatbelt and told her to turn right onto the main road.

'How did you get here this quickly?' She asked as she battled through the heavy Christmas traffic.

'My helicopter,' he said, shortly.

'Oh.'

Millie couldn't begin to imagine a lifestyle that included having your own helicopter, but had to admire this new, coldly efficient Alex. It must be the business-like side of him that had enabled him to do so well in the city. Concentrating on driving, she followed Alex's directions and tried to ignore her bladder. She hurtled into the tree-lined, landscaped business park, blessedly traffic free, and sped down the main drag.

'Drop us off here,' Alex commanded.

Millie skidded to a halt in front of an anonymous-looking grey office block. Even before she'd pulled on the handbrake, Alex and the mysterious Gavin shot off and disappeared through the revolving doors in the glass atrium. Unable to find an empty parking space, she abandoned the Fiesta on a corner and sprinted after them.

Chapter 38

She arrived as Alex and Gavin were having a measured argument with the receptionist.

'I think you'll find we have every right to speak to Douglas Feniman,' Alex said, with quiet authority. 'And to see my brother, who we believe is being held here against his will.' He bent forward and read her name badge. 'Otherwise, Janette, your company will have to deal with this man,' he gestured to Gavin.

'You have no right to detain my client without his permission,' Gavin smiled genially, but Millie sensed the steel behind it. 'I also believe there may be a Section 20 Assault charge to consider?'

Janette hesitated, looked from one man to the other and picked up her phone. She listened intently for a moment and then said, 'Mr Feniman will see you now. Fifth floor.' As they all trooped to the lift doors, she added, 'I'm afraid he will only see your legal representative.'

Gavin nodded to Alex, patted him on the arm and stepped into the lift.

Millie hopped from one foot to another. She looked at Janette hopefully. 'I don't suppose I can use your loo?'

Chapter 39

She came out to see Alex staring through the floor-to-ceiling windows of the foyer. He wore a grim expression and was resolutely ignoring the tray of coffee on the table behind him.

'Did you know anything about this?' he asked, without turning.

'No, nothing.' Millie said indignantly and collapsed onto one of the blue sofas. Looking more closely she saw they were decorated with tiny elephants. 'The first I knew of any of this was when I saw the lunchtime news.' She gazed up at Alex. He had his arms crossed and was scowling. 'You don't think I had anything to do with it, do you?' Her elbow hurt, so she rubbed it.

His shoulders dropped. Taking off his specs, he rubbed a tired hand over his face in a gesture that made him look very like his brother. Replacing them, he turned abruptly and came to sit next to her. Seeing her rubbing her arm, he asked, sharply, 'Did the bastards hurt you too?'

Millie shook her head. 'I tried to tackle one of them but, honestly Alex, he was like a mountain. I fell on my bum and knocked my funny bone.'

Alex gave a weak grin. 'Mil, you do go for it, don't you?'

'Didn't get me very far, did it? They still got away with Jed. I just hope they haven't hurt him too much.' Her bottom lip quivered and Alex put a reassuring hand on hers. 'Everything will be alright now, though, won't it?' she asked.

He stroked a hand down his stubble. 'Hopefully.' He stole a glance at the receptionist's desk and lowered his voice. 'If what Jed says is true, then Blue Elephant have a lot to answer for. If not,' he tensed, 'Then we're looking at slander and, depending on what evidence Jed has, maybe even a libel case. We can counter that, of course, with the assault charge. I just wish Jed had spoken to me before he took it to the press.' He sighed. 'The company apparently warned him there would be repercussions if he went public. Must be more to it than just this Fair Trade stuff. That wouldn't be enough to send the heavies in.' He stopped and shook his head. 'But Jed always rushes in. I suppose we'll just have to wait and see how this Feniman bloke reacts.'

'Who is he?'

'CEO of the UK division.' Alex looked grim. 'It all depends on how clever Gavin can box.'

Millie's stomach flipped. 'Do you think he's any good?'

'The best barrister money can buy. He claims. We were lucky we got him to come, he was just heading off for his Christmas break.'

They sat in silence. Millie watched a few half-hearted flakes of snow fall from the dirty-looking sky. 'Mary's Boy Child' played quietly in the background and an enormous, clinical-looking black and silver Christmas tree stood in the middle of the atrium. She'd never felt less Christmassy. Closing her eyes, she whispered Eleri's mantra, 'All will be well.'

'What did you say?'

Blushing, she repeated it and then explained its origin. 'Did you manage to catch up with Ri when you were in London?'

Alex gave a short laugh. 'I spoke to her on the phone but she made it perfectly clear she had no wish to see me.'

'Oh.' Millie put a hand on his arm, noticing for the first time that he was grey with fatigue. 'You really care about her, don't you?'

Alex leaned forward and put his head in his hands. 'I love her, Millie,' he said, simply.

'And I believe she loves you.'

Alex sat back up. He stared in astonishment. 'Then why the hell did she run off to London?'

Millie licked her lips. She was dying for a coffee but nothing would tempt her to the Blue Elephant stuff in front of her. She hesitated, then launched into why she thought Eleri had left.

When she'd finished, Alex was scowling again. 'There's a grain of truth in it, isn't there?' she said, gently.

'What, that I disapproved of her past?' He blew out a long breath and nodded. 'Of course.' He glanced at Millie and she saw the misery in his face. 'But I would have talked it over with her. Tried to understand.' He gave a grim smile. 'To be honest, I think at the bottom of it all was jealousy. I wasn't sure I could cope knowing all those other men had had what I hadn't.'

'And now?'

'And now? I'd just like the chance to hold her. Tell her how I feel.' He gazed at the floor in misery.

They sat in silence, each lost in their own thoughts. A ping announced the arrival of the lift. As they sprang to their feet, Gavin led a white-faced Jed out.

The barrister nodded at Alex. 'All sorted, old boy.'

Millie ran to Jed, just stopping short of hugging him. 'Thank God,' she said.

'Hello Mil,' he replied with a wan smile. 'Happy Christmas!'

Chapter 40

Having dropped Gavin back at the airport, Millie drove the brothers to the hotel. The drive was interminable. A slushy snow fell, grid-locking the shopping and commuter traffic. Millie had to concentrate hard on the stopping and starting queues. It was December-dark and the headlights hurt her tired eyes. Jed sat in the back, his long legs bent up in her small car. In her mirror she could see him slumped against the door. He was holding his right arm with clenched knuckles. No one spoke.

When they arrived, Coral clucked around them. 'Will you look at what happens when my back is turned for five minutes?' She took charge of Jed. 'Let's get you upstairs and I'll get that dressing changed.'

Millie watched their departure curiously. Jed's bloodied arm had dried to a dark stain. 'I think those bastard Blue Elephant morons must have hurt him really badly,' she said to Alex, as he led them into the tiny kitchen which led off the office.

He flicked the kettle on. 'I think you'd better sit down, Millie. I'm afraid that, once again, Jed hasn't been entirely truthful.'

Millie pulled out a rickety old stool and perched on it. 'What now?' she sighed, too exhausted to be angry.

Alex came to her and leaned against the peeling Formica unit. 'Jed was in Colombia and it's true he was liaising with coffee growers on behalf of Blue Elephant. Then, and we now know why, he began to ask some uncomfortable questions. The political situation is much improved in Colombia for visitors to the urban areas, I think there's even rather a good tourist industry. However, in the more remote, rural parts, where the coffee plantations are often found, it's still under the rule of gangs.'

'These *bandas criminales*?' Millie put in, wondering where on earth Alex was going with this.

'That's right.'

'But I thought they were just to do with drug trafficking?'

Alex shrugged. 'Yes and no. It's a murky area. Coffee is an important cash crop.'

'But what has this got to do with Jed?'

'Jed was obviously getting too close to the murky stuff. They ran him out of town.'

'Oh!'

'It's rather worse than that, I'm afraid. They shot him.'

Millie saw the room spin. Bonelessly, she slipped off the stool and, just before she hit the tiles, found herself propelled to the chesterfield in the office.

'Are you alright?' Alex leaned over her in concern. 'Here, sip this water.' He held a glass to her lips until she'd recovered the strength to hold it herself.

'I'm fine,' she flapped at him, embarrassed at her show of weakness. 'Jed was shot? I thought he was ill.'

'He was. The wound became infected. It's true he was very feverish but it was down to the wound, not a disease.'

'Why didn't you tell me?' She struggled to sit upright. 'Why didn't either of you tell me?'

'Ah, nothing to do with me, that one. All Jed's decision. He didn't want to worry you.'

'That's why he had a nurse,' said Millie as realisation dawned. 'That's why there was blood running down his arm when the heavies man-handled him.'

'I think the wound reopened. Shame. It had nearly healed.' Alex went into the kitchen and poured boiling water into a teapot. 'Tea?' He called through. 'I've rather lost my appetite for coffee.'

Millie didn't care one way or another. She just wanted to see Jed. He'd been shot! 'Was it bad?' she asked Alex as he returned bearing a tray.

'Only superficial. Jed said his collar bone was more painful when he broke it skiing.' He put the tray down on top of the untidy desk. 'But I suspect he was trying to be brave. Apparently the medical team at the Blue Elephant office patched him up while he was there. So they're not all bad.'

'While they were interrogating him, you mean?'

Alex laughed. 'I'm hoping it wasn't quite like that, Millie. Think it was more a sort of robust conversation.'

'No wonder he looked so ill when he came out. I thought it was just the questioning.'

'Oh good heavens no. Jed's tougher than that.' Alex seemed

much more cheerful. 'He's just had to rest quite a lot and needs to build up his strength.'

'He does that,' Coral said, from the door. 'All nice and clean and re-bandaged. I've put the patient in the blue sitting room.' She nodded to the steaming pot. 'And I could murder a cuppa.'

'Do you want to take a cup into him, Millie?' Alex asked. 'Do you feel strong enough?'

Millie felt foolish. 'Perfectly thank you. I never faint. It was just the shock. It's not often you hear the man you love has just been shot.'

'Get in there with you,' Coral said. 'I'll bring you a tray. His Nibs has been moaning for one as well.'

Millie wobbled to her feet. She was desperate to see Jed but had absolutely no idea what she would say to him.

'I'd start with a declaration of love,' Alex twinkled at her, alarmingly reading her mind. 'It would work for me.'

Chapter 41

'Hello Jed.' Millie felt ridiculously shy. He was sitting in the chair by the window again. He looked much better and was wearing a clean shirt and jeans, his injured arm in a snowy-white sling.

'Millie.' He smiled at her warily.

She sat in the chair next to him. 'Coral said she'd bring us some tea in a minute.'

'Ah. Tea. The cup that cheers.'

'Allegedly. We've all probably had enough of coffee. How are you feeling?'

'Much better, thank you. The painkillers Coral insists on doping me up with work wonders.' He gave her a keen look. 'Has Alex told you what happened to me?'

Millie nodded. 'He said you'd been shot. Oh Jed, I can't believe it! Is it ... was it very bad?'

'Not really. The bullet scraped past my upper arm. It's only a flesh wound, hasn't done any real muscle damage. I might have a scar, though.'

'You look quite pleased about that.'

'Well, it'll be something to show for my efforts.' He grinned.

'It could have been much worse.' Millie shuddered. 'And you didn't tell me!'

'Didn't want to worry you.' He reached forward, took her hands in his one good one and gave a great sigh. 'Millie, I didn't want to risk implicating you. There could have been all sorts of repercussions, legal or otherwise. I couldn't have lived with myself if anything had happened to involve you. Look, it could have been worse, but it wasn't. I'm fine.'

'Was it scary?'

Jed sobered. 'It had its moments,' he said, eventually. 'I don't think I'll be returning to that part of the world any time soon. Even if they'd have me.'

'Alex said they chased you out of the village?'

'Yup.' Jed nodded. 'It was quite a night.'

'How did you get out?'

He shrugged and then winced as the pain in his arm made itself felt. 'I'd made a few allies by then. They shoved me in the back of their pick-up under a stinking tarpaulin, fixed the arm up a bit and got me to the airport.' He gave a rueful grin. 'I suspect the back of that truck was where I picked up the infection but I'm not going to complain.' He shot a quick look from under dark lashes. 'They probably saved my life.'

'Oh Jed.' Millie felt her insides go to liquid. She'd been so close to losing him completely. Then she had a thought. 'Will there be any repercussions for them?'

'That I don't know.' His face clouded. 'It's a complex situation out there, Millie. I hope not. I really do.'

'It really was James Bond stuff, wasn't it?'

Jed grinned. 'Like I said, it had its moments.' His hold on

her tightened. 'I can't tell you how glad I was to get out.'

'Was it worth it?'

He blew out an enormous breath. 'I think so. It's not just the Fair Trade thing. Most of Blue Elephant's customers don't give a damn about that.' He frowned. 'There's so much exploitation going on. Child workers, Millie, some as young as eight or nine, labouring when they should be in school getting an education. It's wrong.'

'And you think Blue Elephant were buying coffee from these plantations? The ones with the child workers?'

He nodded. 'I know so. And can prove it.'

'No wonder they were cross with you.'

'Yeah.' He laughed. 'Probably a bit of an understatement there, but yes, I think you can say my time at Blue Elephant is well and truly over.'

'Has that Gavin bloke sorted it all out for you?'

'Let's say he and the company came to an agreement. I've passed all the legal stuff onto him now, so it's out of my hands. Thank goodness. Although I might have been tempted at one point by a life of espionage I think I'd just like to take it easy for a while. Let Gavin handle it.'

'Good.' Millie breathed out. 'Oh Jed,' she said impulsively. 'It's so good to have you back and safe.'

'Is it, Millie? Is it?'

'Of course it is,' she answered briskly, wary of wading too far into the emotional depths.

'I haven't thanked you.'

'Whatever for?'

'For sorting everything out.'

'I didn't do anything, Jed. It was your brother and Gavin who got you away. I just rang Alex, as you asked.'

Jed stroked a thumb over the inside of her wrist. 'But you put everything into motion and without you I'd still be stuck in that office block avoiding difficult questions.' He stiffened. 'And they fucking hurt you, Millie!'

She pulled a face. 'Hardly. I helped the situation out enormously by falling over. Ruined my best pair of tights.'

'They shoved you over, you mean. Are you sure you're alright?'

'I'm fine,' she smiled at him. 'Only my pride hurt. And my tights.'

'I owe you a pair. God, I was so frustrated. I couldn't get to you. Think I landed a kick in the groin for one of them, though.' Jed's eyes gleamed in satisfaction.

'Rough at Eton, was it?' Millie couldn't resist poking fun. Relief at having him back, without any further threat of legal trouble, was making her giddy.

He shrugged. 'The rugger training came in handy. Millie, I —'

Coral chose that moment to bring in the tea tray. 'Just pull up that table, will you now, Millie, and I'll put it on there. There you are, the cup that cheers and never inebriates. A nice cuppa is just what the doctor ordered. None of this mucky coffee stuff.' She looked at them as they dissolved into giggles. 'Now, what did I say?'

Chapter 42

After sharing a pot of tea with them, Millie was chased out by Coral claiming her patient had to rest after all his excitement. Millie, with a reluctant glance at Jed, who she had to admit was beginning to look pinched with fatigue, got in her car and went to collect Trevor. Lacking the energy to update Tessa on everything that had happened, she was relieved when her friend was more interested in bitching about Zoe, who she claimed had just broken Sean's heart. Millie sympathised halfheartedly, grabbed an overexcited and underexercised dog and drove home.

Once in the flat, she was overcome with weariness. It felt as if she'd driven around half of Devon. She couldn't believe it had been a few short hours since she'd left that morning.

She dropped onto the sofa. 'Yes, you'll have a long W.A.L.K in the morning, Trev,' she said to a peevish dog. 'I think we both need our beds. Oh bugger,' she let her head flop back onto a cushion. 'I've got a wedding meeting with Biddy tomorrow.' She eyed Trevor gloomily. 'That's just what I need. Come on, bed. And just for once, you can sleep with me.'

Chapter 43

Biddy was in a cheerful mood when Millie arrived the following morning, even if she did greet her with an accusing, 'You're late. I've got some coffee on,' she added, over Elvis's vocal welcome. 'No? Oh, suit yourself. Tea then?'

They settled in Biddy's bedroom. Millie looked about her in awe. It was sumptuous. She hadn't known quite what to expect, but it wasn't calming blues and greys and luxurious fabrics. She sat on the chaise longue (now that she *had* expected) and waited, as Biddy got changed into her wedding outfit in the adjoining dressing room.

'Arthur rang this morning,' she yelled through. 'I've heard all about your excitement yesterday. I understand young Gavin Patel is handling it?'

'Yes. It all seems under control now, thank goodness. He seems on the ball.'

'Yes, he would be. Bright boy. Arthur's furious at what that Blue Elephant place has got up to.' Biddy's voice went muffled, as if pulling something over her head. 'Although I think all that stuff is a load of old nonsense and an excuse to charge folk more. Still, Arthur said it could have ruined the town's

Fair Trade bid. I see the place is still shut this morning, so maybe there's some truth in what Jed said. Got to say, it's changed my opinion of that young man. Quite the hero.' Biddy emerged. 'What do you think?' she barked. 'Of the outfit, I mean.'

If it hadn't been Biddy, Millie would have said she sounded nervous.

She smoothed down the skirt and repeated. 'Well, girl, what do you think? It's a hard thing to get right when you're my age.'

Millie took in the cream silk skirt and matching jacket. 'It's perfect, Biddy.'

'Really?'

'Yes, absolutely perfect. I like the over-sized buttons.'

Biddy fiddled with one. 'Thought they'd be a stylish addition.'

'Did you make it yourself?'

'Of course. I've made a goose down-trimmed cape to go over it in case it's really cold.' Biddy hesitated. 'Can I let you into a secret?'

'Of course you can.' Millie wondered what was coming.

'I'd always hoped to wear my mother's wedding dress. I've kept it nice all these years but when I tried it on it looked all wrong.' Biddy's face crumpled. 'Should have realised how silly I was being. Mother was nineteen when she got married, not an old codger like me, and big-boned to boot.'

Millie rose and went to her. 'You're the least old codger-type person I know. And you look fantastic. Really elegant. Arthur is going to be so proud of you.'

Biddy's eyes sparkled with unshed tears. 'Well yes, just as it should be,' she huffed. Then she sighed. 'Such a shame, though. Mother's was a beautiful dress. She cast a hopeful glance at Millie. Would you like to see it?'

'I'd love to.'

'Let me get changed, then. Wouldn't do to get this grubby, would it? Oh this is fun. It's just like having one of my girls around. We used to have a gay old time.'

Millie sat back on the chaise, honoured that Biddy wanted to share the dress with her. Then she remembered who Biddy's 'girls' were and giggled.

'Arthur reckons they'll pull out of town,' Biddy shouted from the dressing room. 'Scandal will be too much. And they certainly won't be welcome.'

'Who?'

'Speak up, girl.'

'I said, who will pull out?'

Biddy returned, dressed in a grey polo neck and matching slacks and carrying a navy dress bag. 'Well, Blue Elephant, of course. Good riddance. Can't abide places that aren't dog-friendly. They made such a fuss about me taking Elvis in and he's an assistance dog. It's allowed. Made a stink about that, I can tell you. Used to know that Dougie Feniman. Born in a bottle but never got further than the cork, they said about him. Liked the garden, especially the *weeds*, is all I'll say.' She tapped her nose. 'Still, least said, soonest mended.' She lay the dress bag on the bed and unzipped it. 'Well, what do you think?'

Millie, mind reeling from the news that Blue Elephant

might be no more and wondering what role Biddy might have had in its demise, tried to focus on her question.

'I'll hold it against you, then you can see it better. Hold still, girl, stop your fidgeting.' Biddy tried the dress up against Millie, but sucked her teeth. 'It's no good. The best way to see it in all its glory is to try it on.'

'Oh Biddy, I couldn't.'

'Stop your nonsense. Mother would have loved to see a pretty young thing like you wearing it. She waited fourteen years for me to come along and I still didn't grace her with the mother of the bride role. Go on,' Biddy thrust the dress into Millie's hands and pushed her in the direction of the dressing room. 'I'll help you with the buttons. They run all the way down the back.'

Chapter 44

It was the most beautiful dress Millie had ever worn. Staring at her reflection in the long mirror in Biddy's walk-in wardrobe, she couldn't get over the transformation. Gone was the leggy, slightly quirky girl in striped woolly tights and flippy skirt. Instead, what she saw in front of her was a bride.

The dress was cut on the bias, making it skim every curve. It was made of a deep- cream velvet and had long sleeves and a cowl neck. With her dark hair cut in its long bob and falling over one eye, Millie thought she looked like a film star. A tear traced its way down her cheek and she hurriedly scrubbed it off. She was near tears too often these days. Once, she had hoped to marry Jed in a dress as splendid as this. Now, her relationship with him was in ashes.

She was hardly aware of Biddy coming in until she heard the woman suck in a breath behind her. 'Oh, my dear. It could have been made for you. Here, let me do up the buttons and we'll see if it really fits. You've lost weight, girl, so it should be perfect.'

Millie sniffed. 'I've been on the misery diet.'

Biddy concentrated on the line of buttons, which reached

from neck to the curve of Millie's bottom. 'Mother got married in 1939,' she mumbled. 'Just before the war started. That's why she had to wait for me. Dad was out in the desert for the duration. Reckon he could have had leave but he never did.' She put her hands on the girl's shoulders and stared at their joint reflection. 'There. Fits you like a glove. Oh, Millie don't cry.' She hurried off. 'Here, let me get you a tissue.'

'I don't want to mess up the dress,' Millie sobbed, taking one from her.

'Nonsense. As if that mattered a jot.' Biddy waited, handing over tissues until Millie's tears were spent. 'There, there. Blow your nose, now. Better out than in, I always say.'

Millie did so, hiccoughing. 'Sorry, Biddy. Don't know what came over me. I'm always crying over something at the moment.'

'Don't you?' The older woman gave her a shrewd look. 'Here's me blathering on about *my* mother, who's long gone, when a young thing like you hasn't got one to see you looking so beautiful in that frock.'

Millie stared at her reflection, with its reddened nose and tear-stained face. That her mother would never be there for her wedding day overwhelmed her with sadness. In all her misery over Jed, it hadn't occurred to her. 'No chance of me getting married, Biddy.' A fresh wave of sobs erupted.

Biddy found a new box of tissues and handed more out. 'Go on with you, of course you will. And your mother would have been so proud, my dear. Of you. Of everything you've achieved.'

'Would she?' Millie looked hopefully at Biddy. 'That's good.'

She sniffed. 'I'd better take this off. It's a truly beautiful dress, Biddy. Thank you for letting me try it on.' A little teary gulp came out. 'It's just a shame I'll never have a reason to wear something like it.'

She drove home deep in thought. Grief for her parents tugged at her. Their loss compounded with her sadness over Jed and nearly overwhelmed her. She was exhausted through crying so much, washed out with the emotions of the morning. Well, she decided, as she coerced a reluctant gearbox into third and forced herself to be more positive; if she wasn't to have a happy ever after, maybe she could help another couple achieve it.

Chapter 45

Eleri threw her rucksack into the back of Alf's taxi. It was parked up in the usual spot at Axminster station.

'Davey's place, my lovely?'

She hesitated. 'No. Take me to The Lord of the Manor hotel first.'

Alf's eyebrows rose. 'Going up in the world, are we?'

'Maybe, Alf. Just maybe.'

As Alf's taxi ate up the miles on the journey to the hotel, Eleri gazed out of the window, watching the familiar landscape speed past. Alf had the heating on full and she wished she was outside. It was hovering around freezing again, but today had been blessed with a clear blue sky. It made her feel cautiously hopeful. Was Millie telling the truth when she'd said Alex was in bits? That he was in love with her? Could it be true? The cards were telling her the same – that misunderstandings abounded but happiness could be theirs. She should have trusted them. She believed in them for other people, so why had she ignored their message when it came to herself and Alex?

She thought she knew why. Deep down, part of her

wondered if what he had inferred was true. That she wasn't good enough for him. She'd said as much to Millie during their phone call last night. Eleri smiled as she recalled Millie's robust response. She'd never heard her friend swear so much. As the taxi approached the hotel, Eleri repeated her beloved mantra.

As she got out and paid Alf, she looked up at the imposing, ivy-covered walls. The scaffolding had finally come down, she observed. The building's true majesty had been revealed. It would be incredibly hard work, but she knew Alex would make a success of the hotel; she'd read it in the cards. She'd like to share it with him, knew she was right for the task. But was she really good enough for him? More importantly, would he accept her for what she was? She straightened her shoulders. There was only one way to find out.

Chapter 46

The foyer was deserted. From somewhere in the depths of the building she could hear a man and woman quarrelling. An enormous tree had been erected in the hall and someone had begun to decorate it. Boxes of red and green baubles lay abandoned and a heap of red tinsel was spilling off the chair in the corner. Some was draped over the elderly stag's head. His disdainful expression made it clear that he thought all this frippery was utter nonsense.

'Eleri! Thank the good Lord for all things holy.' Alex appeared from the office. He hurried over and grasped her hands in his. 'Don't ever do that to me again,' he said, urgently. Nodding to the raised voices, he explained. 'Jed and Mother having words. We'll leave them to it, shall we? Put your luggage there and come with me.'

Eleri, amused at his description of her battered but beloved rucksack, left her hand in his and followed him. She was surprised to feel nervous.

He took her to the old stable block. 'Do you remember we discussed converting it into self-catering accommodation? Finished this week,' Alex said. 'I rather wanted your opinion.'

The building had been partitioned into units, each with its original stable door intact. He unlocked the door of the first, labelled Star, presumably after a one-time occupant, and led her in.

'I didn't come here to discuss interior design, Alex.'

Alex viewed her, gravely. 'I know, but I'd like to hear it anyway.'

Eleri took in the pale wood of the kitchenette, the aqua walls with the subtle silver and green highlights, the king-size bed with its canopy. Sleeping underneath its shimmering green and blue drapes would be like swimming, she thought. It was all as she'd suggested. But she'd just outlined ideas, made a few mood boards, drawn up some sketches. Alex had made them a reality.

She whirled around in delight and faced him. 'It's wonderful,' she whispered. 'Everything I could have hoped for.'

'All your ideas, Ri. I just got people in to create it.' He took a step closer and feathered the lightest of touches down her cheek, as if hardly believing she was real. 'Please, please don't leave me again. I couldn't bear it. I've been an utter fool. Can you ever forgive me?' He kissed her very lightly. 'I love you, Eleri *cariad.*'

She smiled a little at the Welsh endearment on his very English lips. 'Despite what I was?'

'Because of who you are. Someone so far superior to me that I couldn't recognise it.'

They kissed, exploring one another, making magic.

Alex broke away. 'There are rumours,' he said, with a smile.

'Rumours?' Eleri tensed.

'That you are descended from a mermaid.'

'Oh that.' She relaxed.

'Are you?'

'What do you think?' She reached up and smoothed back a lock of his hair, luxuriating in being able to touch him.

'I'm a man of science,' he said, as an answer. 'Of numbers and logic.' His face contorted, as if trying to get his head around it. Reaching into his pocket, he brought out her misshapen bangle.

Eleri's eyes lit up. '*Duw*, so that's where it was,' she cried. 'It's my favourite. It was my great-grandmother's.' She took it off him, eyeing it curiously. 'However did it get into this state?'

Alex's face fell. 'I'm so sorry. I did that to it.' He cleared his throat, embarrassed. 'It was in my hand when I overheard your conversation with Zoe.'

'Ah.'

'I'm not proud of my reaction, Ri. I had no right to feel as I did.' His ears pinked. 'Put it down to the old green-eyed monster. I intend to do everything I can to make it up to you.'

Eleri shook her head. 'Nothing to forgive. I should have stayed around, talked it through with you. I just got frightened and running off was the easier thing to do.' She kissed him.

'I'll buy you another, or get that one repaired. It's the very least I can do.'

Eleri slipped it back into his pocket with a smile. 'No, don't do that, *cariad bach*. You keep it. Don't you know? If you take a mermaid's most prized possession, she has to stay with you.'

'Is that why you came back? Because I had your bangle?' Alex's brow furrowed, trying to make the leap. 'None of this makes the slightest sense to me.'

Eleri shook her head and regarded his confusion fondly. 'I came back to tell you I love you and wanted to find out if you'll have me. Oh Alex, I've given my body to many men, but I never let go of my heart. Not until I met you. And it's yours, Alex. My heart will always be yours.'

He put his arms around her, bringing her close and they kissed again, this time passionately. 'Does that answer your question?' he asked, desire making his voice hoarse.

'Nearly.' She put her head on one side.

Alex raised his eyebrows. 'I think I might know what you mean,' he said, deliberately slowly. 'Well, it would be a shame to waste a perfectly good bed. And there's a rather nice one just behind you. Shall we try it out?'

'Only fair, I think.' She led him to it, giggling in relief. It was going to be alright. Everything would be alright.

Later, much later, two thoughts crossed her mind. One, that it was always a shock when nice boys made love so expertly. Two, and just before she let herself be swept away by the waves of pleasure, that being in this sumptuous bed with Alex was as good as swimming. She sank down onto him, surrounding him, loving his ecstatic groans and corrected herself. No, it was better. Far better.

Chapter 47

'Jed. I fail to understand you or your actions.' Vanessa drew herself up to her full height. They were in the blue sitting room and had been arguing for an hour.

'Well, not for the first time.' Jed scowled.

She blew out a frustrated breath. 'I don't understand you. I never have.' She deflated a little. 'I only want you to be happy, darling.'

Jed shook his head slowly. 'No, you want me to be happy doing what you think I ought to do. It's not the same.'

'Your father and I have given you every privilege,' Vanessa snapped.

They'd been going round and round in circles. Jed shoved a frustrated hand through his hair and then winced as he'd used his injured arm.

'Darling, do sit down. You've gone awfully pale.'

He sank onto the sofa. Arguing with his mother was taking it out of him. He almost preferred facing irate, gun-toting coffee growers, He was relieved when Vanessa sat next to him. At least he wouldn't have her hovering over him, accusingly.

She put a tentative hand on her youngest son's hand. 'I only

515

want you to be happy, Jeremy, I really do,' she said, sounding more conciliatory. 'Why did you have to go off to God knows where and get into so much trouble? Your poor arm.'

Jed thought for a second. 'Ma, what did your parents think when you went to modelling school?'

Vanessa looked askance at the change of subject and then answered. 'They thought I was mad.' She laughed slightly.

'Why?'

She sat back. 'I expect they thought modelling wasn't a suitable career for the likes of us. Or rather *them*.' She touched off a flake of lipstick and concentrated on the stain of red on her fingertip. 'They were the sort who believed in the class system, Jeremy.' She corrected herself. 'Actually, it wasn't that. They didn't think people like us should aim any higher than we were entitled to. That we shouldn't stick our heads above the parapet.' She made quotation marks with her fingers. 'We were the sort who became bank clerks and secretaries.'

'Can't see you as a secretary, Ma.'

'Quite.'

'How did you persuade them to let you go? You were very young when you began, weren't you?'

'I used the example of Twiggy.'

'Twiggy?'

'Yes. She came from quite ordinary beginnings and became a global icon. I thought I could do the same. And was on my way until I fell in love with your father.'

'You don't regret marrying Dad?'

'Of course not. He's the love of my life. And he gave me you and Alexander.' She patted his hand. 'But that's not what this is all about.' She plucked a fleck of tinsel off his shirt. 'We ought to get back to decorating the tree. This place really isn't looking nearly Christmassy enough. We could have one in here too. Blue and silver to match the decor.'

'Ma, it is what this is about, in a way,' Jed said, in an attempt to stop her avoiding the subject. 'If you'd become a secretary your parents would have been happy.'

'Oh darling, they would have been ecstatic. Would have put all my grammar school education to good use. What's your point, Jeremy?'

'Don't live your expectations through me.' Vanessa chewed her lip and remained silent, so he continued. 'Ma, I fully appreciate all you and Dad have done for me, I really do. Money is a huge luxury and it's enabled me to do so much.' He thought for a moment of how the lack of it had restricted Millie and what she'd hoped to do. He would have helped her, if she'd let him. 'But I don't want to end up being money's slave. This last year has made me realise how powerful money is. What it can do when it's used well instead of being frittered away. It can help rebuild a theatre roof, or provide windows in an art studio. Or provide an education for child workers. That's the sort of life I want. To use my money to do good.'

'Charity, you mean,' his mother bit out.

'If you like. I prefer the term investment.'

Vanessa looked around at the blue sitting room. She wasn't ready to concede quite yet. 'And just what is your brother thinking in taking this pile on? It's going to eat cash.'

'You could be right there. He knows what he's doing, though.'

'And he's given up on a promising career in the city.'

'A promising career that was destroying him.'

Vanessa humphed.

'Mum, I think you should be proud of having raised two sons who have the confidence to take on the world and win it their way.'

'With your father's money.'

'I can't argue with that. You've both enabled us to be the men we are.'

'Even if it's not what I want for you both?'

'Even that.'

Vanessa was silent again. She stroked the velvet on the arm of the sofa. 'I'm not going to win this, am I?'

'No, Ma. Although I don't like to think of this as a battle.' He reclaimed her hand and squeezed it. 'And, as far as Alex's hotel goes, at least it means you'll have somewhere nice to stay when you come to see us.'

Chapter 48

Coral brought in the inevitable tray of tea. She was unusually subdued, having learned to be wary of Jed and Alex's fierce mother. 'Now don't be tiring yourself, Jed.'

'I won't. Thank you, Coral.'

'Would you carry on with decorating the tree, Carol?' Vanessa demanded casually. 'We seem to have got rather waylaid.'

'Ma, she's here to nurse and not do odd jobs. And the name's Coral.'

'Whatever,' Vanessa continued, unabashed. 'Could you see to it? I hate to see the entrance hall looking quite so untidy. After all, you're not doing any nursing at this minute, are you?'

'Well now, wouldn't I be glad to, Mrs Fitzroy-Henville?' Coral's eyes were amused when she met Jed's embarrassed look. 'As long as you promise me to get the patient upstairs for his afternoon rest at three o'clock. Sharp now, mind. I'll not be happy to have his routine upset.'

Vanessa, unused to being answered back by those she considered staff, bridled.

Once Coral had left the sitting room, Jed let out a guffaw.
'She got you there, Ma.'

'Well, really.'

'You'll have to be mother, Mother.' Jed gestured to the
teapot. 'One arm in a sling makes me impossibly clumsy.'

Vanessa concentrated on pouring tea. She handed him a
cup. 'You do seem to insist on surrounding yourself with the
most extraordinary women, Jeremy.'

'You haven't met Eleri yet.'

'Who's she?' Vanessa looked startled. 'Not another one of
your charity cases?'

'Nothing to do with me. Eleri belongs to Alex.'

Vanessa sank gracefully back onto the blue velvet. She
sipped her tea. 'I simply don't understand where I went wrong,'
she cried. 'All those perfectly suitable girls you both knew
and you end up stuck in the West Country with two women
with the most bizarre names.'

'I wouldn't insult Eleri, if I were you. She'll put a curse on
you.'

Vanessa regarded her son over the bone china. 'You are
talking in jest. Aren't you?'

'Not entirely sure. There's definitely something magical
about her. Alex is crazy about her. And she's been brilliant at
getting this place sorted. I think she has some interior- design
training.'

Vanessa sniffed. 'Well, I have to say this sitting room is
looking marvellous. I look forward to meeting her.' She gave
an enormous sigh. 'And what's happening with this Millie
person? I suppose, if I have to have some kind of witch around,

I can tolerate a café owner as your girlfriend. Just. If this is really the sort of life you want.'

Jed put down his cup, all levity gone. 'Ah, as far as I know, she's about to be whisked off to Tuscany in a Maserati.' His face closed. 'She didn't want me, Mum. Millie doesn't want anything to do with me and especially not my money.'

Chapter 49

In the little flat above Millie Vanilla's, the local evening news blared out of the television in the corner. Millie, with a blanket over her to keep warm, patiently watched the news items about the Santa Special on the local steam train line, about the magnificent tree going up in Plymouth and something about a traditional nine lessons and carol concert happening in Exeter cathedral. Her own tree twinkled in the corner. Despite having next to no money, Millie couldn't bear the idea of Christmas without a tree. She'd pleaded with Les in the Berecombe garden centre and he'd given her the top of one that he'd just trimmed.

The item she was waiting for came on. It was the same journalist as before. Chloe something or other. Millie turned up the volume and concentrated.

'I'm standing in Berecombe's high street, outside the Blue Elephant café, which is at the heart of the recent controversy. I have with me Dennis Hall, leader of the town council and chair of the trading committee.'

The camera panned out to include a self-conscious Dennis. He was pink-nosed with cold.

'Mr Hall, can I ask you what the latest development is? Is the café likely to reopen?'

Dennis puffed himself up to answer. It came out in a rush. 'I can confirm that, as of this week, Blue Elephant is pulling out of Berecombe. What's more, having received hard evidence that the company's trading procedures do not meet the very stringent standards laid down by our trading committee, we will not renew the lease of the building to it or to any company not adhering to the Fair Trade status, which has just been awarded to our town.' He grinned.

'A shock development, Dennis.'

'It is indeed, Chloe.'

'So Christmas shoppers will have to look elsewhere for a coffee to warm themselves up with?'

'They will indeed.' Dennis looked straight into the camera. 'But can I reassure any shoppers or visitors to our town that they are most welcome and that we have a wide range of places in which to eat and drink. We also have a wonderful selection of independent little shops in which to do your last minute Christmas shopping.'

Millie grinned. 'Doing a great job of bigging-up Berecombe there, Dennis.'

'Thank you, Dennis. And many congratulations on achieving Fair Trade status.' Chloe turned to camera and Dennis faded from shot. 'And I have to say the town of Berecombe is looking really lovely this Christmas. The lights are up in the high street here and looking splendid and the tree is in its usual spot on the prom. There's still a lot to welcome the shopper in.' She smiled through chattering teeth.

'But I have to say, a hot coffee would be great right at this minute. Can I come back to the studio now?'

Millie hugged Trevor to her, not quite believing what she had just seen. Jed had been right. The story had made Blue Elephant too hot to handle and they'd simply shut up shop and gone. She supposed they might open in another town in the South West but Berecombe – and Millie Vanilla's – was safe.

'Oh Trev,' she said, into his fur. 'I think it might all be over.'

Chapter 50

Jed, watching the same news bulletin on the portable television in his room, sat back against his bed head. Gavin had done an excellent job. Blue Elephant was finished in Berecombe and maybe in the whole of the South West.

Looking around at the shabby, yet to be re-decorated, walls of his room, he wondered if he had any future in Berecombe, or whether he was finished in the town too.

Chapter 51

Dora, her feet on Mike's lap, as they lounged on the sofa in their Islington townhouse, sat up with a jerk. She'd been idly scanning the Devon news on her iPad.

'Mike, darling, you'll never believe what's happened.' She gave him an edited version. 'Could we nip back home, do you think?'

He ruffled her hair fondly. 'Don't see why not. Need to measure up the new house anyway. Maybe we could pop in and see your folks?'

'Do we have to?'

'Well, they'll have to know at some point. Oh darling, not again?' he added, as she leaped up and dashed to the downstairs loo, her hand cupping her mouth.

Chapter 52

Millie Vanilla's was looking its absolute, Christmassy, best. Snowy white linen cloths covered the tables and white chiffon tie-backs with ivy decorated the chairs. Most tables bore Eleri's glass vases with masses of white lights. Others had branches painted white and hung with frosted stars and hearts. Green napkins were tied with holly twigs, with the red berries making a splash of colour. Zoe had re-dressed the tree in silver and white and on top sat an angel with fluffy white wings. Strings of white lights hung from a central point and covered the ceiling. Once the lights were dimmed, it would be magical.

Millie hugged Zoe and Eleri to her. 'Thank you for all your hard work,' she said, her eyes brimming. 'I couldn't have done it on my own.'

'Well, natch.' Zoe put in. 'You needed our expertise.'

Millie hugged her closer. The girl had worked like a demon. 'You sound a bit happier.'

'Not any happier.' Zoe shrugged. 'Just content I've made the right decision. Me and Sean had a heart to heart last night. Cried a lot,' she admitted, 'But agreed we'd try to stay mates.'

'Ah *cariad*. Not easy.' Eleri reached a hand around and squeezed the girl's shoulder.

'No need to ask how you are,' Zoe retorted. 'You haven't stopped grinning all week.'

'Have to confess to feeling pretty pleased with life,' Eleri giggled. 'All thanks to matchmaker Millie.'

'Least I could do.' Millie surveyed her café with immense satisfaction. 'Wasn't sure at times we'd pull it off, but actually, Millie Vanilla's makes a pretty good wedding venue.'

Zoe snorted. 'The best!' She gestured outside to the line of lanterns leading to the flower-decked arch. 'Much better decision to go with fresh flowers. Must have cost a packet, though.'

'Alex's wedding present to the happy couple,' Eleri explained.

Zoe peered out into the dark. 'I'll just go and check the chairs. That front row looks wonky and Biddy won't stand for that.'

Millie and Eleri watched, amused, as Zoe tweaked the chairs into exactly the right position.

'Have you decided what to do with the café, Mil?'

Millie shook her head. 'About the only thing I've made up my mind about is to shut down over the winter. At least that will cut down on overheads.'

'No other offer come in?'

'No. And not likely to at this time of year. Businesses at the seaside get sold when they're busy. I've picked up trade from Blue Elephant closing, but not really enough to see me through until next season gets going.' Millie sighed. 'This might just be my – and Millie Vanilla's – swansong.'

Eleri put her arm around her. 'All will –' she began.

'I know, I know. All will be well.' Millie forced a grin.

'Of course it will,' said a familiar, actressy voice. 'I'm here. Hello honeybun. Happy Christmas! I've come to claim the afternoon tea Mike promised me months ago. Have you missed me?'

Chapter 53

Dora! Millie ran to her friend and engulfed her in a hug. 'Whatever are you doing here? And Mike too. Come in, come in and shut the door. It's freezing out there.'

She introduced them to Eleri who, after greeting them and whispering something in Dora's ear, said she would go and check on the canapés.

Dora, looking shocked, asked who she was, so Millie explained.

'Astonishing eyes,' Mike said. Noticing Dora had gone pale he added, 'What's wrong Dor? What did she say to you?'

She turned to him, still looking stunned. 'She said, good luck with the baby.'

He frowned. 'But we haven't told anyone yet.'

'Baby!' Millie screeched. 'What baby?'

Dora pouted. 'Yup, you'll have the pleasure of witnessing me balloon into an enormous lactating cow.'

Mike came to her and put his arms around her. 'Think the lactating comes later.'

Dora rolled her eyes. 'Ever the expert. I'm up the duff,' she continued to Millie. 'Preggers. I believe the current parlance in Islington is, *we are having a baby*. Only three months, though, so keep it to yourself, Mil.'

'Oh, how lovely.' Millie went to them and hugged them both all over again. Tears threatened once more. 'That's so wonderful.' And it was. But she couldn't quite stop a little worm of envy. Everyone else seemed so happy. Mike and Dora. Alex and Ri.

'Thanks, hon,' Dora said. 'We're down here to try to make amends with my parents. Thought a baby onboard might force a reconciliation. And if not,' she shrugged, 'Well, it's their loss.'

'The idea of a grandchild might do it. I'm sure it will. They were saying the other day how much they missed you. I ate at Samphyre and we got talking.'

'Get you, eating at my parents' swanky restaurant. Who took you there?'

Millie pulled a face. 'Long story. Tell you later.'

'You might just be able to do that – we'll be around a bit more. We're buying the chalet bungalow on the hill,' Mike explained. 'The one I rented in the summer. So we thought we'd drive down, do the present run and some measuring up at the same time.'

Millie squealed again. She clapped her hands together. 'Does that mean you're coming back to live in Berecombe permanently?'

'Millie, do stop screaming, it's bad for the baby.' Dora grinned. 'It'll be our holiday home. We'll get back here as often as we can. After all, the sprog has to have sandcastle-making lessons from the best godmother in Devon.'

Millie looked blank.

'I mean you,' Dora added gently. 'Enough with the screaming,' she warned, as Millie launched in for another hug.

Once everything had calmed down, Dora insisted on an update on everything that had happened. 'Amazing,' she said, once Millie had explained. 'Good old Berecombe. Who would have thought so much went on? Makes our London life look positively tame, doesn't it, Mike? And Biddy and Arthur are getting married here?'

Yes, this evening.'

'On Christmas Eve? How romantic!'

'That's Biddy for you.' Then Millie's face fell. 'I don't think there's room for you, though. We've only got thirty places.'

'Oh, don't worry about that.' Dora swayed for a second. 'Could I sit down for a second, hon?' She eyed the extravagantly dressed chair.

Mike shot forward protectively. 'Are you alright, Dora?' he asked.

She flapped a hand at him as he pulled out a chair for her. 'I'm absolutely fine. Feeling a little light-headed, that's all. Must be all the excitement.'

'It's because you haven't eaten anything today,' Mike scolded.

'Morning sickness,' Dora said, as explanation. She pulled a face at Millie and wagged a finger. 'Never, ever get pregnant.'

'Not much chance of that at the moment,' Millie replied, with rancour.

'Don't tell me you still haven't made up with Jed, honeybun?'

'I'll fill you in when you've got a few spare years. Tell you what,' Millie added as a thought struck. 'Why don't you come along for the evening do? Biddy and Arthur would love to see you. We're having a huge bonfire on the beach, loads of fireworks and I'm doing a nice line in espresso cocktails to go with the cake.'

'We'll do that.' Dora rubbed her invisible bump. 'Non-alcoholic for we two, though.' She fluttered her eyelashes. 'After all, I *am* pregnant.'

'And I'm joining in for sympathy,' Mike said.

Millie saw a glance passed between them. 'Oh Dora. Oh Mikey. I'm so pleased for you.' She bent to kiss Dora and then hugged Mike.

Dora levered herself, dramatically, from the chair. She put a hand to the small of her back and held the pose, waiting.

'Do you need some help?' Mike offered his arm. He shook his head and winked at Millie. 'Only three months and milking it for all its worth. We'll see you later, then.'

Dora drew herself up. 'I *am* carrying your child, Michael Love. The very least you can do is offer me your hand.' She cast a glance to the kitchen and added, 'I'm still wondering how Eleri knew about the baby.'

Laughing, Millie saw them to the door. 'I'll tell you all about her sometime.' She waved them off. As the Mercedes purred along the sea front road, she saw a grey Golf take its parking space. A tall man opened the boot and took something out. With a skip in the beat of her heart, she realised it was Jed.

Chapter 54

'Hello Millie,' he said softly. He held out a tray of white rose and holly buttonholes.

'Thank you.' Millie frowned. 'Another present from Alex? He's being very generous.'

'From me, actually.' Jed stared at her. 'You don't know, do you?'

'What?'

'I'm the best man tonight. I'm Arthur's best man. I've been popping in to see Daisy, and Arthur and I have ended up good friends. We worked together on the Fair Trade bid, along with Dennis.'

'Oh.' Millie swallowed. It was going to be a stressful enough event without having Jed's disturbing presence around. 'I thought Dennis was going to do it.'

Jed nodded. 'He was, but his daughter's just had a baby so he's gone up to Bristol to see them. Arthur understood. It's his first grandchild. Two months early.'

Millie softened. 'Then he'll be over the moon. He's very close to his daughter. Lots of babies around, suddenly,' she added, trying to keep the longing out of her voice.

'Sorry?'

'Nothing.'

'I'll put them on the present table so guests can pick one up as they come in.' She inhaled the sweet scent of rose. 'They're gorgeous. I like the holly leaves.'

'Prickly and strong, like Biddy.'

Millie thought about her recent encounter. 'Yes. But kind too.'

'Very. Once you get to know her. Always helps when she keeps her clothes on, though.'

Millie giggled, remembering the hot day back in the summer when they'd encountered Biddy and Arthur sunbathing naked. She took the tray off him and couldn't help but breathe in Jed's wonderful smell. Sadness that she and Jed couldn't be together overwhelmed her. It was made all the more poignant by being surrounded by all the wedding happiness and baby news. She would have loved to have his baby. Pulling herself together, as she'd never been the sort to give in to self pity, she turned away to find a space for the buttonholes. She said briskly, 'How are you? How's the arm?'

'Better. Much better, thanks. Still gets stiff, but I'm doing the physio. I'm being such a good boy that Coral agreed to go home for Christmas. Actually,' he screwed up his face. 'She and Ma didn't get on too awfully well.'

Millie turned back to him. 'You do surprise me,' she said, drily. 'Shame. I like Coral.'

'She likes you too. Said she'd be in touch. Wants the recipe for your lemon drizzle.'

Millie batted her eyelashes at him. 'I only go so far for friendship.'

He laughed. 'I think Ma would like you too. If she got to

know you.'

'Why? Does she want my lemon drizzle recipe too? Can't see your mother in a pinny.'

Jed shook his head. 'Only if it came from Harvey Nicks,' he acceded. '*I'd* like her to get to know you.' He sounded curiously hopeful.

'What good would that do? I'm probably out of Berecombe as soon as I've cleared my debts.'

Jed started. 'To Italy?'

'Italy? Why would I be going to Italy?'

He blew out a breath. 'Savio?'

'There's no Savio, Jed. There never was.'

His shoulders slumped in relief. 'Thank God for that. He left the hotel days ago but he didn't say where he was going.' He bit his lip, embarrassed. 'I wondered if it was to here.'

Millie looked at him enquiringly. She kept her mouth shut. She hadn't a clue where Jed was going with this.

'You said you were getting out of Berecombe. Have you had another offer for the café?'

Millie shook her head. 'No such luck.' Picking up one of the buttonholes, she traced a finger over the rose's cool silkiness. 'But I don't think I can stay. Not in the long term. I can't see a way I can make the business make enough money. Not without rethinking the place.' She put the buttonhole carefully back in place.

'You could accept my offer,' he said, softly, sounding distinctly nervous.

'What offer's that, Jed? You can't still want to invest, surely?'

'My offer to marry you, Millie.'

Chapter 55

Millie stared at him. She thought she'd begun to speak, but nothing had come out.

'I've got two offers actually, but the first and most important one is, will you marry me, Millie? I love you. I'll never stop loving you and I want to spend the rest of my life with you.'

Millie found her voice. 'You're not serious?'

'Deadly. Who else am I going to get to feed me in quite the same way as you?'

Millie's legs gave way. She sank on a chiffon-covered chair. 'But —'

'But nothing.' Jed got down on one knee. 'I always said that if I ever proposed to you, I'd do it properly.' He took a deep breath. 'Emilia Fudge, will you do me the honour of becoming my wife?' He reached into his jacket pocket, took out a box and flipped the lid. Inside was an old-fashioned ring; a small diamond surrounded by tiny rubies. He held it out. It wavered slightly in his hand as she didn't respond.

'Jed, you said it was all over between us,' Millie managed, croakily.

A frown creased his brow. 'Did I? When?'

'When I came to see you at the hotel. Just after you'd got home. When you were ill.'

'Oh that,' he said, cheerfully. 'Are you holding me to words said under the influence of several mind-altering drugs?'

'I thought,' Millie tried to gulp the tears back. 'I thought you meant it.' Her lips quivered.

'Oh God, Millie, I'm sorry.' He looked aghast. 'There were days when I thought Alex had morphed into a giraffe. I didn't know what I was saying.'

'But you haven't said anything to me since?' Millie stuttered. 'About us, I mean.'

'Well, *you* told me it was all over. In no uncertain terms. I didn't want to believe it, but then you had me thinking you were about to run off with an Italian millionaire. Jeez, Millie, the thought of that nearly finished me.' He sobered. 'Getting shot for you was nothing in comparison.'

'What do you mean you got shot for me? Oh, do get up,' she added, irritably.

Jed looked chastened. 'This isn't going quite as I'd hoped.' He sat in the next chair, putting the ring box on the table between them. 'Millie,' he began, taking her hands, 'You must know that everything I did, joining Blue Elephant, the James Bond stuff, it was all for –'

'For the town. Yes I know. I saw it on the news. You did it so the town would get its Fair Trade status. And it's important too,' she added hastily, 'That we drink responsibly sourced coffee. I get it. And I agree.'

'I did it for those reasons, yes. But really I did it for you. I did it all for you, Millie. So that you could keep your café.

Because,' he took a deep breath. 'I did it because I am hopelessly, impossibly, in love with you.'

She stared at him, trying to take it all in. 'You did it for me?' It came out on a squeak.

'Yes.' He shook his head a little. 'I don't know what else I can say to convince you.' He brushed a hand over his eyes. 'But if you tell me it's all over, and I know you've said that before, if you tell me there's no hope for us, I'll go away and never ever bother you again.'

'You said once that you'd prove yourself worthy of me. Is that what it was all about?'

'I suppose. Maybe.' He screwed up his face. 'It got a bit out of hand, though. I thought I might get a few dirty facts on Blue Elephant. Then I saw those poor kids working until they dropped. That made it all get a bit serious.' He looked at her from beneath dark lashes. 'Didn't think I'd get shot, though. I'm really not hero material.'

Millie began to giggle through her tears. 'Stop talking, Jed. Stop talking now or you'll spoil it.' She slid forward. 'You're a hero to me.' She rested her hands on his shoulders. 'I love you, Jed.' She kissed him. 'I love you so much.'

'And?' he asked, as they emerged from the kiss. He nodded to the ring.

'What about your mother?'

He smiled. 'She's given us her blessing. That's my grandmother's ring. I thought it was more you, somehow, than some huge solitaire. Ma gave it to me to give to you.' He arched a brow. 'If you say no, you'll have to answer to her.'

The tears began in earnest. 'Oh Jed. How then, could I

possibly say no?' She kissed him again and he slipped the engagement ring onto her finger.

Chapter 56

The wedding was a triumph. Everyone said so. Biddy was complimented on her beautiful outfit, the food was devoured and the champagne flowed. The service, held against the shifting black sea, was simple and moving and fragranced with the scent of a hundred white roses. The dogs carried out their roles impeccably, without even so much as a cocked leg against the wedding arch. Worn out by their arduous role, they snuggled up with Trevor in his basket by the radiator. They'd be put safely in the flat once the fireworks began. Biddy had even thrown her bouquet and, to everyone's delight, Berecombe's favourite café owner had caught it.

Millie put a protective hand over Jed's ring that she'd put safe in the pocket of her specially made green apron. She looked around the café and glowed with pleasure. Now most of the wedding was done, she could relax. The happy buzzy sound of contented people filled the space. She hadn't realised how many friends she and Biddy had in common. And they were all here tonight. Tessa and family, Zoe and her parents, the Levis from the B&B, Percy the butcher, George Small and Old Davey too. Even the Simpsons were here, looking far more relaxed now the pressure of owning the Lord was off them. They'd nodded to Alex and had a brief conversation. Then he'd returned to Eleri, a bewitched look on his face.

Just as the speeches finished, Dora and Mike sidled in.

'Are you sure the happy couple won't mind?' Dora hissed.

Millie shook her head. 'They'll be delighted to see you. Biddy's been on the fizz all evening. She loves everyone tonight.'

Once she'd spotted her, Biddy launched herself at Dora and engulfed her in a bear hug. 'Dora, my girl. How wonderful to see you. How's your dear father?'

Dora decided she didn't want to know how Biddy knew her father and looked relieved when Jed, in loosened tie and flushed from the success of his impromptu best man's speech, joined them. He put an arm around Millie and kissed her on the temple.

'Have you two made up? In the time I've been at my parents, have you two got back together again?' Dora asked, eyeing them.

'What's that?' Biddy boomed.

As an answer, Millie blushed.

Jed tightened his hold. 'Actually, Dora, we've more than made up.' He winked at Millie, who tried to shush him. 'Millie has made me the happiest man possible. She's agreed to marry me.'

It was meant for Dora's ears only, but Biddy chose that moment to hear perfectly. 'What's that?' she yelled. 'You two getting married?' She clapped her hands together. 'Marvellous. Simply marvellous,' she said it so loudly every guest heard.

In the rush of congratulations, Millie, embarrassed, blushed some more and tried to deflect the attention back onto the wedding couple.

'Nonsense, child,' was Biddy's rebuttal. 'On a day full of good news and happiness, let's pile on some more! And, you know,' she added, as a cunning gleam appeared in her eyes, 'The celebrant is over there drinking your delicious espresso cocktail. There's a beautiful wedding arch still out on the beach. The lanterns are still lit, the burners are still going. You could avail yourself of the amenities. What's more, all of your friends are here as witnesses.'

'What do you mean?' asked Millie, thoroughly flustered.

'She means, my love,' Jed put in. 'That we could get married tonight too.'

'Oh, don't be so ridiculous,' Millie began. 'We couldn't possibly. It's Biddy and Arthur's day.'

Arthur joined them and heard. 'Nothing would give us greater pleasure than for my wife and I,' at this Biddy simpered, 'To share our happiest of days with you. Jed, my man,' he clapped him on the shoulder, at which Jed tried not to wince. 'You have become a trusted friend and you've been a wonderful best man.' He winked. 'Although we won't tell Dennis that.' He took Millie's hands. 'Emilia, my dear, Biddy and I wouldn't have met if it weren't for you. Allow us to make this happen for you and Jed. And, dear girl, I would be honoured if you would let me give you away.' He hesitated. 'Let us, in our own unique and very humble way, act as your parents tonight and give you a wedding to remember.'

'Oh Arthur.' Millie blinked back the tears and hugged him.

She turned to Jed. 'What about your parents? They ought to be here too.'

'Oh, don't worry. Ma won't let us get away with it. She loves any excuse to buy an unspeakably expensive hat and we'll have to do it officially anyway. If you can tolerate a marquee on the lawn up at the Lord and as much Pimm's as you can drink, we can do it all again, properly, in the summer.' He took Millie's hands and drew her to him. 'Nothing, my sweet Millie Fudge, would give me greater pleasure than to make you my wife under the starlight and in front of our friends.' He kissed her.

The noise of the cheering nearly took the café roof off.

'Well,' Millie said, beyond flustered now. 'I don't seem to have an option.' She blushed even more.

'I don't think you do, Mil,' said Dora grinning. 'And I'm all in favour of a repeat performance. By the time the summer comes, I'll be able to get into a killer dress.'

'Dress!' Millie clapped her hand to her mouth in horror. 'I can't get married in a green pinafore. It can't happen tonight, I haven't got anything to wear.'

'Rubbish,' Biddy bellowed. 'There's a perfectly good frock at my house. And we know it fits you. We just need someone who's sober enough to drive to collect it.'

'I'm happy to,' Mike offered. Biddy gave him directions and he disappeared.

Dora took Millie's arm. 'And, unless Trevor objects, please can I be bridesmaid?'

'Of course you can.' Millie hugged Dora to her. 'Oh no Dor! What about a ring? I can't get married without a wedding ring.'

'Haven't you still got your mum's?' Dora suggested softly. 'That way, maybe your mum can be part of all this madness too.' At the threat of more tears from Millie, she added, sternly, 'Come on, up to the flat with you.' Grimacing at the state of Millie's hair, she yelled for Tessa. 'I think we need all hands on deck.' Glancing over, she saw Zoe. 'Can you keep our guests fed and watered until Bride Number Two is ready? And Eleri,' she said to the girl, who was trying hard not to look too smug that all had ended as predicted, 'Could you take the dogs for a quick walk? They look like they need one.' She looked down to where they were weaving in and out of each other with excitement. 'Yes doggies, you'll have a role too. Come on everyone, we have magic to create!'

Chapter 57

If possible, it was even chillier when the second wedding began. The guests, fortified by rum-laced hot chocolate and warming food, didn't seem to mind as they took their places again. As the strains of 'Silent Night' drifted up into the cold air, they settled back in anticipation.

Biddy started proceedings off, keeping a tight hold on the motley collection of dogs, and Dora followed, throwing white rose petals. They drifted gently to the sand, like snowflakes.

And then, as Arthur escorted a blissfully happy Millie along the lantern-lit, sandy aisle, a collective sigh merged with the shifting swell of the sea.

'Magical,' whispered Eleri, sitting next to Zoe and gripping the girl's hand.

Millie did indeed look magical. The white cloak glowed softly and a gentle, salt-slicked sea breeze ruffled the goose down. Biddy's white rose and ivy bouquet, studded with crystals, caught the flickering light and sparkled against the night sky. But what most delighted everyone was Millie's expression of complete and utter happiness.

'She looks gorg,' Zoe breathed.

Tessa, sitting on Zoe's other side, wiped her eyes. 'She does.' She gave a gutsy sigh. 'Zoe, bab. I'm sorry it didn't work out with you and our Sean.'

'Me too.'

'Still friends?'

Zoe leaned into her. 'Still friends.'

'Don't be a stranger, you hear? Ken's still got high hopes for you.' She tucked Zoe's spare hand under her arm. 'Our Millie suits vintage so well.' She sniffed. 'And that cloak Biddy made is ace. Love the fluffy trimming. Looks perfect over that velvet dress.'

'Millie would look lovely in anything,' Zoe added, loyally. 'You did wonders with her hair, Tes. Those white roses look fabber than a very fab thing.'

Tessa foraged for a tissue. 'I can't believe Biddy's got in on the act.' She bit down on a laugh.

Eleri joined in with the conversation. 'Well, it takes someone fierce to wrangle three doggie wedding attendants. Take it from me, I know.'

'They're not ring-bearers again, are they? Arthur had a hell of a game getting Elvis to stand still last time.' Tessa blew her nose.

'No,' Zoe giggled. 'Alex has got it. He's Jed's best man. Obvs.'

'Obvs,' said Eleri and Tessa as one.

Then they concentrated on the wedding and sighed in teary pleasure as Millie reached Jed. The couple turned to one another, their faces radiating love.

As Millie and Jed were declared man and wife, a starburst of fireworks lit up the night sky.

'Well, we've done it,' Jed whispered, against the cacophony of cheers and the noise from the display getting into its stride. 'In starlight too.' He glanced up. 'Although the stars seem to have disappeared. Maybe it's just the light from the fireworks making them fade.' He looked into Millie's eyes. 'Or maybe they couldn't compete with my wife's beauty.'

Millie rolled her eyes. 'Corny,' she said, secretly delighted.

Their kiss was interrupted by Biddy yelling her congratulations and promising she'd take the dogs to the flat. 'Could murder a cup of coffee,' she added, as the trio dragged her off.

Millie giggled and turned her attention back to her husband. She put her arms around his neck, careful to avoid his injured arm.

'All I've now got to do is get you to accept my second offer,' he said, his breath misting in the night air and mingled with the scent of roses.

'What's that?' Millie asked as she reached up and kissed his cold-pinked nose.

He took a deep breath. 'I'd really like to invest in the café. I want to make Berecombe my home, Mil. *Our* home. I want to make Millie Vanilla's the best place it can possibly be. Whatever plans you have for it.' He stopped and looked nervous. 'A conversation for another time, maybe, and I understand if it's no longer what you want. I think, though, with money invested and the competition out of the running, we can make a go of it. Together.'

'Together.' She kissed him again. 'I like the sound of together.' She felt the tension leave his body and was touched that he cared so much about her feelings, about what she wanted.

He nodded at the happy and slightly tipsy guests making their way over for honeyed sausages, cooked in the bonfire. 'You know, something like this would be brilliant. Millie Vanilla's as a wedding venue.'

'Just what I was thinking,' Millie breathed. She pulled him closer. 'I accept your offer. Oh, my darling Jed. I accept.'

They kissed again, not noticing the arctic cold, or the magnificent fireworks exploding around them.

'You know,' Millie said, as she emerged from the kiss. 'I think I may have broken my bad run with fireworks.'

Jed looked puzzled.

'I'll tell you later,' she giggled.

'There is one more thing.'

'Another offer, Jed?' She tilted her head, flirtatiously.

'I suppose. More a request, actually.'

'What?' Millie slid her hands under his jacket. Mostly to bring him closer but more because the cold was beginning to penetrate even her loved-up bliss. 'Make it quick. I think I've lost all feeling in my feet.'

Jed quirked a brow. 'I promise I'll warm you up later. What I'd like to suggest is that you close the café for the winter.'

She nuzzled the enticing line of his jawbone. 'Why?'

'I'm planning on taking you for a very, very long honeymoon. To all the places you've ever wanted to go.'

Millie gave a shivery giggle. 'Can we start somewhere warm?'

'How does hot sand, warm seas and a Caribbean island

sound?'

'At this moment in time, I'd settle for a hot-water bottle.' She grinned. 'But I think I'll cope with a Caribbean island or two.'

The softest, coldest touch landed on Millie's nose. And then on her eyelashes. And then one more on her cheek. She looked up. Had someone thrown more rose petals?

Snowflakes floated down from a dense black sky. They spiralled around them like confetti. Proper, fat, magical snowflakes, which began to settle on the sand.

'Oh,' she sighed. 'Jed look, it's snowing.'

Jed looked about him as the snowflakes thickened and whirled around them. He could hear cheers coming from the wedding guests crowded around the bonfire. They were congratulating Arthur on finally getting his forecast right.

He tightened his hold on Millie. 'I thought you said it never snows at the seaside,' he teased fondly, loving her childish delight.

'They say it only happens once in a lifetime,' she whispered, as she kissed him yet again. 'Like true love, it only happens once in a lifetime.'

Epilogue

On a hot Devon day in July, the owners of the most successful go-to café in Berecombe tied the knot again. This time Millie and Jed were married officially.

The bride looked ravishing in white tulle, the groom impossibly handsome in a morning coat. The guests milled about on the smooth green lawns of the newly named Henville Hotel, sipping champagne and nibbling tiny crackers spread with caviar.

And the mother of the groom stole the show in a lime-green designer outfit and an enormous feathered hat.

Acknowledgements

A huge thank you to Julia and Natalie for the seasidey details and putting up with my endless questions. Wendy Lou Jones and Evonne Wareham for talking me through the idea and Bella Osborne for her workshop on plotting with Post-its which started the whole thing off. Margaret Graham for many of Biddy's sayings. Lynn Forth for all the giggles and the slut-red chardonnay jelly recipe and my Mum for raiding her memory for old-fashioned bakes. Also, many thanks must go to Michele Clack who diligently researched designer fashion. Finally, grateful thanks for the love and support of The Anti-Doubt Crows – and for putting up with me at meetings. I'll be quiet next time.